# Fearful Symmetry

# FEARFUL

# SYMMETRY

### Greg Bills

A DUTTON BOOK

DUTTON
Published by the Penguin Group
Penguin Books USA Inc., 375 Hudson Street,
New York, New York 10014, U.S.A.
Penguin Books Ltd, 27 Wrights Lane,
London W8 5TZ, England
Penguin Books Australia Ltd, Ringwood,
Victoria, Australia
Penguin Books Canada Ltd, 10 Alcorn Avenue,
Toronto, Ontario, Canada M4V 3B2
Penguin Books (N.Z.) Ltd, 182–190 Wairau Road,
Auckland 10, New Zealand

Penguin Books Ltd, Registered Offices:
Harmondsworth, Middlesex, England

First published by Dutton, an imprint of Dutton Signet,
a division of Penguin Books USA Inc.
Distributed in Canada by McClelland & Stewart Inc.

First Printing, June, 1996
10 9 8 7 6 5 4 3 2 1

REGISTERED TRADEMARK—MARCA REGISTRADA

LIBRARY OF CONGRESS CATALOGING-IN-PUBLICATION DATA

Bills, Greg
    Fearful symmetry / Greg Bills.
        p.   cm.
    ISBN 0-525-94081-2
    1. Married people—California, Southern—Sexual behavior—Fiction.
    2. Single Men—California, Southern—Sexual behavior—Fiction.
    I. Title.
    PS3552.I473F4   1996
    813'.54—dc20                                              95-48327
                                                                  CIP

Printed in the United States of America
Set in Bernhard Modern and Palatino
Designed by Julian Hamer

PUBLISHER'S NOTE
This is a work of fiction. Names, characters, places, and incidents either are the products of the author's imagination or are used fictitiously, and any resemblance to actual persons, living or dead, events, or locales is entirely coincidental.

for Jeff

Many people will not understand how I could trust Hitler for years despite my friendship with Manfred George [the Jewish editor of the Berlin evening paper *Tempo*]. I will try to answer this difficult question with absolute honesty. In our conversation George quite understood that I was impressed by Hitler's personality. However, I made a crucial distinction between Hitler's political notions and his personality. They were two entirely different things as far as I was concerned.

—Leni Reifenstahl


When the stars threw down their spears
And water'd heaven with their tears,
Did he smile his work to see?
Did he who made the Lamb make thee?
—William Blake

# Glass

0

Recently, an exhibition of biological oddities was held in Russia. To raise funds for their struggling museum, the curators unveiled a long-unseen collection of specimens, freakish things afloat in jars. Foremost among the exhibits was the work of a celebrated anatomist, one of embalming's greatest artisans. His work was limited to children, infants taken before the age of baptism. Each of his studies was emblematic—a hand, a face, the span of a ribcage; each delicately detached, its tender veins infused with wax, flesh still fresh with life's last breath. The unnatural terminations of each exhibit were obscured at the wrist, at the neck, the joint, by a band of hovering lace. The anatomist did not wish the viewer to be distracted from the fineness of his work by a search for the point of division from the body—and so each amputation was collared.

Before I knew the Lambents, I felt that I was a child of the jars, with heart and head, hand and eye, drifting discretely. I believed that my consciousness and the world's regarded each other with mutual detachment. And I never assumed that any tempest could stir me—placid, passive, and eloquent—under glass in my preservative sea.

# Villas del Sol

# 1

I didn't mean to fall in love with them. I guess nobody ever does mean to fall in love. But it happens, and love brands itself on your brain matter. It's like a new street appearing overnight in the city you've lived in your whole life. The street is one-way—you can't turn around and get off it—and it curves up ahead so that you can only see far enough to know that you're veering into the unknown.

Chaz and Muriel Lambent. I called them angels, not because of their beauty (though they were both exceedingly handsome) or because they took me under their wings (although they did), but because they had the amoral grace of angels. Angels are not governed by the rules of man's salvation; by their nature, they are already saved. When they light on earth, they are free to act as they please, secure in the knowledge that they are beyond judgment, that nothing here can bring them to ground. They cannot be soiled with guilt, and so they are always innocent. Which might lead you to believe (as I did) that angels are inherently good. But remember that Lucifer was an angel. And even after his fall, the devil maintained his purity.

When I drove Muriel's mother to the morgue in Santa Ana to identify the bodies, I had hoped my belief in their enchanted status would die in the clinical light. But seeing them splayed on their stainless steel pallets like heaps of cold gray clay served to heighten their grace. Their arms slumped unnaturally in their sockets; their closed eyes were filmed along the seams, their mouths slack. But these human failures only seemed to confirm that some unearthly essences had broken their containers and escaped. As I stumbled afterwards down the corridor behind Miriam's flapping raincoat, I could not make myself believe that the clear light that Chaz and Muriel had possessed was extinguished along with their battered forms.

I'm agnostic about almost everything. Yet, if I can't accept that the Lambents are true angels, I must at least concede the existence of their souls—gone from their bodies, gone (I hope) from the world, but deathless, enduring, and radiant. Yeah, I know it sounds like I've gone overboard in describing them. But like I said, I loved them.

## 2

People would have bought tickets to watch Chaz and Muriel. Their lives were fascinating to observe, lying somewhere between the stately rigor mortis of a *tableau vivant* and the sweaty stomach-churning of a sideshow. They might have installed spectator portals in the walls of their house like the ones at that human zoo where the Dionne quintuplets were raised. Although in my particular case, I guess they did.

Their condo was in a four-unit building directly across a landscaped path from mine. From my bedroom window I had an unimpeded view of the side of their house. I could look directly into their bedroom, which was positioned slightly to the right of mine, or peer down at the big greenhouse window in their kitchen or into the sliding glass door that led from their living room out onto their fenced patio. Sometimes, when there were people bustling in and out of the Lambent house, I felt like an entomologist poised above a termite hill. Other times, when Chaz and Muriel sat with cocktails under the round white paper lantern hung over their tiny box of a patio, I fancied myself to be B. F. Skinner. I would call their number and let it ring until Muriel stood and slid open the screen and reached inside for the phone. Then I would hang up. I suppose watching them chatting happily together made me a little jealous.

My adventures in behaviorism occurred after I knew them, but I had been watching long before then, when we had only exchanged a few words. I had just moved in, and I would sit at my desk by the window with assignments from work and stare distractedly. Or when I was bored and lonely, I would stand in the dark and hunt for solace in the world outside. If I leaned against the glass and peered out at a very oblique angle, I could see between the surrounding buildings to a sliver of the community's artificial lake and beyond. Our complex, a series of stucco buildings with terra-cotta tiled roofs, was called Las Villas del Sol. The development across the water was Las Casas de la Luna. Our walls were pink; the Casas were brown. This was the only difference I could discern, and it made for dull viewing: California Nondescript. By default, the condo across the sidewalk won my attention.

I never felt like a Peeping Tom; perhaps I sensed that they accepted my gaze. Besides, my rooms were equally exposed.

# 3

My name is Peter Keith. I have one of those names that always gets reversed; if necessary, I am prepared to respond to Mr. Peters. Chaz would sometimes call me Keith, and I don't know if this was a manly, gym-class sort of thing or if he thought it was my given name. Chaz claimed to have a poor memory.

I moved to Irvine and Las Villas del Sol in the summer after I graduated from JFSD—the Jane Floe School of Design. Unless you work in one of the disciplines taught there, you probably haven't heard of it, but it is well respected in its field. Jane Floe, the school's late founder, is famous for nothing now, but she made quite a splash with some very ugly furniture in the forties and fifties. My favorite pieces of hers, which are displayed in the administration building's lobby, are a series of ergonomic purses. They are literally handbags—gloves with cunning zippered pockets and pouches attached. The best ones are "lab assistant" red rubber models with retractable lipsticks concealed in the index fingers.

Granted, they were not the most auspicious examples of good design, but the school is in Santa Monica, not far from where I grew up, and offered me a scholarship. It was not an obvious career choice for me. I had always excelled in verbal subjects. But I also thought myself to be socially maladroit, and I believed visual artists were given greater leeway to be personally inarticulate.

In my studies I was drawn to woods and glass and metals. For a while I wanted to design tableware: knives and forks, pitchers and cups. As I completed my course work, I interviewed with several firms in the field, but the one I hoped for didn't call me back and the two that were most interested didn't have any immediate openings. By springtime, I panicked. I had to consider my other options. Besides studio work I had taken classes in material culture, consumerism, and writing; the summer before, I had interned, irrelevantly I thought, for an advertising firm. I called the firm for a reference, and they offered me a job in their Orange County offices. So after training to be a designer, I became an adman.

They needed me in two weeks. The day I turned in my final portfolio, I drove down the 405 freeway, bought an *Orange County Register*, and sat in Denny's drinking coffee. I spread a map out and circled the Newport Center, where the firm's offices were, with a red marker. I looked through the classifieds for each of the surrounding cities (I had no idea what they were like) and wrote down all the affordable listings on a notepad. The second number I dialed at the pay phone next to the men's room was for Lonna, the realtor for 416 Avenida de las Estrellas, one of the thirty-six Villas del Sol. An hour later I drove into Irvine, and Lonna gave me the tour. Two floors, lots of windows, vertical blinds, walk-in closet off the bedroom, tile counters in the kitchen and the bath, keys to the association pool, weight room, and tennis courts. Except for the rust-colored stain in the off-white bathroom carpet, it was immaculate and anonymous. Lonna said it was only ten minutes from work (she fudged the time a bit), and I had four days to pack, rent a small truck, load and unload before my job started on Monday. I didn't care; I took the place.

When I moved in, I was twenty-five and convinced that everything that was ever going to happen to me had happened already, that the rest of life would just be repetitions and variations. I wasn't jaded or cocky. I was just well acquainted with the grooves and contours of my existence. All the essential stops were circled in red with the best routes worn by travel—it was an old map.

I believed that I had already had my great love and lost him. And I was confident that this was the mold from which all subsequent romantic dramas would be struck. Twenty-five was a dangerous age.

# 4

At first glance he looked like a jungle cat. Not bulky lion in the veldt but sleek fanged death in the trees. He had close-cropped ice-blond hair and a slender face full of prominent bones. His beauty was disconcerting, not cute. After studying him for a while, however, his ferocity seemed to slack off until something almost dull-witted and ruminant emerged from his round plaintive eyes and drooping lower lip. The fleeting glimpse of keen ferocity was soon forgotten.

I was unloading the rental truck when I saw him first. I had taken a crate of books inside and was heading out again to trace the path around the back of the building to the parking lot. Lonna the real-estate agent stopped me just outside my door. She had rushed over from the realty office with the spare key. I felt the spine of the key through the plain white envelope that held it as I watched her shift between two eucalyptus trees towards her car. She slipped her agency badge from the lapel of her blazer and tucked it into her purse as she walked. It was Friday at the end of the day.

The key settled into the crease of my palm as I flapped the white wings of the envelope's empty ends on the way back inside. The man came down the path in the opposite direction, bringing the dog home from its walk. The dog panted, its long tongue lolling from the side of its mouth, and the man puffed too, a mist of sweat glowing in his cropped hair. He was wearing a peach tank top and khaki shorts, running shoes with white socks scrunched under his large calves. The dog was a block of yellow sandstone, broad and low. Its head was a squat mass of hide and flesh, undistinguished from its shoulders. It strained at the end of a nylon leash in a black leather harness. On a broad strap across its chest, gold-stenciled letters spelled out a name: CISSY. The dog had dug its nose under a jade plant and was rooting in the dirt. "Hey, girl! Get out of there!" the man scolded, then looked up and spoke to me in the same heavy breath. "Hi! Moving in?"

"Yeah," I said.

"Signed that contract yet?" he asked and gestured with his eyes to the envelope. He yanked at the dog's lead to pull it out of the flower bed. "Reason I ask is that you want to make sure your landlord doesn't stiff you for the association fees on top of the rent."

"This is the spare key." I shook the envelope for emphasis.

"Hey, we could keep that for you. We live right next door here. In case you got locked out or something."

"That's okay," I said. "I've got a friend who lives nearby." This wasn't true, but I wasn't going to hand over my key to him just like that. I'd had my brief recognition of his predator gleam.

"Let us know if there's anything we can do for you."

"Sure. I will."

"Be seeing you." He gave me a half-handed wave and pulled the dog over to the redwood wall of his patio fence. He unlatched the hidden gate and dragged the dog through and into the house, leaving the gate swung open behind him.

As I moved towards my own door, I saw him come out again. He pulled his tank top over his head and threw it onto a picnic table. He uncoiled a green length of garden hose and twisted the head of the nozzle to spray his hair. I stood watching ropes of water coil down the spine of his broad tan back and darken the seat of his khaki shorts. He dropped the hose and tossed his head, scattering bright drops in the sun.

I went inside and set the envelope in the kitchen drawer I had designated for important documents. That seals it, I thought. I was officially moved. I had never lived alone before. I had lived at home with my parents, then with roommates from JFSD, and I couldn't quite believe that anyone would pay me enough to afford so much space for myself.

I opened the drawer again and wrote on the outside of the envelope with a felt tip: SPARE KEY. I knew I wouldn't forget what it was. But just in case. And while I wrote the words, I was thinking, that was for me. A truly shameless come-on. And he did it for me.

# 5

I didn't speak to my neighbor again for weeks. In fact, I avoided him. I must have told myself that I didn't want to get involved in another hopeless romance. A romance that would eat out my load-bearing beams from within until I collapsed like a termited house. Things had ended with Brad eighteen months before—*only* eighteen months, I must have stressed to myself. Brad had revealed that he was "almost married" to a former lover, whom he patched things up with and left me for. My neighbor was married too, I assumed. He had said "we" a few times, and I had spotted a woman, briefly, in the kitchen on the night of the day he stripped for me. I believed I wouldn't tolerate that kind of unsatisfactory compromise again.

Also like Brad, the man was older. I had expected Brad to take the lead, take care of me—everywhere but in bed. And even if I always got my way, I assumed it was his initiative that moved us forward or pushed us apart. I suppose I required and waited for the same assertion from my new obsession. But realistically, fear was the reason I didn't speak to him again.

I am a shy man by nature. So shy that every time my parents moved from one area of Los Angeles County to another, which was often, I would be hours late to my first days at the new school because I was afraid to ask the city bus driver for directions. I wouldn't ask the kids at school either. I would just ride around, making transfers all over the city until I recognized the neighborhood where my mother had dragged me to meet the principal (she always insisted on meeting the principal). This wandering would go on for three or four days until I figured out the routes or called the information hotline to check the schedules. The anonymous exchange of the telephone was the one social interaction I could cope with.

My timidity had become less crippling with time—my friends at Floe had helped—but I wasn't cured. Whenever someone approached me, for conversation or sex or friendship, I froze. I couldn't make the polite, the companionable, second move. Or the third. Or the fourth. I would run, and the person would need to chase after me. I think I was waiting for someone to race up and tackle me. I find it remarkable now that anyone made the effort, but I guess some people thrive on the adrenaline of pursuit and capture.

Although not my neighbor, apparently. My efforts at avoidance proved unnecessary. After moving day, when I saw him at all on the path or in the parking lot, he would respond to a look in his direction with a nod or a curt "hello" but with no indication of interest dilating his dimly shining irises. I began to think I had exaggerated his shower with the hose into a grand flirtation. I had always worried that I was too prone to fantastic elaborations, to spirit-of-the-staircase internal dramas, and so I berated myself for the fabrication.

And at the same time, I began to jerk off constantly, replaying the sheet of tensed muscles in his back as his arms stretched the hose over his dripping head.

# 6

"Have you met the Lambents?"

Irena Delgado stood over the trash can sorting the circulars and subscription offers from her serious mail. Her hair was jet black and quite long, but because of the intervention of natural oils or hairspray, it was stiffly immobile. When she bent to convey her junk mail into the garbage, her coiffure did not shift. As she looked up at me, I saw that her bangs parted in the center, then looped over to her ears and straight down like a perfect pair of stage curtains framing an incredibly tanned, incredibly haggard face. I didn't know Irena's age. In California, it is dangerous to assume that a woman with a face like the creased underside of a leather glove is ancient; the sun can be harsh here. But she had mentioned Social Security more than once, so I assumed she was comfortably past retirement age.

There were four condos in each building at the Villas del Sol, and Irena lived at the opposite end of mine. She had not flinched from the challenge of pursuing me; she had barreled heedlessly into my psychic space and set up her vending cart. She was the sort of person my mother called loud, but with Irena it wasn't a matter of volume or flamboyance. It was the force of her personality that seemed to shout you down like a TV picture with the brightness knob twisted up or the endless plunking of a sour key by a piano tuner searching for pitch.

I was defenseless against her assaults. When I left my place for my first day of work, Irena was out spraying her window with blue glass cleaner. When she heard my door close and my key turn the deadbolt, she scooted down the sidewalk to introduce herself. I was nervous about getting to the office on time and tried to excuse myself, but she had an unswerving agenda. "I'm so glad there's someone to replace the curtains in there. Those old ones are in tatters." I hadn't planned to change the curtains, but by the second time she mentioned them that week, I felt guilty and hung new ones on the weekend.

At the carport, the laundry, or the mailboxes, Irena was always lying in wait, and I soon felt that my head had been stuffed full of Delgado trivia. Yet all the details made a rather enigmatic whole because Irena spoke as if I had been attending family holidays with her for the past fifty years and all her references must be drearily self-evident. For instance, I knew that she was a widow, but all she had said of her husband was that he died in "that awful business at work."

It was three weeks after I moved in when she first mentioned the Lambents. I had been reading the table of contents in the *Village Voice* and thought I had missed some connection in her story and the Lambents might be the dignitaries she had met over cocktails during the

Eisenhower Era. "No," I said in response to her query. "I don't know them." I stood shirtless, in cutoffs and sneakers, leaning a shoulder against one of the posts holding the roof over the mailboxes. I held my mail and the newspaper in one hand, and flipped the pages with the other.

"Oh, Peter, you must meet Chaz and Muriel. At the Homeowners' Association meetings, they crack everyone up with their humor. They're just the life of the party."

"Yeah? Where do they live?"

"Isn't it hot today?" Irena hooked her finger through the large ring on the zipper of her toast-colored nylon tracksuit and tugged it down to reveal a necklace of raw crystal on a gold chain resting against the pressed emerald green T-shirt underneath. It was so hot that I had taken off everything I could, including my underwear, and I realized that, if she looked in the right spot, Irena could see through the stringy hole in the seat of my shorts. I turned sideways feeling inappropriately dressed. In Irvine even the dowdy dress with some semblance of style, and the preferred fashion is expensive leisure wear—children's playclothes for affluent adults. It was clear that the unwrinkled fabrics of Irena's sports outfit and the unspotted leather of her running shoes had never been played in, much less exercised in; the mailbox was the furthest she would travel on foot without taking her Cadillac. "You must have seen them," she said. "They're right across the way from you in five-twenty."

I let the *Voice* fall closed and stood straight. "Chaz and Muriel . . . ?"

"Chaz and Muriel Lambent. They are treasures, those two. So sweet and charming. Chaz works at . . . um . . . and Muriel does something too. And they are always coming around for charities and doing political things. Social butterflies. It's not a week goes by without them having some function or party. And with such small floor space, I don't know how they do it. Last time, Roy—Roy Garamilla, who lives behind us—counted three Rollses, a Ferrari, and a Bentley in the guest lot. And even here in Irvine, where everyone has to have their foreign car and such, that's quite a list. But they're not snobs or stuffy at all. You'd like them, Peter. They're always saying that they wish some younger people would move into the Villas."

"I think I'd be too intimidated." I realized as I spoke that I meant this sincerely.

"No, no," she said. "They're not like that at all. They're very personable. Very personable indeed."

# 7

After speaking with Irena Delgado, I began lingering at my windows in earnest. Through some perverse inversion of effort and effect, I did not observe Chaz again for days but Muriel came into constant focus. Until then she had been invisible, and maybe it was the naming of her that summoned her, created her, brought her down into my view. She would saunter along the paths of the complex, sometimes with Cissy the dog, sometimes without. I could never figure out where she was going or where she had been. She was probably engaged in some mundane task like getting the mail or buying the groceries, but whenever I looked out and spotted her she was already in my line of view, walking. Sometimes she would move around their building to the front door of their condo, and I would lose sight of her behind the bushes at the corner. Her hands were always empty, except for the leash, and she never rushed.

Muriel Lambent was not starlet beautiful but handsome like the more interesting movie queens: like Katharine Hepburn or Lauren Bacall. During the day she wore her hair in a honeyed braid down to the middle of her back; at night she often pinned it up in a French twist like those blond ice maidens in the Technicolor Hitchcock films. Her face was quite long, particularly her nose, which dropped spectacularly from her forehead to her lips like a Modigliani sculpted in flesh. In profile, in certain lights, her face seemed beakish and haughty, the queen of interstellar bird women, but her unflattering moments were few. And she never looked less than striking.

She was petite, but her gently curvilinear silhouette was lithe and gave the impression of a much taller woman. If she were a vase or a floorlamp, she could be praised for her good design—her excellent projection into space, her balance and clarity of outline. Muriel would have earned the highest praise from my studio instructor, Gino Ardt: he would have said that Muriel possessed "realized form." Everything about Muriel succeeded—figure, face, hair, clothes, stance, gait—and there was nothing conjectural, nothing in her appearance to suggest that any ideal professed in her conception had been compromised in her execution. Any evidence of artifice, in the drape of a blouse or the blusher on a cheekbone, was subsumed. She was the thing itself.

But danger coils in these metaphors. And not only in the possibility of sexist reduction. Unease enters the analysis when the focus shifts from studio to shop. When Muriel is regarded as a construct, the temptation can arise to advance her prototype into production (for comparison, instead of "women" as a category for improvement, you might substitute "inner-city children," say, or "homosexuals," or "Aryan youth"). Jane Floe, in the obscurity of her undergraduate days, wrote an essay. She assessed modern architecture according to its awareness of the limits of the human body. Then, in the penultimate paragraph, she impulsively rotated her argument and asked whether it was not man's craft but mankind that required adaptation, whether the clarion call of certain "Germanic" philosophers for a refined, perfected man would soon allow architects to expand their vision and their reach—"new People for the new Cities," she wrote. When this essay surfaced from among her collected documents after her death in the seventies, it created a stir—at least in the JFSD student paper. When I was enrolled there, it had become standard practice to lampoon the school administration with a caricature of Dr. Floe dressed in Supergirl tights and large swastika earrings.

I hope that Dr. Floe was wrong about human advancement because the earth would not survive a race of Muriels.

# 8

After a week of observing Muriel, I sat at home at my desk, ignoring the campaign for bottled water I was supposed to be copyediting, and reproached myself for transforming her into an abstraction. I had reduced her to a kaleidoscope of cubist planes, and although she couldn't know that I had conceptualized her, I felt that she had been wronged. I might have resolved to close the blinds and reassert her privacy, but I didn't. I decided to make my study of the Lambents deeper, more deliberate, and move my attention from their physical surface to their behavior. At some point in this decision, the future twisted out of my control.

I decided to keep a log on my computer. I would observe them for half an hour, twice a day: once before sunset and once at night when the lighted rooms beyond their uncurtained windows were most clearly visible. If I hadn't misfiled the document under MISC JOB QUERIES, I would have purged it long ago. But for the benefit of accuracy, I will repeat it here (with minor additions):

Day 1: Wednesday, 6:23–7:00 p.m. Nothing happened until five minutes before the end of my scheduled watch. The man, Chaz, opened the screen of the sliding glass door and carried a pitcher of water out onto the patio. He bent down I guess to pour the water somewhere then went inside. I can't believe I'm doing this.

10:03–10:33 p.m. Above the shaggy growth of the herb garden in the greenhouse window, I can see part of the stovetop near the opposite wall of the kitchen. Through the sliding door, I can see a rectangle of beige carpeting. Near the door, there is a long white phone cord dangling from the counter and over the back of what looks like a Barcelona chair—world's most expensive dentist's office furniture. Furthest in, before the angle of the top of the door cuts off my view, I can see the back legs of a dining room chair. They are dark and curving and belong to who knows what. Upstairs, the bedroom window is dark. As should be obvious, I didn't see anyone. At 10:30 I decided to open my window [at the time I remember having qualms about allowing another source of sensory data into my study], and heard the muffled beat of dance music from I guess the partially opened door.

Day 2: Thursday, 6:30–7:02. This is a stupid idea. If I'm really this bored I should go to a movie or call up friends or get back to work. I thought I saw the dog's eye and a tuft of ear through a gap between the fence boards. Isn't that exciting.

10:10–11:32. I sat with the light off in my usual spot at the edge of the desk by my printer. After staring at the sidewalk until 10:35, I stood up and decided I wasn't going to waste my time with this shit. Then the woman came with the box. She was wearing a bright fuchsia dress in a light-catching fabric, sashed at the waist with a floral scarf. She had another darker scarf or a close fitting hat on her head. I couldn't see her face. The box was brown cardboard, plain, about the size of a thirteen-inch TV, with the flaps loosely folded over the top. She was coming from the visitor parking and walked quickly to the Lambents front door around the corner. In a few seconds, the dog started to growl and bark. A few seconds more and Chaz dragged the dog out on the patio with his fingers yanking on the harness. Left alone, the dog continued to yowl and snap with her slobber dripping down the glass. Some minutes later at the limits of my perspective, I saw the hem of the fuchsia dress and one sandaled foot on the beige carpet. Then nothing. I waited another forty minutes until the woman emerged, again moving quickly. She pulled up the scarf or wrap from her neck to cover her head. She tilted towards the light at the corner of the building and I got a glimpse of her oval face and a diamondy flash from a jewel piercing her nose. She didn't have the box.

Day 3: Friday, 6:30–6:59. The dog has been out on the patio all day barking and pressing its scrunched face to the glass. Frenzied and fiendish. It found a sheet of newspaper and tore into it with its jaws and front paws. Chaz came to the door in a pair of red paisley boxers and began to talk to the dog. I think he said, "You hungry baby (buddy?)? Are you a hungry puppy?" He [Chaz] scratched his [own] stomach then disappeared back into the shadows. Later, I heard a vacuum.

10:00–10:32. They must have gone out. All the lights are off in the house. Only the bare bulb fixture on the patio is lit for the dog. [I learned later that the Lambents regularly left the lights on when they left the house. They must have been doing something in the dark.]

Day 4: Saturday, 11:00–11:30 a.m. I think they're having a party. Twenty minutes ago, two men in white coveralls appeared bearing large plastic coolers, wine crates, pink cardboard pastry boxes, also large sacks of crushed ice. Chaz and Muriel shifted their dining room table into the corner by the door. I can't see it because it's covered in white linen. The Barcelona chair has been moved somewhere inside. A woman in jeans and florist shop T-shirt has just come with three large bouquets: gladioli and birds of paradise.

I never added any entries for Saturday at 6:30 and Saturday at 10:00. I kept watching. But, by the end of the day, something had shifted in me, and I knew there could be no continuity between the writer who began the journal and the man who was expected to finish it. The document ends with the flowers.

# 9

I spent the rest of the day at home at my desk trying to work. Jock Kurtz, the head of my department, had asked me to think up something interesting for a client presentation on Tuesday. Kurtz had no expectation that I would come up with a serviceable proposal; he wanted to provide me with experience and make me feel like a "team player." He felt that my mind had been curdled from theoretical knowledge in design school and it was time to learn the dynamics of the real world. "You know, Peter," he said, "it's give and take. It's all fucking give and take. We're the masters of nothing. You've got the clients at one end, the market at the other, and us taking it in the face and the ass at the same time."

This wisdom from Jock Kurtz had its merits although I didn't share his conviction that we were somehow responsive or responsible to the consumer. At Floe, we had been instructed that our foremost consideration should be the needs of the people, but in advertising it seemed to me that our task was to seduce the people into needing whatever the client wanted to sell.

The product under my consideration that weekend was a cordless juicer. The line of development behind this product was clear to me: the technology of two marginally useful concepts—the rechargeable electric screwdriver and the small-scale electric juicer—had been merged to create one decadently pointless device. Then it was advertising's job to make the public feel a little more inconvenienced, a little more deprived, because they didn't own one. We had to sow dissatisfaction before we sold its cure.

The clients wanted to imbue the juicer with upscale glamour, and the ideas that had made it to the mock-up stage at the agency all tended towards tropical luxury. A couple—newlyweds—recline on a pristine white beach while the wife, in her bikini and sun hat, feeds an orange into the machine. As if anyone who could afford resort living would want to squeeze their own fruit. I was trying to imagine a scene with Sir Edmund Hillary. While Sir Ed was planting the flag and claiming Mount Everest for the Crown, his faithful Sherpa would be nearby grinding up a nice mango and orange tonic to quench the great explorer's thirst. I couldn't remember the Sherpa's name or if I had ever known it. I remember he had taken the photograph of Hillary at the summit, but he had been erased from history like all the other hired hands of Great Men, who carried the bags, or tested the piranha-churning waters, or tumbled into the rain-slick crevasse halfway to the head of the Nile. I guess the lesson was not to be left holding the camera at history's terminus.

I sat staring out the window, fantasizing about the whole series of great explorer advertisements that could be spun off from my original idea. Occasionally I would make a sketch or try to think of some catchy copy, but chiefly my mind drifted over Everest and down the Congo with a creative satisfaction having only the vaguest connection to practicality. What I really did during these hours was monitor the Lambent house.

After the initial flurry of activity that I recorded on my computer, the afternoon proceeded quietly until Chaz opened the glass door and led the antic dog into the house. Then he came around from the front door to hang a string of electrified Chinese lanterns around the outer perimeter of the patio. While he was fixing the wire to the boards with thumbtacks, Irena Delgado wandered the walkway towards him. Her sole purpose in coming down the path was to snoop into her neighbors' party plans, and, lacking self-irony, I felt indignant on the Lambents' behalf. Lacking shame, I leaned closer to the open window. ". . . Just having a few friends over," Chaz was telling her.

"I'd love to meet your friends. They must be so interesting," Irena said. She lifted the coil of wire and lanterns from the ground and played it out as Chaz advanced along the length of the patio. They were both wearing gray sweatpants and blue T-shirts and looked like a misbegotten construction crew.

"Oh, Irena, I think you're more interesting than any ten of them combined."

"Chaz, that's sweet of you to say. But I'm sure your friends are all well read. I'm sure they've done things."

"We've all *done* things. Doing things does not get you points."

"I'd still sure like to meet them sometime."

Chaz ignored her second bid for an invitation, and when the last lantern was tacked around the far corner of the fence, he thanked Irena with his hand on her shoulder. "Give them our apologies at the association meeting tonight."

"We'll sure miss you."

"You know what we want, Irena. You'll have to be our voice there tonight, okay?"

"I'll try, Chaz. You know I'm just not very forceful."

"You'll do fine. You've got Zu-krall looking out for you." He squeezed her arm and turned to go inside.

"You know what," Irena shouted. "Now that you've said it, I know that I will."

# 10

The guests began arriving shortly after ten. I was surprised that any party would dare to start so late in the Villas del Sol, where the midnight curfew of the noise ordinance was fiercely enforced. But even then, with my limited knowledge of the Lambent state of grace, I didn't assume that the regulation would apply to them. Perhaps their stellar performance at all those association meetings had won them an exemption.

Not surprisingly, the guests were all gorgeous. In the warm pastels of the lanterns, they were glowing confections. Those who weren't beautiful were striking, or imposing, or eccentrically, uniquely riveting. The anticipation of arrival buzzed in the air like the first act of the Academy Awards. Someone is coming, whispered the frisson of the night, some face, some frock, some shoulders in rare leather, some cocky breath-catching stance. I couldn't move away. I was a fandom of one that night (unless Irena had found the means to see around the corner, with a fisheye mirror and a periscope sprouting from her patio).

There were two factions among the guests. Women strolled by in designer gowns—not limited runs but custom originals, so well worked, so fresh that they announced their obsolescence like petals floating in a crystal bowl—that would be worn for this night alone then cast off to the consignment store, too notorious to risk flaunting again. Often these women were accompanied by men in well-cut Continental suits or tailored English tweeds. There were no tuxedos; the men's dress was aggressive, unwilling to serve as a neutral field for the ladies' flash.

The other guests were Gothic Bohemians, dressed in black; with leather, multiple earrings, tribal tattoos; fifties cocktail dresses; punk haircuts, raccoon eyes, and shaky, nicotine yellow fingers. This group was more disheveled than the other but more dedicated to fashion. At home, the gowned women would slip off their frocks and flop into sweats, but the Bohemians would never drop their guard. Their self-stylization was relentless and meticulous. Their stained, wrinkled T-shirts and duct-taped boots were prized.

The two options in attire never mingled—not outside—and I wondered if the groups could be labeled "his" and "hers" or if they were inextricably mixed.

In addition, three women in saris slid past, including—I realized—the woman from Thursday night with the box; also a tall man in a burnoose, and at least one discernible drag queen, an African-American with a Louise Brooks bob and a chartreuse flapper gown.

From time to time, one of the guests would turn the corner and reach the front door, but usually, by instinct or radar, either Muriel or Chaz or both would step out under the lanterns to greet the arriving party. The Lambents' outfits belonged decidedly to the coutured contingent. He wore a dark gray, loosely structured Italian suit with soft black loafers. He had slicked and stiffened his hair with gel, and it had a darker, golden glow. Her gown began in a tight, deep red, pailletted bodice and concluded in a flared black calf-length skirt. Her hair curled up in the Hitchcock twist. Her bare shoulders were tan and faintly freckled, and around her narrow throat she had fixed a choker of gold links and huge (faux?) pearls. Adding white cotton gloves, she would have passed for a cool jazz chanteuse fallen through time from 1959.

The Lambents were unfailingly gracious; they shook hands, and hugged, and brush-kissed cheeks with European ease. Their voices were too softly modulated for me to hear, but their guests responded with bright laughter and coos of appreciation. After standing outside a few moments with each group, they would guide the newcomers in towards the bar and the buffet. Soon I would see the same feathered hat, or cracked-heeled boots, or beaded gown stripped of its blue satin wrap drifting past the table in the corner to load treats on asymmetrical bone china plates.

Needless to say, I wanted to be there. I couldn't imagine what I would wear, or what I would say, or what I would do other than seek a quiet vantage and gawk. But I knew I could find my place there—unlike Irena, who would bob around conspicuously like a thumbtack in a flute of champagne.

As the arriving partygoers slowed to a trickle, Muriel and Chaz no longer stepped out to meet the stragglers. The sounds of chatter, jazz, and shifting tableware rose and ebbed within the stuccoed walls. Someone shouted "Yes!" and the cluster of people by the sliding door turned to face the room beyond my gaze. There was some activity around the corner at the front door as a few guests departed into the night, then a lull punctuated only by the syncopation of the music. Muriel looped the cord of the vertical blinds over her hand; the slats trailed across the glass from the opposite corner as she pulled, then rotated them into place, blocking my view. I continued watching at the edge of my desk, drinking from a two-liter bottle of mineral water.

The light dimmed under the blinds and in the empty kitchen, replaced by a sickly blue flicker from deep within. I heard murmuring. Then shouts. Then the heavy silence of prolonged, suspended breath.

# 11

I waited. And waited. And waited in the dark for more stimulus from the gathering below. After a time the rumble of conversation returned, and the CD player began to shuffle among reggae, mbaqanga, and zydeco, but the blinds remained drawn. I had squandered the whole day watching the preparations only to be excluded when the evening reached its peak. "So long, farewell, auf Wiedersehen, good night." I sang the ditty of the dismissed children in *The Sound of Music* and straddled my desk chair. I pulled off my tank top and looked at my chest in the dim light from the window: lightly dusted with dark hair and displeasingly pale.

I closed my eyes and leaned against the rounded seat back. With curled fingers I brushed my nipples, moved down to scratch my stomach, then stroked the line of hair under my navel. I looped the elastic waist of my sweatpants under my balls and found my dick in the dark shadow under the desk. I licked my palm and slid wet fingers down.

I realized as I gripped myself that I had been aroused all day. I had not been erect—it hadn't been purely or even primarily sexual. It hadn't been lust but another Biblical sin: covetousness. I wanted their life. I wanted to be absorbed into their bloodstream. I wanted their attention.

When I was little, my father—in one of his countless business incarnations—took me with him to a clothing retailers' trade show. It is unlikely that he volunteered to take me; my mother must have had a competing activity that day. I don't remember the circumstances, only the grip of his thick fingers around my wrist as he led me down one cluttered row after another in the caverns of the convention center. At the rear of one hall in a partitioned booth, a mannequin manufacturer was premiering its new fall line. There were men, women, children—anatomically detailed in their nakedness but with bodies pale as frost. My father stopped to look, and I was frightened at first as prospective customers pulled limbs from sockets and rested stiff, snowy palms against their own. But as they stroked torsos and stretched jointless arms, my fright melted into fascination—and into something akin to envy. A sales representative detached a woman's head from her body, lifted off her masking blond wig, and settled her bald pate like a ripe melon in my father's hands. He turned it slowly, examining the finely wrought features, and I struggled to get his attention by yanking at the hem of his jacket. He didn't look at me but moved deeper into the display among the frozen ranks of the mannequins, who were being spun and lifted by other fleshy, living hands. For the moment, they were more alive to him than I was, and I ached to be treated with such interested scrutiny—from my father, my mother, from others.

I craved the same defining recognition from the Lambents.

All the love I had made with myself in the previous month had been undertaken with Chaz Lambent predominant on my mental screen. I had embroidered his back beneath a sheath of water and his stomach above paisley shorts into a tapestry of desire. I would rock back on my bed with both hands tugging at my dick and see Chaz stepping slowly towards me, his hair slick and water dripping on his shoulders, his nipples aroused into dark knots, his stomach pushing in and out with his breath, his solid dick curving gently up before him with a drop emerging from its head. And I would wait with my mouth rolled open to catch that clear sticky bead on my tongue. And I would hover, suspended on that moment, on that saline dot, until I came.

Because I was angry at my exclusion, I tried not to conjure Chaz as I sat at the desk and whacked. I pictured a hot-looking Asian man who had come into the agency Thursday afternoon in a seersucker suit with a silver hoop in his ear. A few strands of pomaded black hair slipped from his widow's peak and curled perfectly against his forehead. I had stared at him while he was turning pages in a portfolio, and when he looked up and noticed me, he gave a shy swallowed smile and then dropped his eyes to the table. I should have waited until after his appointment. Instead, as soon as he looked away, I ducked out of the office and did not return until he was gone.

I tried to bring him back in my mind; I tried to crush the thin blue stripes of his seersuckered shoulders against my cheek. I tried to reconstruct a scent for him of coconut milk, male sweat, and cardamom. But he kept splintering, his seersucker clouding into gray Armani, his scalp sprouting white shocks. I was pumping fast now, gripping hard. And Chaz was saying, "What can I do for you? What do you want, buddy?" I wanted him, I wanted him, and I didn't know what I wanted him to do, but I wanted. I didn't think of a place for him to touch, an opening for his tongue, a landing point for mine. I only wanted—coveted—needed—milked myself towards his love.

I was fierce. I rocked back in the chair until my legs were straight with every muscle braced and tense. I pulled down on my balls, arching my back, my buttocks straining against the seat. Chaz, I thought—this moment, your tongue, your dick, your bristle hair, thighs, voice, eyes, now.

I shot with soft spatters across my chest: as warm as skin then cool, thick as jam then liquefying, with the rangy scent of the dull-sheened trees under my window at work. I stood up instantly, shocked back into the dark of my bedroom, and rushed to the bathroom for tissue before I dripped onto the carpet.

I wiped myself off and returned to scoop my shirt from the floor. As I slipped into it, I peeked down at the closed blinds. They were full of light but still impervious. I sat down again, fumbled for my computer switch, and turned on the desk lamp. My face glared at me, reflected in the window glass. My hair was a mess. This was my first thought, and I combed through the dark tufted tangle with both hands. My face continued to scowl disapprovingly with thin lips set, eyebrows curling, and eyes sunk like black seeds in their sockets. Enough people had told me I was attractive to establish some doubt in my mind, but I didn't really believe them. My image in the glass, overlaying the Lambents' cloistered party, was an accusation of inadequacy.

# 12

I really don't know what happened next. I know that time passed, but I don't remember how I filled it. The memory of those hours has been elided along with life's many other moments of white noise between stations, like the *Us* magazine read before a wisdom-tooth extraction, like the discussion of Exene Cervenka's solo albums between sex and bed. I might have gone downstairs to fix a sandwich or watch television. I might have stretched out on the bed and slipped into a weary, dreamless sleep. I do know that I shut off the desk lamp and left the window.

Long after midnight I undressed and prepared to slip into the cool envelope of sheets on my bed. I felt along the window's edge for the cord to drop the blind. Below me, the interior of the Lambent house lay exposed again—at least the familiar trapezoid of flaxen berber carpeting. The guests were gone; the overhead track lights blared at full strength. The dishes had been cleared from the ring-stained linen tablecloth, and the cardboard box brought by the woman in the sari sat at the edge of the table with its top flaps neatly sealed with tape. Muriel knelt on one knee by the door with her lower body absorbed into the vague mass of her full black skirt. She dipped a large yellow sponge into a bucket of sudsy water and blotted a dark wine-colored stain in the carpet's weave. She squeezed pink water into the bucket and blotted again. Tiny soap bubbles netted her fingers, and her gold and ruby ring glistened wetly.

She swiped at the stain, which grew broader and less definite, from a red continent to a rosy cumulus cloud. She swiped loose hair from her forehead with the back of one hand and squeezed the sponge with the other. She looked out the window, and up. She laughed. I had no doubt that she had located me beyond what must have appeared to her a blank, black glass. My nakedness was invisible, but she saw it. And she knew. She knew that I had been watching all day, and she knew that her upturned gaze was making me hard. She seemed to giggle while she lathered the sponge again, and I yanked at the cord until the blind tumbled into place.

I had been caught. I lay on top of the sheet and shivered. Then I reached over for my phone and called Anthony.

# 13

I first spoke to Anthony when I was still at JFSD and living in the Consulate with Clara and Judy and the ever-changing fourth roommate whom we referred to provisionally as Sam (my lover Brad was the third or fourth Sam). We called the building the Consulate because it was packed with foreign students attending Floe and UCLA. Our four-bedroom apartment was on the top floor: the Ambassador's Suite.

In the summer of the year before I moved to the Villas del Sol, I had been bored and irritable in my room at the south end of the building—furthest from the bathroom and the furnace, coldest in the winter, hottest in the summer, but with the best view: of a swath of Santa Monica stretching down towards the ocean. Brad had left me in the winter, but I was nowhere near to closing my emotional accounts with him. I never conceived of seeing anyone else. Clara and Judy, whose relationship operated on a definite estrus cycle, were in full heat and could not be depended on to distract me. And the apartment's other room was either empty or occupied by one of the anonymous summer Poster Children who would rent the room after reading a flyer on a campus kiosk.

I had spent every week that summer working on a tea kettle. Most of the instructors at Floe were unrelentingly fixated on the practical, and they required you to take your idealizations into the shop and craft them, to transubstantiate your fancy into fiber, clay, and metal. My kettle had a pyramidal body with a thin tubular spout like a watering can, and I had finished a prototype in June. When I presented it to Professor Ardt, he took it to the sink, filled it, and set it on his hotplate. As the water boiled, it frothed and squirted from the spout onto his bench. "This is a beautiful thing, Peter," he said. He pursed his full red lips until they rose from his heavy, white-flecked beard. "But it isn't a kettle. And I can't prepare my darjeeling in a sculpture." He extended my deadline for the project until the new term started in September, which I had assumed would be ample time.

Hypothetically my kettle should have functioned flawlessly; the physics behind my design was sound. But the prototype wouldn't work. By the middle of July I had given up design and delved into hit-or-miss experimentation in the shop, reconfiguring the spout and moving the join up and down the side of the body.

After another day of flailing uselessly around my workbench, I came home to an empty room with nothing else to think about or look forward to but my fucking kettle. I flicked on the television and watched situation comedies until I felt like screaming, then I pawed through the uninspiring stack of books on my nightstand. At the bottom was the magazine I had grabbed outside a bar during my only solo trip to West Hollywood.

It was one of those gay news throwaways with a glossy cover and newsprint pages full of porn video reviews, arcane nightclub gossip, and lots of classified ads for masseurs. I flipped back to the large advertisements for phone sex numbers. I wasn't looking for sex but for entertainment; I had never called one before.

Most of the numbers connected the caller to a party line for a session of bodiless cruising, but the number I selected was a live fantasy line—essentially a bordello for vocal prostitutes. I chose the number mainly because of the accompanying monochrome photograph. A tall brown-haired man in torn cutoffs and work boots stood on a rock in the center of a mountain stream. One of his hands bent behind his neck and the other grasped his thigh with his face raised in heavy-lidded ecstasy. What intrigued me was the shadow of another man, maybe the photographer, that stretched darkly across the water and over the stone at the model's feet. It seemed to prostrate itself, as if Mortal Shade were cowed by Beauty (I was *that* kind of Romantic).

After I dialed, I heard a recording, a man's husky voice, asking me to enter my credit card information on my telephone keypad— which I did—then to choose my preferences from the menu and enter the corresponding number. Was I looking for an active or a passive man? Press 1 or 2. Were my interests oral? Anal? J/O? Press 3, 4, or 5. Pressing 6 would open another menu with a choice of leather, cowboys, or three-ways. Pressing 7 yielded Daddies, rubber fetishes, and S&M. I panicked and hung up.

I called again immediately and punched "1" at the appropriate moment. In the long silence that followed, I had the feeling that I had been swindled. I pictured the line curling out of my phone and over the hills to a strip mall office in Van Nuys where a man in loafers and a button-down oxford sat between the cloth-lined gray walls of a phone-bank cubicle and tried to decide which persona he would adopt to deal with me before switching on his headset. I was certain it would be the same man who answered if I had requested nipple clamps and whips. I had chosen a dominant man because I couldn't imagine shouting sexual orders at some wage earner lost in ennui and a mug of decaffeinated coffee, who would offer an occasional moan or mutter, "Do me."

I felt humiliated and was about to hang up again when Anthony came on the line.

Our first conversation sputtered in a vacuum for quite some time. I was not forthcoming with details to embellish the fantasy, and Anthony was not particularly imaginative. He had a deep voice, caramel-hued and pungent like scotch, and if he had been lying on top of me in bed with his arms wrapped around my chest, I might have found his words unavoidably intoxicating. But I was full of doubt and aware of the distance between us, and my hand never strayed below my hips. While he forged ahead saying, "Take it, yeah, take it. You want it, yeah, you want it. Mmm, doesn't that feel good? I'm going to fill you up, boy," I pictured his small, pronounced bald spot and the grocery list he was composing on the back of a call record.

I looked at the clock on my desk and realized how much money I had already spent. "Wait, wait," I said. "How do I know you're for real?"

"You can hear me, can't you?" He sounded as if he had heard my plaintive plea too many times before.

"Yeah, but it's disembodied. It doesn't mean anything."

"You're paying for a phone fantasy, man. What—you want me to come over?"

"No. But how do I know you're not just eating doughnuts in an office next to a copy machine somewhere?"

"No, look, they forward the calls to me at home."

"Really?"

"Okay, listen." I heard a rattle and a scrape, then sounds of a boombox chugging with rap rhythm, laughter, sirens. "Hear that?" he asked. "You've been out the window, man. This is Venice Beach."

His demonstration had its intended effect; I believed him. And the irritation in his voice seemed authentic. I felt his reality. I pulled down my shorts, then kicked them off and made Anthony describe himself.

He was five foot ten, one hundred eighty-five pounds. He had black hair and brown eyes, a hairy chest and stomach, thickly muscled legs, and long eyelashes. His penis was ten inches plus; I don't recall what he said about the condition of his foreskin. He was a bodybuilder, an aspiring actor—the phone sex thing was only temporary, he claimed—and he told me that he wanted to shove my face into the pillow while he fucked me. I came prodigiously onto my stomach.

# 14

By the night of the Lambents' party, I had been calling Anthony for over a year. On rare calls he would help me bring myself off, but usually we just talked. I didn't delude myself that he was a friend; I thought of our meetings as counseling. My phone bills made the conversations seem legitimate. An hour with him was no more expensive than a session with most therapists, and I felt no pressure to be cured.

Anthony had given me his personal access code, and when I punched it in that morning, I was surprised that he answered. His voice sounded hoarse and sleepy. "Hey, what's shaking, Jerry?" (I called myself Jerry Mouse, because there remained limits to my desire for disclosure.)

"I'm . . . I think I've fallen for somebody."

"Like 'in love' you mean?"

"Well . . ."

"That's cool, Jerry. It's about time."

"I don't know him though."

"Whoa-oa."

"I know who he is. He lives across the way, and I've watched him a lot but—"

"Don't get obsessed, man. Don't turn all John Hinckley on me. That's how presidents get shot."

"No. I'm not going to *do* anything. He's married. And his wife . . . they're both these incredible people. Stunning. I was watching their party tonight, and afterwards, she was cleaning up and she looked up to my window, and it was like she knew and approved of it." I heard the breathless, frenzied edge in my voice.

"Oh man, Jerry. You've got to come up for air. That's what phone sex is for, so you don't have to do this stuff in real life."

"I'm not crazy. I think I just want to meet them."

"Jerry. Look, Jerry." I guessed that Anthony had been instructed to use his clients' names as often as possible for intimacy, but each time he used my pseudonym I cringed. "Before you get involved in this thing, make sure you've got an escape route. This shit's not like a burning house, man. Nobody's gonna see the smoke and come save you."

He was silent, and I was certain he was adjusting his assessment of my character from "nice, lonely introvert" to "borderline psychopath." Instead, he continued brightly. "Hey, Jer. Can you do me a favor? I've got my girlfriend Dixie here, and she thinks all my callers are sick old farts. Would you talk to her a minute and show her what a nice guy you are?"

"I don't know," I said doubtfully. At the same time I spoke, I heard a woman's voice squeal "To-neeeee!" in the background and realized I would rather keep my remaining illusions about Anthony.

"Oh, come on, buddy. She's a great lady. She's from Corpus Christi, Texas. She's a dog groomer."

I heard a loud clunk, then a scuffling sound, then the woman screeched "To-nee!" again, then she giggled. "Um, hello," she said tentatively into the phone. "Hi, Jerry. I'm sorry about this. It's all Tony's idea." She had a faint Southern accent, a light mist in the valleys of her vowels. "I'm Dixie."

"Hello," I said. I stood and looked out the window. The lights were off downstairs at the Lambents.

"I know you're probably thinking, 'Well shit, I've paid all this money and Tony isn't even gay.' But let me tell you, Jerry, he's bisexual for sure. Honestly. I met one of his ex-boyfriends."

"Well, good."

"You don't think I'm being too forward, do you? I think it's wonderful that you've got this place to call and get your rocks off. I wish they had a number for women. I mean I guess they probably do somewhere. But it's not as acceptable, you know? Women are supposed to be immune to a cheap thrill. Not that I think that's all this is. Just a cheap thrill, I mean."

"It was nice to meet you, Dixie," I replied, then rested the phone softly in its cradle. So much for advice from Anthony, I thought.

# Ground Zero

# 15

I muddled through dull Sunday and weary Monday and a contretemps on Tuesday with Jock Kurtz at work. He said my explorers concept for the juicer campaign was interesting but didn't place the product properly. He gave my proposal no more than a cursory glance before he left the office. Wounded, I followed him into the hall and asked him why he had given me the assignment if he had no intention of considering my work seriously. He said the point was moot since it was already too late to take my ideas to Vince Sullivan, who was in charge of the account, but the work had been good seasoning for me. I asked him why he didn't get me transferred—if he didn't think I was qualified—to the graphics department, which was at least closer to what I had been educated to do. He said that he just might do that and shut the door to the washroom in my face.

On Wednesday I remembered the key. I couldn't simply walk

over and introduce myself to the Lambents—that wasn't in my nature—but Chaz had suggested that they might keep my spare key, which was reason enough to visit them. I thought of the key while staring at the strobing face of my home computer screen. When I looked up and out the window, Muriel was jogging the path towards the patio with the dog on a short lead. Her hair was braided, and its honeyed length slapped against her curving back at each stride with almost palpable weight. She wore a black Lycra tank suit under shorts of saturated yellow. The dog, Cissy, had parentheses of froth at the corners of her mouth.

I knew that if I waited for a more proper occasion, I would never have the courage to act. I bolted down the stairs and dug the envelope with the key out of the kitchen drawer.

By the time I flung myself out my front door and raced around the corner, Muriel had opened the hidden gate onto the patio and was coaxing the dog inside. "Dammit, Cissy. Come in here and get a drink before you pass out." Her voice was full and warm, a little scorched around the edges, perhaps by cigarettes.

I realized that I was advancing towards her with a familiarity I couldn't claim, and I stopped moving abruptly in the middle of the sidewalk. "Excuse me," I said.

Muriel looked up from the dog, whom she had finally managed to pull into the confines of the fence, and latched on to my face. "Oh, hi!" she exclaimed and smiled. I detected the tiniest, unreadable pause before she spoke, but I knew I would be in danger of losing my resolve if I attempted to decipher it. I ignored the temptation for analysis and raised my hand to give a goofy wave.

"Hello," I said. "I live . . . you probably know . . . I live next door to you here. I'm Peter Keith."

"Yes, I know, Peter. Your arrival did not escape me." She pressed her hands to the frame of the gate and extended her left leg behind her to stretch her calf muscle. "Chaz said he spoke with you, and we've been meaning to get over there and introduce ourselves. But the stream of time slips on." She reversed legs. "Anyhow, I knew we would catch up to each other someway. I'm Muriel. Come in." She stood up to leave room for me to cross the threshold behind her.

"Really, I was just—"

"No, come in." She spoke firmly although with great patience. "Cissy tends to wander off with the door open."

I edged around her onto the redbrick paving inside. I took careful note of the portion of the patio that was invisible from my window. A narrow border of earth planted with flowers ran along the inside of the fence. In the far corner, sheltered from my usual vantage, was a standing sculpture or birdbath; it looked something like a prickly pear cactus fashioned from hunks of rusting sheet metal. On the topmost of the twisted arms or branches, plain metal cans had been welded, and these were filled to the brims with water. Under the metal tree, Cissy lapped determinedly from a white plastic dish.

While my head was turned, Muriel had shut the gate, then bent at the waist to grip her running shoes. Her braid had slipped along her back and curled around her neck; the fine, light hairs at her nape were damp. Muriel rolled her shoulders until the knots in her spine, visible within the scooped back of her tank suit, seemed magically and serenely to align themselves. "I apologize for the ludicrous rudeness of this," she said from between her shins. "If I don't stretch out, disaster follows."

"That's okay. I really didn't mean to bother you. Your . . ." Husband, I was going to say, but their relationship seemed suddenly uncertain. "Chaz, when I spoke to him, said you might be able to keep a spare key for me. I didn't think I'd need to, but then Sunday I got locked out and had to force my way through a window."

"You did?" Muriel rose slowly, settling each vertebra, and her pale face flushed. "I didn't notice. That shows you how useless I am at Neighborhood Watch." She didn't see me crawl through the window, of course, because it didn't happen, and I wondered if she was aware of the truth. "We'd be happy to keep a key here for you. Let's go in." She stood very near to me and smiled. She touched my shoulder. Then she stepped past me and slid the glass door open.

She receded into the dark inside, and I took my first step into the Lambent house.

# 16

There were three of the chairs. Two on one side and one on the opposite side of a massive mahogany sideboard. Even half blind from the sun outside, I was slowed by their luminous beauty. I had managed to skirt the Barcelona chair near the door with barely a glance because it was buried under newspaper and beach towels and didn't interest me. But these chairs were quite extraordinary. They were also mahogany, lighter than the sideboard yet still dark and lustrous. They had vaguely shield-shaped backs with a splat in the center pierced to resemble delicately twining fern fronds. The front legs curved gently out then curved gently back in cabriole style, ending in lightly filigreed outward-turning feet. The seats were upholstered in finely worked gold cloth, slightly threadbare along the slope of the seats' perimeters.

I stopped following Muriel and stood before the chairs. Stylistically they seemed to belong to the last quarter of the eighteenth century—a more subdued rococo adopted by English craftsmen. Except for the worn cushions they were in excellent condition, and I wondered if they were truly of the period or flawless copies. I wanted to touch one, to lift one and test its strength and weight, but I didn't dare.

When Muriel noticed I had paused, she returned to my side. "Aren't those great?" she said and pulled the elastic from the end of her braid. "They were my grandmother's. When she sold her house, she gave them to me." She worked the strands of the braid loose and shook her head.

"They're beautiful. They look like they should be in a museum."

"They were, actually. They were on loan for years."

"Then they're really eighteenth century? Are they Chippendale?"

"Apparently they correspond to an etching in Hepplewhite's Guide, but nobody can say for sure."

"They can't actually attribute any furniture directly to Hepplewhite, right?"

"I guess not." She sat casually on the edge of one of the chairs to untie her shoes. It shocked me at first, like someone striking a match on a Delacroix, but then I recognized that it was, after all, a chair. And it was *her* chair and therefore none of my business. "Are you interested in antiques, Peter?"

"Sort of. I trained as a designer."

"Really? That's wonderful." She used the toe of one shoe to push off the heel of the other. "Chaz said that you were a writer."

I hadn't said anything to Chaz on this subject, but I didn't dwell on the incongruity. "I work in advertising down in the Newport Center."

"Why not a design firm?" she asked as she jumped to her feet. "Come on, I'll show you my other chairs."

I was glad that I didn't have to answer her question. I would have been embarrassed to explain my occupational plight; it seemed like a failure of character. I trailed after her into the front room. In her bare feet she seemed more diminutive—I could nearly stare down at the top of her head—but her body, whenever it tensed, was supported by pronounced muscle. Her hips were narrow, and her buttocks, in the yellow shorts, almost boyishly small and solid.

The next room was full of chairs and very little else. They lined up against the walls in exhibition fashion with few concessions to the use of the room as living space. A sofa and armchair were arranged before the rack with the television and stereo, and across the room by the large front window was a Victorian "cosy corner"—the mutant child of a couch and a bookcase, which bent in the center to form a right angle. The upholstered armrests at either end of the V were bolstered by tapestry throw pillows, and the shelves above the seat back were stuffed with paperbacks and knickknacks.

"Can you tell I'm a collector?" Muriel laughed. "My grandmother did everything. Armoires, credenzas, canopy beds, garden benches. She had a Gothic ceiling shipped from a chateau in Dijon. I couldn't escape the collecting curse. It's like a yeast culture. She gave me one little piece—a writing table—when I was twelve. And my interest started bubbling, and it needed to be fed more and more. Fortunately, I've stuck with chairs. At least they're convenient for parties."

She gave me the tour, and while we walked around the room from artifact to artifact, some part of me wanted to impress her with my expertise, with casual references to yoke rails and stretchers and tubular steel construction. But the quality and unfathomable price of her collection left me quiet. Most of the pieces were twentieth century and almost all of them represented some pivotal movement or designer. She had a rosewood Eames lounge chair, a cubical Le Corbusier armchair, an austere Shaker bench, and a boldly colored chair formed of planes and angles from the De Stijl group. The most amazing piece was a desk chair of carved walnut in the style of François Rupert Carabin. A naked woman was carved, on her knees, with her torso bent over and supported by a sawhorse forming the rear legs of the chair. Her arms were curled to her chest with her hands reaching back at her shoulders. She held a massive slate against the nape of her neck which rose to form the back of the chair. The chair seat sat on the small of her back; the twin domes of her buttocks peeked out beneath the front to be burnished by the touch of seated calves. She was a slave trapped in the material of the chair.

"It is degrading in so many ways," Muriel said. "I imagine all the men who thoughtlessly sat on her, and some days I just want to free her. But then I remember she doesn't exist apart from the chair. She *is* the chair."

I rested my hand on one of the side cushions of the Le Corbusier. "I can't tell you how impressed I am."

"But I'm sure you could make one just as good, Peter." Muriel took my hand in her own—which was warm and slightly damp— and led me to the cosy corner. We sat on opposing cushions near the converging angle, and she placed a palm on each of my cheeks. "Peter," she began. "When we become good friends . . . and I know we will . . . I want you to design a chair for me. Will you?"

"Of course," I said, and understood that I would have no choice.

# 17

"Muriel thinks you're the cat's pajamas," Irena said. "I saw her in the laundry and she just went on and on about you."

I had rushed home during my lunch hour to retrieve some papers I forgot, and Irena intercepted me before I reached my door. She was wearing forest green leggings with rubber pads strapped to her knees and oversized, spotless gardening gloves. After the contract gardeners finished trimming the bushes and ground cover, Irena would circle around the building with her own gardening kit to tidy things up. Her fingers were wrapped around a pair of needle-nosed shears.

"She barely knows me," I said and glanced down at my watch. I couldn't think of anything I had done to impress Muriel or anything I might have said that Irena didn't already know. After examining the chairs the day before, I had forgotten about the key in my hand, but Muriel reminded me as I prepared to leave. She tore the envelope in half, poured the key into her palm, and slipped it onto a ring with an impressive number and variety of other keys. When I asked if we should label it with a piece of masking tape, she said, "I won't forget."

"False modesty is the virtue of fools, Peter." Irena made a few inconclusive snips at the edge of a box hedge. "She says you're a wonderful artist. Besides, Muriel has great discernment. I believe she may be a sensitive. One of those people who can perceive auras."

"Oh, Irena." I gave her a mild scowl.

"I know, Peter, I know. Before the seminar, I doubted it myself. But once you peel off even the tiniest corner of the veil of skepticism, you see that almost anything is possible."

"Does this have something to do with Zu-krall?" I tested out the term Chaz had used with her, but as a fervent light grew in her eyes, I regretted it.

"Oh yes," she said. "The Green One. The One Who Comes in a Circle. If you like, I have some literature or—"

"Thanks, but no," I said quickly. I would rather have been killed by a ten-ton truck than talk about her seminar any further. "I'm afraid I cherish my skeptical veil," I added and slipped around her into my house.

# 18

Whenever she saw me sitting at my desk upstairs, Muriel would rise onto the balls of her feet and wave. We didn't speak for the rest of the week, but each time our eyes met through one and sometimes two panes of glass, I felt that our relationship had grown a little warmer and more intimate. As if our auras had arranged some secret rendezvous.

However, while Muriel became increasingly visible, Chaz had disappeared. He may have left town or spent the week in bed, but, for whatever reason, he was absent from view; he had even vanished from my fantasies. When I jerked off, I filled my canvas with men I had seen at work or in the grocery store. For the first time in months, I had an erotic dream—an erotic dream with Muriel, not Chaz, at its core. While it was not unprecedented for a woman to appear in my head in this context, it was rare enough to shatter my sleep and leave me awake for an hour.

I was running along the beach on the Balboa Peninsula. (I assumed it was Balboa, because the white sand stretched along the Pacific without interruption for miles.) The sky was full of birds.

I was running in an inexplicable panic. And Muriel ran beside me. As we ran she placed one hand on my ass, and one on my stomach, and somehow another at the back of my neck. And she said, "Don't worry. I'll catch you."

Until she spoke, I didn't know I was falling. But then I felt the downward pull, and the sand was wet and warm and parted easily as we slid sideways into it. We were embracing face to face, and our bodies were drawn very close until our clothes disappeared and I was inside her. She surrounded me as comfortably as a pool of sun-warm water. I wanted to rock waves into her with my hips, but we were still falling and there was no way to gain leverage. "When you learn to swim," she said decisively as if she were answering some question of mine. I woke up with an aching hardness and finished the tangent begun in the dream with my hand.

When Muriel left the house to take her run with Cissy the next morning, I peered down intently into my kitchen sink as if I hadn't seen her. After the dream I felt wicked and awkward in her presence in a manner that I had never experienced with Chaz. I had already used and discarded so many men—real and imagined—for self-gratification that one more could not affect me. But, as a woman, Muriel retained the privilege of singularity.

At that moment I believed I might never speak to Muriel again, for a complete disconnection from the Lambents would have fallen within the normal trajectory of my shyness. I did not like variables, I avoided situations with indefinite stresses, and my relationships with people foundered more often on imagined violations than on real conflicts.

With Brad, I had been tempted to allow myself to break with him before he could discover my failings and nurture a disaffection, but my roommate Judy had convinced me that I couldn't afford to be brittle, that in order to embrace life I had to accept the possibility of failure or the need for adjustments. My friends at Floe had all been interested in yanking me from my socially maladjusted shell, and I had absorbed their lessons. I had held fast to Brad against an incredible fear, and when he left me, I was not prepared to make another commitment to uncertainty.

But Muriel was oblivious to my hypothetical abuses of her person and tenacious in her forward friendliness. She knocked on my door at six o'clock one Saturday bearing a rectangular platter under crimped foil. "Do you like pad thai?" She whisked off the cover and revealed a beautifully arranged nest of delicate noodles, squares of bean curd and bright pink shrimp, dusted with crushed peanuts, and bordered with watercress and curled shavings of carrot. "Whenever I cook, which isn't often, I always make enough to stock a small, chic restaurant for a week. So it would really be a big favor if you could take this off my hands." She executed a small, ironic geisha bow with her head and knees as she handed me the platter.

"It looks delicious. Thank you."

"Taste. Taste," she said and offered me a fork. I took it and wound a few strands onto the tines. "I would have brought you chopsticks, but I just learned last week that they aren't used in Thai cuisine."

I chewed the noodles and the flavors melted across my tongue in an effervescent blend of peanut, lime, tamari, and hot pepper. "It's amazing," I said.

"Good. That makes it easier to admit that this is all part of a shameless plot." She rubbed her hand along the back of her neck, and I noticed that while her hair was twisted up into a chignon, she was wearing a Brown University sweatshirt and a short, pleated gray skirt. With its contrast of hairstyle and outfit, her image fluctuated as if she were teleporting from one cosmos to another. "Frankly, Peter, I need an escort for tonight. Our friend Zorna is performing in a cabaret show and Chaz has opted out. He says experimental cabaret is the cultural equivalent of carpet bombing—too much destruction aimed at too few targets. But I say he's a snob. Will you come?"

"Sure," I said without hesitation. "I'd be happy to."

"Cool." She rocked back on her heels with her hands behind her back. "Nine o'clock?"

"I'll be ready. What should I wear?"

"Black. Dress in black." She grinned. "You can't go wrong with black."

# 19

The Ground Zero Cabaret was located in the basement of a plastic parts supply warehouse near the railroad tracks in Santa Ana. It was in a business district between neighborhoods, a cultural divider. The bilingual signs flip-flopped as we drove north past the carnicería with the huge plastic cow above its door and the joyería with giant engagement rings and enticingly cheap prices painted on its window. The stores' English names were stenciled in small black letters along the bottoms of the signs as a concession to any stray Anglo eyes; the shopkeepers weren't expecting much business from the English speakers, who tended to drive through these areas in the heart of Orange County with quick trepidation or skirt them entirely.

These were the neighborhoods where the women who scrubbed the floors and watched the children of Irvine went home to sleep. The buildings seemed more real to me, more substantial, than the Villas del Sol. Few of the neighborhoods I grew up in could be described as gritty; people I met from the East would chuckle and say, "L.A. is *not* a city." But my childhood streets had held the glow of inhabitation. Like tree rings or salt rime markings, they bore the traces of their evolution. In Orange County, however, every neighborhood was an Athena born fully formed from some developer's head, and while I might admire the technical achievement, the totality of a realized vision, I could not shrug off the feeling that I was living in a construct. I had never felt the inherent artificiality of human civilization so keenly.

At another time the battered doorframes, barred windows, and grime-streaked bricks of the Santa Ana streets might have unsettled me with thoughts of crime and bleak, crumbling lives. But that night I felt relieved, lightened, almost hopeful.

Rather than the likely Volvo or Mercedes, Muriel drove a 1967 copper brown El Camino—those mutant car-trucks trapped in nightmare fusion. The seats were covered in acrylic leopardskin, and a green tree air-freshener dangled from the rearview mirror. As we turned onto a dark drive, I looked towards the fading streetlamp through the back window, then down at a piece of grease-blackened metal hunkered in a corner of the truck bed. "What's that?" I asked.

Muriel glanced back, then smiled with both hands draped over the wheel. "I don't know. It was there when we bought the Lady, and we thought it might be some part of the car and we'd need to have it installed."

"The Lady?"

"Lady Lazarus," she said and spread a palm against the dashboard. "I love her. She's like the car in a road movie. Jolene, in the Dolly Parton song? Jolene would drive this car." Muriel sang, "Jolene, Jolene, Jolene, Jo-*lene*."

She pulled into a narrow space between two cars under the raised platform of a loading dock. "This is it?" I hunted for a sign that would indicate we had arrived. "There's not much in the way of advertisement."

"This is not the sort of place one just drops in on. Like fugu, an acquired taste." She laughed and slipped her legs from beneath the steering wheel with her knees pressed close. She stood and shimmied her hips to adjust the drape of her jet, sequined cocktail sheath. She grabbed her satin clutch purse from behind the seat. "Let's go," she said. "Or we'll miss Zorna's curtain."

I had dressed in (mostly) black as instructed—black jeans, black jacket, white T-shirt, and black boots—and as Muriel and I squeezed down the steep, crowded cement stairs into the muggy, crowded lobby, we were absorbed completely into an inky sea. Those few men and women who had dressed in burnt orange or sickly yellow or princely purple still looked as if they had considered wearing black, had in fact slipped into somber turtlenecks and granny gowns, and had only at the last moment decided to change.

Everyone in the throng knew Muriel; I shouldn't have been as surprised as I was. "Where's Chaz?" they asked and stared at me with the keenest interest their jaded faces could summon. I was used to slipping in and out of crowds, unobserved—at least this was my perception—and the attention reflected from Muriel made me uncomfortable. We were like mismatched salt and pepper shakers, and because I was both a complete stranger and an instant addition to the innermost circle, they felt the need neither for familiar sympathy nor for polite deference. Their gaze was nakedly clinical. After encountering a few coteries of Muriel's friends on the way to the buttoned-leather doors of the theatre, their scrutiny became unbearable. While Muriel spoke with a Pre-Raphaelite woman in black lace with a red cameo choker and auburn ringlets, I excused myself for the bathroom.

In the vestibule outside the toilet, an olive-skinned man in a red-and-black checked silk shirt sat on the edge of the sink. Another man, who wore a bomber jacket cut from a black velvet painting of blown yellow roses, stood between the first's spread legs and inserted his tongue into the other's ear with patient precision. I sidestepped them, but the toilet was locked. I didn't need to use it; I left.

When I emerged from the back hall, the crowd was shifting—some going into the theatre, some coming out. Muriel crossed through the thinning traffic from the tiny bar tucked into the corner. If I had thought of Chaz and Muriel drinking, I would have pictured them watching absinthe cloud through a blue haze of kif, but Muriel handed me a can of Coors. She shifted the clutch purse clamped to her side and raised her own can. "Cheers!"

"How much do I owe you? Is there a cover charge?"

"It's on me. Actually it's on the house. Because Chaz and I help out with fund-raising when we can."

"I don't normally drink Coors."

Her red lips tightened with real concern. "I'll get you something else."

"No, it's fine. I just hate to support the Coors family when they've given money to such appalling right-wing groups."

"That's okay then," she said with a relieved smile. "I thought you didn't like the beer."

"I'm serious. I think—"

"Oh, Peter. Don't worry." Muriel brushed her fingers along the sleeve of my jacket. Her gaze shifted watchfully around the room and halted at the bottom of the stairs. "There they are. We'd better hurry before Audra and her sisters reach us, or we'll never get in." She turned, and I followed her through the heavy double doors into the cabaret with the condensation from my untasted beer dripping from my fingers.

# 20

The cabaret had a thrust stage (if any platform the size of four connected card tables can properly be awarded that term). Above the stage at its halfway mark, a pair of black curtains were parted and gathered as neatly as Irena's hair. A single track of spotlights beamed down from a girder. Three rows of round gray formica-topped tables were arranged around the lip of the stage, and further back against the walls there were several red leather banquettes probably stripped from some defunct Italian restaurant. Muriel led me to the only available center stage table, which looked pristinely untouched, and we sat down on the japanned black, bentwood café chairs.

The room was dim, with light from the melon-shaped red glass globes on the tables. We had arrived for the denouement of an experimental sketch. Someone in a tatty gorilla costume was shining a flashlight beam on a man and woman in leotards and tuxedo shirts who were tied together at the wrists with a length of rope. They paced around each other until they were bound chest-to-chest in the coils. They spoke in turn: she said, "You've become so cold. I should have listened to Mother. And now I feel—" And he said, "You don't let me breathe. I shouldn't have married you and become—" Then they both shouted, "Trapped!" as the gorilla switched off the flashlight.

"Maybe Chaz was right to skip this," Muriel whispered under the scattered applause as the house lights rose to a dim glow.

I looked around the room at tables packed with the highest concentration of beveled haircuts, nose rings, and pallor I had encountered in Orange County. "Where do all these people come from? I can't believe they live here."

"Don't be so starstruck, Peter," Muriel responded. I had attempted to sound ironic and mildly disparaging, but she had seen through my cover; I was bedazzled. I suppose that I had been intimidated for too long by individuals who wore their cultural sophistication with the casual élan of worn jeans and slouchy jackets, and the opportunity to be effortlessly admitted to the ranks had lured me into their thrall. "Most of the people here merit less scrutiny than Irena does during one of her least brilliant asides at the homeowners' meetings."

It was the second time one of the Lambents had praised the discreet fascinations of Irena Delgado, and I was prepared to ask Muriel what quality my neighbor possessed which made her such an exemplar. But the lights were doused, and Zorna began her performance.

Although the Louise Brooks bob had been usurped by a waist-length corkscrew fall and the chartreuse tasseled gown replaced by a gold lamé halter and crimson velour pedal pushers, I had no difficulty recognizing Zorna from the Lambents' party. A single spot found her upended on a cushioned stool in a kind of headstand with her right leg shooting straight up to a pointed toe in a high-heeled clog and the left bent at the knee with the foot braced against the other shin. Jazz combo riffs throbbed from the sound system.

With her weight supported on her shoulders and elbows, Zorna swiveled her head to the side to look at us—at Muriel and me specifically, it seemed—and began to mouth the clipped, throaty intonations of the voice from the speakers. She kicked languidly at the air. The song was "From This Moment On."

As Zorna pulled herself upright onto the stool, Muriel leaned towards me and whispered, "Anita O'Day."

Zorna's performance was amazing—not because she was flawlessly synchronized but because her enactment poured the songs into new, unfamiliar vessels. With each Cole Porter lyric, she embodied the white voice of the female singer of a gay composer's work, and she also reincarnated the black idioms that served as the composer's inspiration. She danced, strutted, pouted; she was black and white, man and woman, straight and gay, sincere and satiric. Her appeal wasn't purely cerebral; she was hilarious and poignant.

When Zorna left the stage briefly for a costume change, Muriel looked behind us and raised her hand. With disconcerting speed, a waitress placed fresh beers before us on small white napkins. "Chaz likes you very much," Muriel said between sips.

"Really? But he doesn't know me. And don't tell me he's in touch with my aura."

"What?" she asked, but a crescendo of gushing strings made further conversation impossible.

# 21

Zorna's second set was more bizarre and less successful. In a powder pink teddy and knee-high green vinyl "wet look" boots, she performed to passages from Andrew Lloyd Webber and Sondheim with dada snatches of dialogue and helicopter noise. In the best section she donned a black Stetson for a Johnny Cash medley—"Folsom Prison Blues," "I Walk the Line," and "A Boy Named Sue." At the act's conclusion, she synched her lips to a recorded voice that might have been her own and introduced Polly Morpheus. Polly emerged from the dark with a bubble bouffant and a creamsicle organza prom dress. They performed a duet from Carol Burnett and Cher, and when the spot went out, the audience thundered.

The next act was announced as "Agony of the Rose." A cute young man with dark eyebrows carried a table onstage. He began to snip the heads of roses from their stalks and arrange them on an ornate oval hand mirror while weeping sonorously. Muriel tugged my sleeve and said, "Come."

We stood and weaved our way among the tables to the wall at the side of the stage. She parted a curtain and waited for me to pass ahead of her into the hallway beyond. She guided me around the corner and down a short flight of steps then knocked on an unlabeled door. For a few seconds, we stood in the drafty hall as a tape of screams and wails began to play inside the theater.

A person in a quilted bathing cap and three-inch false eyelashes opened the door wearing a floor-length tangerine dressing gown. "Muriel! My star!" Zorna hugged her. "Come in."

Beyond the door was a room smaller than my walk-in closet, crammed with tables, chairs, and wheeled garment racks, a space Zorna shared with Polly. "I would offer you refreshments," Zorna said, "but we don't have any."

"Oh, this is Peter Keith." Muriel coaxed me forward into the room with a hand to my back.

"Hi," I said.

"I'm Zorna." She spread a hand across the front of the gown. "Some of Zorna. And there's some of Zorna over there." She gestured to a row of wigs on Styrofoam heads across the room. "And some over there too." She nodded her chin towards a black plastic garment bag hanging from the rack.

"You're such a put-together woman," Muriel said, flicking one of the wigs' black tresses. "It's quite intimidating."

"Not Woman, my princess. I am Diva." She burst into a laugh. "But every diva needs to let her hair down."

"You were wonderful tonight," Muriel said and Zorna looked demurely at the floor. "I just want to congratulate Polly before she goes on again." She slipped around Zorna's back and left me standing awkwardly alone in the doorway.

"So, you're the new one," Zorna said and fixed me with the clinically speculative look I was growing accustomed to. Her face was rounder, less sculptural and severe without a huge wig to frame it. "Muriel's new friend."

"Chaz couldn't come, and I'm their neighbor, so . . ." I allowed my voice to trail off. I didn't want to explain my presence further; I didn't know how.

"Chaz is such a very, very busy man."

A silence followed as I watched Muriel in the opposite corner with Polly, trying on a quilted silver bolero jacket and giggling. "I thought you were brilliant. Your act was really wonderful."

"You know what I want to hear." Zorna grinned. "Come on over here." She pulled me to her side and hugged me, and I tried not to shrink away. The physical contact made me feel intensely self-conscious—and obscurely excited.

"I liked how it questioned all these assumptions about race and gender. It seemed really well thought out."

"Great. Great," Zorna said. "But how did I look?"

"You looked gorgeous," I replied. And she did, in a hyperreal flurry of lashes, blusher, and painted lips. Some light shone under Zorna's gloss that attracted me although I couldn't see its source.

"Girlfriend!" She kissed me on the cheek. "Muriel picked a winner."

"I saw you going into their party in that green dress and thought you looked quite stunning. I was very jealous that I wasn't invited." I flattered Zorna because it seemed so easy; she seemed to lap up adulation. Actually, I hadn't paid much attention to Zorna at the party, but the jealousy was true.

Zorna released me to arm's length and bent her head slightly to look down into my eyes. "Chaz and Muriel give great party, yes ma'am. But you have to know when to make your exit. I always leave early. That's my rule." Zorna leaned into my chest and whispered, "And you should make it yours."

"Telling him all my secrets, huh, Zorna?" Muriel stood at my side and squeezed my shoulder.

"Princess, you don't have secrets. When you're gonna shit, they put up a billboard with the time and date."

"That's only so I can make some money on the ticket sales."

"Go on, girl." She brushed her hand in the air and laughed. "I've got to help Polly with her props. Thanks for looking in. But next time, would a dozen long-stem yellow roses hurt so much?"

"Next time, Zorna." Muriel stretched up and kissed her along her cheekbone then left the room.

"Nice to meet you," I said and began to follow Muriel out.

Zorna pointed a finger at me. "Be good. They don't have to be, but you *do*. Bye." She waved and spun around to commence an immediate, heated critique of Polly. "Your tits are slipping, girl. Looks like you're pregnant with twins."

We didn't stay for Polly's act. I followed Muriel down the dark hall and into an open stairwell that led up to the parking lot. In five minutes we were heading home.

"Would you get my smokes?" she asked. "In the glove box."

I rooted around inside and pulled a nine-by-twelve manila envelope and several cassette tape cases into my lap. I found a pack of Camels and handed them to her.

"Bless you. I thought I might be out." She touched the red coil of the dashboard lighter to a cigarette, then took a long drag. "Did you like it?"

"Yes, very much."

"Oh, that's for you." She pointed to the envelope in my lap with the hand holding the cigarette, and a fragment of ash dropped to the leopardskin. "I made you a present."

I bent open the clasps and pulled out a sheet of paper. It was heavy and thickly spongy, handmade, with dark flecks on its surface. On one side, within a neatly drawn rectangle, was a carefully calligraphed verse.

"This serves as a piece of life philosophy, I suppose. I find belief in little bits. In poems, snatches of song, what someone says to me. I can't manage more than bits, like a crow gathering up her shiny nuggets of foil. I don't even believe them all at the same time. But it's a nice poem."

In the intermittent illumination of the street lamps, I read the verse. It was from Emily Dickinson:

> How many schemes may die
> In one short Afternoon
> Entirely unknown
> To those they most concern—
> The man that was not lost
> Because by accident
> He varied by a Ribbon's width
> From his accustomed route—
> The Love that would not try
> Because beside the Door
> It must be competitions
> Some unsuspecting Horse was tied
> Surveying his Despair

# 22

At that moment, I thought the poem was an invitation, although it might as easily have been a warning. I was naïve enough to believe that it couldn't be both.

I was convinced that Muriel knew I had been watching them, that she knew I was intimidated by her other friends—the competition's Horses—and that she didn't want me to suffer like Dickinson's despairing Love.

The poem had two examples of Fate's fickleness, but each time I read the verse, I glossed over the first, ignoring the man who had grazed unknowingly within inches of death. I stuck the paper to my refrigerator with a magnet and vowed that I would not fail to try the Door, to cross the threshold into the Lambents' domain.

One night that week I went to the University of California library in Irvine and checked out every book I could find about chairs. I wanted to give something to Muriel—a sketch, at least, or a diagram—to show my good faith in honoring my pledge.

Beyond a few technical exercises in drafting class, I had never worked with furniture. I had certainly never made a chair. I knew that chairs were like miniature buildings, dwarf skyscrapers, microcosmic cathedrals. Master architects, whose grandiose schemes for underground cities and endless towers remained forever lost in blueprints and elevations, had nonetheless created actual chairs—the truest expression of their thoughts pushed into the material world. These men (for, from the evidence of books, there were few women who toiled as prophet-architects) were secure in their belief that they were the capable creators of worlds; their vision, which could reshape continents, might also be directed with a laser's fineness to the shaping of a demitasse or a spoon. Dionne Warwick was wrong to conclude in song that "a chair is not a house." A chair *is* a house, a building, a city; a chair is the world.

My chair for Muriel could not be a copy. She owned too many originals to be satisfied with some apprentice attempt at Queen Anne elegance or second-rate Memphis funk. I wanted to make for her something wholly new. I wanted to speak to her in the language of the lathe and the vise. So I turned to books not for form but for inspiration.

Many of the illustrations in the histories of the chair were taken from the paintings of artists like Hogarth or Nicolas Maes. A Dutch woman would sit sewing near the window, and the chair at her side would be dimly seen: a simple turned leg in a shaft of sun, a prayer book lying open on its dark lap. While studying the pictures in this context, my eyes were drawn away from the figures at the center and into the corners of the rooms. The sitters were people who sat on the edges of settees; they were ladies who draped gloved hands on the back rails of chairs. But they were ephemeral; they would not endure the razing of time while their furniture would.

I stared for an hour at the painting of Mr. and Mrs. Andrews by Gainsborough. The couple stared back at me. Their faces were composed, self-satisfied. They posed before a tree's thick trunk at the left of the canvas, and all the land visible to the right and out to the horizon beyond belonged to them; they were its stewards and the recipients of its riches. He stood, wearing a tricorn hat, a hunting coat, black breeches, and white stockings wrinkled comfortably at his crossed ankles. A black shotgun dangled flaccid from the crook of his elbow. His dog waited at his feet, sniffing his knee for some crumb of manure that had snagged in the breeches' nap while he bent in the field. One hand was shoved into his pocket; the other casually clutched the absent hand's glove. The woman sat, dressed in clearest blue, bluer than the skies above the hills and woods. Her tiny feet were also crossed at the ankles beneath the voluminous panniers of her gown, and in her lap she held a delicate gray fan. Her fingers were positioned around the handle, not to wave it, but as if she were squeezing a bird's slender throat.

She was anorectically thin; he was angular and narrow. They did not eat with pleasure because each outlay for food diminished their capital. Their eyes in oval faces were curious. They were interested in me, but they would not make the first move.

She was sitting on an iron garden seat painted a deep green. The back rail arched up and the legs twisted down in an evocation of tangled vines and curling leaves. The seat back was visible at the woman's left side along with one twisted arm rail and one leg. The other foreleg was just visible between the leaning man and seated woman, almost indistinguishable from the gnarled root of the tree. After the couple had stared at me for an hour with their implacable eyes, I wanted them to go. I wished that he would lead the dog away from the rise and she would gather her skirts of reflected sky and leave the seat vacant, in unobstructed view above the field of ripened grain.

# 23

I went over at Muriel's behest. I was indifferent to baseball and had not watched a game all season. But she stepped out and invited me while I was sweeping my porch, and I agreed. "Chaz would really like you to join him. He loathes watching television alone, but I find it vastly boring. I don't care if it *is* the playoffs. Someone hits the ball and they all move around and around the same square and end up where they started. It's Pavlovian. And say some guy bats the ball into the next state; all he gets to do is run around the bases. Big deal. Will you come over please and get me off the hook?"

"Who's playing?"

"Oh, please. Who cares." She pulled her braid over her shoulder, touched the tip, then batted it back, all while staring at me plaintively.

"Will you be there?"

"Later maybe. I'm going shopping." She said "shopping" with slow relish, as if it were an activity of the Marquis de Sade. "I know it must seem an awful capitulation to gender roles, but I need to get out of the house."

"Mmm," I said without commitment. Although it was Chaz who had first attracted me to the Lambents, Muriel was the person who had become, in some way, a friend. We hadn't done anything together since our night at the cabaret—she had invited me out one night for drinks, but I worked until eleven at the office and then fell asleep on my couch ten minutes after coming home—but we would talk for a few moments whenever we met outside our respective doors. I would tell her about my travails at work: Jock Kurtz did, indeed, have me transferred to the art department where I was "earning my stripes" with ignoble hours spent on the computer and on graphic cleanup work—a demotion, although with the comfort that, by continuing at the same salary, I was being vastly overpaid for the position. Muriel told me about Zorna: she had been discovered; she would be staging a one-person show, "Zorna Swings Songs of Innocence and Experience," at a performance space in Los Angeles. Because we talked, I felt secure enough to consider Muriel an acquaintance, but I didn't know Chaz. I was apprehensive about visiting him alone. "You're sure he won't mind?"

"Peter, he *invited* you. It's his idea. He likes you." She hooked her thumbs in the pockets of her jeans. "So?"

"Okay, sure. When is the . . . ?" Kickoff? Tee-off? First ball?—I had no idea what the beginning was called. "When does it start?"

"Stop by at two. I liked you in the jeans and T-shirt you wore to see Zorna." She smiled. "Now I need to go collect my charge cards." She waved and wandered around the corner towards the mailboxes.

I wondered at the wisdom of her suggested outfit when it was still hot enough for shorts and tank tops, but I supposed that my initial consultation with Muriel about attire had condemned me to accept her advice forever. I finished sweeping, showered, and spent an inordinate time working my hair over with gel and a blow-dryer. I dutifully buttoned up my black jeans and donned a clean white shirt, tucking it in and rolling the sleeves. After arranging the shirt, I had to fuss with my hair again. Then I locked the house and walked next door. I knocked, firmly, and realized that I probably should have brought something—beer, snacks, something—but it was too late.

Chaz opened the door immediately as if he had been lurking in the shadow behind it. "Hey, there," he said and stepped aside so that I could pass into the small foyer. "You're just in time for the national anthem."

I smiled and looked directly into his eyes. Their emerald glint arrested me—I felt the muscles freeze along my spine—then the irises melted into a benign, inviting green. I wanted to avoid formality, I wanted to be at ease, so I asked casually, "Why is it that the only time you hear the national anthem is at games?"

Chaz folded his arms across the stomach of his powder blue polo shirt. "Sports are the only patriotism in America today. Want a beer?"

"Sure." As I continued into the main room, I glanced back and saw his solid legs straining forward behind me in bleached, near-white jeans. "You really think so?" I wanted to keep the conversation running. I was afraid we would exhaust all topics for mutual discourse and end the day glaring sullenly at the television.

"Maybe," he said. He scratched absently along the outer curve of one ear. "What's left to rally round? There's no communism. No races left to hate. And nobody's claiming the next hundred years will be the American Century. So why not baseball?" His voice grew low and serious; his face fell slack. He looked up, embarrassed at being caught thinking. "But I try not to believe in anything too deeply. Makes life easier. Sit down. I'll get the beer."

I sat at one end of the sofa centered in front of the muttering television. Text and graphics swirled giddily around stills of the players' faces. I watched Chaz recede through the archway, guiltily aware of the cheeks of his butt tensing high at each step in the tight hammock of his jeans.

While he was in the kitchen, I fixed my eyes obediently on the screen. The images flipped from batters limbering up to a close shot of the pitcher methodically adjusting his cap—either as a signal or merely aimlessly. I began to sense the presence of all of Muriel's empty chairs arrayed in silent audience around the walls behind me.

I was relieved when Chaz dodged around the corner with two Bohemias cocked in one hand and a bowl of popcorn. He sat in the center of the sofa and gave me the beer. "I think there's been two strikes, no outs," I said.

"Sshh." He punched the volume button on the remote and gazed intently at the screen. "Sorry, I just like to hear the little things. Cleats scuffing in the dirt. Leather ball slapping leather glove. Stuff like that."

I couldn't hear any noises of this category beneath the crowd noise and the mindless banter of the sportscasters. I couldn't imagine that the perception of such intimate sounds was even possible with TV— except maybe with tennis. But I kept respectfully silent.

I resigned myself to a soporific afternoon getting pleasantly buzzed on Mexican beer and relaxed into the back cushion. By the second inning I was actually interested in the game, and I didn't notice that Chaz had dropped his hand to his lap until he began to pull at the top button of his jeans.

I listened to the metal studs slip with a hiss from their looped cotton holes with the same attention Chaz gave to the crack of a bat, but I didn't shift my head. At the periphery of my vision I saw a white strip of his briefs within the spreading triangle of his fly. His shirt lay folded up across his stomach, exposing a band of taut golden skin above the briefs' elastic waistband. My neck ached at the effort of remaining attentive to the television.

Chaz slid his fingertips under the waistband with the heel of his palm resting casually flat against his hip. A few dark blond hairs curled out into view along the straight white edge. Chaz continued to stare ahead, and I risked a sidelong glance. His fingers had sunk deeper into the pouch beneath the exposed Y-shaped fly of the briefs. I couldn't breathe; I didn't know what to do or say, or not to do or say.

He continued to sink his fingers into the rift of his fly. A patch of deeper, denser hair appeared. His hand began to curve, giving dimension to the flesh inside, and within the arch of the briefs I saw a swelling of dark pink skin.

I began to stiffen, and I shut my eyes, clenching the empty Bohemia bottle in my fist.

He pulled himself free of his shorts, lifting his balls out and over the curving line of the waistband.

His other hand pressed at the back of my neck. As he led me slowly down, my entire body jerked with a rigid spasm. The beer bottle flopped from my hand and hit with a soft thump on the carpeting. "It's okay, Keith. It's okay," he said without taking his eyes from the television.

# 24

I never saw the final score; my head never left his lap for the rest of the game. It wouldn't be accurate to say that I wasn't present. I have rarely felt as energized, as fully in possession of my body, as I did that afternoon. But the waking part of me, the critical creature who analyzed and passed judgment, had been enclosed within a soundproofed jar and stored in a far corner of my being. I was alive to the world, and I could crave his pleasure above my own without irony or abasement.

Chaz had guided me down between his legs, and I soon flipped my body around into a near fetal position beside him on the sofa with my face turned towards his stomach and my feet kicked up over the padded arm. Sometimes I lay with my cheek cradled on his thighs and other times I propped myself on an elbow. He made no concessions to my comfort, and I didn't ask for any. I didn't think of my oddly torqued body because my full attention was concentrated in my face and hand and the aching hardness in my jeans.

When he first brought me down, he held up the head of his swelling erection and plugged it into my mouth as if he were making an electrical connection. I was afraid that he would use his hand at my neck to force me down too fast and deep and choke me. But he kept his hand loosely braced, only massaged my neck gently from time to time, and gave me control. He kept his eyes on the game and never looked down.

I was not a novice, and I knew how to make use of a flicking tongue and loosely brushing teeth, but I may have been too eager the first time. I wasn't concentrating on the rhythm, and it took me time to find the right pace. He only shifted once: when I reached down to unbutton my fly, he batted my hand away.

He came unexpectedly in my mouth—three short, sharp jolts—and I panicked and attempted to pull away and run for a sink or toilet. He held me in place with a palm to my back and a hand in my hair. "It's safe, Keith," he said. "Just swallow it."

I looked up at him with what must have been an expression of abject fear, and for the first time since he sat down to watch the ball game, he met my eyes. "Go ahead. I promise you."

I don't know why I believed him; I suppose I just wanted to. Dutifully, I sucked up the heavy, slightly bitter liquid that had pooled around my front teeth and gulped it down. He kept his hand in my hair until I relaxed my head onto his leg. He stroked my cheek and forehead.

For most of the game, I rested in his lap with my eyes turned in, my nose attuned to his warm, slightly raucous smell, and waited until his dick recovered and began to swell again with the rim of the crown becoming a fierce violet. I would take him into my mouth and suck. I had been hard myself for so long that I felt slightly crazed. I wanted to grab myself, but I understood that Chaz would not allow it. Instead I waited hungrily for his climax. There were three or more of them, and after each one I scoured him thoroughly with my tongue in search of any errant drops.

After the seventh inning, Chaz slid out from under me and jacked up his jeans. He grinned at me and climbed the stairs to the bathroom. I heard his urine patter into the bowl of a toilet, and, without reflection, I wished he had saved it for me. I had never fantasized about this before. Water sports had always seemed quaint to me, like Victorian pornography—an interest to avoid in specialized personal ads. But I wanted Chaz intensely. I wanted him to give me everything.

# 25

Chaz returned ready for me to take him again. He had stripped off his jeans and shorts, and his blue polo shirt draped symmetrically over the base of his erection. While he was gone, I had stared at the sofa's fabric-covered buttons, not thinking, barely breathing. If he had taken a few more minutes, I wondered later, would I have sat up and wiped my lips with my fingers? I might have considered what had happened. My conscience had never allowed my desire to fly unfettered. I had always been in control during sex and therefore able to detach from it, to float free and watch and study. But at the Lambents', my head was swimming in it. If I could have pulled up to the surface, I would have fled for home. At the time, I was only happy to have him back.

"Want another beer?" he asked, but his smile said he knew I had no desire for alcohol, for anything but him.

He lay back against the arm of the sofa with his hands under his head, and I rolled over to crouch between his legs. In this position I could take him with deeper, more forceful strokes.

When the game ended, I was resting, exhausted yet still aroused, with my head on his stomach. He had reached down to stroke my hair and tickle my ear with a finger. I was half asleep when Chaz said, "Come on, Keith." He began to stir underneath me. He pulled free and stood. When I rolled onto my back to look at him, he scooped his arms under my shoulders and knees and lifted me into the air.

I wasn't light, and it took some effort from him to carry me up the stairs and down the hall. I put one arm on his shoulder; the other dangled against his side. We paused in the entry to the bedroom. "Get down, Cissy!" he called, and I lifted my head in time to see the muddy yellow dog rise grumpily from the center of the down comforter and slump off the side. Chaz dropped me with a grunt onto the bed, and I heard the shush of air and feathers in the duvet beneath me.

He undressed me brusquely, flipping off my laced shoes and rapidly shucking my jeans down my legs. After he lifted my back to free me of my T-shirt, he held his cheek to mine and whispered in my ear. "Sorry if I woke you. Get in bed and relax. I'll be back."

Chaz left the bedroom, and I slid dutifully under the covers: the airy duvet, a thin cotton blanket, and soft sheets—all white. For an instant I wondered how I had become so easily subsumed into Chad's plans, but I couldn't sustain the thought as my head sunk into the yielding, expansive pillow.

Claws scraped against the sheet a few inches from my face. I opened my eyes to glistening black gums and clenched, numerous teeth. Cissy stared down at me, snarling. Snails of thick saliva began to stretch from the hinges of her wide jaws. Her forepaws dug with determination into the mattress.

"Cissy! Get out of here!" Chaz shouted. The dog bunched her broad shoulders and shifted her legs down onto the floor. I heard Chaz slap his thigh or her flank. She whimpered once plaintively, and I listened to the clink of her nametag against her collar as she sauntered down the hall.

Chaz set a long-necked bottle down on a table somewhere to the side of the bed; I didn't look. He pulled his shirt over his head, revealing a torso like a bronze shield broken by the golden-pink rivets of his nipples and the channels under his arms tufted with brown hair. He straddled me on the bed, pinning my arms against my sides under the covers. He grinned at me, and I smiled back. I didn't want to break the spell and speak.

He edged up along my body until he knelt directly above my head. Then he squatted heavily on my chest and stretched his erection flat against my cheek. "It's cool that your eyebrows are darker than your hair. They really make your face." He drew his thumb along my brow.

I opened my mouth and brushed his skin with my lips.

"Hey," he said. He grabbed his dick and slapped me on the cheek with the shaft then drew back. "Let's see what we have here." He peeled the covers back to my sternum; he touched the hollow of my throat and the crests of my nipples with an index finger. "Roll over,

Keith," he said and climbed off me to allow me to move. I twisted onto my stomach and folded my arms under the pillow beneath my head.

Chaz lightly traced the arc of my shoulder blades. His fingers paused. "What's this?"

"What?" I didn't open my eyes. I didn't want to talk.

"This thing here . . . this speck." His finger circled a spot on my shoulder blade.

"Oh, it's a mole." I had a small reddish brown mole with a miniature tail like a comma on my left side. I couldn't see it except in a mirror, and I rarely remembered it existed.

"I like it," he said. He bent down and licked it with the tip of his tongue. "I like your little speck."

# 26

Chaz was interested in minor details. He liked my eyebrows, and he liked my tiny mole, and he liked the curl of hair behind my left ear, which he unwound, then let flex back into place each time he whispered to me. He began to call me Speck—a secret name to murmur as he explored my body.

He dragged away the bedcovers until only my toes were blanketed and considered me carefully with his fingertips. He stood, and I heard him lift the bottle from the table and unscrew the cap. There was a soft touch along the top of my back; it felt neither cool nor warm nor wet, only motile and frictionless as it spread over my skin and dripped in rivulets down my sides. Chaz wiped the softness down my spine and along my flanks. He rubbed it over the muscles of my upper arms and into the hollows underneath. He hooked his fingers over my shoulders and kneaded at the cords tensed there. The air began to warm around my face, and I smelled the deep pungence of olive. I opened my eyes and looked at the bottle of green oil near the bed.

Chaz massaged my back, pressing deeply and rhythmically into rigid flesh along my spine. He worked the oil over my calves and up my thighs. His thumbs squeezed up into the base of my legs, and I relaxed until my body was puddled and fragrant. I was prepared for the final gesture when he would hold the narrow throat of the bottle in the air above my buttocks and pour a trickle into the rift between them.

Instead, he squeezed a tube of cold lubricant and watery fingers probed in between my cheeks. He worked one and then two fingers inside me. I moaned, and he rocked them slowly deeper. He pressed firmly down into the rounding of my prostate, and my body quivered. I arched my back, upsetting the pool of oil in the valley of my spine. Drops beaded at my waist and pattered on the sheet.

Chaz reached down to the floor. I squinted to watch him lift the condom and the lubricant. I heard the plastic rustle of the unrolling sheath and a wet squirt. Then his fingers were gone, and I felt him loom over me. He moved into me, and my body stretched to take him. He pushed deep once and paused. Then drew out. Then in again. Then he rocked into me swiftly. He made me raise my legs and pushed a pillow under me. His palms pressed into the greasy sheets at my shoulders. His clenched stomach slapped wetly against my buttocks.

I moaned. I knew I could be screaming soon, and I didn't care—as I might have thought I would—that the neighbors would hear and wonder. I went into myself, into the blank of my mind.

I was being fucked. I had been fucked twice before—both times with Brad—and each time I had lain on my back with my legs in the air, feeling vaguely cramped and uncomfortable—trapped. When I fucked Brad, my mind was alive, channeled to a fine point of discrimination at the head of my dick. I could enjoy the act and the thought of the act simultaneously. When I reciprocated at Brad's urgings, my thoughts stretched taut and squeaky around me, preventing any contact, containing my release.

But with each thrust from Chaz I felt pushed out of myself, out into the slithering sea. I suppose I was writhing under him on the slick sheets. But I don't remember the bed or the room. I remember being opened, opened wide enough to surround the world and feel its pulse, its beat, inside me.

I knew when he was ready to come; I could feel it in every muscle, on every plane where our bodies touched. He made low, muffled animal sounds, and I shouted, "God! Oh God!" I came, spurting into the sheets, in the intermezzos of his fierce, climactic thrusts.

As Chaz sank on to me with his full weight, exhausted, I understood that I would never escape this sex. I would replay it—whole —forever in my mind. It wasn't just Chaz or me alone; it wasn't a place in time, an event. It was pivotal, an entity with its own identity and claims to love and memory.

# 27

After Chaz rolled free of me, he tugged the condom loose and tied off the salinated tip with a neat knot, then dropped it to the floor. I turned onto my back, and Chaz held me until I fell asleep.

It was night when I woke. The sound I heard was a faint, slicing hiss like satin being drawn across marble. I jerked my head up and realized that I had returned to the stream of time, to the thick of my life. For the first time, I worried about Muriel. She would be returning imminently; she should already be home. There would be no excuse I could make. It would take me weeks to understand for myself what had happened; I certainly couldn't explain it to anyone else. She wouldn't forgive me, and I wouldn't want her to.

It took an instant for the fear to tumble through me, as my arms reached into the dark for security. Fabric bunched and shifted in my hand. It was slippery but dry, unlike the oil-sodden sheet.

I was about to sit up. I felt intensely naked, and the skin of my entire body was alive under a sheen of oil. I was prepared to raise myself on my elbows when I discovered the mirror on the ceiling. I had been too oblivious to notice it before. It was a vast oval with a gilt baroque frame whose fripperies played out then vanished into the shadows of the ceiling. Around the edges the glass seemed to have rumpled and darkened with age, but the center was clear. Before I could understand what I saw reflected in its depths, I imagined earthquakes and falling shards, and I panicked. My heart jumped, but nothing moved in the mirror, and I took a breath.

I saw myself stretched naked in the center of the large bed, my body long and shimmering, my arms pulled in at my sides, my dick at rest against my thigh. On my right, Chaz slept on his side, turned away from me. He too was naked, and his spine curled against my arm.

To my left, also on her side, also curled away from me, draped in sheer black, was Muriel. Her elbows were bent with her hands cupped under her head. Her hair spread loose and golden behind her on the pillow. The material I worked in my hand, which made the mild sussuration I had heard in my sleep, was the hem of her negligee. I released the fabric and it sussed out of my hand.

"Peter?" Muriel whispered. I continued to watch her in the large, dark mirror; she didn't open her eyes. "I thought I'd just take a nap till you both woke up. Then we can go out to dinner."

I didn't respond. From above, with my body a straight line and theirs curled away from me, we looked like a fleur-de-lys, like an exclamation point and two parentheses. And the parentheses faced out to enclose and hide the entire world beyond my singular exhalation.

# 28

"I can't tell you how glad I am that things have worked out." Muriel knocked back the slushy remnants of her drink and shifted her bottom on the black-spotted, hairy white cowhide seat of her barstool. We were working our way through a second pitcher of margaritas and an elaborate platter of quesadillas in the bar of a Mexican restaurant across the street from where I worked. We, the three of us, each sat on one of the ridiculously tall brushed-steel stools at an even taller pedestal table. I had drunk more than I ever had in such a short time; Chaz was nursing his second glass; and Muriel was both drinking thirstily and slathering one stringy wedge of quesadilla after another with mesquite-smoked tomatillo salsa and lemony guacamole, then happily noshing on them.

Muriel wore skin-tight jeans tucked into black cowboy boots and a ribbed, flaxen yellow cowl-necked sweater. Chaz wore blue oxford cloth and chinos, and I was dressed in Chaz's comfortably frayed tuxedo shirt and my own black jeans. I had spent twenty minutes in full steam under the Lambents' shower to wash the skin of oil from my body, and I still felt subtly greasy and thick. Correspondingly, I felt a hazy barrier between myself and my engagement with the world. When I said, "I feel kind of weird," I wasn't responding to Muriel but reporting on my own internal condition.

"Oh, don't, Peter. It's wonderful," she said and poured herself another margarita. "Chaz and I have been looking for a suitable lover for a long time. And I think we both feel blessed that we found one. I, for one, can't wait for you to eat me out."

I must have blanched, even in my detached, tequila-addled condition, because Muriel added quickly, "Assuming, of course, you want to, that is." She looked down at the ceramic ramekin of salsa, bit her lower lip, and blew a little huff of air in embarrassment. Chaz smiled (I thought) sardonically.

My stomach was shuddering. "Excuse me," I said and dropped gracelessly off the stool to charge for the men's room. The doors were branded with hieroglyphics of cows: one with udders, one with horns. I pushed through the bull door, knelt before a toilet bowl, and rapidly gushed away the contents of my stomach. I instantly felt less nauseous, less drunk, and more connected to the world. It may have been the too-copious tequila that made me sick, but at the time it seemed more like an augury for the condition of my soul. I couldn't explain why sleeping with my new friend's lover in abject secrecy would have been preferable to receiving her consent and encouragement, but it would have been. I couldn't actually disapprove of what had happened; I had no higher moral ground on which to stand. Besides, in the murky bottom of my mind, beneath the nausea and moral queasiness, I knew I reveled in a private vertigo of anticipation.

I stood and latched the stall door behind me and stared at the chalky, lagoon-green tiles ahead. I studied the phallic lever thrusting from a circular steel plate in the wall above the commode. Around the circumference of the plate was a ring of embossed letters: SAN-AM-ARCO LTD. MADE IN USA. My eyes twitched around and around the circle rereading the empty phrase until I felt ready to vomit again.

When I had finished being ill and could think of no other reason to linger in the dimly lit, ammonia-scented men's room, I washed my face, toweled off with a fistful of stiff brown paper, and went back into the bar. Chaz beamed at me and clapped his arm around my shoulder when I came within reach. "Feeling better, Speck?"

"Yes. Much." I sat down on my stool before a large tumbler of clear iced liquid.

"Water," Muriel said. "You should always drink plenty of water to forestall a hangover." I continued to stare at the ice cubes. "Go on. Cheers!" She tilted her half-full margarita to sip. I hoisted the heavy glass and drank.

"Let me tell you a story," Chaz began. He held the finely manicured nails of both hands out on the table in front of him.

"A true story?" I asked, because I wasn't in the mood for some well-meant but noncomforting fiction.

"It doesn't really matter, does it?" Chaz drummed his right index finger rapidly against the formica table, which was illustrated with turquoise cartoons of saguaro cactus, steer skulls, and coiled lariats. "There was a girl when I was in college. Named Jennifer. We had the same faculty advisor and ended up in several classes together. She was the kind of girl who always dressed neatly, studiedly. Preppy surreal, I used to call it. She wore these beautiful tartan skirts, the kind you close off with a big gold safety pin. She said they were actually the colors of her mother's clan, believe it or not." Chaz looked at me directly, and I looked at him—not into his eyes but at the vertical spikes of his near-white hair.

"She was a lesbian for a while, I think for political reasons—for the feminist agenda. Then her girlfriend dumped her when she found a box of rubbers in Jennifer's tote bag." He dipped a tortilla chip tentatively into the salsa, then lifted it to watch the red liquid coalesce along the chip's edge. "We had an Italian cinema class together. De Sica, Visconti, Rossellini, Fellini—the whole gang. We had Marcello Mastroianni out the wazoo. And in every discussion group, Jennifer was dismissive. Of Visconti especially. And she despised Fellini. She respected Pasolini, grudgingly. Then we started on Antonioni. And she entirely loved him. She shit bricks over *L'Avventura*. Then they screened *Red Desert*, and she snapped. She started screaming in discussion group. Seems she couldn't forgive Antonioni for using color. 'Singing in the Fucking Rain is in *color!*' I remember her choking out the word. 'Gone with the Fucking Wind is in *color!*' She couldn't deal with it, and she dropped the class." Chaz ate his chip finally, crunching it unhappily.

"And?" I was amazed at my surly tone. I had never had an extended conversation with Chaz before, but I already felt at ease in being insolent with him. I suppose my afternoon with him made me feel entitled.

Because Chaz seemed disinclined to continue, Muriel took over, with the assumption that the message of his story was obvious. "We've been bored, Peter. Not bored with each other. Not by any means. But we don't want to get stale and rigid. We wanted someone else to share our loving. And I'm happy we can be honest with you now. That we don't have to pretend anymore. And don't let anybody say you can't have Technicolor if you want it." Muriel leaned into my side, with her stool creaking under her, and kissed me, softly, on the lips.

# 29

Muriel's chair would have wings. I decided this early in the planning stages, before I pulled out drafting paper and graphite pencils with needle-fine leads and got serious. From the outset I knew that the design would need to be realistically simple because I would be required to master all the construction techniques involved, and because I couldn't overtax the capabilities of my father's workshop where I planned to build it. Consequently, I wanted its features to be striking.

The wings would serve as the arms of the chair, soaring free from the frame of the seat rail with the curve of a boomerang or a bird's wrist. The arm rails would arch, supplely rounded on top and filled in below with a thin flange of wood—stretched like an opposing thumb and forefinger and their uniting web of flesh. The flange might be scalloped along its free edge or carved with a delicate motif suggesting feathers.

The seat would be square with a drop-in cushion. The legs would be slender, slightly tapering and with exaggerated knees rising above the seat rail like a jaguar's limbs crouched in preparation for a fatal pounce.

I had more difficulty envisioning the back. Initially I imagined a stark backboard, an upholstered rectangular block. But in my early sketches the solid back seemed incongruous with the delicate arms, a concrete slab with inadequate wings. I finally settled on a more curvilinear outline: on some pages, a pie wedge narrowing sharply as it approached the seat; on others, an inverted tear. As I flipped through my notebook, I recognized the form I had been approaching: a peacock's tail, provocatively upraised, its plumage slowly spreading.

With its tail and wings, with its lithe, tensing leopard's body, Muriel's chair would be mythological beast, a sacred monster, with a deep velvet shrine and a cult of mysteries.

# 30

I sat with Muriel on her patio in a yellow canvas director's chair drinking sun tea. I looked at Cissy curled in an undifferentiated, doughy lump inside the screen door. She had emitted a pro forma snarl when Muriel first invited me in through the hidden gate, then settled back into her dreams. "What kind of dog is she?" I asked.

"The mystery breed. Her mother was an English bulldog. But her father was . . . a night of passion. A mastiff, maybe. A shar-pei." Muriel reached up from her chair to refresh her drink. She had brought out an insulated bucket and a pair of genuine ice tongs, which I found somehow disconcerting.

Having worked until nine for three nights, I had demanded (and won permission) to leave at noon on Friday. I had been heading out in cutoffs and floppy rubber thongs to wash my car when Muriel burst like a *Laugh-In* girl through the gate. I required very little coaxing to drop my coiled hose and bucket of sudsy water in exchange for iced Earl Grey and macaroons.

After our day of baseball and margaritas, Chaz had once again vanished from view. I never saw him when I looked out my window, and he never called out to me or knocked on my door. Of the many attitudes I might have adopted—feeling anxiously aroused, or distressed, or used and discarded, or angry—my most basic response was relief. I had been given a reprieve, a chance to contemplate the wisdom of my acquiescence, and I took it. I did not attempt to track Chaz down; I would not make the next move.

Whenever we met, I continued to talk amiably with Muriel. She had retreated from her strident seduction at the Mexican restaurant, and this was also a relief. I was content at the time to design her chair in secret and keep our encounters on a neighborly plateau.

"I'm such a bad person," Muriel said and looked over, perhaps with the expectation that I would object to her assessment. When I failed to speak, she smiled and looked down to guide her right thumbnail speculatively under the clear-polished nail of her left index finger. "Once again I have lured you into my scheme with refreshments. See, I have a favor to ask. I need to take Cissy in for her shots, and without someone to hold her while I drive, she can become unreasonable." She glanced inside at the dog, shapelessly inert in a pool of light. "I know it's an imposition on your day off, so I could pay you if—"

"Of course you can't pay me. I don't know if Cissy will approve of me though." It became apparent that I would not be washing my car.

"No. Cissy is an angel. I would recommend long pants, however, in case she decides to stand with her claws in your lap. Should we go?"

I went home to change into jeans and met Muriel and Cissy in the El Camino out in front in the visitors' parking. Muriel looped her fingers under the dog's collar and pulled her over to the center of the seat. After I climbed in and slammed the door, Muriel released the collar, and Cissy shifted onto my lap. She braced her back legs against my thigh and launched her front legs onto the tiny padded ledge below the passenger window. Cautiously, I stroked her back and the ruff of wrinkled skin under her chin, but she ignored my touch, treating my body as if it were a convenient booster cushion. Muriel drove out of the Villas del Sol and onto Culver, the street that traverses the length of Irvine.

The uninitiated would not suspect that a city enclosed them. The street had six broad lanes—three in each direction with a carefully groomed greensward down the median. At the roadside, beyond the meticulously marked bike lanes, were sidewalks that stretched through grassy, tree-lined buffer zones between the traffic and the walls. There were miles and miles of walls along Culver: brown brick walls, ivy-laced stucco walls, terra cotta walls with spines sheathed in curling brick. The walls had been designed to act as sound barriers, as privacy screens, as a discouragement to trespassers, and as a demarcation for the quasi-independent villages of Irvine.

Each development in Irvine had its own homeowners' association, its own property management company, its own architecturally coordinated and color-coded shopping village, and its own name chiseled on elaborate (but tasteful) tablets and displayed at the beautifully landscaped corners of major intersections. There was no discernible center to the city, no recognizable concentration of business or culture. If Irvine were invaded by a foreign power, there would be nothing to seize, no symbolic district to hold and defend. Irvine had been born with its hooves down, ready to run on its own; its master plan was already in place. It had evolved with the ordered certainty of replicating DNA, and often, while driving the clean lines of the streets, I would forget where I was in the city, as if I were in the midst of a hologram representing every fraction of Irvine at once.

Cissy grew restive in my lap and began to whimper and shift her weight from leg to leg. Whenever her thickly padded feet moved, her claws left behind rows of divots in the fabric of my jeans. "How much further?" I asked.

"Not far," Muriel said. "Gladewood." She reached over to pat one of Cissy's tensed flanks. "Isn't she a sweetie?"

At the next intersection we turned along a side street, then into the drive of a nondescript shopping center. We continued around the corner of the supermarket and the frozen yogurt store to an outbuilding of offices. While not actually identical to the complex down the block from the Villas del Sol—our coral pink façades were modelled on the Spanish Mission style and these were cocoa and beige with shingled roofs and wood trim—Gladewood Plaza exuded the same attractive, distressing anonymity. "How come you and Chaz live in Irvine?" I asked and steadied Cissy as Muriel swung sharply into a parking space.

"It suits us," she said. "Don't you think?"

I thought, No, I wouldn't say that. But I would need to consider it further.

# 31

The loose ends of the receptionist's head scarf stirred in the breeze from the door as it opened, and she reached up to secure it without lifting her eyes from the large chart on the counter before her. She held a thick red Magic Marker, which squeaked across the paper as she filled in a bar graph. When we passed the electric eye at the door, a soft chime rang, and she waved her fingers airily in our direction, still without looking up. "A minute, please," she said and continued to squeal the marker while shifting the gossamer wrap to cover her brown shoulder, bare above her blue sari.

"Hello, Mrs. Rabindagore," Muriel said while bracing the leash around her wrist to restrain Cissy from bolting.

The woman looked up at once, beaming; the furrows of concentration eased from her forehead and revealed the red caste mark above her nose. "Mrs. Muriel! How nice you are looking today!"

"Thank you," she said. "I love the bracelet. Is it new?"

Seven or eight gold bands jingled between the woman's wrist and her elbow, but she caught one stamped along its length with a pattern of half-moons and held it delicately away from the soft, dark hairs of her forearm. "Yes. It is from Manjula." She lowered her voice. "Because her brother is so much the stingy one."

Muriel offered a conspiratorial grin, then squeezed my biceps. "This is my friend, Peter Keith."

"Enchanted," she said. She dipped her head slightly and allowed the bracelet to fall against the others bunched at her wrist with a click.

"Is Dr. Gupta ready for us? We have an appointment."

Mrs. Rabindagore pressed a button on the console of the telephone. "Jamma? Jamma? Mrs. Muriel is here." An awkward silence crept through the office while we waited for a response from the intercom, punctuated only by a peep from a caged parakeet behind the reception desk and the whimpers of Cissy as she tugged against her collar. "Jamma?" the woman tried again and smiled at us sheepishly. "My daughter is perhaps assisting Doctor with a spaying." She slipped from her stool and nearly disappeared below the counter. "I will go. A minute." Her sandaled feet padded down the hall into the darkness.

"Mrs. Rabindagore is Manjula's brother's mother-in-law," Muriel quietly informed me. "Manjula sponsored them and paid their way here. Her brother, his wife, his wife's mother."

"And Manjula is . . . ?" I was confused.

"The vet," she said. "Jamma, her brother's wife, is her assistant." She yanked on Cissy's lead. "Settle down, would you."

We stood in the hush for a while near a love seat upholstered in vibrant orange corduroy and a small glass and tubular steel end table stacked with trade magazines. "I was wondering," I began, to fill the silence, "how did you know about the bracelet? How could you keep track?"

"Lucky guess. Manjula is always buying her jewelry." Muriel strummed her fingers against her thigh. "Look, you keep Cissy under control, and I'll go see what's going on." She unwound the strap of the leash from her wrist and closed my hand around it. She looked reassuringly into my eyes, then wandered down the hall.

I sat on a couch and reined Cissy in until she was forced to sit on the rug at my feet. I dropped a year-old copy of *Today's Veterinarian* into my lap and flipped through pages of advertising for cordless clippers and delousing spray. While skimming halfheartedly through an article on laser orthopedic surgery for cats, I heard Muriel knock firmly at the end of the hall. I looked up as the door opened a head's-width, pouring light onto Muriel's face. She spoke towards the light in a low voice until a woman in a white smock emerged. The woman turned to peer in my direction. Her oval face phased into view within a firmament of copious dark hair. She grasped the stems of her glasses and adjusted them. She said, "Him?" in a hushed, doubting voice. I couldn't see or hear Muriel's response, but the woman touched Muriel tenderly just beneath the low-scooped arm of her sundress. Muriel stepped into the lighted room and shut the door while the woman clicked along the contoured linoleum towards me.

Other than the clatter of her stride, there was nothing inelegant about the woman who approached me (and responsibility for the noise lay with the old linoleum, not her footwear; on concrete or marble, her footfalls would have rung out cleanly). Her work boots were black leather with riveted steel plates at the toe and heel; they seemed suitable for no other occupation but nightclubbing. Nubby brown trousers gathered at the tops of the boots, then rose to disappear at the knees under an intensely white lab coat. Above the broad, impersonal ice field of the coat, her slender throat supported an intense, composed face. Her irises were magnified into huge glinting black stones under her rimless glasses. She had lustrous dark hair folded back in successive waves from her face. Without the flash of the diamond stud in her left nostril, I would not have recognized her as the sari-clad woman with the box. "Hello, Peter?" she said and extended a small, soft hand, dimpled at the knuckles. "I'm Manjula Gupta, a good friend of Muriel."

"Pleased to meet you," I said and carefully released her fingers.

"If you will lead Cissy, we can see to her now."

Manjula lifted a clipboard from a rack behind the counter and kept her head bent to study it as she retreated from the desk. I yanked on Cissy's lead until she stood then led her to the open door near the head of the hall. Manjula waited inside before a high stainless steel table. "Come in." She bent and braced one arm under the dog's tail and another across her chest then hoisted Cissy until her claws clicked on the metal tabletop. Manjula stared directly into Cissy's eyes. "Hello, girl," she said then looked along the dog's flank at me. "You will need to steady her while I administer the shots."

"Wouldn't it be better if Muriel held her?"

Manjula began to pull small packets from drawers and set them in a high-sided metal tray. "Muriel is assisting my sister-in-law with the suturing down the hall. Don't worry, Peter. Cissy knows me."

"Muriel is suturing? What is she suturing?"

These weren't the questions I wanted to ask, but Manjula recognized this. "We went to school together for two years," she said and reached over to place my hands on Cissy: one just above the dewclaw of her hind leg, the other curling under her throat. "Like this. Yes."

"She went to veterinary school? Did she quit?"

"I suppose she wasn't interested anymore." Manjula filled a syringe and ticked it with a fingernail to free any air bubbles. "No, it would be better to say that her interest was satisfied." She pressed the plunger until a tiny spurt of clear fluid jumped from the needle tip. "Hold her steady now."

Manjula approached with the silver tray, and Cissy must have sensed its portent. Her legs tensed and quivered, and she tried to back off the edge of the table. My grip remained firm on her leg, but the skin under her head squirmed like furry pudding. I wrapped my arm around her and pressed her side tightly against my chest to keep her in position. I saw the needle tip sprout from Manjula's palm as she smoothed her other hand along the dog's flank. Our heads leaned close above Cissy's spine, and I smelled a sharp waft of Chanel No. 5, warmed at Manjula's throat—it was the one perfume I could readily identify because my mother had worn it unrelentingly throughout my childhood. As the needle neared, Cissy writhed in my embrace, whimpering and snarling in a single exhalation.

"Hold still," she said. "I mean you, Peter." I had been too engrossed in quelling the dog's flailing to notice the pinstick in the crook of my elbow bent under the curl of Cissy's tail. "I'm so sorry. Don't worry," she said, before I could advance to the next stage of panic. "I'm going to remove the needle slowly. We don't want to tear an artery or contaminate you. Hold still."

I strained up to see beyond Cissy as Manjula cupped her free hand to my elbow. She slowly pulled the needle away, and although it was concealed in the cloak of her fingers, the needle did not appear connected to a syringe but to a blood-filled, snub-bottomed vial.

She slipped her hand into her pocket, and the needle disappeared, replaced by a wad of cotton gauze. She grabbed Cissy's collar and gave me the compress. "I am deeply sorry," she said. "Go sit and let me get you something. We have juice or dog chews." Manjula laughed. "Or would you like a Tootsie Pop?"

# 32

Manjula carefully bandaged my needle stick, and after Muriel appeared in the examination room, rolling off squeaky latex gloves with puffs of the powder lining, the two women gave Cissy her course of shots. I was introduced to Jamma, a slight girlish woman in jeans who jingled subtly when she walked—a phenomenon I attributed to an unseen anklet of tiny bells. The four women and I chatted and laughed our way out into the foyer again, and Mrs. Rabindagore, as she struggled up onto her stool, promised with an unknowable level of sincerity to prepare a feast for me at some unspecified time in the future. I told her I would be thrilled while Muriel nudged her recalcitrant dog out the door. We were soon settled once more in the El Camino with Cissy in my lap as we made our way down Culver. After leaving the clinic, Muriel made no further attempt to disguise her subterfuge.

"Should we stop for coffee?" Muriel asked.

"Sure," I replied and shifted Cissy's leg, which she had wedged uncomfortably into my crotch.

"I hope it didn't hurt too much."

"I'm okay." I could just feel the twinge of a nerve where I imagined the needle hole to lie.

"Guppie should get the blood work back from our friend Ray in a few days." Muriel turned right onto Harvard Avenue.

"Blood work?" A spasm of unease coiled down through my intestines.

"Then we'll know that we're safe."

"Safe?" I turned my head from her and looked, stunned, out the side window. The street curved in the direction of the ocean, and on my side the buildings receded to reveal the innermost reach of Newport Bay, a finger of wetland stretching between the University of

California and the business sector near the airport, left untouched as a nature preserve, a memory of the land's original design. "You want to know if I'm safe? By what right do you think you can do that?"

"Peter. Peter," she said, half to comfort me and half in dismay at my reaction. "It's because Chaz and I want to share everything with you. We want to get to know you deeply, right down to your blood and bones."

"Didn't you consider that I might already know?" I had been tested twice, in bitter resentment after Brad moved out: six months apart, both times negative. "Don't you think you should have asked me?"

"Peter." Muriel pulled onto the shoulder of the road. On a slight rise beside the car was a ribbon of pavement at the perimeter of the wetlands for the use of joggers and cyclists, and beyond, tufts of dried grass stirred now and then by arriving and departing birds. "I wish that Guppie had just come right out and told you. But she was within her rights to do it her own way."

"This is all a fucking game to you."

"No, Peter. We didn't ask because—well, because neither Chaz nor I are very good at moral arguments. We don't like to talk about ideas when we can act on them. It just seemed simpler, more direct, to do it this way."

"To lie to me?"

"Cissy had an appointment for shots." Muriel jerked the car into PARK and pulled her braid over her shoulder to study the curling tip. "I don't lie, Peter."

"Bullshit."

She met my hard glare with a steady, unreadable stare of her own. A large tear pulsed from the rim of her left eye and slid, snaillike, down her cheek. Her fingers fumbled for the door handle. As the door swung open, she flew out and scrambled up the gravel embankment to the jogging path. Cissy jumped into the driver's seat, and I leaned sideways to snag her collar before she could bound out. She whined plaintively at Muriel, who ran off along the track, then twisted her head to snarl accusingly at me.

I reached around her and closed the door before flipping the key to shut down the engine. Cissy crouched on the seat, lowering her head between her shoulders, growling. I backed out the passenger door and slammed it as Cissy launched herself. Her claws scrabbled at the ledge, and she tilted her head to thrust her jaws through the open crack of the window. A froth of saliva scudded down the glass.

As I stepped over the rise to stand in the damp ground at the edge of the salt marsh, my rage returned. Anger grew loud in my head, filling my ears, filling the silent air around the cry of birds and the diminishing barks behind me. I stuffed my hands into my pockets and kicked at the salty crusts of dried, rumpled earth. Reluctantly, almost involuntarily, I scanned the perimeter of the preserve for Muriel.

I found her in the distance, crouched low on the gravel inside and below a bend of the path. Her arms wrapped her knees with her fingers locked under her armpits. Her face was upraised to watch the birds in flight above the wetland, but from my vantage her features blurred into brushstrokes. Her sundress was a light smudge among the dead plants and brown soil—a white pink—the color of a cherry Slurpee sucked until the ice was almost drained of tint.

I watched her, both of us immobile, until I could no longer sustain my rage. A coldness crept into me, an absence. I walked towards her. A lizard, thin and gray as a twig, skittered across my path, and I paused to watch it disappear into a scrawling line of yellow brush. When I started forward again, Muriel stood with her arms folded, waiting for me.

As the distance closed, I resolved to hold firm to my sense of injustice. But my righteous indignation crumbled into scraps of wounded pride and embarrassment when I saw her red eyes and the toothmarks she had bitten into her lipstick in the effort to keep her mouth from trembling. "Look," I said and waved my hand emphatically (and no doubt enigmatically). "I didn't mean to call you a liar. But what else am I supposed to think?"

"You don't understand us." Muriel rubbed her palms against her thighs. "Chaz and I have a certain way of being. We have this one way of seeing. We have to. We have no choice." She reached to touch my chest, then drew back. "We want to know you, Peter. But to do that, for us to know you, you have to accept us, a little, on faith."

"But how can I ever trust you again, after this?" I began the question in a bitterly rhetorical tone, then realized I honestly expected an answer.

Muriel took my hand and led me up the embankment towards the car. She didn't respond. Because I did not shrug off her hand, she knew that she didn't need to.

# 33

We drove over to Newport Boulevard, then down through Costa Mesa and Newport Beach towards the Balboa Peninsula, which seemed a ridiculous distance to travel for coffee. I thought we might be heading for the ocean, but within blocks of the beach Muriel turned onto a side street and parked in front of a renovated warehouse. The casement windows were painted a deep indigo; the largely featureless walls were softened with a rosy cream. Stenciled in green above the open door within brackets of tole-style flowers was the name THE LADY COW and in smaller, darker letters beneath it: COFFEE.

"What time is it?" Muriel asked.

I looked at the gray face of my watch. "It's three-twenty."

"Good." She jumped out of the car, pulling Cissy along behind her. I followed and waited while she knotted the leash around the leg of a wooden bench outside the door.

"Is it safe to leave her tied up out here?"

"She won't get away."

"No, I mean, she won't try to take a bite out of someone?" After my tête-à-tête with Cissy, I had been reluctant to get back in the car with her, but the dog had forgotten our conflict and resumed her air of indifference towards me.

"Cissy knows how to behave." Muriel climbed the stoop into the dim interior. "What will you have?"

I joined her inside. The counter was fronted with a glass panel revealing three shelves of pastries, brownies, muffins, and croissants, arranged on blue and black speckled stoneware plates. I stared in; I had always been fascinated by the duality of display counters.

In one of my father's many careers, he had managed an oddments store full of buttons, tassels, beads, fabric trim, and bolts of exotic cloth. The store was located in a ten-year-old strip mall that had already suffered an irreversible decline into seediness—a victim of the transitory nature of fashionable commerce in Los Angeles. Inside, however, my father's store was smearless, dustless, and impeccably organized. I used to wander down the central aisle, peering into the cases where the goods were neatly and attractively displayed under sealed, polished glass like museum vitrines. Then I would exert my privilege to slip around the back where the counters exhibited a different face. There, the cases were open to the air, the backs of the trays were labeled with prices and serial numbers on peeling masking tape, and hidden from public view were stacks of paper bags, a bottle of glass cleaner, a box of Magic Markers, invoices, and a pair of red leather pumps pushed out of sight underneath and forgotten by my mother or Miss Kensey the Salesgirl. It had thrilled me as a child to observe a tray of nautical buttons through the glass and then to run behind and locate an exposed pile of brass knobs stamped with anchors and understand that they were the same buttons in the same tray.

"Peter? What did you want?" Muriel asked again, and I looked up from contemplation of the baked goods to a woman with straight black hair in a long-sleeved dress patterned in Wedgwood blue roses. Muriel determined from my inactivity that I wasn't going to respond and told the woman, "Make that two lattes." She pulled a ten-dollar bill from a clam-shaped turquoise coin purse and dropped it on the glass above a row of bagels. "Will you bring them out to the patio? And a carrot cake. Two forks."

As Muriel led me among the tiny tables crowded with clusters of mismatched chairs, I popped out of my revery and noticed the abstract watercolors for sale on the walls above shelves of carefully selected cow-themed bric-a-brac—cookie jars, rusty toys, weathervanes, idols, surfing cow figurines. "Come on," Muriel muttered as we slid out the rear door. She motioned me to a table under the adjacent window. The whole length of the coffeehouse was visible inside.

"What's the rush?"

"It's almost three-thirty, right?" She gently turned my wrist to see my watch. "Irena will be here soon."

"We're meeting Irena?" I stared through the building at the rectangle of light from the open front door.

"Not precisely. But she'll be here."

"How do you know?"

She didn't respond before the woman from the counter arrived with the frothy mugs and a square of dark, chunky cake capped with cream cheese icing. After Muriel had ripped into several packets of raw sugar, tasting her coffee after each addition, she gestured towards an elderly man seated alone in the shade of the lattice at the far end of the patio. "I call him the Knight Errant. He's very polite." The man wore a blue blazer opened over a yellow polo shirt. He had a slight potbelly, a large nose, and cavernous jowls. His eyes were watery and the clearest blue. He stared out through the lattice at the boat engine repair yard across the back street. "He's an Austrian émigré. He comes every afternoon to flirt, very genteelly, with the ladies behind the counter, and play chess with the students when they show up."

"You come here a lot?"

"Sometimes." She sliced off a slab of cake with the side of her fork. "Here's Irena," she whispered.

# 34

Our neighbor entered the coffeehouse as if she were boarding a small, possibly unseaworthy dinghy. She paused on the stoop, settled one foot and then the other on the tile flooring inside, then paused again. She removed her sunglasses, which were large, oval, black, and gave the impression of sheltering blind eyes behind them. She blinked twice and opened her mouth as if to yawn away the darkness then slipped her glasses into a green felt pouch and into her sizeable purse.

"Do you guys run into each other here all the time?" I turned to

Muriel, who shaved off a final helping of carrot cake and pushed the remaining portion and the clean fork onto my side of the table.

"Well, I've never actually talked to her." She inserted the morsel of cake into her mouth. "More to the point, she's never noticed that I'm here."

Irena waited near a condiments table crowded with pitchers of milk; a plastic bear full of honey; shakers of sugar, chocolate, and cinnamon; and trays of napkins and stir sticks. She held on to her purse's shoulder strap with one hand and draped the other over the flap concealing the zipper. She looked ahead at the cash register expectantly but continued to stand outside the invisible zone that exists around sales counters to divide the truly desirous from the merely curious. No one moved forward to assist her.

"So how did you know she'd be here?" I sipped from my mug and swallowed a dollop of warm, slightly bitter, whipped milk. "You must have followed her here. You spy on her." I felt indignant on Irena's behalf; she seemed misplaced and fragile in her trim, shiny brown tracksuit, her crystal necklace, and petite white running shoes.

"Peter, you're so judgmental." Muriel smiled; she did not take me seriously. She viewed my protest as perfunctory, a tissue of moral rectitude that I threw out to assuage my conscience and which I would be relieved to have dispensed with. I considered the likelihood that she was correct; I was genuinely curious about Irena and the source of her fascination for the Lambents. Perhaps I was only deflecting my own sense of invaded privacy.

Irena looked at her watch. She took a single step forward and raised her arm at the elbow as if she were preparing to hail an approaching cab. "I'm going to go ask her to sit with us," I said.

"No, you won't." Muriel spoke curtly. "She won't want to, and it will only upset her. She's here to meet someone."

"How would you know?"

"It's like you said, Peter. I'm a spy. A spy in the house of love." She shifted her eyes to the window again. "Now, this is touching. She always knows exactly what she wants but can never remember the name for it."

Inside, the woman in the blue rose dress was questioning Irena, who strained up on the balls of her feet like a small child to read the chalkboard menu over the counter. The sound of their voices reached us through the open door less distinctly than the vision of their faces through the window, and it seemed a poorly dubbed movie—some old neorealist film in Italian or French.

"Now a café au lait," Irena said, faintly, as she pointed to the sign above her, "that's the one with milk and . . . not espresso."

"That's right," the woman replied. "It's steamed milk and coffee. No foam."

"Oh," Irena looked briefly wounded. "But I like foam. I like foam, and milk, and chocolate."

"I could make you a hot chocolate with steamed milk?"

"No, no, I want coffee. Espresso."

The woman leaned over the counter to look up with Irena at the menu. "Maybe what you're thinking of is a mocha. That's like a cappuccino with chocolate in it."

"Yes!" Irena's furrowed face opened out like a firework, a sudden bloom. "That's it. An Italian cappuccino!"

"But the Italian cappuccino doesn't have chocolate. Maybe you'd like a—"

"Of course it does. Little shavings of chocolate dusted all over the whipped cream."

"—a Viennese cappuccino," the woman concluded and fixed her long hair behind her ears.

"Viennese cappuccino," Irena muttered, almost to herself, almost inaudible to us, her audience on the patio. She unzipped her purse and stared down into its open mouth. "I should write that down."

"She never has a pen with her," Muriel whispered. "If she's lucky, Shauna is at the counter and remembers what she usually orders."

Irena paid for her cappuccino, then remembered her frequent-buyer punch card, which entitled her to a free drink. While the woman keyed numbers into the register to issue a refund, Irena licked at the chocolate-and-cinnamon-coated whipped cream cap of her drink with little jaunts of her tongue. She eased her returned money into her billfold, then carried her slender glass mug steadied before her across the room. Although the indoor space was nearly empty, she selected a table in a seemingly undesirable corner, behind a pillar and under a low-hanging planter. "I think she chooses that spot," Muriel explained, "because she's afraid someone is going to play the piano—although no one ever has—and she wants to be as far away as possible."

Irena studied the chairs in her vicinity and selected a slender armless chair in maple with a simple urn-shaped splat down the center of the back. She canted the chair at an oblique angle to her table and sat. She adjusted the slacks of her tracksuit at the knees, then crossed her legs. She fiddled with the collar and zipper of her top, then rested her hands before her like two curving shells.

"What about Cissy?" I whispered. "She must have recognized her."

Muriel shook her head. "Cissy always comes with me. Irena tells me that she sees a dog just like Cissy all the time, but she can never remember where." She grinned. "Now, quiet." She reached out to touch a finger to my lips. Then we waited out the pregnant minutes of the afternoon along with Irena.

# 35

I was swirling the grainy bottom of my latte when Irena's guest stepped in. He was a tall man but so broad in the shoulders and waist that he seemed rectangular, a slab of flesh. His hair was elephant gray and sheared close to his skull. His face was doughy except for his nose, which crooked out between his eyes like a knurled root. Mysteriously, it was clear to me that he had once—long ago—been strikingly handsome.

Over crimson sweatpants, he wore an astoundingly garish short-sleeved shirt with a pattern of what looked, from our distance, like bullfighters in electric pinks, yellows, and blues. Before acknowledging Irena, who watched him expectantly across the room, he ordered a cup of coffee and a slice of an elaborate torte topped with a heaven of shaved white chocolate and strawberry minarets. He placed the dessert in front of Irena and sat down on the chair opposite her.

She smiled at him weakly, then looked down at the layers upon layers of frosting and spongy cake. He rubbed at the base of his throat and sniffed loudly. He sipped at his coffee. After a few minutes, when he had drained his cup, he took her hand in his on the tabletop. They did not speak.

They didn't speak for a full twenty minutes, and when a loud crew of college students arrived to mask the sound of Muriel's voice, she told me, "That's her ex-husband, Bert."

"She told me she was a widow."

"Yeah, that's what she *says*." Muriel reached into the neck of her sundress to scratch her shoulder. "But didn't you ever wonder about that accident at work? About her uncharacteristic vagueness on the subject?"

"I didn't think it was any of my business."

"Well, it bothered *me*. I made it my business." Muriel's voice descended into a thick whisper. "He molested both of their sons. One of them needed surgery. That's how she finally found out, when it could no longer be kept secret."

Irena's gaze remained locked on the table, on the rococo dessert she wouldn't touch. She didn't cry; she didn't open her mouth to emit the smallest noise. But her fixed expression continued to fall; her downcast eyes glistened with increasing despair. Even with her hair pulled back in a cloth-covered magenta band that matched her T-shirt, Irena's bangs were swagged like theatre curtains—parted to reveal the mask of tragedy.

"She got a restraining order to keep him from seeing them. But the court put the boys in a foster home anyway. They said she did nothing to stop him, even though she didn't know. Her lawyer got them back eighteen months later. Bert did time, and she got the divorce. I have copies of the court records if you want to see them." Muriel pulled packets of sugar from the bowl and began to arrange them in a circle. "She still loves him. She reminds me of a Western schoolmarm who keeps a secret flask of scotch in her skirts, for rejuvenating purposes. She can't admit to needing him, she can't excuse him, but she can't give him up. For her, he's this dangerous cordial."

I looked in at his hand folded over hers on the scratched, gummy table.

"I sit here and watch over her and wait. Perhaps there will be an opportunity to do something for her."

After half an hour, the man stood up to leave. He placed his hands on Irena's shoulders and leaned down to whisper in her ear. When she (and Muriel and I) had watched him go out the door and climb into his brown sedan across the street, Irena twisted around to explore the torte tentatively with her fork. Her face did not brighten. Muriel rose quietly to her feet and scooped up her coin purse. "Let's go. Down the back steps," she said, then added, "There's nothing else we can do."

As I scooted my chair back, the émigré gentleman passed behind me. He paused in the threshold to hook the top button of his blazer and shrug his shoulders. He walked straight towards Irena with his hands clenched together over his stomach. "Beg pardon," he said, and Irena glanced up, startled. "I have seen you in this place before. If I am mistaken I mean no offence, but does that man hold you against your will?"

Irena shook her head and managed a strained smile. I looked back, while Muriel descended the wooden steps at a break in the lattice, and watched Irena make a game attempt to stab a strawberry on the tines of her fork and pop it jovially into her mouth.

# 36

I had been propped up in bed, half asleep, in the midst of an Angela Carter story, when the night cracked open. The phone rang, and I jerked up, losing my thumbhold on my place in the book. I lifted the receiver and heard Chaz speaking coolly and directly into my ear before I had the opportunity to say hello. "Stand up," he said. "Stand up on your bed."

"What?" I reached out to my watch on the nightstand. It was 12:45 A.M.

"Come on, Speck," he coaxed. "Stand up and show us."

I sat up, and the sheet slid from my chest to gather in folds around my waist. I ran my hand through my hair, blinking.

"That's it." It was Muriel's voice, lowered to an artificial, theatrical growl. She had replaced Chaz inside my head. "You look hot like that. I like the knot of hair under your arm. Stand up, sugar."

Untangling the phone cord, I got out of bed and crept towards the window.

"No. Get up on the bed so we can see you better."

"Where are you?" I asked and cautiously climbed up on the mattress—not, I convinced myself, to comply with their requests but to discover how they were observing me. I saw myself reflected back in the glass, thin and pale, with rumpled hair and asymmetrically sagging white cotton briefs. I saw through my outline to the indefinite huddle of the Lambents' building across the walk. The rectangle of their bedroom window was blank, but I suspected they waited there, watching in the dark.

"Lookin' good, Speck," Chaz said. "Now take your hand and run it along your neck, over your chest, touch those small pink nipples with your fingertips."

"Chaz," I protested weakly. "Muriel." I shielded my eyes ineffectually with my hand and stared at the unresponsive black glass.

"Go on," Muriel whispered. "Touch the hollow between your pecs."

I clutched my hand to the front of my throat feeling my blood course rapidly along its channels.

"Don't be afraid," she said in her throaty, glamour queen voice. "No one can see."

I slid my hand down until a finger poked at my xiphoid process. I shook my head and laughed. "I'm afraid I'm not cut out to be a go-go boy."

"Relax, sugar. Slow down," she said. "Caress yourself."

I kept shaking my head. I suppressed a nervous, strangled giggle.

"Turn on your radio, Speck," Chaz said. "K-Dance. KDNS."

I squatted down and switched on my portable stereo. A pulsing beat rippled out of the speakers. The station was already set, and I wondered if it was a coincidence or if they had binoculars that could read the dial. I listened to the rapid electronic throb and the woman's voice, undulating low in the mix, like a wraith: "Ride the beat, ride the beat, ride the rhythm to my heart, boy." I stood again and was lost to myself. I felt my mind and body separate like decoupling train cars, on the same track but at an increasing distance from each other.

"Just listen to the music," Chaz directed me. "Sway in it."

I suppose I did as instructed; the room seemed to shift in the wash of the song. From my vantage on the bed, my perspective of the room was odd and new, but it didn't seem dangerous or embarrassing to move this way in my own place.

"Mmmmm." Muriel purred, satisfied. "Now cup your chest. Now stroke your stomach. Rock your hips. Feel the beat there."

My hand moved down my body, skin finding skin. My fingers dipped under the waistband of my briefs then out and around the slope of my rocking buttocks.

"Now put down the phone, Speck. Just dance."

I allowed the receiver to drop onto the bedspread and threw my arms over my head. I swam my way into the layers and layers of beats towards the song line, a soulful, operatic wave. "Ride, ride, ride, ride, ri-ee-i-ee-i-ee-i-ee-i-ee-i-ee-ide!" I raked my hands down my sides and twisted up the sides of my briefs into a G-string, then shucked them off. I forgot the Lambents; my tired body forgot itself. I shimmied down, then thrust my hips. I grabbed my crotch and turned and spread my buttocks and slapped my ass. I leaped and thumped over the bed, groaning the box springs. My erection bobbed before me, off the beat. I grabbed it through the dense corkscrew hair at its base and wagged it. Then danced again.

Songs mixed seamlessly, end to end, and I tunneled through them. I washed in them. When a commercial for auto insurance interrupted, my breath was heaving into my throat, my stomach swelling and compressing. I spiraled dizzily down out of the canceled cloud of music. I allowed my body to fall back, sodden with sweat, onto the bed, and my shoulder smacked against the cold plastic receiver.

I lay for a moment, breathing, then picked up the phone and puffed wordlessly into the speaker.

"Why don't you come over," Chaz said.

# 37

The art nouveau bed in the Lambents' room arched up at the head and foot in asymmetrical waves. It was a huge thing, larger than king-sized, making it—on this basis alone—an anomaly among antique beds, which are almost invariably cramped and small. Beyond its initial cost, such a bed would incur no end of expense for its owners: it would require a customized mattress, customized sheets and bed-covers, and likely a customized load-bearing underframe.

The head and footboards were inlaid with the most complicated marquetry I had ever seen, in painstaking slivers of countless varieties of wood. At the head, gowned women stretched from behind a cathedral of slender trees; some clutched lilies, others held wreaths of nettles. At the foot, other women knelt on round stones above a rippling river and dipped cattails into the water. Although the mythological tropes were not familiar, the women seemed elemental: dryads and naiads perhaps. Despite the marquetry's exacting detail, its striving towards the pictorial limits of its medium, it seemed less capable of expressing the human form than a cruder carving might. The women had been reduced and refined into a decorative motif without a claim to mimetic life. Still, the overall effect was stunning, and I marveled that I had not noticed the bed on my previous visit to the room.

The bed was fitted at mattress level with brass rings attached to plates sturdily embedded inside the four corners. I noticed these only because a slick black dog leash was tied to one of the rings, then looped around Muriel's wrist. The rings must also have been a cus-tomized addition, unless the bed had been purchased at the estate sale of some fin de siècle French dominatrix.

I concentrated on the bed and its accoutrements to avoid making eye contact with Chaz, who slouched barechested in olive-drab khaki shorts against the dresser across the room; and, more urgently, to escape an examination of Muriel, who stretched naked across the plush, luxurious duvet. I was less distressed by her body, which divided the bed from her raised arm down to her crossed feet, as translucent and glossy as an icicle, than I was by the sheath of slick black rubber over her face. The mask covered her entire head in a featureless void; there were two shining silver grommets opening at the eyes and a neutral row of three grommets at the mouth. In the silent room, her breathing was audible, with a faint wet squeak, like a finger rubbing the side of a balloon.

Chaz had let me in and led me through the lightless house to deposit me at the foot of the bed. When I finally found the courage to look down at Muriel, I smiled. "You look like the villain in a Mexican wrestling movie."

They didn't laugh with me; Muriel made no sound, and when I looked over nervously at Chaz, he was not smiling. I leaned forward in my sweatpants against the curling rim of the footboard, and my dick began to swell against the wood—a reaction I didn't expect or want.

"Are you kidding?" I asked slowly. Their intentions seemed clear, but I couldn't accept it. I remember thinking that if I were already apprehensive about making love to a woman, to Muriel, I certainly didn't want my first experience to be with a woman who was bound and masked. I stared down in shock and sickening arousal; I thought I could see the glint of her eyes behind the tiny holes in the mask. I strayed to the tuft of rusty blond pubic hair, then twisted around to look at Chaz. I felt, in a clot of panic, that Muriel had been obliterated, that her soul was absent.

"Spread your legs." Chaz looked past me, and I heard a soft shushing behind me, of Muriel's limbs shifting across the cover of the duvet. Chaz reached into a small carved chest on the dresser and removed what looked like looped strips of yellow cloth. He divided the material into two coils and handed one to me. He gestured to the opposite end of the footboard. "Tie this off on the ring."

I didn't move at his command but weighed the loops in my hand, and they were surprisingly heavy. As they shifted on the hook of my fingers, they emitted a slight, bell-like clink. I squeezed them to feel the ovals of chain inside the sheath of silk. "Shit," I muttered and allowed the chain to slip link by link from my hand and patter dully onto the carpeting.

Chaz grabbed my arms from behind, and as I struggled forward he pinned my elbows to my back. His voice breathed hot against my throat. "Don't, Speck. Don't be this way. You owe us your respect." He released me, and I stumbled over to stand with my arms folded by the door. The mask shifted on its pillow in my direction.

"I don't—" I began. I was going to say, I don't owe you anything. But as I spoke to the Lambents in their carefully draped and lighted room, I located a new track in my head, a new channel whose walls blurred as I raced between them. I flew towards a conclusion, but the idea I sought receded before I could name it. Its memory shape, its vast undemarcated bulk, fixed my tongue. I recognized that I was indeed bound to Chaz and to Muriel, if not by obligation then by some equally unappeasable force. "I don't understand."

"There's nothing to understand, Speck," Chaz said, more genially. He walked around to my edge of the bed to finish tying off her feet. "Just empty your head. No preconceptions, all right? And take off your clothes."

# 38

I did what I was told to do. I stripped off my jersey and sweatpants as Chaz directed and lowered my head between Muriel's legs as he instructed. I remained there, my hands braced on her thighs, after he left the room. I convinced myself that it was kindness that led them to devise their plan, that they intended Chaz's assertive presence and Muriel's effective absence to create a sense of capability in me; they hoped the extremity of the situation would jump-start our encounter with a minimum of awkward preliminaries. Even then, I was keenly aware that this analysis was a comforting construction on my part. There was no reason to assume that their motivations were benevolent and explicable, but I had to create a comprehensible explanation or I wouldn't endure.

I crouched beneath the keystone of Muriel's arched legs and lowered my face towards her. I was fixated on physiology, on the mechanics of pleasure rather than its sensation. I couldn't lose myself in Muriel as I had in Chaz, perhaps because on that day I had been guided by Chaz and now I was expected to be the active partner. Muriel could not have been more passive, with her shackled legs carving heavy channels in the goosedown, one arm twisted up in the leash, and the other idly circling her nipples with a fingertip. I could not stop thinking. I thought of feminist theory, of the objectification of women; I fought against acute self-consciousness, against fear; I tried to forget the inverse law of arousal—that an increase in thought would decrease my erection. I struggled to submerge myself.

I was soon deep inside Muriel. First I opened fleshy lips fringed with fragrant hair; they parted, as soft as warm butter. I stroked them with the tip of my tongue, driving the blade in between. The skin within her was as soft-wet and delicate as the lining of my mouth. I tightened my tongue and prodded the pebble at the end of these inner lips, nudging its delicate hood. I circled it slowly, steadily as Muriel circled her aureoles. Circling. Circling. Her body poured its liquors up to interlap with my saliva, to wash across her lips and mine, salt and musky sweet.

Her spine roiled up, and I dodged my hands under her small, tight buttocks. I pulled her up in the air, her back arching, and buried myself, nose and mouth, inside her. She sounded out a low growl, from her throat not her mouth. The smooth skin of her thighs against my neck and shoulders chilled and heated in shivering waves.

I tried not to monitor my reactions any further and risk spoiling them. I felt myself losing grip, falling into a wash of desire. I reached up without looking to rub her stomach, to knead the small soft handfuls of her breasts, to brush the contours of her clavicle. I felt for her cheek, the defining bone of her jaw, and my damp fingers adhered to the powdery rubber like a bathmat on a wet tile floor.

I pulled my face away from her—cold as liquid met air and dried on my cheeks. My eyes darted the room; Chaz had not returned. I looked up at the giant mirror. I was enclosed, naked, in its gilt frame, enclosed naked in a golden arc of legs. The mask arched its neck to stare at me from the reflection. My fugue began to diminish, my erection to fall, until I snatched at a kernel of anger. I climbed over her, straddling her chest, to unknot the leash and free her hand. "Take it off," I said coarsely.

Her loose fingers lifted in the air like blown leaves, then landed gently on my thighs. She made no further move to comply. "Take it off!" I shouted, but she remained motionless.

I squeezed my thumbs under the rubber rim of the mask and tugged up. It came off slowly with a squelching noise. It was moist underneath, and a transparent goo inside slithered down to my wrists. After the nose and the cheekbones, the mask came away more quickly. I pulled the crown away from her slicked hair, and tossed the deflated mask onto the other pillow.

Muriel smiled. Her lips seemed pale without a trace of lipstick. But her face was very red and greased as if she had been skinned, as if the black rubber were her epidermis.

"I have to see you," I said. "I have to see you to know you want me."

"That's sweet of you, Peter." Muriel wrapped her arms around my back and pulled me onto her to hug me. "I'm glad you said that. I love you for that." She kissed my lips. "But for tonight, I want this face."

She shrugged lightly from my embrace and reached out for the mask. With both hands, she began to work at the top of her head and donned it expertly. The forehead, eyes, cheeks, nose, mouth, and chin filled from within. She placed her palms at the sides of her head and gave the mask a sharp jerk to the left, and with a damp, flatulent burp of air the mask shifted into place.

# 39

The difference with Muriel, the difference with a woman, I found, was a matter of emphasis. Between men, regardless of ebb and flow, of position and role, closure is always anticipated. The result would be (or should be, ideally) two jolts of fluid, a dual progression of imploded tension and exploded release. But for women, I sensed, there was no end. There would be climaxes, rolling crescendos, but the erotic statement would chug on, a harmonic progression, like a minimalist symphony, until exhaustion or a partner's withdrawal provided a period. And then sensation would subside, in waves, like a diminishing isotope.

I discovered myself easily, almost accidently, inside Muriel. Unlike male anatomy with its reluctance towards penetration, Muriel's body welcomed me effortlessly. There was none of the anticipatory negotiations of fingers and wetness. I slid unimpeded into her soft sheath.

I planted my knees and tightened my buttocks to rock into her. My hands swallowed her small breasts and compressed them. Her nipples rose beneath my palm. She lay pinned beneath me like a butterfly prepared for taxonomy, and the only variation in activity available to me was to increase the intensity of my thrusts. I rocked faster and wondered if it hurt her. I couldn't tell; the mask rendered her moans into one dark, thick, inexpressive sound. I wasn't satisfied. I unhooked Muriel's legs from their cloth-coated chains, and she wrapped them around my waist in a surprisingly muscular vise.

If I shut my eyes, I could ignore the unceasing glare of her rubber countenance, her eyes of silver seed. I allowed my hands their primacy. They rippled along her sides—smooth, supple, pliant. I traced each muscle corded in her untied but outstretched arms and in the flat, solid planes of her thighs. I licked the shining lobe of her right breast, its fullness and feathery softness, slowly, with a spread tongue to moisten each miniature diamond demarcation of her skin.

She was warm beneath me, and her slickness spread, coating my cock and matting my pubic hair. Our bodies melted in a fragrant puddle. I rocked waves in the cup of her pelvis.

And, suddenly, I *wanted* to fuck her. I had fashioned an image of Muriel inside my head to replace the bound and masked figure underneath me, and I believed at last that we were united in the huge art nouveau bed, together creating sex. I was stunned in my admiration for human design: how perfectly we fit, how elegant our coupling. I fit into her without force or adjustment like a perfect joint.

Muriel squeezed her thighs to urge me on, and I saw her smile on my eyelids' screen—a slow eruption of mirth. I saw the frond-frail wisps of blond hair unraveled from her braid. I saw her polished teeth with one bottom incisor slightly overlapping another. I heard her laugh without using my ears, a sound that began as a slight catch in her breath, then sallied into warm, low rhythm.

"Peter," she whispered into the actual world, almost soundlessly, so that the mask did not vibrate. "You fill me, Peter. I love you in me."

I thrust faster as she spoke. My balls were wet with her. My thighs were soaked. I smelled my own sweat, pungent in the damp hollows of my body. I was fucking Muriel. My muscles tensed and strained. Our bodies flexed hard and soft in unison.

Her arms flew up from the bed and clutched the rigid tendons in my neck. Sweat dripped from my nose and channeled cool across my nipples. I lifted my chest from hers and dug my palms into the bed.

As the pressure built within me beyond the possibility of subsidence, I felt Muriel's body relent. Her desire spread out into a broad plateau, diffuse and faint, evaporating out through her system, stippling her flesh like the faded freckles of her back.

But I couldn't wait for her to build again. I came in fast, relentless beats. I had meant to pull out in time. Earlier, I had planned to slip into a condom. But I had forgotten both of these intentions, coming, shuddering out to the end of passion. I had wanted to come with Muriel, and that hope went unfulfilled. My body twinged with regret, and I allowed it to wash over me, to hide hotter, more frightening emotions. I pulled myself away from her and rolled, landing on my back with a pillow wedged under my shoulders. "I'm sorry," I said. I opened my eyes and looked sharply off to the side to avoid the great glass overhead and what its reflection would reveal. My gaze rested on the carved box on the dresser.

Muriel's fingers brushed my cheeks. Her hands wrapped my head, cradling my face below my ears. Her voice buzzed from its wet cage. "No one who can fuck like that has anything to be sorry for."

# 40

It seems simple at first. It seems impossible. There is the idea suspended for inspection in a golden mental light. And there are the plans, diagrammed and quantified, with the cold beauty of hypothesis. And then there are the materials: smooth planks, and dowels, glues, screws, sandpaper, and varnishes—all radiating unexploited, fresh potential. Until the saw bites its first wood, until the thumb tests the grain of the new cut, there is nothing to belie future perfection. But neither is there indication in the stack of wood nor in the folder of graphs that anything will come of it, that effort could wrest from such inert components a functional object, a work of art, a chair.

I decided to reveal nothing to Muriel until my project was complete. Originally I had intended to include her at every step; I had been eager to present her with something tangible and had gotten as far as matting a detailed drawing finished with a watercolor wash. But I realized that it would be truer to our relations, to the out-of-the-blue progression of our intimacy, if the chair were to appear on her doorstep, complete and unheralded. I buried the drawing in a box in my closet.

I bought the supplies and hid them under a blanket in the back of my car. I selected white oak for the chair because it was easily available, relatively cheap, and because it seemed apt: a firm, common, American base material for a winged chair. The boards were thick and heavy when I lifted them from the rack in the lumber yard, and as I stood strumming along the grain with my knuckles in search of knots, I admired the pale wood with its yellow undertone, a complexion very much like Muriel's.

When I woke after sex with Muriel, we had brunch—Muriel, Chaz, and I—then I drove my materials up the 405 freeway to my parents' house.

After decades of disappointing retail experiments and hapless entrepreneurial schemes, my father had been blessed with tardy, miraculous good fortune. He decided to retire and sell his current business, a sporting-goods store, at the peak of the real estate boom. The developers paid dearly for his property and building—which was quickly razed to erect a glitzy, five-story, block-long shopping mall. In the last fraction of their lives my parents were finally able to afford the life they had always anticipated. They purchased a two-bedroom house in an older neighborhood of Brentwood and a pearl-gray Lincoln Town Car. My mother, whom I had long suspected of latent agoraphobia and a profound level of indolence, rarely found reason to depart from the air-conditioned comforts of 1717 Acacia Avenue. She ordered boudoir fashions from catalogs: silk kimonos, cashmere pullovers, harem pants, and astonishingly salacious lingerie, which—to my relief—she never modeled for me. I refused to contemplate what the purchases revealed about my mother, who had disdained underwear advertisements in the newspaper during my childhood and had lambasted Carol Burnett for appearing on television in a dress "slit way up to there."

My father's discretionary purchases had been more consistent, if more costly. My father had always insisted on serving as his own handyman, his own carpenter and auto mechanic. Quintessential childhood hours with my father were spent in some act of refurbishing or repair. While I crouched near his legs splayed out from under the front of the family station wagon and handed him tools with the imagined proficiency of a surgical nurse, he would regale me with tales of shoddy workmanship and inferior service. He had a particularly intense contempt for society matrons who could not find their gas tank, let alone change their spark plugs (an accurate description of my mother, although without the corresponding social status). I vowed, secretly, as I hunted through yet another mason jar for the required three-quarter-inch washer, that I would make enough money at whatever career I chose to hire skilled workers to perform all these mind-numbing tasks for me. I suppose it was the last laugh of my father's life philosophy that I arrived at his house as a budding craftsman in need of his tools.

In order to fulfill his gospel of self-sufficiency, my father outfitted the garage or basement of each home he inhabited with a formidable array of equipment. He had developed relations with the proprietors and staff of every hardware store in Los Angeles and the Valley, and no power tool was too specialized or esoteric to escape his interest. Any savings he might have realized from his self-service attitude were almost certainly consumed by his hunger for hardware novelty. However, his well-stocked workshop was of great benefit to my project.

As I unloaded the wood and the plastic bags of supplies from my hatchback and stacked them on the lawn in front of my parents' house, my mother watched from the picture window. She held one of her long mentholated cigarettes in one hand, and in the other clutched the green ceramic ashtray I had made her in junior high. She looked at me quizzically, then slipped from between the opening in the sheer curtains and disappeared.

I carried the boards and bags around the house to the back door. I knocked and then entered. From the landing inside, one set of stairs dropped down into the workroom and the other brief set climbed into the kitchen. I found my mother there tamping grounds into the filter of her espresso maker. She was wearing a loose caftan with a print of peach and magenta flowers on a jade ground. The sleeves slipped down her forearms to puddle at her wrists, and she pushed them back. "You like coffee, don't you, Peter? You used to say, Mommy, how can you drink that dirty water? But I guess we can't expect our children to avoid their parents' vices. You want steamed milk with it?"

"Whatever you're having." I wanted to get to work, but I sat obediently at the bleached pine table in the breakfast nook and sorted through the disheveled heap of the Sunday *Times*. "Where's Dad?"

"Peter." She looked up from arranging demitasse cups under the spouts of the machine. "He's touring elder hostels in Europe. I told you." She pressed a red button, and a dark drizzle of liquid ran into the cups.

# 41

It was possible that she had told me; I tended to use my mother's extended phone monologues as a mantra for meditation. But it was more likely another example of my mother's propensity to elide the essential.

My nephew was a year old before my mother disclosed that my sister had given birth. Perhaps she assumed that my sister and I were so distantly connected that I wouldn't be interested. Meg was twelve years older than I, and although she lived at home until she was eighteen, she was a roving teenager and remains almost completely absent from my memories of childhood. I was convinced that by some bizarre genetic circumstance my parents had produced a second, only child. I was six when, according to my mother, Meg "ran off" with "a young man" to Saginaw, Michigan. Meg did not say good-bye to anyone, but as a courtesy (or to avoid being classified as "Missing" in a police file) she telephoned my mother en route. After that call, I thought Meg had disappeared entirely, except for the occasional noteless, return-addressless, grocery store Christmas card, which my mother would see fit to display on top of the television. I remained ignorant until one day when I was conscientiously writing thank-you cards for my high-school graduation presents. Searching for envelopes, I walked into the "den"—the small spare bedroom in our apartment in the Valley—and found my mother fitting a pair of tiny tennis shoes, miniature blue denim overalls, and picture books into a box. When I asked about the package, she paused, briefly, then told me it was a gift for my nephew's birthday. Meg was living with a young man, "a different one," in Pensacola, Florida, and her little boy, Tyco, would be a year old on June 28.

I did not get angry with her immediately; I had no reaction for most of the day—not even questions. I remember speculating that my mother was being protective, cushioning me from a mortal blow to our family happiness. I imagined that she had bolstered herself at the time of my sister's departure with a determination to correct her mistakes in parenting and raise me more successfully. As part of the project, my sister had to be excised from discussion.

I was in shock and didn't know it; the evening was full of chrysalis hours for my mind to prepare itself for new understanding. That first night, I treated my mother's decision not to tell me of my sister's whereabouts as if it were a reasonable proposition, as if after careful consideration she had chosen the best course for us all. I suppose I wanted to believe that my upbringing had been sensible, that I had been deprived of all knowledge of my sister for my own good. And, after all, I couldn't pretend that I had fretted with concern for the past ten years; I couldn't claim a bond with Meg that we didn't share. I couldn't, on reflection, state that I had felt the loss.

But as I sat up in bed that night listening to the traffic pulse from stoplight to stoplight on the major thoroughfare outside the apartment complex, my mind turned an irreversible corner. I knew that in growing up everyone detached from their parents, but, for me, adulthood cracked my life like a broken bone. My family life had not been an idyll until then, but it had been unexamined. My mother's lies of omission, her deception, her treachery—as I called it then—had leached unobserved into the bedrock of my childhood and left a toxic sinkhole. I knew that I risked being melodramatic, but I could no longer assume that any of my long-held beliefs about my family were true.

In the morning, I found my mother carefully removing the paper backing from a rectangle of adhesive shelf paper. I asked her out to lunch in a calm voice, suppressing any tincture of the fresh rage I felt. To avoid the necessity of leaving home, my mother countered my proposal in equally serene tones with an offer to make sandwiches and serve them on the balcony. I declined politely; I would not confront her in her own territory.

My mother outfitted herself carefully in a cream linen suit and packed her purse with prescription bottles, Kleenex, cosmetics, packages of premoistened towelettes, and sunscreen as if she were embarking for a foreign country with unreliable supply lines. We climbed into the seven-year-old LeSabre I had inherited from my father, and I drove with spiteful speed down the left lane of the freeway, knowing my mother would have preferred hugging the right shoulder, nearest the exits. When I parked in the lot of the Sherman Oaks Galleria, my mother looked up from the nervous study of her lap, puzzled. For our conversation, she would have selected a quiet restaurant with padded booths as deep and cloistered as the first-class seating compartments of a luxury train, and I grinned with perverse satisfaction as I led her to the food court, where a thousand fourteen-year-old girls would surround us in audience.

When we were settled in our sticky molded plastic chairs with plates of steam-table Chinese takeout, my mother pointed at me with the tines of her white fork and spoke with surprising crispness, "So what is it you've brought me all the way out here to talk about?"

She had stolen my initiative, and I responded with the first question that floated to my lips. "Does Dad know?"

"About Meg?" She stabbed a gray lump of chicken. "Of course."

"Then everyone knows but me." I was suddenly, helplessly disconsolate. I dug a hole in the center of my side-order of rice with a chopstick; I made a volcano with soy sauce.

"Why is this a problem for you *now*? You've always known you had a sister. You could've asked."

If she had stopped speaking, if she had held to her usual dictum of restraint, I might have forgiven her longer silence. Despite my anger, I was ready to accommodate her view. I had forgotten my sister when it suited me, and I had no right to be outraged. Convenient obtuseness was a trait my mother and I seemed to share. I glared down at the shriveled pea pods on my plate.

But my mother could not tolerate my sullenness and did not let the matter rest. "It's not our fault, Peter. Your sister is strong willed. And it's those young men: that first one, and now this new one." She sucked at the straw of her iced tea, closing her eyes as the dark beverage worked its way into her mouth. "And the baby, Peter, is black."

She spoke the last word with great difficulty and finality, and her features tightened around the eyes to put a period to the conversation. I stared at her a moment as she returned to plucking morsels from her greasy stir-fry. I realized that this detail was the revelation that she had withheld until the last moment to convince me of the benefits of my ignorance, her trump card, her pièce de résistance. At the bottom of my mother's well of deception was her strange racist fastidiousness: she could buy a black baby clothes and toys, but she couldn't—until pressed—tell her son that his nephew existed. I laughed, loudly.

My mother glanced over her shoulder at a group of lunching women in secretarial print dresses with bright white bows at their throats. "Why are you laughing?"

"I didn't really bring you here to talk about Meg." Of course, I had done exactly that, but my statement became true as I spoke it. "I wanted to talk about me. This thing with Meg has made me realize I don't think I can hide it anymore." I had always expected my own revelation to arrive after months of mental preparation and under a pall of seriousness, but I felt buoyant. "I've known for quite a while now that I'm gay."

"What?" She spoke with frustration, as if she hadn't actually heard me. She set down her fork and leaned visibly into the table.

"I'm gay. Homosexual. I'm attracted to men," I said and smiled. I couldn't control it; I burst with nasty joy directed at my mother. I continued in a louder voice, loud enough to incite surreptitious twists of the secretaries' heads. "I'm queer, Mom. That's my secret. I'm a faggot." I laughed. It was a cruel laugh, and I have regretted it since that moment. But the sensation in my chest, the sound as it escaped my throat, scoured out an unacknowledged pain inside me.

While I was watching the uncomfortable secretaries, my mother had produced a tissue, and she closed the hinged jaw of her purse with a snap. I wasn't certain if she was preparing to cry, if she had something stuck in her teeth, or what. "I'll take a taxi home," she said, dryly. And then she stood.

# 42

My mother did not forgive me. But I did not remain unforgiven either. My confession, my "coming out," was a revelation my mother found so unprecedented, so indigestible to her system that she simply spit out the hard truth of it like a fruit pit. On that night after I returned home from the mall, and for months thereafter, my mother appeared to have forgotten the reason for her dramatic exit from the food court. She continued to treat me with her usual coolly rendered politesse, and I wondered if she had misunderstood me. She believed, perhaps, that I had fabricated my admission out of spite.

I recognized later that she wasn't deceived in the matter; instead, she had consigned my revelation to the realm of the truly unspeakable—the category in which my nephew had languished for a year. If my sister had lived in California, I understood, my mother would have treated her as if she were unmarried and childless or, if circumstances absolutely required acknowledgment, as if her husband and child were not black. At the greatest extremity, and only then, would she have recognized my sister and her family at face value and pretended that the issue didn't matter to her. The sliding scale of her consciousness was rooted in necessity. And because I took no overt action to force her attention, she did not allow a consideration of my sexuality to impinge on her thoughts.

For my part, I wanted to apologize. I regretted that the unveiling of my true identity had been just a bitter footnote to our contention over my sister's story, but more important, I didn't want to be the kind of man who would punish his mother for her inadequacies of understanding. However, my mother's lack of response made it all too easy for me to delay broaching the subject again. When the reasonable time for apology had passed, I became determined to make my good intentions known by deed rather than words. I vowed to tolerate my mother's more insufferable qualities with poise and grace. It was a vow I had kept while living at home as an undergraduate —although after leaving for Jane Floe and my room at the Consulate, I had maintained my cordiality principally by avoiding my mother whenever possible.

I had not been home for such a long time that, despite my efforts at nonchalance, my arrival with stacks of wood and material carried the weight of a major event.

After espresso and a conversation crafted entirely of effortful pleasantries, I carried my supplies into the basement workroom and began tentatively to set up the table saw. My mother appeared at the end of the workbench, her arms folded into capacious sleeves. Beneath the caftan her body seemed somewhat stouter and rounder than I remembered it. "Oh, there you are, Peter," she said casually, as if, in her perambulations about the house, she had found herself quite by chance in the narrow, unfinished room tucked behind the furnace and the water heater. "Did you say this was something you were doing for work?"

"I didn't say." I lifted a board onto the edge of the table. "But, no, this is just a personal project of mine."

"Your father hasn't been down here in ages." My mother extended a hand out from her nimbus of fabric and lightly, speculatively brushed along the grain of the new wood with the pads of her fingers, as if she might find some clue to my intentions.

"I don't see how he could, what with being in Europe and all," I said and lifted my sheaf of plans and a tape measure from my satchel. Vow or no vow, my mother was a bane to my concentration, and I endeavored to sound appropriately sour to deter her from lingering.

"I mean before he left. One day last winter, your father was building a birdhouse for the yard. He came up for lunch, and I don't think he ever went back down. He stopped, just like that. He lost interest." She looked around her at the shelves, pegboards, and cupboards filling every inch of the wall, searching for remnants of the abandoned project.

Despite myself, I followed her gaze as it swept the room. Everything was properly stored and stowed away; everything was in order, almost obsessively prim—if a little dusty—like one of my father's notions shops. There was no half-constructed birdhouse in sight, and I began to wonder if his project had been a fabrication to mask some other activity conducted in the basement. Perhaps my mother was thinking the same thought; she had something on her mind. However, I wasn't interested in pursuing it. "Well," I said, with what I hoped was an air of finality. I spread my diagrams out along the free space of the workbench to my right.

I expected my mother to feel rebuffed and drift upstairs, but she remained firmly planted by the saw with her hands spread on the board. She asked her next question with unswerving directness: "Are you still a homosexual?"

I was stunned. In the years since our talk at the Galleria, the word had never formed on her lips, nor had any of its synonyms. "Still," I said, making a determined effort not to flinch. I saw no advantage in telling her that my self-definition appeared to have broadened; she would not take any comfort from my tales of Muriel and Chaz.

"Was I a good mother to you, Peter?" She fiddled idly with the lever of a vise bolted to the end of the bench. Under the light from the window, the gray hairs in her helmet of dark curls shone like wires. "I think sometimes that if I had been more attentive as a mother, this would be different. But sometimes I think I should be more supportive of this."

She did not explain what "this" was, and I did not feel inclined to ask. "I don't have any complaints, Mom. I had a happy childhood, all in all." I hooked the lip of the tape to the edge of the wood and began to unwind the yellow metal strip from its chamber.

My mother held the end of the tape in place with her finger. "I worry I haven't done enough, that this was my fault."

"It's okay. Nothing was anyone's fault." I was strangely pleased that my mother and I were having a heartfelt talk, although I didn't know exactly what we might be saying to each other. All our indefinite pronouns made me weary, and I needed to get to work. "Excuse me now, Mom. I need to cut wood here."

"I'll help," she said cheerfully. While I marked the wood with a pencil, she rolled up the sleeves of her caftan and tucked them in at the shoulders so that her arms were encircled by huge doughnuts of cloth. She donned a pair of thick plastic safety goggles; she resembled the Empress of Pluto.

"That's not—" I wanted to tell her that her aid was unnecessary, that I could manage perfectly well on my own. But she was uncharacteristically eager to spend time with me, and I couldn't refuse her. "All right, you can steady the board at the end there while I cut."

"What are we making?"

"A chair," I said. I didn't elaborate but smiled with perverse satisfaction at the idea of my mother assisting me with a gift for Muriel. I imagined the result of my mother's handiwork carefully displayed in the Lambent Hall of Chairs.

# 43

I pressed Chaz down against the mattress with the butt of my palm. The golden cords of his back tensed as I forced his legs apart with my knees and entered him. Nothing, no latex, no hesitancy, slipped between my flesh and his.

Except for two desultory sessions spent on my back, I had always taken Brad, his face buried in the sinking surface of my futon, his hands stretching above his head, clutching at the corners of a pillow. I was ambivalent about assuming power; I shied from the responsibility of control. But when my blood grew fierce enough, I felt a switch turn, a valve open, onto a flood of confidence. With Chaz, energy surged in me easily. When Muriel let me into the house and I saw Chaz standing at the top of the stairs, lean and wet from the shower, I had no doubt that I would have him.

Muriel had poured me an iced tea, but I excused myself and pursued Chaz up into the bedroom. I was not myself—not my expected self—but my bravado was not artificial. My actions felt precise and true.

I grinned and grabbed Chaz, squeezing one cheek of his butt as I kissed him. My other fingers combed through the white damp spikes close to his skull. Our lips interleaved, and I chewed at the flesh couching his lower teeth. My tongue spelunked the cavern of his mouth. I toppled him onto the bed, kicked off my shoes, groped out of my clothes. I bent against him, tugging at his tough nipples with my teeth while strumming his solid stomach with my palm. We didn't talk; there was nothing to be said.

Chaz moaned as I turned him over—a thin, wet string of vowels—and I appreciated his exposure of tenderness. I couldn't have wanted him more.

As I rocked into him, I filled my head with distractions to hold myself off. I thought about my coffee-table tome on Shaker furnishings, I tried to recall the names of swatches from the Pantone color book, I attempted a chronological filmography of Fassbinder. But I found all these details immeasurably exciting. They did not deflect me. I propelled myself into Chaz, shooting deep; without pause, I flipped him over and worked at him.

As he came, Muriel's finger flicked at one of my buttocks. "What are you boys up to?" she asked with the haughty air of an Edwardian governess. I turned my head to see her, in an atypical lacy oyster peignoir, her hair neither braided, nor twisted, nor swept into a chignon, but full and loose against her shoulders. She smiled wickedly.

I grabbed for her wrist and pulled her to the bed, then shoved her to her knees. "I want you to eat every bit of this," I said and guided her lips towards the pearl drops fanned across Chaz's chest.

Muriel swept her hair back in her fist, spread the blade of her tongue, and cheerfully began her work.

# 44

We had a lot of sex. I had never imagined myself to have a particularly earth-shaking libido; I had always envisioned my lust as a mouse scuttling at the back of a cupboard after midnight. I had pleasured myself when I felt inclined, I had undertaken a couple of affairs of no significance, and I had found one real lover in Brad. I imagined I was satisfied. But with Chaz and Muriel, I was engulfed in a ferocious brushfire of desire. My craving cut a swathe through my days, torching trees to their roots and melting metal walls. Hour by hour, day by day, I hurled myself towards their inferno heart of pure light and heat.

I would come to their door directly after work to have dinner with them, and rush home to shower in the brown predawn light. When I moved to Orange County, I had meticulously bulwarked myself into a complacent life alone, but in a few weeks with the Lambents, the weave of my routine had come unraveled, the glue of my identity unstuck.

Initially, my visits to the Lambents had been divided discretely from the rest of my schedule; they were diversions that could be marked off on a calendar and encompassed by unlimited periods of reflection in the neutral beige space of my apartment. I had purposely left the walls stripped of all ornament except for a poster for a Kandinsky exhibition, full of vague geometries that suggested absolutely nothing to me. I wanted to preserve the condominium's assertive blankness as a haven from the aesthetic undertow to which I imagined myself susceptible. But soon I met each morning with a mad dash from their door to mine to avoid Irena's curious eyes. When the time spent in my place became limited to a brief dance around the bathroom to the beat of FM radio and an even briefer pause in the aisle of my walk-in closet to select a shirt or a tie, it was no longer realistic to reckon the Lambents a diversion, an eddy in the current; they *were* my life.

Once my encounters with Muriel or Chaz had been exclusive. While I was in bed with Muriel, Chaz would absent himself; when Chaz wrapped his arm around my waist, Muriel would slip off unobtrusively. But quickly, this division of activity was abandoned, and we became a threesome. I had feared it would be awkward, a triangular tango, but we moved with grace, balletic, under the broad dark mirror.

Our sex continued in a pattern of (relative) normalcy; the oil, mask, and chains had disappeared, and I did not miss them. I did not need props or rituals to lose myself in the Lambents. Even now, I can taste a residue of the thoughtless bliss that soaked those days. It was within the firestorm of my love for them that I have best known the unearthly levitation of Beauty. I felt buoyed as if wings were forever lifting at my shoulders.

# 45

I slept with the Lambents, I spent my days with the Lambents, but I didn't know them. It seemed that the volume of the Lambents was locked for me; I could brush my palm along their thick hand-tooled spine, test their weight in the crook of my fingers, admire their gilt-dipped edges, but I couldn't cut into their pages and find their text. Or if their secret chapters were laid open before me in some subtle manner, I couldn't read them; I was Lambent-illiterate.

My attempts to glean morsels of insight into their history were met with disdain. When, over breakfast, I asked Muriel if she had grown up in Southern California, she answered with languorous contempt, "Oh, Peter. Really." Her response was not a negation—not the typical denial of an Easterner who wished to distance herself psychically from the lifestyle she was now successfully exploiting. Muriel spoke to preclude any possibility of further discussion, and I wish I could claim to have imitated her reticence and kept my own stories hidden like a clutch of pearls. But when we talked, which was often, my life was at the center of our discourse. I told them about Brad, about my parents, about my rogue sister and her invisible family, about the intrigues at the Jane Floe School of Design, about various machinations at work.

One of the senior associates at the agency had been lured away to manage a senatorial campaign, and through some mysterious process, everyone in my department had been bumped up a notch. I was now entitled to sit in on meetings with clients—weirdly enervated sessions in which large-scale mock-ups and storyboards were paraded before corporate PR reps, who would shake their heads over the width of a graphic line and say, "This border doesn't really say 'comfort,' does it?" I would come home outraged and exhausted, anxious to vent my irritations, and the Lambents seemed eager to empathize.

Whenever I wasn't the focus of discussion, we talked about art—favorite movies, antiques, paintings—or bantered, glancingly, over current events. Chaz regarded any issue touched by politics with icy cynicism, and Muriel affected an attitude of perfect disinterest. To my dismay, I would find myself defending basic tenets like the democratic process or freedom of expression. Chaz and Muriel seemed to regard such rights and duties as social pleasantries—desirable perhaps but without personal implications. I began to believe that their attitude was not deluded; I could not imagine any circumstance, any totalitarian dystopia (or any liberationist revolution for that matter) in which the Lambents' mode of being could not persist, or even thrive. By some pact with the cosmos, they had been given the carte blanche of heaven.

Although I apprehended them on every level but the physical as if through frosted glass, I was incapable of decelerating my growing need for them. I wanted to spend all available hours in their presence. When I was with them, I was the focus of attention, with the inevitable cost to the privacy of my mind and body, but with the apparently infinite reward of resting couched and enveloped in their regard.

It was a shock to my sense of well-being to discover a hint of encroaching boredom in the Lambents. I had been lying naked in the art nouveau bed, following the overhead meanderings of the mirror frame whose golden peaks and runnels seemed stiff yet mutable like the cap of a baked meringue. Muriel sat on the edge of the bed in a pair of laddered Danskin tights and her oversized Brown sweatshirt. She looked straight up to converse with my image in the glass. "Isn't it time for you to clean your house?" she asked, without apparent inflection.

Her assessment was, of course, literally correct. I had spent so few hours in my apartment in the last weeks that its surfaces were shawled in gray dust and anointed here and there with shrugged-off socks and carelessly forsaken glassware. And she was accurate in her implication that there was no reason for a twenty-five-year-old man to expend a late afternoon as an odalisque on a well-plumped duvet. What troubled me about her comment was that she had somehow been given pause to ponder the situation, that the febrile intensity of our relations had slackened sufficiently to allow the mundane to intrude.

I felt now as my mother had upon the arrival of her gray hair. I was very young, but I remember her seated at her vanity table on a white wire-backed ice cream parlor chair, crying, her elbow bent, the hairbrush fisted like a scepter. It wasn't her first gray hair—more likely her fifth. She could dismiss the first four as freaks of pigmentation, false alarms. Yet while she had plucked the offending strand and another might not creep into view for months (they would forever remain stark and few), she knew that there would be no end to them.

As I looked up into Muriel's mirror eyes, I felt with the same certainty that her question was but the first in a long strand of up-coming dismissals.

My pessimism was rewarded by Chaz the next day. The three of us were watching television when he announced his intention to drive to Trader Joe's and pick up some wine. I rose when he did. I had a particular reason for following him out to the carports: I had never seen the car Chaz drove—we had always taken Muriel's El Camino—and I was curious.

"Can I tag along?" I asked as we crunched through peeled curls of bark on the walk under the eucalyptus trees.

"Sure. You can drive," he said and subtly shifted his direction across the pavement towards my car.

We drove to the shopping center, and Chaz spent several minutes selecting a cart using some obscure criteria. He wheeled it carefully under the door's electronic eye, then through the opening glass into the store. He skirted the unadorned shelves of bargain-priced specialty foods and halted in the liquor department. His selections from the open crates of cheap, decent wines were educated and rapid, like a skilled scout's at an estate auction. He racked the bottles deftly in the bottom of the cart.

"What's all this for?" I asked and rocked queasily in my high-tops.

"Some libations for home, and some for a little get-together." He tipped a green bottle against his palm to examine the label, then quickly returned it to its box.

"You're having a party?"

"Not us. Going to a party."

"Oh," I said, unable or unwilling to mask my disappointment that they were going someplace where I wasn't invited, where I was unknown.

"You wouldn't care for these people, Speck." He slipped a final bottle into place in the cart and pushed it towards the checkout. "They're old friends. Old in the sense of worn out. Tired. It's more of an obligation for us actually."

I understood that I was being consciously excluded. My stomach wrenched as I peered down into the bins of imported chocolates. I had been reduced to Irena's supporting position: hanging paper lanterns along the closed border of the Lambents' domain.

Out in the parking lot, my disillusionment bloomed as a fit of pique. I waited until Chaz had unloaded three cartons of bottles into the hatchback of the car, then I kicked hard at the cart, which careened down the aisle of parking slots and clipped the door of a hideous metallic blue Merkur.

"It's not worth it, Speck." Chaz opened his door then tossed a candy bar across the roof. "Here. I bought this for you. Chocolate-Raspberry Truffle."

The worst jolt of the afternoon was that he had intuited exactly what I was feeling but didn't care.

# 46

I drove home angry—to *my* home. And I vowed that I would not allow myself to suffer from my exclusion. I sprawled on my futon couch in front of an MTV video countdown and drank a six-pack of Tecate. The ensuing shipwreck inside my head prevented me from a step-by-step visualization of the soirée I was missing. I was spared from speculation over where the Lambents might have gone, who might be greeting them, what music might be playing on what brand of stereo.

In the following week I struggled conscientiously to avoid my neighbors and to fill the void in my days with incidental activities. After work I bought a thick stack of magazines. I filled out the byzantine membership form at a video store. From a rack in the drugstore, I purchased a slick-bottomed bodyboard made of dense pink polyfoam and took a day off to drive to the beach on the Balboa Peninsula, where I was too embarrassed to take my board down to the water for a show of ineptitude, and instead punished my skin with a sunburn/tan while reading the more esoteric nineteenth-century essayists (Pater, Carlyle, De Quincey) in my Norton Anthology of English Literature.

I was ill at heart, and I knew it. I made an unprecedented number of phone calls to people I had previously blithely ignored. But each conversation made a sickening loop back to the point I was trying to escape. I called my mother, who was eager to know when I was coming up to Brentwood to finish the chair.

I called my sister at the number I had for her in Florida, but I hung up when a child answered.

I called my friends Judy and Clara from the consulate. Judy answered and was initially pissed that I hadn't responded to the messages she left on my answering machine, even though I protested that I hadn't received them. She guessed that only a great love affair would have made me so impolite. "Anyone I know?" she asked. "You didn't get back together with that 'Sam'—Brad, I mean—did you? That would be making mistake number three for sure. But tell me."

Drawing on all my courage and desperation, I asked her, "Could we get together for coffee or something?"

I met Judy on the Third Street Promenade in Santa Monica, and we walked past the wire frames of the topiary dinosaurs to a café for iced tea and french fries. As she eased into a white plastic chair under the awning, she looked up at me, and her pink mouth curled at the corners like licks of flame. "You're up to something. Come on. Spill it."

I sat and made a show of laying out a stack of clean napkins and streaking the top with ketchup for the fries. My story—the story of the Lambents that I had invited Judy out to listen to—suddenly seemed so absurd that I couldn't begin it.

"Come on," she urged more insistently, then bent over to dig her cigarettes from a large canvas bookbag on the ground. I examined the top of her head—the blunt-cut henna red hair held back from her forehead with blue plastic barrettes, eight-year-old style—until she straightened up. I returned my gaze to the fries. "Clara keeps hiding my smokes, ecofeminist bitch that she is. She's having the whole Lesbians of Color Coalition for the Environment over for tofu dogs. Great dykes really, but it means thirty angry activists in my living room when I want to watch those music video awards." She reached into the hip pocket of her blue-and-green plaid sundress and pulled out a lighter.

"You guys having a bad month?" I asked.

"Oh, I could go off on her. But I won't 'cause you've got something you're dying to tell me." She lit up and exhaled a first, satisfied puff. "And I wouldn't dream of interrupting." She glared at me pointedly.

Reluctantly, I told her more or less the whole story of my encounters with the Lambents while she coaxed me on with an occasional "no shit?" I had never talked to her about sex or my personal life in any detail before, and I was jolted by my directness. When I reached the point in the telling where I felt abandoned by the Lambents' party plans, Judy bit on one of her forest green nails and said, "And so?"

"So am I nuts? I shouldn't be hurt—I should just keep away from them, right?"

"Well, Peter," she began languidly and stretched against the rigid seat back. "It's not like we're dealing with the Marquis de Sade here. More like a backup feature in *Swinger's Holiday*. These days, there are photo spreads on genital piercing in *Mirabella*. Well, no, but close. What I'm saying is, do what you want. Just be careful. Think latex."

"We don't—didn't use condoms," I added quickly, brazenly.

"Now that *is* dangerous. Do I need to get you a pamphlet?"

"We've all been tested," I said—and wondered if this was true.

"It's always the cautious, intellectual types whose brains shut off in bed."

"I haven't been stupid," I began confidently, then faltered, "have I?"

"I'm the same. Okay, I'm never cautious. But I want to just get out of my head with sex, you know? Do you want frozen yogurt?" She dropped her cigarette pack and lighter into the canvas bag.

I took this as a cue to gather the cups and napkins between us.

"Another possibility is—all this about whether they're bored with you, whether they really care—do you think maybe you enjoy the agony of it all?"

Muriel called twice during the week to ask me why I had disappeared, and I told her first I was behind schedule in making potato salad for a company party and didn't have time to talk. The second time, I told her that I was seasoning my wok and the oil smoke had set off the fire alarm. Then I hung up as if in a panic and never called her back. I didn't care that my lies made me sound like Betty Crocker's incompetent twin; my disaffection could not be verbalized to Muriel.

I brought work home to occupy my evenings and cleared my desk and tilted the top to serve as a drafting table and, with pretended inadvertence, began to spy on the Lambents again. This was the period when I would spot them on the patio or alone together in the living room and interrupt their mood with an anonymous call. In retrospect, I am certain that Chaz and Muriel were not left puzzled or disturbed by these calls, but at the time, I was convinced that I had created a mood of enigmatic malice.

Two weeks passed before I decided that my actions were profoundly immature, not just the crank calls but my whole approach to the Lambents. I had relegated myself to misery and loneliness because of my wounded pride at feeling shut out of their party plans—for a party, moreover, held in a location I had never seen and hosted by people who wouldn't know of my existence. As my extended snit subsided, I called Anthony on his private line.

It took five rings. After I had determined he wasn't going to answer and had moved the receiver away from my ear, I heard him faintly, "Anthony speaking." When he recognized my voice, he growled, "Hey, Jerry Mouse, where you been, man? I been aching to do you with my love rod. Let me tell you about it."

"No. Look," I said quickly, preemptively. "I have a story to tell you. Remember that couple I told you I was interested in? Well, there have been developments." I briefly sketched the details concerning Muriel and Chaz: the mask, the spying, and the other accoutrements of our ménage à trois. Intermittently, Anthony interrupted me with an incredulous whistle.

As I approached the end of my tale, I had forgotten what my expectation had been in telling Anthony. He was less likely than Judy to offer any useful observations. I certainly couldn't assume that he would be sympathetic. Whatever impulse had spurred me to call him had evaporated. "So I haven't seen them for two weeks," I concluded, allowing my voice to sputter to a stop.

"I gotta tell you, Jerry. The thought of you giving it to those two in their big bed really straightens my johnson."

"I didn't tell you this to get my rocks off." I had been lying on my bed, but I now sat up stiffly at the edge, planting both feet on the floor.

"No, I mean it, man. You prying her pussy with your thick meat while she's wearing this mask. And you and the other dude going at each other while she stands around watching. That's some weird shit. Really makes me want to pump my lovebone."

I pictured Anthony as he had described himself with the fists of both hands milking some monstrous Tom of Finland phallus between his legs while I talked. I had managed to arouse my phone sex counselor. Some weird shit, indeed. I didn't want to escalate the situation, although it seemed somehow inappropriate to hang up. I scanned my mind for responses that would spoil the mood. "Is your girlfriend around? Dixie."

"I'm sorry about that, man. That was unprofessional. That kind of shit can get me fired."

"No, I'm not complaining. I'd just kind of like her advice."

"Dixie's not here," he said, losing interest in the subject. "Now tell me more about the mask. You said it's got holes in it. They big enough to stick things in?"

# 47

My next encounter with the Lambents was the indirect result of the aggressive helplessness of Irena Delgado. Irena needed a ride; she was relentless in her pursuit. And there was never a question in her mind that I would offer my services.

I was coming in from work, exhausted, the fingers of both hands hooked through the handles of plastic grocery sacks. My brown wool pants had bothered me all day, and after being crushed beneath me against the car seat, they felt unbearably damp and scratchy. Unable to use my hands, I wriggled to adjust them as I walked. As I completed the curved path around the large fern at the corner of my unit, Irena loomed from my doorstep. Under the dying sun, in her black-

and-white checked sweater and black stirrup pants, she looked monochromatic and dour. "Peter, I was just about to knock."

I had avoided Irena since the day of the coffeehouse surveillance, fearing perhaps that my knowledge of her hidden misery would be reflected in my eyes. Despite evidence to the contrary, I had never judged myself capable of keeping a secret. "What can I do for you, Irena?" I averted my eyes and ruefully studied the crunchy smear of a smashed snail on the sidewalk.

"I hate to trouble you when you've just come home from work," she said, in a tone that indicated she was not remotely vexed about her presumption. "The traffic these days. It grinds you down so. Mark my words: people's life expectancy is going to go down. Down." She pointed to the black puddle of snail. I dared a direct glance at her. Her eyebrows had been painstakingly penciled, her lips meticulously outlined and painted. Her immutable curtains of black hair had been fussed over and shellacked into a shell of molded fiberglass. Her necklace glinted, new-polished. Irena was going somewhere.

"When I first bought my villa," she continued, as if she were clearing up a matter of historical confusion on my part, "all of this wasn't here. The congestion. Irvine was practically a frontier town. Who'd have thought."

On the frontier of master-planned megacommunities, I thought, but I rather liked Irena's vision of gaslit strip malls and pony-riding FedEx agents. My hands were growing numb from the milk jug and the heavy cans dangling from my fingers, however. "Excuse me a minute, Irena. I need to get these groceries inside." I suspected she would love to follow me into the apartment while I unloaded the sacks, but I wanted to preempt her disapproving comments on the mess lurking indoors.

"Oh, I didn't mean to keep you." She moved closer to me as I inched towards the door. "The Caddy died. I put the key in and—click—nothing. I'll get Roy, Mr. Garamilla, to take a look at it tomorrow. I was going to ask Muriel or Chaz, but they're not home." She touched fingers to her hair for dramatic emphasis. "So I wondered if I could impose on you to give me a ride to my seminar. I would skip it, only it's our last meeting of this session. It's not far."

"Sure," I said without notable enthusiasm. "I'll come knock when

I'm ready." I turned and dumped a handful of sacks onto my door-mat to fish out my keys.

"Wonderful," she said but lingered. "Only, the seminar starts at six-thirty." Her smile coaxed me to hurry.

"In the same way that braille represents but is not the same lan-guage as written English, Zu-krall embodies, but is not identical to, Harmonic Consciousness." Irena paused from the rote tone she had adopted in order to spray a pulse of wintermint Binaca onto her tongue. She capped the little vial and dropped it into her purse.

I had changed into jeans and drunk a large glass of orange juice. The relief these acts provided was intense, and I ferried Irena calmly out of Irvine and onto the 55 freeway towards Costa Mesa. I had barely registered the complex, arcane monologue that Irena was de-livering until a few of her repeated refrains began to circulate invol-untarily through my head like the hooks of a pop song. "Chaz said something about that."

"Yes, Chaz is very knowledgeable. He's read all the contact journals."

"So what is it? Zu-krall?"

"Call him what you will. Or her. His manifestations are various. You shouldn't think that we who study the Circle are not all good Christians. After all, why should Earth be the only planet God sends a messiah to?"

Her point seemed sensible to me, if irrelevant, but I didn't respond immediately. Traffic slowed ahead as the freeway ended, transformed into Newport Boulevard, the main street through Costa Mesa and Newport down to the ocean. I flipped on my signal and peered over my shoulder to merge into the left lane. "So Zu-krall is the Alien Jesus?"

"No!" Irena raised her voice and sounded quite angry. "He's *our* Jesus. Of course, he is many things, including the Fourteenth Mani-festation of the Polycyclical O, but . . ." She took a slow breath, then proceeded more calmly. "But you see, the important thing to under-stand is that the past is as changeable as the future. Say you had a bad childhood, and that makes you unhappy in the present. What you would need to do is change the past, give yourself a happy childhood so you can be happy now. It can be done!" While we waited at a light, I looked over at Irena, but her head was lowered. She worked at adjusting the sleeves of her sweater. "When Zu-krall manifests himself physically on earth, he will be the Jesus of the future. But when the change comes, he will become—no, he will always have been the Jesus of the past."

"A sort of spiritual appropriation, huh?" I asked, but Irena was silent. I looked out at the plain, single-story storefronts along the roadside. Until my eyes had been attuned by Irena's presence, I had never noticed that there were so many tarot readers, psychics, and New Age bookstores on the street. "Does Zu-krall look human?"

"Turn there," she said and pointed to the next intersection. I shifted the car into the left turnout lane. "He's very much like us. In the photos, his skin radiates a kind of watery green light. And he has multifaceted eyes."

"Photos?"

"He consented once to be photographed by Monica Lupenhaus, the woman who receives him and holds the seminars. Just turn into the parking lot here, and you can let me out at the building."

I pulled up to a plain door, opening into the back side of a row of stores. Irena climbed out and stood inside the arc of the open car door adjusting, straightening, smoothing, and primping for her entrance. "Is Zu-krall one of those guys abducting humans from their homes?" I asked.

She looked at me with horror. She had not registered the flippancy in my voice, and I felt rather sour at having frazzled her. "Oh, no! Not those horrid gray people. Zu-krall has come out very strongly against the anal probe." Irena touched up her bangs to no perceptible effect, then leaned into the car and spoke sweetly. "Thank you so very much, Peter, for bringing me here. Now, there's just one thing. I'm going to ask Barbara Lyman to drive me home, but if she can't . . . well, do you think you could stay for an hour until intermission? I'll come find you then and let you know. I'd invite you in, but it's an advanced seminar tonight."

"I'll be across the street in Triangle Square. In the bookstore."

She smiled. "Wonderful." She lowered her voice to a whisper. "I think Zu-krall's coming tonight! I hope I'm not late." I watched until Irena disappeared into the light beyond the door, choosing her steps carefully in her high heels.

# 48

Triangle Square was a cunningly designed multilevel complex nestled in the acute angle of the intersection of Newport and Harbor Boulevards. The development did not possess the necessary critical mass to become a shopping mecca like South Coast Plaza, but it was too capacious and pretentious to be properly designated a strip mall. It was sleek, upscale, vaguely glamorous. I parked in the tiered garage, which was located at the center of the Square's design, and after checking my watch to plan for Irena's eventual arrival, I toured the attractions.

A series of open-air escalators glided up beneath a whitewashed, red-tiled canopy held aloft by a series of pillars. On the top floor there were movie theatres, trendy Mexican and Italian restaurants, a yogurt store, and other concessions. On the ground floor were the bookstore, coffeehouse, and shops. At the far end of the structure was a giant sporting-goods store, a flagship, full of expensive, elaborate, self-congratulatory display—interactive vitrines, life-sized statuary, numerous computer terminals, and banks of video monitors celebrating exertion and litheness—a corporate shrine, a mausoleum of fitness. There was also a giant music and video store and a virtual reality game room. Beneath all this, on a basement parking level, a subterranean supermarket glowed pristinely. Inside its cavernous hall, long aisles of product stretched back, separated by unusually wide expanses of hygienically polished floor tile. As in the sports store and the music store, the goods simultaneously shimmered with freshness, vibrated with novelty, and posed with almost incantatory quietude, with sepulchral perfection.

I walked off the escalators and through a food court arranged with tables, chairs, and black-framed windbreaks like Japanese screens in canvas and clear plastic, then down another set of escalators onto street level, where I paced the perimeter. I admired the façades and the vistas; they were all attractively wrought. The governing principle was postmodern, but like the pun of "Triangle Square," the ironies had been normalized by familiarity. Outsized, "weathered copper" lanterns dangled from hooks over the central court; Spanish styles from mission and adobe to Moorish were plundered for gewgaws; magnified decorative motifs loomed from the walls, while vestigial cupolas, domes, and minarets bloomed above. But all these borrowings and juxtapositions offered no commentary, only pleasures. Postmodernism was dead as a philosophy but alive as a palette of tropes. I could not imagine Triangle Square at fifty years, at seventy-five; I could not imagine that the architects had considered its persistence either. The sporting-goods store would make a cool nightclub in five or ten years if the parent company reckoned with deficits and decided to clear out. But in twenty years the whole enterprise would seem somewhat embarrassing. For the present, however, I was charmed by its mixture of the timeless and the obsolete.

When I looked down to eye level again, I found myself between a square fountain platform and the inescapable Gap outlet. The clothing stores in the Square all focused solely on leisure: besides the Gap, there was a store for outdoor wear, one for ready-to-wear casuals, a T-shirt vendor. The clothes on display promised sport, play, fun, and activity, as did the posters for coming movie attractions, as did the array of romances and spy thrillers in the bookstore windows. As I strolled towards the bookstore, I heard the spirit of the place, of Orange County, the combined voice of its architecture, its merchants, its concealed history (of what had been razed to make way for the new). It muttered from the elevated planters and the benches of glazed ceramic tile, saying: Here is a world you need never leave, here are pleasures and products and sustenance without consequence. There is nothing beneath the surface, no subtext to disturb; there is no end. It told me that I would be young forever, that I would never die.

# 49

I selected a prominent bench in front of the periodical racks of the bookstore and read *Deneuve: The Lesbian Magazine* until Irena appeared.

"Good news," she proclaimed in a voice slightly winded by the uncharacteristic exercise of crossing a street. "It's all worked out for the best. Barbara will take me home."

"You're sure? I could stay. I'm kind of enjoying myself."

"You go ahead. We're all stopping at Earl's house to look at his Kirlian photography. But thank you so much, Peter. You're a treasure." Irena bent to kiss me on the forehead.

"No problem," I said, and from some instinctual code of etiquette, I found myself rising from my seat as she departed. The page spread of a girl-on-girl fashion pictorial slid to the ground. "Have a good time."

"Zu-krall's aura is so strong," she said from the entrance, delighted and mysterious. "I can feel The Change coming all the way over here."

I stood in my spot until Irena scurried around the corner; then I left for my car.

The garage was a series of ascending ramps, switching at each end of the structure like the flights and landings of a staircase. The concrete was washed white, and each floor was emblazoned with its own stenciled signature—black fish on the subterranean floor, then jade seahorses, rust brown Rolls-Royces, golden Fred Astaire silhouettes, purple poppies, sky blue swallows, and on the exposed top tier, silvery crescents of moon—motifs that were repeated as grace notes in tiny spinning weathervanes throughout the complex. I had parked several switchbacks up from the bookstore, and I decided to walk them rather than cross the central court to the elevators.

"Yeah, you wish, you saggy, hairy-lipped cunt!" The man's voice cracked against the concrete and scattered through the garage.

"Fucking shriveled dick! Gimme the keys!" The woman's voice was even louder, shrill, a sonic drill.

The space ahead of me was populated by automobiles but no people. Due to the acoustics of the garage, the voices seemed to emanate from near my head.

"Look fuckhead, gimme the keys! Then you can go stick a broom handle up your ass and lick the shit off for all I care!"

At eye level to my right, the wall opened to reveal the slanted gray slab of the parking ramp that rose around the corner. I looked through the protective fence of thick cables along an aisle between the tires of two automobiles. Two pairs of boots faced off: diminutive black cowboy boots with a hint of pale denim tucked into their tops, and oily, scuffed black workboots. The toes of each nearly touched.

"Bitch!" the man's voice shouted, and the workboots lurched forward. The cowboy boots rocked back on their heels. I heard the heavy thud of a body slammed against metal and a surprised, heavy-breathed scream.

A motion-sensitive car alarm began its series of bleats—HONK-HONK-HONK-HONK, then EE-OW-EE-OW-EE-OW, then REE-A-REE-A-REE-A. The cowboy boots righted themselves suddenly, and along with a guttural sound, the workboots skidded backwards. After an answering thump, another car alarm joined the cacophony of the first—WONKWONKWONKWONK.

I realized that I had been peering for some time at a fight through a gap in the wall. And I knew the participants.

I raced up the ramp and made a sharp turn at the corner, catching at a supporting pillar with my fingers. Over the roofs of several intervening cars, I saw Chaz and Muriel scuffling next to their brown El Camino. Muriel had somehow managed to open the driver's door and was trying to slip back through it. Chaz tugged at her to pull her away. They were both wearing bomber or biker jackets, and from my vantage their arms and upper bodies were an inseparable tangle of black leather.

Chaz shot a hand up and twisted Muriel's braid around his fist. Her head torqued sideways as he yanked the rope of hair. "Fucker! Cocksucker! Asshole!" Muriel screeched and, as Chaz shifted to tug her from the door by the hair, she kneed him in the groin, then followed that with a punch in the same spot as he lurched away. I kept silent and pressed close to the pillar.

As Chaz bent over, Muriel's braid slipped from his hand. She plunged back into the car then quickly swiveled on the seat to pull her legs inside. As she grabbed for the door handle, Chaz snagged the lapel of her jacket. "You little bloody cuntrag!" he panted over the continued honking of the neighboring car's alarm. He adjusted his body weight to drag her from the car. But Muriel had found the handle, and she smashed the door forcefully against his arm. He shrieked but either could not, or did not, try to withdraw his hand. Muriel pushed open the heavy door and slammed it in again. When she eased the door back to hit him a third time, Chaz slumped away from the car and fell out of my sight.

Muriel locked the door and turned over the engine. At high speed, she reversed out of the parking slot, gunned it down the aisle, and banked around the corner, screeching her tires. She failed to notice me as the El Camino roared down the ramp beyond my pillar.

I crept slowly forward to look for Chaz and found him lying on his side, almost underneath the blaring green Mercedes. I think he was making little groaning sounds, but I couldn't tell beneath the din of the alarm. I knelt close to his head, his blond spikes mussed with dust and oil from the concrete. "Hey, it's Peter. Are you all right?"

"Speck," he said and smiled without opening his eyes. He reached out for my arm to pull me down to him.

I pulled him out from under the car and turned him so that his head and shoulders were nestled across my arm. Blood spotted the cement where his arm had been pinned beneath him. It looked like the pictures I had made in elementary school with tempera paint and a sponge or a potato. "You're bleeding," I said. "You'd better not try to move your arm."

"Come closer," he said. He used his free hand to press me to him. I thought he hadn't heard me and needed me nearby to talk. Instead, he kissed me on the lips, stretching his tongue up into my mouth.

"Chaz—" I began, but felt someone kick at my back.

"What's going on, gentlemen?"

I turned my head to see a burly man in a blue short-sleeved uniform with a security company logo on his pocket. He prepared to kick me again with the side of his shoe.

"We were making out," Chaz said, grinning vacuously. "I guess we got a little carried away."

"Oh, God." The guard's faced curdled above me as if from discovering a grisly roadkill. "Take it somewhere else, all right?" When we didn't climb to our feet immediately, the guard completed the kick he had been preparing. "I said get out of here. Now!"

I helped Chaz discreetly to his feet. We kept his bloodied, wounded arm hidden between us as I led him to my car. The guard mumbled into his walkie-talkie behind us, "Couple of queers."

I tried to ignore the man's impatient glare while I unlocked and opened the passenger door. Chaz dropped onto the seat. With his functional hand he cradled his right arm, stiff as a bouquet of crimson flowers. When I climbed in the other side, Chaz turned his head to me. "Can't you see how much we need you?" he said.

# 50

Chaz refused the hospital, which didn't surprise me. Rather than heading home, he insisted on being driven to Corona del Mar. I glanced over through the shadows in the car. Chaz continued to hold his injured arm away from his body as if it were a glass rod or a stick of chalk. "How bad are you hurt?" I asked.

"Bad enough," he said, insufficiently masking the wince in his voice. "We've missed you, Speck."

I stayed in the center lane as we cruised down Pacific Coast Highway. The road hugged the curving contour of the inland side of the bay through Newport, past the Rolls Royce dealership and the conglomeration of office towers where I worked, then narrowed into the main street of Corona del Mar. The town was quaintly small but quietly flush; securities traders and the VPs of plastics firms had been slowly buying out the fraying, graying citizenry for two decades. There was a hardware store, a liquor store, a bank, and a community church, but as the proportion of blue-rinsed perms to tailored linen skirts diminished, quotation marks seemed to hover at the shopfronts—"Deli" and "Drugstore" and "Post Office"—like Norman Rockwell in aspic.

During my lunch hours, I would often stroll through the floral-named residential streets. With the gradual imminence of a glacier, the boxy pastel bungalows were being leveled, their slivers of land overtaken by mock tudor country estates, mock Italian villas, mock Arts and Crafts cottages. The streetscapes were as "unauthentic" as Triangle Square, and more beautiful. The grounds were lushly green, overhung with lissome branches, and bespeckled with a multihued profusion of blossoms. I would see an old house with an entire adjacent lot devoted to lawn and wonder if the retired owners could sense the calm breath of a realtor somewhere waiting patiently for them to die. I ignored the less savory aspects of the neighborhood's gentrification; I loved it for its beauty.

When we passed the town limits, I began to look for Magnolia Street. "What exactly was that about? That fight?" I asked.

"What are fights always about? A difference of opinion."

"Great. Like you fought about what kind of yogurt to get or what?"

"Nothing so important as that." Chaz released his arm with a puff of pain and reached down into the dark. "I think I've been dripping on your seat."

"Chaz, we should find a doctor. We don't need to tell them what happened."

"No need to get testy, Speck. Turn here, I think."

There was no Magnolia Street, as we discovered after several attempts. There was a Marigold, however, and Chaz instructed me to drive up and down its length. He paid no attention to the shadowed houses as we cruised by them, but on the third pass, he finally pointed to a cottage with light behind its leaded diamond-pane windows. "Stop," he muttered.

We sat for a moment in the silence of the car. Then Chaz reached over to pull my hand from the steering wheel and hold it. His fingers were damp, slick from sweat or blood. He leaned across his seat towards me, and his forehead furrowed in pain. His eyes glistened in reflected light from the windows of houses; a snail-trail ran from his nose along the slope of his upper lip. "I'm really scared, Speck. I'm scared all the time."

His hand shook around mine, and I saw the fear rise from the tenebrist shadows on his face, a lost and hopeless pleading. But as with his raptor gleam—the panther gaze I had briefly spotted—his plea flickered and was gone. Like the glow of polished marble or the tenacious sheen of a Mapplethorpe lily, the impermeable Lambent glaze reasserted itself.

# 51

After knocking, we waited on a covered porch, perfectly set-designed with a hammered brass pot of begonias and a cushioned swing. Muriel answered the door, and this did not surprise me either. "What took you so long?" she asked. She had shed her leather jacket and stood just over the threshold, arms crossed, in a black cashmere sweater. The cowl neck draped perfectly at the base of her narrow throat.

"Speck got lost," Chaz said and shifted past her nonchalantly. For an instant, I saw through the darkened patina of the evening: Chaz had delayed our journey; he had been reluctant to arrive.

"Ow," she said, watching Chaz cross the front room. "Did we break something?" She spoke sympathetically, but her eyes scanned his body with clinical attention.

"Yeah," he said, and in the same breath, "I'm hungry."

"Mrs. Rabindagore is seeing to that," Muriel said and turned her face to me. "She did promise to have you over to eat, as I recall. It's good to see you, Peter. We've missed you." She stretched up to kiss me briefly on the lips. "Go sit. And I'll round up Manjula to see to that arm."

"I don't want to stain anything." Chaz clutched his elbow carefully, standing in the central circle of an elaborately enspiraled Persian rug. "I think I ruined Speck's upholstery."

"A shame," she said as she reversed to exit through an arched portal at the rear of the room. "We'll have to buy you a new car."

I snapped back with irritation, "I don't want a new car." Her blitheness was grating.

Muriel stared at me and changed the subject. "You'll be needing a drink. We were sipping retsina. But the possibilities are almost limitless."

"Beer," Chaz said and sat carefully on a triangular camp stool.

"Beer," Muriel repeated with mocking gruffness and stepped through the arch.

Unlike the porch, which was as orderly as Grover's Corners, the interiors of the house (Manjula Gupta's house, I gathered) were a wild amalgam: subcontinental pop art. There were exquisite dhurrie rugs on the hardwood floors. Art deco sofas covered in white canvas and draped with saturated red and purple patterned scarves. On the mantel of the white stone fireplace a bronze Shiva danced the end of the world, while in the painting above him a blue-faced cartoon Krishna drank deeply from a bottle of Orange Fanta.

I chose a sling chair across the round expanse of a teakwood table from Chaz. Someone had fashioned an elaborate mandala from tiny bleached seashells on the glass top. I looked over at Chaz, but his eyes were shut tight—both to the room and to me.

Behind us was a wall that had been treated to a thick impasto of eggshell paint then varnished to a high gloss. Three rosewood frames were vertically stacked and centered over the table. The first frame held Manjula Gupta's undergraduate diploma from Dartmouth, the second enclosed her Doctor of Veterinary Medicine certificate from the Craven School in San Francisco, and the third preserved an article from the *Orange County Register*. Two years previously, Manjula had received a commendation from the GOP Women's Service League of Orange County. In the accompanying photograph, she was shown in full-dress sari, receiving a plaque from Representative Halford Bryndon, the cryptofascist congressman from Fountain Valley.

"Excuses please." The soft voice murmured very near my ear, and I jerked my head from the article, startled. Mrs. Rabindagore leaned towards me, holding the wrap of her sari to her shoulder; the fabric was formally stiff and shiny, cobalt blue with borders of pewter. "Mrs. Muriel is telling me you are wanting refreshments."

"Oh," I said and glanced over at Chaz, who sat upright but seemed otherwise unconscious. "Thank you." Out of politeness I rose halfway from my chair, but Mrs. Rabindagore had already turned her back to me. She bent over the table sweeping the miniature shells into the cup of her palm. The concentrated effort of the mandala was brushed away in an instant.

I noticed her daughter Jamma waiting in the center of the room gripping the handles of a heavy copper tray. She wore a denim shirt and a blank frown. When the round table was cleared of shells, Jamma set the tray down between Chaz and me. She withdrew quickly from the room without looking at either of us. "Please," Mrs. Rabindagore said, bowing slightly, "if there is anything else?" She followed Jamma out with her fistful of seashells, her bracelets slipping up and down her slender forearms.

On the tray sat two beers capped by upended glasses, a plate of bubbly fried naan bread, and two white ceramic bowls of bright orange paste which, from the aroma, seemed to be carrot pudding. Both the pudding and the bread were puddled with clarified butter. I breathed in the sweet, salty warmth of the food, and hunger lurched inside me. But Chaz had not stirred, and it felt like betrayal to eat without him. I sat staring down near my feet at ornamental gourds in a grapevine basket until something happened to break the stasis.

Muriel burst into the room, swinging by her arm from the doorjamb like a musical comedy chorine. "We're ready," she said brightly. "Bring your beers."

"I didn't realize this was a party," I said.

"Why not?" Muriel spun herself out of the room.

I stood, but Chaz hadn't opened his eyes so I touched him on the shoulder. "Hey. They're going to take care of your arm now."

Chaz raised his head slowly, then bolted to his feet. "Let's go." He nudged me ahead of him into the hall beyond the archway where Muriel was waiting.

"Why *not*?" I continued, still upset. "You two were just slamming each other around a parking lot less than an hour ago, and now it's playtime?"

"How else were we going to get you to visit us, Peter?" Muriel smiled and opened the door into the garage.

Manjula stood at a sink mixing a white gruelly concoction in a bowl. Her jeans gaped at the knees, and her white coat hung open to reveal a bandeau of blue and black batik. Her navel was pierced with a diamond glinting like the stud in her nostril. "Hello," she said.

"Guppie," Chaz said, with the most cheer he had yet exhibited. "You're looking hale and hearty today."

"I would not say the same of you. But we will repair the discrepancy." Manjula smiled. "Hello, Peter. Help Chaz onto the table, would you?"

The garage was outfitted with a complete clinic. One wall was lined with cupboards fronted in matte black. A counter held a stainless steel double sink, an instrument sterilizer, some kind of centrifuge, a microscope. There were several high-voltage arc lamps on adjustable spring arms, and in the center, an examination table. Rather than the slightly dished metal surface of most veterinary tables, the rectangular top was upholstered in forest green vinyl. Stirrups were bolted to the far end; there was a raised cushion at the near end. I helped Chaz lift himself onto the table with his legs slung over the side.

Muriel had slipped around behind the table; she pulled the jacket from Chaz's shoulders. He winced as she tugged his arms from the sleeves. A net of dried blood lines was laced down his arm, and a purple swelling bloomed from the flesh under his elbow. She dodged around the table and reached out to lift his arm. He shied from her, then submitted. I moved away from them both to stand between the poles of the stirrups.

"Well, it's definitely broken," she said. "But it appears to be a closed fracture. All the blood is from the contusion up here. Three or four stitches maybe." She softly stroked the lip of a clotted wound on his biceps.

Manjula approached Chaz in latex gloves. "First, I'll need to do a reduction. Think you can take the pain while I set the bone?"

"Wait," I said. "Shouldn't he be X-rayed first?"

"Why?" Manjula asked as she grasped his arm above and below the swelling.

"I don't know. To see if there's bone chips or something."

"I'm a doctor," she said coldly and torqued Chaz's arm until he shouted. "Why don't you take your friend somewhere, Muriel?"

Muriel smiled at Manjula and dandled her fingers along my shoulder. "Come, Peter. We'll go over here and gossip about Guppie. She's touchy about her degree."

Reluctantly, I allowed her to lead me around a carpeted partition into an office or consulting room. We sat in a facing set of yellow canvas director's chairs beneath a full-color cross-section diagram of female genitalia. "There are girls here in Orange County with parents from the Old Country," Muriel began. "It doesn't much matter what Old Country that is—Pakistan, Iran, Sri Lanka, Thailand, wherever. The girls drive five-year-old Volvos and have their own charge cards, but they don't have sex. Not officially. But such strictures are more often honored in spirit rather than in the flesh. When these girls have skipped a period or two and sneak a home test into the upstairs bathroom to find that something is growing inside them, they don't tell their parents, who would be livid, who might very well make them marry the awful boys, the passing fancies, who provided the semen. Rather, they call our Guppie, who clears things up for them. She really feels for these girls."

Muriel jumped up, giggling, and pointed left and right on the diagram. "These, Peter, these are the Fallopian tubes." She hunted along the floor. "She has a pointer. Really! With a rubber tip." She stood up stiffly and spoke in her mock governess tones, "Now, Peter, as you will see, a D&C is performed thusly . . ." She snorted air through her nose.

"You're pissed to the gills, aren't you? Come sit down."

She nodded. "Restina—res—res—retstina."

"Okay." I gave up trying to settle Muriel into the chair. "If Manjula cares so much about these girls, why doesn't she open a legitimate clinic?"

Muriel put a finger to her lip. "Discretion. The girls prefer it this way. Listen," she said and pointed up with the finger. I heard the bass notes from a stereo pounding faintly through the ceiling. "Sonic Youth. Guppie's brother is in the apartment upstairs studying for an engineering exam." She sang and danced in little jerking steps, then fell back into the chair. "And Guppie makes a lot more money doing it this way. See the fridge by the desk there? Open it. Go on, open it!" She punched me in the chest when I didn't move. "Open it, goddamnit!"

I finally stood up and reached for the handle. "That's where she keeps the fetal tissue," Muriel said. "In little jars to sell for research." Some sick curiosity made me pull the door free of its soft rubber

suction. The two shelves inside were lined with rows of canned pine-
apple juice and slender blue bottles of mineral water. "Ha!" Muriel
called and bounced out of the room.

I skulked more slowly around the wall. Manjula had cleaned the
dried blood away from Chaz's arm, and there was a small bandage
over the cut on his biceps. She was occupied dipping strips of cloth
into the white paste she had mixed. His arm was bent at the elbow
and covered with cotton batting and some kind of rigid splint. Manjula carefully overlapped the plaster bandages.

"Speck?" Chaz called. "Come sit with me."

I crossed the room and hoisted myself up onto the table beside
him. Muriel was dancing by herself in the corner to the softly thudding bass. Chaz clutched my knee with his free hand. He leaned to
kiss my cheek, and for a moment I forgot the women and turned to
give him access to my lips.

Muriel sang out loudly to the driving song from above—although
her tongue mangled the angry lyrics—and swung her head and her
braid. My love for the Lambents returned instantly like a radio station
jumping from the static fog; I felt my reservations vanish. Then just
as rapidly I felt intensely weird, self-conscious, and pulled away from
Chaz on the table.

Muriel peeled the black cashmere sweater from her chest; she was
naked underneath. Her breasts glowed firm and voluptuously
creamy, displayed against the backdrop of surrounding tan like
peeled halves of Asian pear. "Who wants a tit?" she asked. She
swerved close to me, then darted away. She looked at Chaz. "Not
you." She stood next to Manjula, whose gloved hands were coated
with lumpy white plaster. "Taste," Muriel said childishly. Manjula
laughed. She leaned sideways and flicked her tongue across a rising
nipple.

# 52

We ran down the ramp skirting the hill, onto the cove of sand at Little Corona beach. The lights of unimaginably expensive houses shone on the cliffs overhead. Muriel took my hand and pulled me along the cool, damp sand. My feet were bare, and my shirt, untucked and unbuttoned, billowed behind me as we ran. Chaz kept pace with us, his bent arm swinging in its carapace of plaster. "Watch for rocks," he warned, and soon we were scrambling over them, black and slickly treacherous in the moonlight.

We scuttled around stony outcrops pushing into the ocean. They were pocked with cisterns bristling with invisible sea urchins. I slowed to a safer speed to avoid plunging into one of the tidepools and receiving a footful of spines. Curving around from one outcrop was another stretch of sand, which we took at a still faster speed. Then, gasping, with her hand tightly fisted on my own, Muriel plunged into a cavity in the wall. I dropped to my knees to avoid slamming my face into the cliff face.

We scrambled crab-fashion over the rough stones and sodden sand until the darkness became inviolable. At last we reached some kind of low-roofed chamber where our quick breaths bounded bell-like from the walls. Muriel roared and pushed me down onto my back.

She, or she and Chaz, were pulling off my clothes. My shirt, pants, and briefs were shrugged off and tossed somewhere near or far in the sightless cave. The wet sand molded coves for my buttocks and my shoulder blades. Wet hands brushed my chest. Salty, wet, gritty fingers stroked my nose and lips. Someone was burying my legs in the heavy cement. They stretched my arms and covered them with silt tunnels. I began to feel the cold. I shivered.

Someone took hold of my dick. It was already hard. I slid in and out of a wet, warm mouth. Then I slid into a wet, warm space without teeth. Then another cave, another hot cove, differently figured. I wondered if my flesh (or theirs) was being scratched and torn by grit. But I didn't care. I turned my head to the side with my cheek in a cold pool.

It may have been my eyes adjusting. Or misfiring. But I thought I saw the moonlight reaching back into the channel of the cave—like the sun at an Egyptian tomb, penetrating, on one day only, past the giant pharaonic couple seated at the gate, through the murk of the antechambers, to illumine on the farthest wall the face of God. I thought I saw the Lambents etched in silver, their naked torsos huddled over me. I sensed the weight of the sand pressing down. And I imagined these words, in a headline or embossed on fine handmade paper: PETER KEITH WAS NEVER SEEN AGAIN. Pressure bunched at the crux of my legs; I poured my wet, salty drops upwards, into a dark chamber.

# 53

"And wear a tie," my mother advised me, to conclude our conversation.

I was dubious and said so. "Why?"

"You have to make an impression on them. Otherwise they take advantage."

"They're salesmen. We're customers. They're the ones who have to make an impression."

"Trust me on this, Peter. I didn't spend twenty years going to trade shows with your father without learning a little something about wholesale."

"Okay," I said. "A tie it is."

My mother had "decided" to accompany me on my expedition to find material to upholster the cushion of Muriel's chair, and while at first I had planned to dissuade her, I realized that she might indeed have valuable insights. In various venues, my father had sold fabric, beads, buttons, and all manner of millinery products; and he always testified that, despite her other shortcomings as a businesswoman, his wife did know "value for dollar."

So I put on a clean, pressed, blue oxford-cloth shirt, and a delicately patterned navy tie and drove north to pick up my mother.

After a few initial weekends of uninspired puttering, I was completing Muriel's chair at startling speed. The basic frame was finished, and I was through chiseling the convex feather-shapes on the backboard. My remaining tasks were: the installation of the scalloped arms, a final sanding, then varnishing, and the assembly and attachment of the cushion. My mother had taken a keen interest in every stage of the process.

My father remained in Europe, trackable (at a ten-day delay) by a series of blandly uninformative postcards and flimsy airmail letters, and evidently the novelty of his absence had finally dissipated for my mother. She was lonely, and for the first time in my life, she seemed cheered by the distraction I provided. She had apparently arrived at the conclusion that the taciturn underpinnings of our relationship, which she had been careful to establish since my infancy, were either no longer applicable or else had never been ideal, and she was therefore determined to lay new foundations. She was anxious to bond with me and had spent almost every moment in the workshop while the chair was being crafted. Now that the opportunity had arisen for her to place her creative imprimatur on the project, she was eager to proceed.

When I pulled up to the house, she swept down from the bench on the front porch and into the car. She was dressed impeccably in a crepey dove-gray skirt suit with matching pumps. She wore a triple strand of pearls and carried a seal-gray leather purse and a clipboard with a yellow legal pad. "Let's go shopping," she said with disquieting vigor.

We drove across town to a wholesale fabric outlet in City of Industry. The front showroom was clean, well lit, and reasonably orderly. It differed from a retail store in that there were none of the embellishments of consumerism. The tables full of paperwork and the pegboard walls and carts with bolts of cloth were well designed but fiercely plain. The room was organized for the transaction of business, not the pleasures of browsing.

But my mother had never indulged in shopping's ephemeral

pleasures. Whenever she could, she ordered by phone, and she approached all other purchases with a steely forbearance. She did not tolerate frittering time away, although her methodical pace often took longer than a more enjoyable, leisurely expedition. Our yearly sojourns to find appropriate school clothes had been grim affairs, and the discomfiting tenor of these trips returned to me in little jolts of memory as we stood over a broad white table stacked with sample books.

Each page held a grid of four to six swatches of cloth in various figurations of pattern and color. Usually on the facing page there was a color photograph of a sofa or an easy chair upholstered in one of the selections from that particular style or "family" of fabrics. Often a smiling family adorned the couch, or a male-female couple snuggled cozily in the corner of a loveseat.

In the archives of commercial design there were thousands upon thousands of photographs of couples on sofas and women stroking carpet pile with manicured nails. After my months in advertising, I was sometimes frightened by the vast quantity of enticements that the world was required to bear. A product had to be designed, then its packaging constructed, then it had to be sold—to the retailer and to the consumer. There were magazine ads, television, point-of-purchase displays, special offerings, trade journal marketing—all of it requiring a special "look," a "style." Imagining this onslaught of artifice would make me queasy, and I would long to look at something naturally arranged like sand dunes or the leaves of a tree, something without an overt intent to catch my eye and please me.

Somehow this nausea was partially relieved by my love for the Lambents: they were contrived in their fashion, but their artifice was fresh to me—tantalizing, yet mysterious, and therefore not available for instant consumption. In apprehending my love for them in this way, I suppose I viewed the Lambents as less than human—but transcendently less, in the way of spirits. They might be conflicted and troubling beings, but their complications lifted me from the murk of fondled carpeting, just-so jam mustaches, and the chiaroscuro lighting of soda bottles.

While I was deep in revery of the Lambents—how after sex we had sat on the beach watching ocean and sky welt in a purple bruise in preparation for the dawn, then left before the coming of the sun-

—my mother dispensed with her inspection of the swatches. "There's no point looking at these little scraps. The dye batch you actually get could be completely different. Excuse me, miss?" She flagged down the sales rep who had originally escorted us to the table.

The woman reluctantly put down the samples of fabric she was carefully gathering and crossed the room to stand opposite my mother at the table. She was younger than I was, in an orange plaid skirt and a white lace blouse, her fawn hair in a mild pageboy. A small sterling silver gnome depended as a charm from her necklace. In a contest of wills, she would be no match for my mother. "Can I assist you?"

"Yes," my mother said. "We'd like to see your stock. Could we go back and make our selections from that?"

The woman's eyes rolled sideways to an office door at the back of the showroom and paused as if she were waiting for someone to feed her the next line of her script. "Mr. Dunbar will be back from lunch at two."

"I'm afraid we don't have time to wait until two. I'm sure Mr. Dunbar wouldn't mind if you took us to the stockroom and showed us what you have on hand."

The woman lined her fingernails against the lip of the metal band encircling the tabletop. "What company did you say you were buyers for again?"

"Here," my mother said and reached into her purse to extract a card. I read it before she handed it across the table:

**Deborah Keith**
Assistant Manager
Keith's Sewing and Notions

The woman held the card in her palm and scrutinized it. After some time she said, "I'll be right back." She stepped out of sight behind the door of the office as if she were going to consult with a superior, although it was evident through the open blinds of the adjacent window that there was no one else inside; she simply needed to escape my mother's penetrating gaze. I was torn between wanting to rescue the woman from my mother and savoring the verve with which my mother had sent her flying from the room.

"We had those printed up for the Expo in San Francisco," my mother said quietly as the woman opened the door to return to us.

"This way," the woman said and made a vague sweeping gesture with her hand. She led us into the warehouse through another door in the rear.

Quickly but thoroughly, my mother proceeded through bolt after bolt of fabric stacked on crude wooden shelving around the stockroom. Many of the rolls were still wrapped in their brown shipping paper, which my mother tore away. The saleswoman looked at me imploringly, perhaps hoping that I could stem the damage, but I kept silent. Soon she left to check on the showroom. Other than two beefy women in sweatshirts who were silently cutting fabric at the opposite end of the warehouse, we were alone. "Find anything?" I asked.

"Not yet," she said.

"I kind of like this." I held up the frayed end of a bolt of linen that had been dyed a delicate salmon color.

"Not linen. And don't be swayed by the price. The expensive stuff is never durable. Remember people are going to sit on this over and over. It may be art to you, but it's still a chair."

"Right. No silk. No linen. Think cotton/nylon blends." She had coached me on this litany in the car.

"So, Peter," she began as if she were going to continue my lesson, "are you going out with anyone these days?" Her tone of nonchalance was unsteady but aided by her upper body's submergence under a shelf. "Do you have a boyfriend?"

Her question left me slightly irritated. I wished that she had undergone her change of heart two or three years before when I could have introduced her to Brad. I couldn't tell her about Chaz and Muriel; I didn't know how I would explain them and didn't want to try. I mumbled, "Not right now. No."

She pulled her face away from a length of tweedy cloth that she was holding to the light and looked at me. "I want you to feel that we can talk about this now. Could you do that?"

"Okay," I said flatly. I wondered where her new outlook had come from—if she had read it all in a book, if a meteor had landed in the backyard and warped her mind with its rays.

"Meg's coming home for a visit. The plans aren't final. But she'll be here soon." Before I could absorb the news of my sister's imminent return, my mother raked her fingers through the paper wrapper of another bolt of cloth. She pulled it out onto a low table in the light. "Peter, this is it."

The fabric was a jewel-pure blue, very faintly textured with narrow ribs, and with a velvety surface. I would never under any circumstances have selected this particular material for Muriel's chair, but my mother was convinced. She would not be deterred. "It's durable," she said. "And best of all, the color's perfect for a chair shaped like ours. See, it's peacock blue."

# 54

We had remained in the warehouse to observe personally the measuring and cutting of the fabric. Then my mother had cajoled the woman into giving us the necessary yardage, which was minimal, at the greatly reduced price of a memo sample—a bargain I found almost uncomfortably shrewd. We returned to the basement workshop with the lustrous blue material, a similar length of muslin backing, and a rectangle of one-and-one-half-inch foam rubber. Before going home, I sanded and varnished the spread fan of the chair back while my mother trimmed, and sewed, and cut the foam to fit the seat board.

I had ordered a small brass plate, engraved with a dedication and my signature. It arrived one morning in the mail, and I drove into Los Angeles to finish the chair.

My mother was out when I arrived, and I let myself in the back door with my key. Before I switched on the basement lights, I saw the chair on the worktable lit faintly by the high windows. With its curving legs, winged arms, and flaring back, and without its seat for grounding, it looked insectile, a praying mantis crouching in the long grass shadows. When I threw the switch, I expected the chair to turn and skitter from the tabletop for a crevice in the wall. Instead, it seemed to straighten and stiffen under the glare of the overhead bulb, poised and proper, furniture again.

There was little work left to do. I rubbed down the chair with a soft cloth, giving the varnish a final polish and searching for any rough edges or irregularities. I needed to attach the seat, but my mother had wanted to finish it and she had taken it upstairs. I stared at a space I had marked off on the seat rail, then searched in my bag for the metal plate. "Designed and Constructed for the Collection of Muriel Lambent," the plaque read, with my signature underneath. Now that it was time, I didn't know whether to install the plate; I didn't know whether I wanted to give my handiwork to Muriel, whether she deserved it. I dropped the rectangle onto the workbench and went upstairs.

As a child I had sensed that certain areas of my parents' house were forbidden to me, and in the Brentwood house where I had never lived, I had always felt like an interloper. But with both my parents away, I shifted from room to room with open curiosity.

My parents were not interested in enduring style, and they did not form sentimental attachments to furniture. When they moved into the Brentwood house, they had abandoned the comfortably worn hodgepodge of furnishings familiar from my childhood and started afresh. They had taken the advice of whichever furniture salespeople or interior designers were involved, and the house had the coordinated impersonal sheen of a showroom. The effect was exacerbated by my mother's fondness for the pristine; a book would not remain open on the coffee table or an envelope by the phone for more than ten minutes.

In planning the kitchen, someone must have shouted "Provençale!" In a band around the wall above the cabinets were a series of baskets, bundles of dried herbs, and a strange wire contraption I decided was a lobster trap. The floor space in the kitchen was overtaken by an enormous butcher-block island with a built-in sink. Its function was uncertain, but it did provide the kitchen with the aura if not the effect of efficiency.

The appointments in the living room had been selected by someone interested in trend analysis, one of Faith Popcorn's progeny, on the assumption that everyone would wish to spend the next decade cocooning in front of the home entertainment center. The room was sparsely decorated, and all the furnishings were turned in towards the giant television and stereo system. The sofas were fluffy white overstuffed marshmallows; the glass tabletops rested on thick pillars of white plaster scored like doric columns. It was difficult to imagine performing any other activity in the room besides watching television.

I eased my way down the hall to my parents' bedroom; it had always been the most unapproachable area of the house for me. I opened the door and stared down for a moment at the blue cambric comforter. Then I ventured along the aisle between the foot of the bed and a dresser with a large rectangular mirror. My father used to keep his collection of pipes there, on a series of stands, but they were missing.

In the master bath, I looked in my father's side of the medicine chest. There were a number of worn toothbrushes but no razor. I slid open the painted doors to the closets. One was crowded with dresses, slacks, peach and ecru blazers, its floor full of sandals and pumps. The other was empty except for a few wire hangers and the incursion of a single garment in a clingy, opaque drycleaning bag.

I heard the key turn in the front door lock, but I continued to stare at the scuffs on the rear wall of the closet where the heels of shoes would have lined up.

"I'm home," my mother called cheerfully from the kitchen. I heard her move down the hall into her sewing room, then approach me from behind. "Look," she said. "It's all done."

I studied the square cushion in her hands, perfectly cut and mounted, lustrous as a peacock's tail. "Where's Dad?" I asked.

"Where is he?" she repeated cautiously.

"He certainly didn't take all his clothes with him to Europe, did he? And all his shoes? And all his pipes?"

"No," she said. "No, he didn't." She allowed the cushion in her hands to slump against her thighs. Then she placed it on the end of the bed and sat next to it. "They're in storage."

"Storage? Mom, what's going on?"

"You remember Helen?" I didn't. When I didn't respond, she scolded, "Of course you do. Miss Kensey, from the store. Well, your dad has left with her."

"What?" I felt blood heat my scalp with anger.

"He put his things in storage until they get back from their trip."

"Dad left you?" I spun to look into the empty closet, then back at her. "Dad left you, and you didn't tell me? Mom, you have to tell people these things. You can't keep stuff a secret. It's ridiculous!"

"I thought otherwise," she said coldly. She covered her face with her hand, and the loose mauve sleeve of her silk blouse slipped to reveal a single silver bracelet. "I thought it wouldn't happen. It might not happen, Peter. He might get sick of her on this trip and come home. You've read the letters. He's still very affectionate to me."

"Oh, Mom. He's been gone a long, long time. Do you really think it's likely if he wanted to . . ." My words were crushed by the weight of my mother's despair; I became aware of my cruelty. "I'm sorry, Mom."

I looked down at her, but she was occupied in tracing the corner of the cushion with her finger and did not return my gaze. I waited for one of us to say something or make some gesture, but neither of us was adept at providing comfort. I closed the doors to the closets —embarrassed for the first time that she had discovered me in the act of snooping—and picked up the cushion. I flipped it over to examine the neatly tacked underside. "This looks great. Why don't we go down and put it on the chair."

"You go," she said without raising her head. I could see that her eyes were wet with tears she wanted to shield from me. "I'll change my clothes and join you presently."

"Okay. But do come down soon." Self-consciously I touched her shoulder. Then I left the room.

When I was ready to screw the seatboard to the braces on the inside of the seat rail, my mother appeared in a creamy rose turtleneck sweater and sweatpants. She had dried her eyes and arranged her features into an expression of weak cheer. "So, Peter . . ." She gripped the seat rail to steady the chair and the cushion while I hammered. "Do you prefer to be called gay or queer?"

"Have you been reading a book or something?" I didn't want to discuss homosexual terminology with my mother.

"I just want to be supportive."

"And I appreciate it. I do," I said and finished attaching the seat. "Either's fine."

Although the chair was not heavy, we worked together to stand it upright, then stepped away to admire it. It was the most beautiful thing I had ever made with my head and my hands. The chair crouched on its legs, it spread its tail, it fluttered its wings. It was anthropomorphic, but not in a crude cartoonish manner. It glowed; it lived. And because it was my tendency to discount my own abilities, I felt a little detached from the chair, as if it had been entrusted to me by some force outside myself and was not born out of my own skill.

"It's wonderful," she said and squeezed my arm. "I'm very proud of you." She shifted around the worktable to study the chair from a variety of angles, and her fingers alighted on the brass plate. She traced her fingertips across the engraved surface and lifted the thin slice of metal without looking down or thinking of it. "I'm so glad you let me help you with it. It's been important to me."

I wished she would put down the plaque; I hoped she wouldn't read it.

"I could keep the chair here for a while if you don't have space for it or . . ." She didn't complete her thought, but I understood. She didn't want to let the chair go. If she could hold on to this one thing that she had helped create, and that gave her satisfaction, then she could prove that not all beauty, not all love, not all happiness was elusive.

I felt the need to hold on to my work as well. I wanted to give my mother the chair for safekeeping. I wanted to make it a gift to her. But the chair's fate was sealed. "Who is Muriel Lam-BENT?" My mother tilted the plate towards the bulb overhead to read it. She struggled to stifle disappointment from rising into her voice. "Is she a friend of yours?"

I nodded. "She's the one who convinced me to try making a chair."

"Then it's for her then," she said with sorrow and finality. She let the plate drop with a clink onto the table.

"I'm sorry," I said.

"Why?" She stared at me across the lap of the chair. To comprehend my apology would be to admit that she had desired the chair for herself, but I knew she understood.

"I'd like you to be the first person to sit on it." I grabbed the chair by the seat rail and lifted it down to a free space on the floor.

"That's all right," she said dismissively and backed away.

"Please, Mom." I pleaded with my eyes until she stepped forward.

"Peter. I hope it doesn't cave in on me." She looked down at the seat—a deep blue outside the harsh light over the table.

"Don't you trust me?"

"Of course." She turned her backside to the chair and sat, slowly and soundlessly. She leaned back, and her face relaxed and lightened with quiet satisfaction.

I smiled back at her.

# 55

From the time I withheld my first sketch from Muriel's perusal, I had always intended to surprise her with the chair's unheralded appearance on her doorstep, and I saw no reason to alter my plan.

After screwing on the brass plate, I wrapped sheets of polyurethane around the legs and back of the chair, and my mother taped the pieces in place. We carried the chair out to the car and positioned it carefully in my hatchback to prevent nicks and scratches from marring the surface on the way home.

It was after dark when I unloaded the chair in my carport at the Villas del Sol. I knelt on the cement under the security light and peeled away the packing sheets. I lifted the chair and carried it along the curving path to the Lambents'. Lights shone from the windows upstairs although I suspected that they were out.

I considered leaving the chair on the square of concrete outside their front door. The overhang of the roof would provide protection from any unlikely inclement weather, and the hedges surrounding the porch would block the chair from casual covetous view. But if the chair were stolen, I would be heartbroken. Instead, I turned along the side of their building paralleling mine to open the hidden gate. My plan was to set the chair inside the patio for safekeeping, but I thought I heard the dry hiss of Cissy's chain skating along the concrete. If she were lurking in the shadows under the rusted bird-bath/sculpture, I couldn't be sure of her reaction. I latched the gate again and carried the chair into my apartment.

According to the blue clock on my microwave, it was after midnight, but as I looked at the chair perched expectantly on the largely empty beige carpet of my living room, I couldn't conceive of keeping it in my place for an entire night, then surrendering it in the morning. I was too ambivalent about my intentions to wait. I dialed the Lambents' number.

Muriel answered cheerfully. "Peter, it's late."

"I know. I'm sorry. But I've got something for you. A present."

"How nice," she said. "We're just on our way out, but if you want to bring it over, we'll leave the door open. Talk to you soon," she concluded breathlessly.

I set the chair back out on the sidewalk, locking my door behind me. Muriel's suggestion that I slip her present into her darkened house seemed odd—even though I had wanted to surprise her—but I was determined to shift the ownership of the chair before I changed my mind. As I followed the bending sidewalk to the Lambents' front door, I wondered where they might be going with such urgency at one in the morning that they couldn't wait for me to cross the path. I opened their door slowly, and as I stood among the chairs in the front room, I imagined how my winged chair would look when it took its place among them. Then I thought of the dog. If she wasn't on the patio she might be lurking inside, and she had never expressed any affection for me. I called out "Cissy!" to announce my presence and hunted for a lightswitch.

I stumbled over the kneeling hulks of several chairs and worried I had scratched something. I gave up. I braced the chair against my hip and felt my way down the hall with my free hand. I decided to leave my gift in the bedroom and lifted the chair carefully, step by step, towards the warm light leaking along the upstairs hall from the grapevine Tiffany lamp on the nightstand. From the threshold I saw the muscled lump of the dog snoring in the center of the duvet. "Hi, Cissy," I said, fully expecting her to answer me. She partially opened the slits of her eyes, closed them, growled throatily, and allowed a shiver of irritation to gravitate from her back leg into her tail. She grew still again, and I felt secure enough to shift my eyes from her.

I arranged the chair in position at the foot of the bed and scanned the room for a pen and paper to write a note—thanking the Lambents for their inspiration.

I did not realize that I was alone inside the Lambents' house for the first time until I looked down at the bureau top and noticed how sun from the window had mildly discolored the varnish everywhere but in a rectangle where the carved wooden box usually lurked. I had grown inured to the mysteries of the room, but the missing box snapped me to attention. I looked around with renewed interest. I could go anywhere in the apartment. Open any closet. Touch any object. To test my power I slid open one of the bureau drawers.

It was filled with three piles of Chaz's brand of briefs, neatly folded and whitely blaring from the shadows of the drawer. I touched them. Unconsciously, I lifted one to my face. I breathed bleach and laundry soap as I felt around the edges of the piles for something hidden. My fingers brushed the bottom of the drawer.

The phone rang.

I dropped the briefs into the drawer and slammed it shut, jumping back and bumping into the massive footboard of the bed.

The phone rang again, and the answering machine on the nightstand clicked on. Muriel's recorded voice whispered from the box: "Born in silks, the princess now lived in penury." There was a pause, then a beep.

"Nothing but underwear in there, I'm afraid, Speck," Chaz announced from the speaker. "Mission accomplished? Good. Look through the blinds."

I didn't move my head for a while. Then I bent down one of the slats. Across the path and over the top of the jacaranda tree near my building, I saw Chaz and Muriel framed in my bedroom window. They sat holding hands on my bed in the spotlight of my desk lamp. They grinned at me and waved. "Why don't you come home?" Chaz asked.

# 56

They had a key, of course. I had given it to them freely. I had pressed it into Muriel's hands. On the unlighted stairs up to my room, I wondered how many times they had visited before. I reenvisioned my days at the Villas del Sol as a sinister version of the Shoemaker and the Elves. I could not calculate which turns in my recent life were the result of chance and which resulted from their sabotage. The missed phone messages from my friend Judy, the radio station preset on the night I danced for them. I saw Chaz and Muriel as spirits creeping through my rooms, leaving spectral handprints on the walls. Tonight they had lured me into their house, tempting me with trespass, so that I couldn't complain; I couldn't say I wasn't one with them.

Chaz and Muriel remained seated side by side on my bed, blond and fresh-scrubbed, a salt-and-pepper shaker pair united. They wore their black leather jackets, attractively scuffed and distressed, and probably purchased that way—although the separated seam at Chaz's shoulder was verifiably authentic. The jacket's sleeve hid the cast on his arm.

"Peter, did you lock the door on your way out?" Muriel asked.

"I locked *my* door."

"You look very tired. What have you been up to all day? We've been waiting for you."

"I *am* tired. So if you guys don't mind, I'd like to get to bed." I didn't have the energy to analyze the implications of their appearance in my room; I was resentful that they were ignoring my generosity in giving up my chair; I just wanted them to leave. "Go home and look at your gift, then call me tomorrow."

"By all means, Speck, come to bed." They stood in unison, and Chaz folded back my quilt and the striped pastel top sheet to form an inviting open triangle.

Muriel knelt at my feet. "Let me get your shoes." She tugged at the laces.

"That's okay," I said, but she ignored me and popped the canvas shoes from my feet. She flipped the strap of my belt from my buckle and unsnapped most of my fly before I grabbed her hand. "I really am tired."

"Look what we bought for you." She leaped to her feet and pulled a glossy shopping bag out from under my desk. She unfurled a length of slinky fabric: a pair of black silk pajama bottoms. "Come try them on, and we'll let you get to bed."

"I'd rather not."

"You don't like them?"

"No, they're beautiful," I said and regretted speaking as if I had been led docilely into a trap. I had allowed their gift to overshadow mine.

"Come on, Speck." Chaz stepped over from the bed and awkwardly attempted to undo the buttons of my shirt with his good hand.

"All right." I pulled away, took the bottoms and the sack from Muriel, and turned towards the door of the bathroom.

Muriel leaned her buttocks against the desk. "Don't be shy. We've all seen your peter before."

"Fine," I said and stood shucking my clothes in the middle of the room. I kicked off my briefs and crouched ridiculously naked while I fumbled for the waist of the pajamas. I scooted my legs awkwardly into the pants and lifted the top from the sack. It was short-sleeved and buttoned halfway down the front. I pulled it over my head, spread my arms, and said, "There, see?" When I moved, the material shifted, slippery and cool against my flesh like the second skin of olive oil I had worn for Chaz. I felt luxurious and exhausted. "They're nice," I said, relenting, and yawned.

"We thought you'd like them."

"Thank you." I looked at them both. "I'm sure I'll love sleeping in them. Now let's go down, and I'll let you out."

"We want to tuck you in, Speck." Chaz stepped away from the bed, presumably so that I could climb under the covers.

I grinned at him and rubbed at my eye with my finger. "Thanks. But I have to brush my teeth and stuff, so—"

"Get in the fucking bed!" Chaz grabbed me by the shoulder and pushed me off my feet. He knocked me down against the edge of the mattress and pinned me in place until he could pull my legs up onto the bed. Struggling, I flipped onto my back and pushed at his chest. Chaz flung himself up and straddled my stomach. He held my arms down with his knees. "Stay still."

"What the fuck are you doing?" I struggled to lift my shoulders. Chaz cuffed me across the face with his cast—not as hard as he might have, but enough to leave my cheekbone buzzing with pain.

"Chaz is just impatient. We did have to wait for you all day." Muriel had turned from us, from our struggle, and was rooting through the contents of my bag on the desk. She pulled out my black address book and flipped among the pages. "Let's see, Judy Dane we've heard of. Alan and Deborah Keith. That's a rather formal listing for your parents, don't you think? Jock Kurtz at work. And who is Anthony? Hmm?"

I didn't answer her; I decided I would refuse even if Chaz decided to smack me again with the log of his cast.

"Let's call him," she said and lifted the receiver of my phone.

"No," I said.

"Okay then." She dropped the phone with a click onto its cradle and slipped the book back into my bag. "Oh, and we brought you something else to match your jammies." She withdrew another bag, a grocery sack, from under the desk.

"Relax, Speck." Chaz smiled and I glared up at him. My cheek felt wetly tender as if it had been scraped or bloodied.

I shifted my eyes to look for Muriel, but she had moved from the desk. She appeared on the opposite side of the bed; the black rubber hood slumped decapitated from her fingers. Its grommet eyes had been covered on the outside with squares of shiny gray duct tape. Her other hand held a capped transparent tube. As she squeezed a dollop of faintly blue gel into her palm and stroked it slowly through my hair with a rake of fingers, my body tensed—with fear or desire, I couldn't say. I knew that soon I would meet with the darkness inside the mask.

# Seraglio

# 57

I cannot vouch for the truth of anything after I was sealed in the close walls of the mask. There was no vision, no possibility of light, and sounds were muffled, sometimes clear, sometimes abstracted through the membrane covering my ears. When I breathed, the air that sucked through the three grommets lined along my lips tasted powdery with a fragrance like the drawer of red rubber balls in my elementary school.

They led me through my apartment and out the door. I strained against their grip on the stairs in my place and scuffled on the porch outside, but they had no trouble shoving and kicking me forward. I told myself that I had no choice but to go with them—I was blind, I was punch-drunk from the crack to my cheek, and I could not outrun or escape them. I told myself that my helplessness was a reality because on some level I wanted to believe it—on some level I was thrilled to be the focus of their attention.

After we had walked for some distance, I realized that we had gone too far to reach the Lambents' door, and a real fear crawled through me. I did not want to be dragged any further into the blank night. "Okay, enough!" I shouted, my voice smothered by the mask. I wondered why Irena wasn't out spectating at the one time she might have been useful to me. I bent forward, then flung my arms back. I slipped from their grasp. I was free.

I stumbled on, reaching up to tug at the mask, and crashed into some knee-high ground cover bordering the walk. As I searched for firmer footing, I was tackled from behind. I tumbled down, breaking pliant stalks and a nest of tiny sticks with my shoulders, my head. "You're gonna hurt yourself, Speck," Chaz whispered into my ear. He—or he and Muriel—jerked me upright and grabbed my arms. Cold bracelets clicked around my wrists. "You're trouble, sugar," Muriel whispered, and they pulled me to my feet by the shackles.

Our neighbors didn't hear our tussle. Or they chose not to investigate.

The Lambents put me in an automobile—I couldn't tell if it was Lady Lazarus—and we drove off into the invisible night. I sat between them. Muriel was behind the wheel, and Chaz held my arm firmly above the shackle at my wrist.

"Where are we going?" I asked, but my voice did not escape the narrow aperture of the grommets. Or they chose not to hear me.

We drove for a long time. At first the terrain under the tires vibrated through the car, vibrating through me, and I was aroused, apprehensive but stimulated, jazzed by new sensations. Denied the primacy of sight, my skin—the body's largest eye—began to see with fresh intensity. I felt the silk pajamas stretching across my chest, the hot bracelet of fingers on my arm, the sweat beads that dripped from my hair inside the mask and chilled on the nape of my neck, the hot, dry air from the car's vents blowing at my legs and lap.

However, the novelty of experiencing my flesh as a carpet of nerves dissipated, and I found myself cast into a void. Driving became a condition, an existential constant in my diminished new world, and my mind unstuck itself from the contemplation of the physical and drifted. I did not have dreams, which dip their lines into the solution of the brain and accrete with crystals of story—of cravings and terrors; I floated suspended in a dilution of mind where every thought was equidistant and hazy. My head dropped back like a flower on a broken stalk. When the car lurched to a stop, I jerked forward into a waking state, but without the comforting surety of waking, the embrace of the known and familiar.

When the car stopped moving, I was deposited abruptly into my body, perilously exposed and alone.

The door on the passenger side opened. Muriel's small fingers slipped between my own. "We're stopped for gas," she said. She spoke the words very close to the covered shell of my ear, her lips perhaps swiping the elastic surface, and each syllable was a loud raspberry from a brass horn—blat-blat—through the membrane.

"Shit!" a voice said from outside the driver's window. "Shit, is that so he won't bite no one? You people from the state hospital?" It was a low voice with a slight drawl, a small-town Western voice.

"No, you can come closer," Muriel said. "He's perfectly safe, I assure you." She squeezed my hand enmeshed with hers.

"I ask 'cause that's how all them psychos look on the videos we rent in there."

"Our brother was burnt over ninety percent of his body," she said. "He needs to wear the special prosthetic until the skin grafts heal."

"Well, gee, I'm sorry to hear that. Hope I didn't offend you . . . you both, I mean."

"No, no, we know his appearance is shocking. In that one small way, it's a blessing that he's deaf. This," she said, lifting our linked fingers into the air, "this is his only contact with the world."

"He's lucky he's got such a pretty nurse to take care of him. Um, that'll be fourteen seventy-five."

I knew that my last chance to speak had arrived; I needed to shout out before the man left for his cash register in the station. But I sat stone silent, wrapped in my imaginary skin graft.

This was a test. When I reconstructed the conversation later, I couldn't be certain that there had been another man—a gas station attendant. It might have been Chaz with a slightly lowered, mock hayseed accent. Because every sound grew damp and muddy within the mask, I couldn't have guessed. I will never know, but in either case, I had been offered an escape to see if I would grasp for it. Since I didn't speak when there was no gag to prevent me, the Lambents could feel secure in my consent. It was another twitch of the shoulders as I crawled down the one-way tunnel into a trap. I've often speculated that, if I had reached up to peel the tape from the eyes of the mask and spotted Chaz with his hand on the gas pump, they would have laughed, and taken me home, and offered me margaritas under the round paper lantern on their patio. We might never have driven on to our destination.

# 58

I had fallen asleep, and Muriel shook my shoulders to rouse me. I tried to swat her hands away and my arms moved in tandem within the manacles. "We're here," she said in her distorted, bleating voice. "The Hotel Seraglio. Chaz has gone to register."

I felt Muriel reach into the space behind my seat and pull something over into my lap then across into hers. "You'd like it, Peter. It's a sultan's palace. It's got minarets covered in gold spray paint, lit up with these green and purple garden lights. There's grillwork on all the windows. Just like the Alhambra." She giggled. "That's funny. This is the Abduction *to* the Seraglio!" She laughed louder, then began to hunt through the sack or package she had pulled from the back. "Now, Peter, will you be good so we don't have to carry you to the room?"

I didn't respond. I doubted her word about the Hotel Seraglio, but I had to believe her. If I didn't accept the reality of the surroundings she described, then I was left in the midst of nowhere.

# 59

I was bound to a bed at the Hotel Seraglio with what I guessed were the same silk-sheathed chains that were kept in the carved box in the Lambents' bedroom. When I saw the empty rectangle of varnish on the bureau top, I should have anticipated the chains' future use.

Already time was slipping from its track. The hours seemed unrecoverably vast since I had stood at their window watching them seated on my bed like the monolithic figures at Abu Simbel, serene while the stars swarmed millennially overhead. I was beginning to lose my grip on my inner clock as if steam gradually obscured its crystal face. It was Sunday morning, either early and dark-skied, or later and filling with pearl light. I couldn't guess; the status of the sun was unavailable to me.

The chains at my feet were secure but slack enough to permit me to bring my inner ankles to within about six inches of each other. My hands were cuffed together just above my head; the handcuffs seemed to be attached to the bed by a single chain locked to the cuffs' central links. When I lifted my hands, then dropped them into place, or when I spread my legs to their widest expanse, lengths of wrapped chain slithered off the edges of the slick fabric beneath me with tiny snake hisses.

I concentrated to catch these faint sounds through the muffle of the mask. A tree branch or loose wire tapped gently and erratically against the glass of a window. Somewhere to my right, a faucet dripped metronomically: plink-da-da-plink-da-da-plink. I suppose I listened this intently in order to have some nutrient for my mind to consume, however ephemeral. I combed my senses for some landmark to fix my location in the universe.

The available sounds were trivial and inhuman because Chaz and Muriel had led me into the room, then abandoned me. I heard the door close on their voices discussing breakfast. Although I also suspected that they had not gone. I imagined them poised together, their breaths in shallow unison, observing me with curious detachment like Gainsborough's Mr. and Mrs. Andrews painted at their garden bench on the hill.

# 60

When I focused on the sensation, I became aware of the hot, sticky underside of the mask pressed flat against every contour of my face. I felt the cheek Chaz had bruised intermeshing, fusing, with the rubber as it healed. I panicked, and my breath panted out with difficulty through its constricted passage. I writhed on the bed and rubbed my head along the pillow underneath me to try to scrape the mask from my head. But like peeling the skin from a basketball, there was nowhere to begin. By rocking my neck back and forth, I could lift the bottom edge in a flap from the nape of my neck, but when I readjusted my head to roll it off further, the rubber snapped firmly back into place.

At some point, my digestive system turned the morning corner in its cycle, and my need for relief grew fierce. For the moment, this was the most frightening and humiliating consequence of my entrapment. I knew then that the Lambents were watching me, waiting for the wet drops to further emblacken the black pajamas, waiting for the fragrance of defecation to steam into the room. But I refused them. I held still against the spasms of my body until they subsided in cramping diminuendos. I felt weirdly victorious. I was confident that I could easily lie motionless and silent until they grew bored.

Then the door to the room opened with a paint-loosening scrape against the jamb.

"Let me up! Let me go!" I shouted, tensing every muscle in my body. "Goddamnit!"

"We brought you date shakes," Muriel said with manic brightness.

I heard shuffling around the bed and the rustling of a paper sack. Someone pushed another pillow under my head. An icy cylinder pressed against my neck. I tried to shrink from it, but a hand brushed the damp chill along my throat. Fingers probed under the bottom lip of the mask and peeled it back from my mouth until a double thickness of rubber flattened my nose. I gulped avidly at the fresh air while a plastic straw probed insistently at my tongue. I gritted my teeth against it. "Let me go."

"It's good. Really," Muriel insisted. "I know it sounds a little weird. But just try a sip."

"Fuck you."

The curled rim of a waxed paper cup spread against my lower lip, and a tongue of freezing slush sluiced out onto my clenched teeth. As the slush poured back along my gums, the fillings in my molars rang choruses of pain into my nerves. I opened my jaw in agony, and glops of searingly sweet, cold fluid splashed onto my tongue. I couldn't breathe through my crushed nose, and I had to swallow some of the shake, and cough, and breathe from my mouth. There were hard knots in the shake, and they scratched going down, forcing me to cough again.

"Careful," Muriel said and patted my chest ineffectually. She slid her hand under my neck and lifted my head further from the bed. "Here's a swallow with less datey bits in it." She tilted another tablespoonful of shake into my mouth, which I managed to swallow more successfully. As the cold dripped down my esophagus and dropped into my stomach, my hunger ignited. I didn't know how many hours it had been since I had eaten. I thought, what if this is the last food today? Forever? I swallowed greedily as Muriel dispensed the shake onto my tongue. "See, Chaz?" she said. "I told you it was good."

"All right. I'll drink mine," Chaz responded. I felt his hands brush my stomach while releasing the drawstring at my waist. He tugged the silk bottoms down below my knees.

Plastic clattered; thick liquid plashed onto my belly and between my legs. My nerves fizzed with shock, then settled into a register of unutterable cold. I felt his beard against my skin as Chaz licked with small circular motions around my navel. I shriveled from the cold; my dick withdrew into a button of flesh until Chaz licked off the frozen milk and tugged me into his mouth.

I began to rise. I didn't want to, but I couldn't prevent it. His lips massaged me, and I savored the warmth, although sometimes he pulled away, and when he returned there would be a new puddle of cold around his tongue. I moaned and kicked against the bed with my heels. Muriel sank two sweet milky fingers into my mouth.

# 61

I slumped into the slick spread, my body cooling, dappled with pockets of moisture. I couldn't focus my mind. I remembered a television commercial I had seen for a device that inserted a needle into eggs; the needle would spin or shudder and scramble the egg without ever cracking the shell. I felt scrambled inside my skull—all my thoughts, yolk and white and chalazae, indeterminately mixed.

The chains uncoiled softly from my ankles; the cuffs were unclenched from my wrists. "It's time for your morning ablutions, Peter."

Hands grasped my biceps and brought me to my feet. My internal gyroscope spun crazily, and I stumbled between the Lambents as they led me to the bathroom. My feet curled up against the chill of the floor tiles when they pushed me. They set me carefully on the seat of the toilet and closed the door.

After my stomach cramps subsided, the satisfaction to my body was immense—the chance to relieve myself, to sit upright, to be away from the Lambents and free. I fumbled my hands along the wall until I found the toilet paper dispenser. I swabbed at the syrupy patches of milk on my legs and stomach and wondered where the date shakes had come from. It might mean that we had gone inland. We might be in the Coachella Valley. The dates and the Arabian Nights hotel would be appropriate.

Brad and I had taken our only vacation together to Palm Springs during my spring break. It was a Southern California cliché, but I had a wonderful time as a tourist. We took each other's pictures beneath the massive concrete dinosaurs at Cabazon. We went club-hopping down Palm Canyon Drive at night. We toured a date farm, gnawing grainy, sticky flesh from the pits of complementary medjool dates, walking among the columns of date palms, and reading the crumbling plaques on the freak-grafted fruit trees outside the gift shop, where orange, lemon, and grapefruit-bedecked limbs arched from the same trunk. Everything seemed oddly askew like an art installation; I was ecstatic. Brad was less thrilled, but he acquiesced to my plans. He held my hand in the dark as we sat in the date garden's tiny theatre with a pair of senior citizen couples and waited for the beginning of the instructional slide show *The Life and Loves of the Date.* On the screen, a bleached color slide presented two elderly women: one in a prairie bonnet and ankle-length gingham skirt, the other in a "mod" peach polyester pantsuit. They held opposite handles of a basket mounded with the dark lumps of dates, and smiled. And smiled and smiled and smiled. And smiled, until it became clear that the show was never likely to begin. I laughed at the absurdity of our patience.

I pulled Brad out of the building, and we kissed in the covered portico to the consternation of one of the older couples who followed us out. As we crossed the parking lot, he hooked his thumb into the back pocket of my jeans and spoke regretfully. "I wish I understood what you get out of things like that. I wish I knew why they interest you."

"But it's so fascinating," I said, "the images, the structures people create to explain themselves." I wished he understood too, but I didn't think I could explain it to him. I was afraid he would find me superficial, a sucker for artifice, but I couldn't help myself.

He slid his arm around my shoulders and suggested we go back to the motel.

I pretended to mistake his meaning because I wanted to take him to the Living Desert Museum, where acres of real desert had been bulldozed to make way for cultivated desert dioramas. "There's still a couple hours of light left," I said and drove to the museum. When we arrived, the gates were closed for the day. We ended up back at our motel room anyway, where I made love to him on the floor in the draft from the air conditioner.

I don't know if Brad noticed that I had consciously chosen the museum over making love with him. At the time, I didn't notice it myself because I believed that Brad was in control of everything in our relationship and I only made minor adjustments within the larger machine of his desire. It was never true, but I believed it.

I believed it until this moment of isolation in an unseen bathroom. Until the Lambents, I had never experienced the true nature of control, and I was no longer certain I craved it.

After I finished at the toilet, I touched my way along the edge of the vanity to the sink. I rested my fingers on its porcelain slope and steadied myself. I stole a moment before I flushed the toilet and washed my hands. There might not be time to rip away the mask before they decided to come for me—and my body was too sore to risk another flight—but I could lift the tape from the eye grommets and see where I was. It disturbed me that I hadn't thought to do it earlier. I reached up to stroke my uncovered lips and the flattened bump of my nose under the rubber. I slid my finger along my cheek to feel for the edge of the duct tape.

"Time for a shower, Speck." I heard Chaz twist a tap and send a flood of water thrumming into a tub. He had been inside the room with me. Chaz helped me out of the black pajamas and guided me to step over the rim of the tub. I felt the water patter dryly against the mask's face.

# 62

"Born in silks, the princess now lived in penury."

Muriel began the story quite suddenly, after I had decided no one would ever speak. After my shower, I had been returned to the bed. One ankle was chained, and although my hands were left free, I left them folded together on my stomach—strangely thankful for the chance to simply relax. Muriel sat on the edge of the bed; Chaz stood or sat somewhere else in the room, invisible. I could hear the faucet's drip again and the scratching at the window. Muriel's voice rippled into the stillness, pure and undulant, like a ribbon of enamel.

"They watched her as she walked through the bazaar of the coastal city—the merchants from the doorways of dim shops, the vendors from their carts, the women peering through the lattices above. They watched not because she was beautiful, for her beauty languished beneath an unwashed face and a gown that was little more than rags. They watched because she was blond.

"For the Sultan's subjects, her yellow hair was as unsettling and mysterious as any tribe of headless men or flock of colossal birds. She was an affront to Allah. She walked the streets without a veil, strutting about with her head unclad and her fierce tresses fanned as proudly as a golden peacock's tail. She was a white-hot mote hurled brashly into God's eye. They hoped the Sultan's viziers would send men to arrest her; the Koran's word was Law, and her lawlessness was irrefutable. However, they realized that their city was a great port, tolerant, by commercial necessity, of strange visitors and novel activity. And they knew that among the forty-eight honorifics preceding the Sultan's title, the three he most prized were 'The Wise, The Merciful, and The Mild.' Their Sultan was disposed to close his eyes to the blasphemies of strangers, while explaining that their ways were not ours. Knowing this, the citizens watched the woman and waited, attentively, to discover a reason more damning than blondness to bring the heretic to their ruler's attention."

Muriel stretched out on the bed next to me. She took my hand. Our bodies touched at the shoulder and at the shin.

"The beacon of her hair alone was sufficient to alert the fishmonger as she crouched below his cart and attempted to slip a flayed fish beneath her gown.

"He shouted, 'Thief!' and she ran, dropping her pilfered dinner in the dust. He chased after her, and when the other men saw her flaring down the narrow streets towards the harbor, her hair a comet's tail in her wake, they joined the race.

"They cornered her against a yellow wall where nets had been strung up to dry in the sun. Having trapped her, the men were uncertain. A male thief would be beaten to the ground and then borne to the palace gates. But a woman? A woman with blond hair? She was like a perishable fruit, best packed in sawdust, best treated as if any jolt might bruise. Only if the fruit burst, if, through the slit in the skin, it displayed its sweet red meat, would they dare to consume her.

"They crept forward warily until one man, a spice merchant, reached out to snatch at her gown. She shrieked, and her fear emboldened them to take her in their clutches. Frailty in women was a quality they understood. They took hold of her limbs and bore her up in the air to the nearby storehouse of a leather merchant. They sat her down on a stack of splayed hides and surrounded her.

"The Blond Woman had not lost her fear, but she had recovered her fire. She hiked the long skirt of her gown above her waist. 'Is this what you seek?' she asked in the men's own tongue. She eyed them coldly.

"Several men began to dig at their belts, and soon they would have been upon her if someone at the rear of the crowd had not asked, 'Where did you come from?' His voice was soon followed by shouts of 'How did you get here?' and 'Are you a demon-spawn with that hair of gold?' It became evident that the men would rather have her story than her body—at least they would rather have her story first.

"She said, 'I would tell you my tale, which I promise is as delirious and tragic as any you have heard, but I am too weak from hunger to begin.'

"The leather merchant understood her needs and dispatched his servant, a boy who returned with the speed of incantation bearing a tray laden with steaming dishes of food, followed quickly after by another with a chalice of honeyed wine, by a third with a bowl of luscious fruits, and by a final boy carrying a heavy pitcher with a jewel-encrusted handle and a basin worked to resemble an oyster's shell. She was rapidly surrounded with enough dainties to rival the hospitality of the antique palace of Solomon or of the Sultan's itself.

"The men lingered by the walls of the shed while the Blond Woman wiped the smudges from her face and washed her long shimmering hair over the basin. They watched her transformation with rapture. Another merchant dispatched his nephew, who returned with a tunic of rich brocade, the colors of palm leaves and pomegranate, a gown suitable for the Sultan's most cherished concubine.

"The Blond Woman finished her bath and donned the gown. She reclined on the hides and nibbled at the foodstuffs and sipped the sweet wine. She knew that none of the men would dare touch her now. A clean face and fine clothes had restored to her the prerogatives of her former class. When her hunger and thirst had been sated, she gestured for the men to sit at their leisure around the dais of hides so that she might begin her story."

# 63

I heard a light metallic scraping like that of keys or coins scooped from a tabletop. The door to the room squeaked open, and Muriel paused in her story and did not speak again until the door was slammed definitively shut. I assumed that Chaz had taken the car keys and gone out.

Muriel squeezed my thigh through the thin silk; she lifted a pinch of material and rolled it between her fingers.

"The Blond Woman sat and tucked her legs beneath her," Muriel continued. She had lowered her voice until it sounded more intimate, more clearly intended for my ears alone. "As she spoke, she smoothed and plaited her hair, and each man felt that he had been invited into her bedchamber to nestle at her feet. 'I am not from your kingdom,' she began. 'Or from the kingdom across the water, or the one beyond that.

" 'I come from the North,' the Blond Woman said. 'My father was a baron, a nobleman,' she explained. 'His entailed lands were vast and prosperous. The fields were fertile and green. When the earth was broken with a plow, the soil gleamed black as raven's wings and moist as cake. The castle stood on a hill above the convergence of two rivers; it had been the baronial seat for centuries.

" 'When my father married a cousin from a distinguished branch of the family, it was the chief desire of the Old Baron, my father's father, that the union produce an heir. Yet my father was a sick man, having what the physicians called a weakness in the blood, and he and my mother were unable to consummate their union and conceive a child. The Old Baron could not accept the end of his family's reign and the loss of their lands, and in secret he encouraged my mother to get herself up with child in any fashion she could. Better a bastard with alien blood, he asserted, than an ignoble end for the lineage. So he dispatched vassals to procure likely partners for the task. They found a traveling strongman who had come to the city for the Summer Fair, a savage lion-maned mountain of unequaled brute force. They scrubbed and shaved him and brought this beast to my mother's chambers.

" 'I was the product of that sorrowful night of unsanctified love,' the Blond Woman exclaimed. She touched the brocade spiral at her breast, and the merchants sighed in sympathy, so enrapt were they in her strange tale.

" 'Soon after my birth, the Old Baron died, and my father assumed the weight of the family mantle by taking to his bed. So precarious was his health that he required servants to bear him from room to room in a padded chair. My mother reacted with keen frenzy. She knew that were her husband to die without a son, her reign as baroness would end.

" 'I believe that she engaged in questionable alliances with various grooms and stableboys, but without fruitful effect. In desperation, to extend the fragile thread of my father's life, my mother uprooted the family and bore us towards warmer climes. South and south and south we traveled in our household caravan to douse my father in the healing sun. Alas, the daily cruelty of the journey did him in. My father died far from home.' Here the Blond Woman looked down, then paused to refresh her cup from a pitcher at her side."

Muriel rose from the bed. I heard a running faucet, and then she returned to sit near my chained foot.

"The merchants waited in tearful silence until the Blond Woman chose to continue. 'With fearful heart,' she said, 'my mother dispatched a letter to Court. But the messenger returned with the dire news. Her enemies had uncovered the scandal of her unions with the festival strongman and the many who followed him, and used it in their campaign against her. She could not return to face such shame.

" 'My mother cast about for options. With the servants dismissed, with the fortunes of the family coffer reduced to a few worn coins, we were lodged at the bleached-white inn of a port at the borders of Christian empire. All manner of sailors and traders passed by our window.

" 'And, yes, my mother gave her body to the rabble for a price. And, yes, despite the terror to my heart and mind, she sold my childish body as well. What else did she have to barter? And when the dark men came, who said they were merchants from a nearby city yet spoke with strange and broken accents, she was well prepared to sell me outright. She pressed my hands into theirs for a journey she could not know the finish of.

" 'They were slavers. And my mother must have guessed this, for the payment they offered was great. They presented her with two silken purses dangling heavily from drawn cords. I was carried off like a sack of flour, screaming "Momma!" through the village streets while my mother worked the knots of the purses. When she spilled their contents on the table before her, she was met with a heap of stones. In a rage she scooped a fist of pebbles to fling in the slavers' faces and raced to the dock. She found them, and accused them, and tossed her stones. One of the men produced a curved blade and cut her down. And so, before my body had taken its first bloodrush into womanhood, I saw my mother halved like a ripe fig with its wet seeds spilled into view upon the ground. Before I could take a final communion and taste the succoring body of Christ upon my tongue, I was tossed aboard a ship bound for heartless infidel land.

" 'I fear to detail for you this horrible interlude full of wet coughing and infernal heat. The hold of the rotting vessel was crowded with girls like myself, commoners, but all fair of hair and blue of eye. The oldest among us had not reached the age of maturity, and the youngest were barely out of swaddling. We tended each other as best we could, huddled fearfully in our dark and squalid quarters. The passage was long, and the food scarce. Some of us, alas, did not see the journey's end.' "

Muriel leaned against my leg, and I felt her pulse racing in the flesh of my thigh.

" 'Upon arrival, we were marched through the streets of a foreign port and led into a fenced alley behind the slave market. Young boys my age with almond eyes hung from the bars outside the dim rear of our cell and gawped at our blond hair and sapphire eyes. One lanky youth smiled at me and motioned me over to the wall. I hesitated but did as I was bid. Two of his friends held onto his feet as the boy dangled headlong into our cell. He stretched his arms down, and when I stretched my hands up to him, he took them. Before I could make a decision to leave the other girls, I was hoisted into the air and out of the cell.

" 'With dark intentions, the boys took me to an alcove deeper in the alley, but I was not without resources. I kicked one boy in the teeth, another in the shins, and punched the third between the legs. I made my break for freedom.

" 'Alas, such dreams of liberty proved futile, for from hence my tale becomes one of wandering and degradation. For a time, I served as the youngest concubine to a wealthy merchant, a trader, who criss-crossed the desert living in a city of tents.

" 'I completed my childhood within shifting silken walls. I learned to converse in your tongue and in a dozen others, from the discourse of viziers and scholars, to the love tonic of poets, to the lustful whis-pers of the painted harlot. I was not faithful to the trader. I opened my dewy gates for other men in our caravan—men who could teach me things: how to bring a camel to the bit, or rig a sail; men who could give me things: gemstones or caskets of spice; men who could distract me through the long hours waiting in the limbo of shifting sand. But always, I held my heart and head above the rabble.

" 'One day as we camped at the gates of a city, I ran away from the trader and with a few stolen coins set up household to ply my trade as a courtesan. But to my sorrow, no one here in your city would buy what I have to sell. I have been led too far from my ancestral home, and here I seem a monster. With my wild, fair hair, you people think me bewitched. No one dares touch or speak with me. My few grubby coins have all been spent. And so, born in silks, I now live in penury.' The Blond Woman stared down from the hides onto the weeping men beneath her. 'And that, kind strangers, is my tale.' "

Muriel slid up along my side until she crouched near my head. I felt the distant vibration of her fingers stroking the cheeks and tem-ples of the mask.

"So moved were the merchants by the recounting of her woes that as soon as they could rise up on their weak legs and wipe their eyes on their sleeves, they called for a litter and bore the Blond Woman to the gates of the Sultan's palace on their own shoulders. Their Sultan was a wise man, and they knew he would have the remedy for her misfortune."

Muriel's fingers left my face, and when she spoke again, her voice arose from further off in the room. "Oh, good," she said. "It looks like Chaz is back with your dinner."

# 64

The preparations for my meal were complicated and tedious. My wrists were shackled to the bed once again while the chains at my feet were readjusted. After the ankle chains were reapplied, I was pulled by my shoulders to sit upright with my back against the head-board. A pillow was fitted to the small of my back. Their care with the restraints was unnecessary because I had no immediate plan to run away. I couldn't imagine going to the police—I couldn't testify where my volition ended and their force began—and I wouldn't get far on my own in the city or on the desert wearing only a pair of black silk pajamas.

Muriel tied a towel or sheet in a bib around my shoulders while Chaz folded the mask away from my mouth again. "I got you a real turkey dinner from Chuck and Edna's Country Kitchen," he said. I could feel the edge of a paper plate against my chin as he held it close, and steam rose up across my lips although my nose was squeezed too tight to catch its aroma.

"First, a sip of apple juice," Muriel said and tilted a cup against my lips. I swallowed a gulp of sweet, cold liquid.

They fed me by hand, scooping the food up onto their fingers and sliding them into my mouth. They gave me slivers of moist, warm turkey, lumps of doughy stuffing, little dollops of cranberry compote. As I licked their fingers, I noticed which ones had the manicured nails and smooth cuticles of Muriel and which had the rougher, hair-ier knuckles of Chaz. I was too hungry to feel infantile.

Muriel pressed a scoop of mashed potatoes onto my tongue and wiped her two fingers off against my bottom teeth. I closed my mouth to swallow and something thick and hard within the creamy mass caught in my throat. I coughed, and Muriel patted my back and gave me another sip of apple juice. "That go down okay? That's how we always give Cissy her medicine."

"What? What was it?" I swung my head as if I could find her

face with my taped eyes. I convulsed my throat, retching, to bring up whatever it was they had given me to swallow. One of them quickly lifted the plate from my lap before it could spill all over the bed as I jerked against the chains.

"Speck! Hey, Speck, calm down. It was just something to help you rest." Chaz set his hand on my chest to ease me back onto the bed.

"Leave me alone! Leave me alone! I can't believe it! I can't believe you're doing this!" I shouted. What upset me most was the tingling that crept through my body. I felt more vividly alive, more real, than I had for years, since the best times with Brad. These shivers were a dangerous sensation, and I fought futilely against them.

"Sssh, Peter. You'll wake the dead," said Muriel. She touched my lips with her fingers. "We have a plug. It fits between your teeth with a strap that goes around your head. I've never liked it myself. It feels really gross on your tongue. So why don't you be quiet, and I'll tell you some more of my story."

"Keep it down, Speck," Chaz said. "And I'll give you some peach cobbler."

# 65

Muriel began the story again after the food was cleared away. "When they reached the Phoenix Gate of the Sultan's palace with its towering bronze doors, the merchants bearing the Blond Woman were met not by guards with cutlasses but by the Sultan himself."

My manacled hands were spread across my chest, and she traced the perimeters of each one with a fingertip, beginning at the wristbone then rising up over the thumb to the index finger; from the nail down past knuckles to the finger webbing, then up and over to the next; ending at the opposite wristbone, then shifting along the chain of the handcuffs to the other hand until the process was complete and ready for repetition.

I could do nothing else but listen.

"Like a pebble, like the merest grain dropped in a still pond, the ripples of the day's events—of the Blond Woman's theft, the chase, her captors, and her remarkable story—had spread through the city, out to the people of the bazaar, in to the women sheltered from view in private chambers, and up through peasants, peddlers, merchants, soldiers, clerics, scholars, eunuchs, concubines, wives, and viziers, to the Grand Vizier, and from the Grand Vizier's lips to the Sultan's ear.

"Upon hearing the strange and tragic tale of the Blond Woman, the Sultan had ordered the halls cleared and the royal carpets unrolled so that he might descend to the gate to meet her.

"At first sight of the Sultan in his magnificent gold and purple robes, the merchants lowered the litter so that they might kneel at his feet. He bade them rise and, extending his hand, assisted the Blond Woman from her cushioned seat onto the ground. She dipped her head slightly in deference to his status and allowed him to lead her forward through the giant brass doors stamped with outstretched wings.

"While the meeting at the gate occupied the Sultan, servants prepared a small room in the palace walls with pillows, rugs, and low tables of tea, sweets, and delicacies as he had instructed. They flavored the air with a suggestion of incense spice, then shifted the royal carpets to guide the Sultan and his guest to this secluded chamber.

"The Sultan sat with the Blond Woman on the floor in the ring of cushions and poured tea into eggshell cups. He placed a chip of sugar between his front teeth before sipping the dark brew, as was the custom of all men in the kingdom. He intended these humble acts to put her at ease. 'I am Sultan-Potentate of this kingdom,' he said, 'and I have been informed of your story, which is as sorrowful as it is startling. When I heard it, I was stricken to the heart and lost to breath. Your tale affected me thus, my dear young lady, because I fear that I am in some way responsible for your plight.'

"The Sultan presented the Blond Woman with a tray of tiny sweets fashioned from nutmeats and honey. 'You see,' he said, 'although my subjects may no longer remember, it was I who established the reward that led the slavers to dog your young life.'

"At this revelation, the Blond Woman started to her feet in shock, and the Sultan took her hand to settle her. 'Please,' he pleaded. 'If there is just cause for you to hate me, I shall not attempt to sway you. But first allow me to offer my own tale, which is as uncanny and perhaps more dire than your own. I hope that it might shed favorable light on my reasons for issuing the edict that ensnared you.'

"The Blond Woman nodded silently. She placed a small dainty to melt on her tongue."

Muriel's fingers brushed my throat at the perimeter of the mask. "Are you comfortable, Peter? Let me shift this." She did something with a soft clatter of chains above my head.

She continued, "After the Sultan settled into the cushions, he began his story. 'My mother was beautiful,' he said. 'No one in the world, not even my family's most merciless enemies, would deny this truth. Her hair was sleek and black. Her lips held the stain of rose petals. Her tapered hands were as smooth as carved mahogany. And like the most beautiful flowers, she flourished, then died young.

" 'As was her habit, she had taken an early morning walk in the garden. While she bent to trail her hand through a reflecting pond, her attendants withdrew to a pavilion erected beneath the palms opposite. When she failed to join them, they returned to the path to find her lifeless, her head slumped against the rim of the pool. I was very young, and her death was explained to me in this way: each soul is a lamp with an allotted reservoir of oil. Some lamps are deep, some shallow; some burn quick and bright, others slow and low. But whatever the lamp's qualities, when the fuel is spent, the flame must gutter out. I took this maxim to heart and demanded that the lamps in my chambers be lit night and day and that a servant be dispatched to fill them on the hour. I feared the darkness that had stolen my mother.

" 'My father, the Sultan, met the news of her death with unassuageable grief. Harder yet was his knowledge that my life might also be unnaturally brief. I was a delicate boy, thin, and easily feverish. Perhaps he sensed that I too possessed inadequate reserves of life; perhaps he feared that he would outlive me as he had his wife. He might have other children, other heirs, but none who carried the life's spark of his beloved.

" 'He became desperate to hold on to me against the predatory dark. Every expert in the kingdom was entreated to provide curatives. I was instructed to change my diet, to drink elixirs, to wear talismans, and perform rituals. Prayer was prescribed. And sleep. And the massage of the body. Yet I remained a weakling, and my father's considerable gloom darkened further. A soothsayer, an ancient hag who was not afraid of the consequences of reporting ill fortune to the Sultan, announced that unless a journey to the Center of the Sands was undertaken, I would not live to my maturity.

" 'My father asked the soothsayer where the Center of the Sands might be and what he might find there. But the old woman would not or could not say. She tucked up her veil, gathered her skirts, and disappeared like a dust cloud out of the city.

" 'A caravan was quickly organized, and, entrusting the government to his Grand Vizier, my father led the line of camels out from his capital. I accompanied him because it was not known from the soothsayer's words whether the journey might be undertaken on my behalf or was mine alone to make. As I looked back at the city walls drowning in the desert hills, I did not realize that it would be the last time I would see my home for many years.

" 'Our adventures, were I to recount them in full, would likely amaze even a princess who has seen more in her young life than the most hardened soldier. We visited fabled lost cities of immeasurable wealth and beauty, crossed vast deserts too hot and arid for a single speck of living green, and were beset by bandits who stole much of our fortune.

" 'And all the time, through strange and distant lands, my father kept his eyes and ears alerted for a sign, some word or mark of Allah, that would guide him to the source of my salvation. At the suggestion of a village chieftain, I was lowered in a basket into a deep, haunted well where female wraiths clutched at my clothing and attempted to tip me from my perch into the underworld before I could be pulled up to the surface. We ventured into the valley where the phoenix had been reborn. The heat of her birth had melted the dunes of sand into purest glass, and we walked among the reflecting hills at night lest we be blinded by their scintillations in the full sun.' The Sultan touched an amulet at his breast—as flawless and clear as a water drop or a tear. 'An artisan fashioned this talisman from its substance.

" 'Many years passed, and although my father was discouraged, he refused to turn for home. Perhaps for as long as the journey lasted, he could imagine that his beloved was in her bridal chamber awaiting him. Yet even this illusion was not enough to soothe his shattered heart, and one night when the Center of the Sands and my redemption seemed no closer than the night before, my father lay down in his tent, never to rise again. His illness was lovesickness, and there is no curative potion for that malady.

" 'When my father's body grew cold, it had been my thought that we would return to the kingdom. Yet the members of our caravan were not interested in the journey home. By rights, I had inherited the sultanate, but to their view I was still a sick and scrawny child as yet without my first tufts of beard. After my father's burial rites, the soldiers and craftsmen, scholars, and counselors ignored my entreaties and scattered to the four winds, and I was left alone with but a few faithful servants and the much diminished contents of my father's treasury chest.

" 'My small party turned in its tracks and trod over our last week's footprints. We trudged on, dispirited, knowing we were too few and too far from home. One night on the road, there entered into camp an old woman dressed in tatters. Her veils were grimed, and her teeth were gone. She begged for food, then sat outside the ring of the fire, sucking at her stewed meat. I cannot explain it, but I was certain that she was the very same soothsayer who had lured my father on this journey with vague prophecies. I sat down next to her in the dust and, with little expectation, told her my sorrowful tale and asked whether she knew of the Center of the Sands.

" 'At this, her eyes brightened, and she gaped at me with her gums. "The Middle Desert," said she. "We are nearby. If you like I shall take you there." She advised me to prepare a camel, to bring food and waterskins, and to carry my father's treasury chest, for some payment might prove necessary at the end of our march. There was need to leave at once, with no time to wake the others, for the Middle Desert could be reached only at night. The heat of the sun would make our path impassable.

" 'I assisted the crone onto the camel, and we plodded off the main road over trackless sand. The morning sun found us surrounded by white dunes; soon the day's fierce light would evaporate the shadows from even the deepest rifts, and the world would become white upon unbroken white from horizon to horizon. The crone bade me pitch the tent beneath a rare rocky outcrop, and instructed me to sleep so that we might travel again at nightfall. I stretched out within the tent, but the old woman continued to sit with greasy fingers clutching her veil tightly to her face. I asked her if she wasn't going to rest, and she explained that she was old. And the old do not need sleep, for in death they will soon have their fill of it.

" 'I shut my eyes for what I thought was a brief slumber, and when I awoke, the moon was playing silver across the sand. I adjusted my clothes and crawled from the tent to find that the old crone had vanished, taking my camel with her. She had stolen the food and the water and my father's treasury box. I was left in a lake of silver sand with nothing but my robes, a small tent, and a cushion for my head.

" 'With a quaking heart, I bundled my few remaining belongings and set off in the direction I hoped would return me through the desolation to the main trading route. Although in truth, alone, without water in the blinding waste, I would soon expire.

" 'I trudged along great drifts under purple sky, the stars fading to make way for dawn. I stumbled and fell to my stomach in the sand, and there I remained, my body too weary to move. I heard the sand hiss and whisper as it settled over me. Slowly, heavily, it built upon my back, its weight growing grain by grain, like sleep.' "

Muriel's hand squeezed my shoulder. "Do you feel it, Peter? Heavy and slow."

She continued, " 'My eyes had closed when I heard the thunder. With effort, I raised my head and saw the veins of lightning pulse above. Circles of flame spiraled overhead. Circles within circles. And from the center a great light plummeted towards the earth, a falling star trailing brilliance. The star was an angel, his head to the earth, his wings folded back like a diving bird's. The dunes glowed bright as he collided with the ground. From the same spinning window in the sky, a sword of light streaked down and pierced his wing in a cloud of sparks. The circles above closed like a shut eye, and the light in the dunes deepened, and reddened, and like an ember, died.

" 'I crept to the hilltop to watch the Angel in the rift below. He shook and writhed about his pinned wing like a beetle caught by the leg. Rays of diamond light flowed from his eyes, and his beams found me crouched above. "You, boy," said he, "you there. Come here." I made no motion, and he raised his hand to beseech me. "I am fallen from heaven," said he. "The Angel bnnf bnnff bnnnfgh . . ." ' "

I had been holding on to Muriel's story while my body slipped away. I had forgotten the mask, the chains, the bed underneath me, the cranberry skin caught between my teeth. I couldn't tell if Muriel's hand remained on my shoulder. I couldn't guess where she sat in the room. Whatever coursed in my bloodstream had systematically shut the valves of my nerves, slid hoods over my synapses. I had focused on her voice, but now it faded as well. I had to struggle to make sense of her words. I flailed inside my head like a goldfish in a broken bowl who discovers that the remaining water is insufficient not only for swimming but for breathing as well. It was not sleep but something less friendly that threatened to bludgeon me.

" ' "And so," said the Angel disfavored by God, "I was cast out of heaven to this lonely place. Here I will remain immobile, here staked, until my radiance crumbles. This desert waste around you, boy," said he, "is born from the dust of angels. It is no accident that you bnnff bnnn . . ." ' "

I struggled against the blanket swaddling my mind.

" ' "Only pull the sword, boy," said he, "and you will be rewarded." I shook my head, feeling too weak to lift a palm of sand. Yet finally I was too much in sway to his radiance to disobey. I bent over his wing, fearing at first that the shimmering blade would burn my hands. When I touched it, it was cool and pulled up easily at my least exertion. I lifted the sword until its point pricked at the air; it burnt away painlessly in my fingers like paper. Soon the Angel was free from his bond and rose to his feet, flexing his wings, stirring clouds of dust. Erect, he was much larger than a man and by every degree more magnificent. As the dawn spread her rose-petal traces behind us, I awaited the Angel's reward.' "

I fell down and down inside my head, touching nothing, leaving no traces.

"That's enough for now, Peter. Chaz and I are going out. Get some sleep."

I obeyed her. Sleep was the last word I heard.

# 66

What happened next may not have happened at all. My memories of that night have the cotton-swathed, asynchronous rhythms of dreamtime. My only argument for their reality is a persistent sense that I was not asleep.

I was standing on a hard floor, and there were bright floodlights in my eyes. For an instant I rejoiced that the mask was gone; then I recognized that my vision remained limited. I reached up to touch my face, but my fingers and my cheek were mutually muffled in a dreamlike tactile numbness.

My head was heavy, and I looked down at the ground with dizzy nausea. The floor was checkered black and white; it was a small square that fell away at three sides into the darkness beyond the lights. My feet were bare, but large and dark, with the long toes of a primate. I raised my hand before my eyes. The palm was thick and deeply lined. The back was coated with coarse black fur. My body was sweating in the heat of the room.

I covered my eyes with my hand to stem the blinding light and heard a murmur—a familiar sound but somehow distorted beyond my immediate recognition. Muriel stood in front of me in a long white silk gown. Stripes of gold lamé crisscrossed between her breasts, and diaphanous sleeves floated from her arms. "Look," she said and lifted the object she had been holding at her side. It was a large rococo hand mirror with a carved and gilded handle and frame. She held the glass up to my face, and I looked. My face was covered in dense fur; my eyes glistened in deep-set sockets beneath a heavily furrowed brow. My mouth, full of jagged yellow teeth, was frozen in a simian rictus. I lurched back in surprise, slipping on the slick floor and covering my eyes from the light with my hands. "The Beast Beholds Himself," Muriel said.

I stumbled back and fell through heavy draperies. The murmur grew, and I recognized its nature: it was a conflation of many voices, laughing. On my hands and knees, I crawled into the draperies, off a stage into the safe blank space beyond. An arm wrapped my shoulders and helped me sit on the floor. "Relax, Speck," Chaz muttered in my ear. "It's just show biz." He eased my head into his lap.

Like the gossamer of a spider's web loosed from its mooring then played out into the breeze, my thoughts unraveled, then dispersed. Whether I departed from the waking world or a dream one, I did not and do not know.

# 67

The first time I woke up definitively, I found myself staring at the front of a bureau. There were fifteen drawers: three wide drawers in each of the outer columns, and a grid of nine drawers in the center. The faces of the middle drawers were square and no larger than the old library card files at the Jane Floe School of Design. The effect of the bureau was vaguely art nouveau with hints of orientalism—like the dangling pagoda-shaped handles on the drawers.

I studied them for a moment with the dispassion of completely disconnected thought. Then I recognized the novelty inherent in the act of observing them: I could see. And I wasn't peering from tiny grommets; the mask was gone. I relished the return of my vision and examined the dresser's asymmetrical top and the weirdly bulging lines of its upright edges. I shifted my focus along the length of the dresser to a chairback that flared before a stretch of white wall. I studied the few inches of the top of the chair that I could see without lifting my head, and a greater discovery than the return of my eyes stole into me. My chair. I could sense each channel and spike in the wood's grain with mental fingertips.

The bureau had also passed through my field of vision dozens of times, but without leaving a clear impression. I had even plumbed the depths of its drawers on the night I had spied Chaz and Muriel in my bedroom, but I had never studied the distinctive handles. I saw that the carved box was still absent and that I was lying naked in the Lambents' bedroom. I lifted my cheek from its nestling spot in a pillow and looked up.

My body shone palely like a frosted glass sconce in the murky mirror overhead. From the unsteady reflection, the covered chains coiling at my ankles and wrists dribbled over the white sheets like yellow stains. I tugged at the links determinedly—but quietly, to avoid attracting the Lambents, who were out of the room. The bonds resisted me with dull scrapes and clicks.

I looked up into my face, framed in sticky tousled hair—at my bleary eyes, heavy stubble, and the purple welt along my cheekbone. I had slept through the ride home, I thought, then corrected myself. I had been drugged throughout the ride home. As I took an accounting of the weight of my body against the bedsheets, the slight discomfort of the chains pulling at my limbs, and the foul metallic taste in my mouth, I prickled with suspicion. Initially, I couldn't determine why I was bothered, but some incongruity prodded at me like the proboscis of a mosquito, slight but irritating.

I had been left alone, and I searched around the room, enjoying the resumption of my sight. It was not until I shut my eyes to blink the stickiness from their corners that I heard the sound. It was the kind of inconsequential noise that visually oriented humans tend to ignore, but my time in the mask had heightened my awareness. Perhaps like Chaz, with his love for the scrapes and squeaks and whiskings of baseball, I had gained new respect for the aurally marginal.

The noise was a steady but arrhythmic pulse originating from somewhere near the window. I turned my head again to locate its source. The cord used for raising and lowering the blinds hung along one end of the slats; at the cord's end was a conical white plastic bauble—one of those mundane objects, like the plastic aglet at the end of a shoelace, whose names are known only to experts, crossword players, and gifted children. From time to time the breeze from the open window would lift the thin cord, and when it fell back, the plastic tip would tap against one of the metal blades of the blind.

The tapping near the window was very much like the tapping I had memorized from the hotel room, even though I couldn't be certain of their similarity due to the absence of the mask's distorting membrane. I realized that I might have been right to disbelieve Muriel from the beginning. We might never have been at a hotel; we might never have left their bedroom. I considered the arguments against this theory, most particularly the appearance of the date shakes. But these shakes were exactly the authenticating detail that would make Chaz and Muriel proud of their deception.

# 68

Muriel opened the door to the bedroom. She slipped sideways through the passage bearing a large variety of shopping bags. Although she arrived in a vintage sleeveless sundress with wavy diagonal stripes of alternating coral and sea green, she quickly reached under her arm and worked a zipper down the side. She stepped from the dress and stood topless in a pair of pearl white panties and green espadrilles. "Good morning, sugar," she said and smiled at me.

"What day is it?" I asked.

"Does it matter?" She reached into one of the sacks on the floor and pulled out another dress, a narrow tube of lightly puckered black fabric.

"Does it matter?" I echoed her sardonically. "I have a job. How long do you plan to keep me like this?"

"We all have our work to do." She lifted the dress over her head and worked it down over her small high breasts, her lean stomach, and mildly flaring hips. She studied herself in the tilted mirror on the chiffonier near the door to the bath. "No, no," she said, adjusting the clinging black sheath. "I should have listened to those nagging doubts at the store."

"I need to get on with my life." I looked at myself in the ceiling mirror, at my stomach concave beneath my ribs.

"Do you have any idea what you would be doing right now? If you weren't here with me? If you didn't know us and hadn't met your kismet? Last week you would have met this guy named Timothy Crane outside Jock Kurtz's office at work—you would still be working under Jock-o—and you would have gone out on your first date in God-knows-how-long. It would be really sweet, and the next date he would buy you a flower, and, oh, how special it would be. And after a few dates he would let you lie on his bed with him and hold him. But he wouldn't let you fuck him because he has just broken up with a lover and he needs time to grieve and be sure it is the right thing to do. And after three months—three patient months—you would get frustrated and the whole thing would desiccate and rattle in the wind like an autumn leaf. That sounds so exciting, Peter. I can see why you wouldn't want to be here."

"I could shout. I could make any kind of noise and someone would hear."

"That's true. Maybe Irena would hear you and rush in to your rescue. That would be amusing." Muriel stood at the end of the bed, her hands on the swooping rim of the footboard. She was right; I couldn't imagine calling for someone to save me. My situation would be impossible to explain to strangers when I could not understand it myself. "Tell me honestly," she said. "This dress. It was a bad impulse, wasn't it?"

Without waiting for an answer, she flipped it over her head onto the floor. The next item she pulled out looked like a roll of gauze bandages, stained faintly pink. From the mirror, I looked down at the top of her head while she unfolded the fabric. It was a transparent babydoll dress with a pattern of tiny stitched roses. "Now this one's a keeper. Just let me find something to go under it. What do you think, some kind of chemise or a body stocking?" She spread the dress across the footboard and dug into a drawer of the bureau.

"Muriel, please let me go."

She turned to me as she stepped into white stirruped tights. "Oh, Peter. Don't whimper." She sat on the edge of the bed and dabbed at tears beneath my eyes that I hadn't realized I was shedding. She held my face between her hands. "The chair is magnificent, Peter. Thank you so much. I'm truly honored."

"Well, good," I said flatly. I smothered any pride and pleasure I might have felt at Muriel's response.

"Now don't be churlish, sugar." She tapped my cheekbones with her fingertips. "I'm going to have a party for you. To celebrate your chair. You like parties, don't you?"

I looked up into her eyes. The pale steady light from the window curled around her head, leaving a shadow across her face. "Who are you? Where do you come from? What do you and Chaz do when you're not fucking with my mind?"

Muriel smiled. "We mean you no harm, Peter. We most assuredly do not."

I did not doubt that she was sincere; they never meant to harm anyone. The Lambents were as incapable of malevolence as they were of its opposite. Such dichotomies were meaningless to them. But, as Zorna had pointed out to me that night at the cabaret while warning me to be good, these distinctions were not without value to me.

"I know what will cheer you up. I'll finish the story." She jumped up and pulled the pink dress over her tights. The short skirt floated on air while her arms emerged lithe and white from the puff sleeves. She looked like Goldie Hawn circa 1969; like a huge, preternaturally sexual child on her way to Easter services.

"Let me go, you bitch! I don't care about the fucking story."

Muriel stared at me icily. "It's *my* story, Peter. My talisman. This story, some poems, my chairs—they're what tell me who I am. I keep them with me always next to my heart. What you learn, Peter—what you learn after years of dissatisfaction and privation—is that you must pursue the things you treasure and cling to them, without hesitation, without constraint. You're an artist, Peter. I'd think you would understand the transformative power of holding fast to Beauty."

I glared at her.

"I don't know where this hostility is coming from. Just free your mind and listen." She sat on the bed below me with her legs tucked under her and draped her hand loosely over my stomach. I began to wonder if the story was the real reason I was chained, if I was the tale's captive audience.

# 69

"So," Muriel said as she stroked her fingers tranquilly around the arch of my thighs, "having nearly completed his tale, the Sultan rose and extended his hand, asking the Blond Woman, if she was not too tired or too weakened by her deprivations, to accompany him on a brief journey into his palace. He led her from the chamber where his story had been spun and guided her along a dim, unadorned passage. He stopped quite suddenly and unlatched a wooden door that stood no taller than a young child's height. He bade the Blond Woman to crouch low and assisted her through the opening.

"From the cramped and lightless hall, they emerged into yellow sun netted through the spiny leaves of overhead palms and reflected softly from the faces of numberless flowers. In the near distance, fountains played and a large stripe of motionless water mirrored the sky. 'It is perhaps fitting,' the Sultan said, 'that we conclude our business together here in this garden where my story began with my mother's tragic death. For it is also here where my story ends with the Angel's descent after flying me home from the Middle Desert'."

The side of Muriel's thumb smoothed the line of hair beneath my navel.

"While the Sultan and the Blond Woman strolled together along the verdant length of the central pool, he explained the nature of the Angel's reward and the strange conditions placed upon it. 'As we flew serene above untrammeled wastes, immense cities, and foaming seas, the Angel explained that in appreciation for my effort in freeing the sword that bound him, he would return me to my father's kingdom. He might also, he offered, restore to me my health so that I might live indefinitely, and fill the treasury of the sultanate with unimaginable riches, and, further, stand guard over my kingdom against the predations of our enemies. His sole requirement was that within the span of one hundred years I find a bride for him who would meet his specifications.

" 'He explained that, as a castoff of heaven, he must be prepared to live among the men of this world, and although his powers were vast, he too must now seek shelter, sustenance, and the ministrations of womankind. I need only procure for him a single, suitable bride.

" 'His was an offer I could not refuse. The chance to repair my delicate health was in itself reason enough. Otherwise, I would be forced to admit that my father had died in vain. I assented to the Angel's proposal, and when we landed at night near this pool, he bared my body and, as I shivered before him, he touched my breastbone, here.' " Muriel reached up and pressed a finger to my chest. " 'At once, a healing light swept through me. It was the green light of oasis. Like a lizard's shrugged scales, my old skin split and fell away, a dry husk borne up by the night wind and tattered into dust. I was reborn into a new strength and exuberance. As you look upon me now, dear lady, you will observe no hunched back nor pitted flesh, yet all the same, I am a very, very old man. The Angel has given me perpetual vigor.

" 'Also as promised, he filled the treasury vaults by some conjuration with gold, and gems and rare woods and fabrics such as I had never seen. Before he departed, he inscribed his enchanted sigil of spread wings on the doors of the palace to forestall enemies from breaching the walls. Then he came to me here in the garden with his instructions.

" 'The woman I should seek for his bride must have fire-white hair to match his own, skin of the palest pearls, and a perfection of form and feature. She must have knowledge and experience beyond that of ordinary women, although with a woman's homely virtues. And if she is to consort with an angel, she must be as strong of body as the strongest man. No harm would come to me or to my kingdom for one hundred years while I discovered this prize, but if no such woman had been found at the end of this period, the Angel vowed to pull the palace down upon my head and wrack my kingdom with pestilence and warfare for a thousand years. With that warning he unfurled his wings and, flying low, disappeared out of the city.

" 'Remember that I was a child when the Angel left, and one hundred years was the equal of eternity. Little did I worry about my obligation for the first fifty years of my peaceful and prosperous reign as sultan. Only as my viziers and attendants became enfeebled by age and died in great numbers around me did I realize that the term of our agreement would someday expire. It was then that I sent scouts to search the land for a woman who could meet the Angel's desires. None were found, for as you have seen, lightness of hair and complexion is as scarce as wings in these environs. I was discouraged but commenced the first edict of reward and saw to it that its contents were broadcast through my kingdom and beyond. It is evident that my search has been forgotten now in this city, or else the people would have brought you to the Phoenix Gate at once. But with each year I have increased the reward and pushed my messengers further afield. It grieves me to think that it must have been one such announcement that led your captors in pursuit of you. Such heinous treatment was never my intention.' The Sultan looked down at the reflection of the Blond Woman and himself on the still waters of the pool.

" 'Now I am aged one hundred and eleven years. It will soon be one hundred years since my meeting with the Angel, and I had surrendered hope that any suitable bride for him would be found. As is the wont of old men, I am more inclined towards thought than action. And in my idle hours I have addressed myself to the nature of the Angel. I have lately begun to wonder whether I have made an unholy bargain. For if, as he says, the Angel was hurled out of heaven, does this not indicate the displeasure of Allah? Must there not be good reason for his banishment?

" 'I tell you my dark thoughts, dear young lady, because I must now ask you to consider consignment to this Celestial Being. The marriage must be undertaken of your own free will. There must be no coercion. And I could not ask your consent if I felt that there were some aspect of the union I had not divulged.'

" 'I am not afraid,' interrupted the Blond Woman. She had plucked a small lemon from a passing tree and held it delicately in her hand. 'Though my body is soiled, I have a virgin spirit. My virtue remains my best and purest guide.'

" 'You consent then?' the Sultan queried.

" 'What better option do I have?' she asked in return. 'Shall I pledge myself to be the wife of an angel, or shall I embrace degradation as a woman of the streets? Yes, I consent.'

" 'Very well,' he concluded. He lifted the Blond Woman's hand and placed it over his own. Their journey through the garden had brought them to the end of the long reflecting pool where a black stone obelisk had been erected on a circular base. 'As I have said, the Angel prizes certain qualities in his bride. She must have hair of fire, skin of pearl, a beauty of face and figure. She must possess a commingling of worldly wisdom and domestic attributes. And all these virtues are indisputably yours. Yet one further value remains to be demonstrated. The Angel requires a wife with a strength surpassing the strongest earthly man. To determine this value, I have had constructed the obelisk you see before you, which sits freely on its pedestal. I have tested its weight against the might of the brawniest workman and the most hulking of soldiers, and no single man has been able to lift it from its base. Each woman who has been recommended to me has attempted this task, and none has succeeded. When your strength is restored to you by rest and the best foodstuffs I can provide for you, I will ask you to attempt this trial as well.'

" 'I would prefer to have this indignity disposed of,' the Blond Woman said. She dropped the yellow fruit from her palm into the pool with a splash. 'For, weary or not, I am a woman of royal blood, untrained and unsuited for manual labor, and such effort can only be humiliating.' Without awaiting the Sultan's permission, she climbed upon the base and wrapped her arms about the slick black stone that rose taller than her head towards the blue sky. With quiet concentration, she lifted the obelisk until the Sultan, standing on the other side, could see the tops of her embroidered slippers underneath it. She then set the monolith in place again with the slightest scrape of stone upon stone.

" 'You are the most powerful of creatures!' said the Sultan, aghast.

" 'I would have you speak no more of it. Such strength is a condition befitting a woman at childbirth and at no other time,' said the Blond Woman, who stepped down cautiously from the pedestal and sat at its edge.

"No sooner had she done so than the Phoenix Gates burst inward with a clamor heard throughout the city. The Angel soared towards the garden, scattering rugs and bolsters, bowls of fruits, prayer books, and ceremonial armaments in the gusts of his wake. Crossing the reflecting pool, he said, 'I accept this lady as my bride,' and reaching down to encircle her wrists, he drew her up with him into the sky. They then soared up and up above the garden until the Sultan saw them as a twin of the sun, shining immaculate and magnificent among the palms' serrated leaves."

Muriel had taken hold of a pinch of my scrotum and rolled the velvety skin under her thumb.

"A marital feast was prepared. The palace was bedecked with unimaginable finery, and the Blond Woman oversaw the cooking of the banquet herself while the Angel remained in attendance aloft. It would be her last act as a terrestrial maiden. It was she who issued the orders and greeted the guests, for the Sultan, after the Ascension in the garden, had withdrawn from view.

"On Feast Day Morn, the Grand Vizier, with some small but pressing question of protocol at hand, sought out the Sultan or, failing that, the Blond Woman. He found them both at the firepit of the great kitchen. The Sultan had been skinned and hung upon the roasting spit, charred black and glistening red. The Blond Woman listened to his fat hiss as it dripped onto the flames while she turned the handle of the spit with care. The Grand Vizier suppressed a sickening gurgle in his throat. 'Allah be praised, woman, why have you done this?'

" 'The Sultan spoke ill of my husband,' she said calmly. 'And what's more, I acted thus because I could. You would be wise not to question me in the future.'

"At this, the Grand Vizier was silent, and for the first time in many years the Blond Woman laughed, and when through laughing, smiled. The Feast Day was remembered with rapture by all who attended, and it has been immortalized in this tale, which now is ended, The Tale of the Angel and His Bride."

Muriel jumped from the bed. "Did you like my story?" Without waiting for an answer, she lifted off her pink teddy dress and slid out of the tights. She plucked off her pearl white underwear and danced a quick, arm-swinging dance in the banded light through the windowblinds. When she stopped, she was breathless. "I want you now, Peter," she said. "Pull your legs together so I can straddle you."

# 70

We had sex, Muriel and I, and when Chaz came home—or came into the room from wherever he had been—he took me into his mouth and braced his knees on the sheets beside my ears so that I could swallow him. I grew hard and stayed hard; I came; I did not protest.

Only long afterwards, after they had fed me and eaten their dinners with me on wooden trays listening to Blossom Dearie singing on the bedroom's small, shrinelike stereo ("I'm always true to you, darling, in my fashion") and only after they had left me to sleep wherever they slept or do whatever they did outside the bedroom, did I marvel at my situation and touch gingerly around the fresh edges of my fears.

My cock was my complicity. I tried to protest, I tried to revolt, but if I could not deny them my arousal, I had no sure basis for complaint.

I was amazed at my submissiveness. I had never believed myself to be a yielding person; I thought I was a shy, detached, observing spirit—inviolate—in my protective jar. In all my time with Brad, he had never penetrated my inner glass seal. His fingers had slipped and slid over my surface, and I suppose when we both thought he held the true pulse of my heart, it was just heat trapped in the Pyrex. But the Lambents' grip was so sure and so swift in finding its purchase on me that there seemed no barrier between myself and the world. I was bothered not by my greater receptiveness in sex, but by this different, more pervasive, lack of volition.

Chaz and Muriel were giddy jailers; my imprisonment was an elaborate, celebratory lark. Because of their joyful, weirdly innocent attitude, I could not hate them despite my anger, discomfort, and hours of boredom. I think I continued to love them; I certainly continued to desire them. I couldn't claim to understand them.

Shifting the chains carefully, I rolled onto my side. They had tucked me in under the duvet before leaving, and I felt less exposed and more comfortable, although I couldn't sleep. I lay for a while with my eyes closed, sifting through Muriel's long story. Somehow it revealed an aspect of her and Chaz, the union of blonds, although I didn't know enough about their lives to interpret the details. I pored over it for clues until, finally, I felt sickened by the mental attention I had lavished on the Lambents. I reminded myself that I had my own life, and that I should be looking for a way back to it. I should be plotting my escape.

My muscles tensed with new energy. Slowly and carefully I moved each limb to test the chains for a hundredth time. In each case, after the slack had shifted a few feet across the giant mattress, there was an abrupt jerk and the click of the final link catching against the ring bolted into the bed. I reached beyond my head to the nearest ring, but it was cold, solid metal, without a hint of a crack to work upon or a loose bolt to free with steady rotation over time. I considered flailing against the rings, trying to pull them free of the bed, but I imagined myself slipping half off the mattress and hanging in midair over the floor, unable to right myself. My wrists were clasped in neatly made bracelets of wrapped chain snapped together with a padlock. I tried to slip my hands from their grip, but with each tug the chains constricted further. I shrugged off the duvet, which had grown too hot after my exertions, and settled into the pillow again, defeated.

# 71

There was sex. And irregular meals. Showers at odd intervals, usually after a particularly messy session with the Lambents left me with whipped cream residue in my hair or honey on my thighs.

The Lambents were not interested in punishment and reward. There was no punishment, beyond the fact of my captivity and a certain amount of neglect. And there were no rewards. Their actions were decidedly arbitrary. One evening Chaz brought in the black pajamas, neatly washed and folded, and I was allowed to dress in the bathroom by myself. I permitted myself a few extra moments while dressing to look in the drawers and under the sink for any overlooked item that might be of use, but they had stripped the bathroom bare. Even my toothbrush, toothpaste, and shampoo were brought in at the appropriate times and removed afterwards. Sometimes I was allowed to wear the silk pajamas all night. At other times I was given only the tops or only the bottoms. More often I was kept naked with a sheet or the duvet or nothing at all to cover me, while my mirror image spread across the ceiling, symmetrically composed.

I didn't know what day it was. I wasn't sure how much work I had missed. I had lost my feeling for the passage of time, and it actually seemed years earlier that Muriel had been rifling through my desk and my address book while Chaz held me to my bed, months since Muriel had begun her story at the Hotel Seraglio, and weeks since the mask had been removed and I listened to the tap of the venetian blind cord.

Some days, some nights, I was drugged; sometimes I wasn't. There was no sense to their actions that I could recognize. I was affected by the Lambents' calendar, but like the astral movements of astrology, their trajectories influenced me ambiguously, indirectly. When it suited their purposes, they would contrive to slip sleep into my food, and I would drift as a dead weight through the hours and the days.

# 72

"Come on. Come on." Muriel urged me to sit up on the bed. "They'll be here." She scooped her hands under my shoulders and lifted me. I was awake but a thin drowsy membrane surrounded me that I could not yet penetrate. I was sufficiently conscious to notice that the cuffs around my wrists were gone, but it was not until Muriel grabbed my shins to slide my feet onto the floor that I realized the chains were missing entirely. The rings on the inside of the footboard were empty. I looked across the room to the carved box, which had been restored to its position on the bureau.

"What?" I asked. Her comment had completely failed to lodge itself in my mind.

"Our dinner guests," she explained patiently. "I hesitate to leave them in Chaz and Guppie's hands for long. So go shower, go."

I stood and, with an unsteady gait, stepped away from the bed. I continued to stare at the bureau until I realized that my chair was missing from the room.

I lurched to the bathroom and closed and locked the door. Although I felt restive beneath my weariness, there were few possibilities for rebellion in the bathroom. Other than soiling the rug, flooding the floor with tap water, or plugging the commode with toilet paper, my options were limited. I acquiesced and took a shower with the hope that the water would pulse away the shroud in my blood. I was free to escape if only I could concentrate.

While I was drying off, Muriel pounded on the door. "All right, all right. Get your ass in gear. They're here." I smiled at myself in the mirror, at the irregular landscape of my growing beard, enjoying her irritation.

When I emerged, Muriel stood at the dresser unloading clothing from my black bag. She pulled out a pair of putty-colored chinos, a white oxford shirt with blue pinstripes, socks, underwear, and my scuffed but presentable penny loafers. "Put these on," she said and tossed the armload of clothes onto the duvet. She returned to snoop in the bag for a number of felt-tip pens and graphite pencils, a legal pad, and my address book.

I slid into my briefs while Muriel leaned impatiently against the door to the hall. "You must be hungry," she said. "I've made that pad thai you liked so much."

Without speaking, I checked myself for hunger and located it, dully, deep inside me. I was awake, but something held the world at bay. I felt as if I traveled inside an unconvincing three-dimensional projection, as if the objects I reached out to touch might prove insubstantial. Consequently, I felt less beholden to acknowledge reality. I took my time to dress and pushed my feet into my loafers. I was cooperating dutifully, but I didn't know if I was being crafty in biding my time or just obedient. I walked to the chiffonier mirror to adjust my hair and scraped a wet, stringy mass back from my forehead. "I need a dryer," I muttered.

"You worry entirely too much about your hair," she said and opened the door.

"What are you doing to me now?" I asked, but she merely smiled.

I followed her out into the upstairs hall—out of their bedroom for the first time in many days—and across to the stairs. Muriel stood behind me to coax me down, and I held on to the bannister for support when my legs seemed unwilling to negotiate the rhythm of bending and unbending required to descend the steps. I suppose I did not expect to find a real dinner party awaiting us at the bottom of the stairs or I would have panicked.

Halfway down, the ground floor became visible. The sofa had been removed and a rectangular table erected in the center of the

Hall of Chairs. There was a white lace tablecloth, copious candles in silver holders, a bowl of fresh-cut flowers, and two people I didn't know.

Chaz sat at the far end of the table in a tan jacket, uncorking a green bottle of wine. Manjula reclined against the back of her chair at his left. She wore a gauzy saffron sari and a look of boredom. She and Chaz were talking in low voices, largely ignoring the other guests.

The man seated on Manjula's side of the table stared down nervously or distractedly at the silverware at his place setting. His body gave an overall impression of bulk and thickness—a bodybuilder's silhouette. The circumference of his biceps was twice that of mine. To show off his arms, he was wearing a Hawaiian-style shirt but in a deep orange and russet African print. The glow of the print enhanced a burnished tone in his milk chocolate skin and lit fires in his dark eyes. His head was shaved close to his skull, and his handsome features were concentrated on studying the shining spoon on the table near his thumb. I tried to recall any clue I might have heard from the Lambents that would tell me who he was. It wasn't Zorna in any of her (or his) manifestations, and I didn't know any of their other friends.

I thought of Muriel unloading my address book from my bag and remembered the night in my bedroom when I watched her flip through its pages. She had threatened to call Anthony that night. From the bottom of the stairs, I watched the man accept a glass of wine, and I knew, with great conviction, that he was my phone sex counselor from Venice. I hadn't expected Anthony to be African-American; I hadn't expected to recognize him in any form. But I was certain.

The woman across the table spoke to me first, however. "Peter? My God," she said and touched her lip with her fingers. "I'm sorry," she continued, apologetically. "You just look a little . . . tired."

I stared at her, probably rudely, while I tried to remember her name. Dee-Dee? Danitra? Dixie. Anthony's girlfriend actually resembled my original vision of her. She had bobbed, rather lank brown hair, a small nose, prominent pink cheeks, and light blue eye shadow. Her voice had a slight, untraceable accent.

"Did you guess who was coming? Muriel picked up the phone at your place when I called about our visit. And she said you love surprises. She set it all up for us." The woman smiled at Muriel, then at me. "Anyway, it's good to finally see you after all this time." She reached across the table to take Anthony's hand. "Oh, and this is my husband, Oscar."

"Hello," Oscar said in a deep voice. I wasn't surprised that he had a different name. He had known me as Jerry Mouse—Muriel must have told them my real name—and I could hardly be shocked at his pseudonym. Yet I was disconcerted that he was married.

"That really puts the lie to your business, doesn't it?" I stumbled towards the table, and Muriel deftly grabbed me by the arm and led me to my seat across from Manjula, between Dixie and Chaz. I should have bolted for the door, but the civilities of the dinner party held me in check.

"Excuse me?" Anthony/Oscar said and looked across the table at the woman for clarification.

The woman, Dixie, shrugged and turned her head to me. "I really like where you're living, Peter. Irvine is a nice city. And the beaches here are really fabulous. Oh, and thanks so much for letting us stay in your apartment. You sure you'll be all right over here tonight? I hate to kick you out of your bed when you're sick."

Chaz handed me a glass of wine, and I glared at him. He returned my gaze with a neutral ruminant expression, a look of mindless ease. I looked down the table to Muriel, who had been saying something to the man about his wristwatch. She sat in my chair with the back fanned behind her, the winged arms rising to bolster her elbows. I said, "If you were going to snoop through my book, you could have at least invited friends of mine."

"Peter," the Dixie woman scolded, "I think it's wonderful that you have friends as gracious as Chaz and Muriel. They've gone way out of their way for us."

"I'll bet they have."

"Look, I guess you're cranky because you've been ill, but you don't have to be rude."

"Oh, have I been ill? Is that what I've been?" I slammed my wineglass down, sloshing red dots onto the cloth, then I jerked to my feet, sending the Hepplewhite chair crashing onto its back on the floor. I flailed around to free myself from the chair legs and somehow stepped on the fern-frond splat with a hideous squeak of torquing, splintering wood. The woman twisted to look at me over her chair-back with concern. My head reeled. Chaz grabbed my biceps from behind. He led me to the stairs.

"So, tell me," I shouted at the Dixie woman. "Does he really have a ten-inch dick or is that just what he tells men on the phone?"

Anthony/Oscar rose to bolt towards me, but Muriel restrained him with a hand on his forearm. "Maybe Peter's not quite ready for company yet. He doesn't know what he's saying. It's just a side effect of the medication. Some more rest, and he'll be fine."

Chaz leaned the blunt weight of his cast into my back as he forced me up the stairs. "Okay, Speck," he whispered in my ear. "You've done enough damage for one night." As we reached the upstairs landing, the light was already failing in my eyes.

# 73

I slept for hours, churning with unremembered dreams. When I woke, I found that I had been reattached as a fixture of the bed—restaked and stretched taut. I lay with nothing to do. I had long ago cracked the code of the pattern buried in the seemingly random swirls of the rococo mirror frame above. I had admired the remarkable soldering of the Tiffany lamp near the bed. I had studied every object in the room for form, content, and execution.

Each element of the furnishings in the Lambents' house was an exquisite example of its category, but they did not work together; there was no synergy. Each piece stubbornly maintained its autonomy from the whole. The condominium exacerbated the disunity. The layout, wall treatments, and fixtures were as blandly impersonal as those in my unit, and the fine pieces stood around the plain walls looking uncomfortably cramped and detached, as if they were just passing through, like a Sotheby's auction at a strip mall.

I had ample time to grow bored staring at the furniture in the room and decided to spend the unfilled hours contemplating a fantasy project that I had begun at Jane Floe—an encyclopedia of the aesthetics of everyday life—a book based not on an overriding theory but on practical observations: what makes a fountain pen beautiful or what dramatic devices a school board meeting exploits.

I thought that I might as well plan entries in my mind during this enforced period of idleness. But my brain had grown recalcitrant and sluggish, and when I thought coherently, I did so solely to berate myself for becoming trapped and for not doing enough to escape. I began to look forward to the appearances of the Lambents to relieve the static mumbling in my head. I listened eagerly when they sat down to tell me their lies.

# 74

"We were twins, raised in a laboratory compound in the middle of a grueling-hot jungle," Chaz informed me. We had finished sex, and he was stretched on his back with his head raised slightly against the footboard of the bed. One side of my face was buried in a pillow, but I could see him in the mirror above from the corner of my free eye. His hand curled proprietarily over my buttocks, and his other arm, in its cast, was bent behind his neck. "Have you heard of the Lebensborn, Speck? Our mother was born and raised in a state home for children. She was taken away from her own mother, who had been interned in a Well-of-Life house to be inseminated by one of several officers in the SS.

"Our father was a geneticist. He studied at Harvard and Oxford as well as in Germany. This was the late fifties, and while he was completing his doctoral work, he was contacted by a group of German businessmen who operated out of South America. They had all changed their names, you see, because I guess they didn't want to deal with the nuisance of facing up to the crimes against humanity they were accused of." Chaz squeezed my leg as he spoke. I didn't like the story he was telling, and I made no comment. More important, I decided not to believe him. "These businessmen offered him a sum of money, a huge sum of money, to come to the jungle and work on a project for them. Their pockets were deep; he'd be able to outfit his lab with staff and equipment unimaginable at a university or a government post. And, at any rate, his specialization was the study of dominant traits in genetics, and this kind of research made people uncomfortable in Germany. So, he accepted.

"He met our mother the week before he left. She was an actress in an avant-garde theatre collective. They were performing a kabuki version of some Brecht play. It was supposed to be oh-so-daring to stage a communist play in West Germany at the time. And everyone, all the academics and bohemian intellectuals, were going to see it. Our father fell for our mother immediately and went backstage to find her after the play. He located her taking off the white pancake makeup in the dressing room, and by the time her face was clean and he saw that she was even more beautiful than he thought, he was already engaged in luring her home to his one-room flat.

"They engaged in intercourse with each other three or four times over the next week, and one of those times, his sperm and her eggs splashed together to create the zygotes that became us. They were married in a little government office; then my father shipped out with his equipment for a new life. My mother promised to join him soon. As soon as she had severed all her ties to the past. Like, for instance, the fact that she was living with the director of the theatre collective, who was surprised to hear that she was married and on her way to a different hemisphere. He threatened her. Then he offered her the lead in his next production, some free-form piece using Kafka stories. So she stayed in Germany. And wrote vague letters to our father apologizing for the delay and pledging her endless love. And in time, she gave birth to blond twins.

"What beautiful, beautiful babies, the nurse said. Real Germans. The nurse smiled when she said it; no one wanted to sound too serious when saying things like that. But our mother knew what she meant. She remembered the home where she had been kept. Hitler is your father, they told her. Hitler is every Aryan child's father. Fine. But she would not raise Hitler's children. She put our bassinet on the open door of the oven and turned on the gas.

"Lucky for us, her boyfriend, the director, came home in time to stop her. She scratched his face, then ran and barricaded herself in the kitchen. Unlucky for her, the director grabbed the chunk of bomb slag he used as a paperweight and threw it to break the frosted window in the kitchen door. It crashed through the glass and beaned her on the forehead, and as she fell to the floor, she impaled herself on the knife she was planning to use to chop up her boyfriend if he attempted to reach into the room.

"The doctors couldn't repair the laceration to her aorta, and she died before morning. The director was prepared to shoulder the burden and care for us, but to satisfy propriety, he telegrammed our father with the news. His announcement was eventually answered by a series of businesslike letters, the last of which instructed him to pack the infants' things and take them and their belongings to the home of a Frau von Ruggen. She was returning to South America to rejoin her husband and would accompany us on our passage.

"And so we left the Fatherland while we were still blind little kittens curled up in a perambulator pushed by the wet nurse Frau von Ruggen had hired." Chaz slapped my ass then shifted his position on the sheets. "We're all fucking Nazis, Speck. Me, Muriel, the neighborhood skinhead, Congressman Bryndon. The world is stuffed with fascist pigs. We can't help ourselves. That's why we invent a society with rules to keep us staked up. Otherwise we'd launch out and chew off each other's faces. People are scum, Speck, and the world is shit."

# 75

On the pillow beside my head, Chaz's feet sat crossed at the ankles. They were solid and evenly tanned, shading to deep pink at the sides of his heels. His toes were very long and tapered, and I wondered what evolutionary purpose they might serve. His feet were clean and without odor even at this close range. I had kissed them before; I had drawn his toes in with my lips. (There were no parts of his body that I hadn't explored, that I hadn't found erotic.) I watched them in their peaceful immobility while Chaz spoke.

"Do you know the jungles of South America, Speck?" He bent my leg at the knee and gripped my shin. "Some places it rains every day of the year without fail. But the rain doesn't break the heat. The wet heat. You never realize that your skin is a living organism, not just something you wear, until it perspires all day every day like a planet with its own weather system. You've read about the rain forests, haven't you, Speck? They're the chemical plants of the world. You can practically feel the oxygen being made. And photosynthesis. A billion billion green satellite dishes sucking up the sunlight. Nobody knows how many creatures are hiding there in the trees. Insects scuttling around up in the canopy without a Latin name. It's the most precious resource on earth, and you know what's happening to the fucking rain forest, don't you? Some days it's blacker than midnight from all the burning.

"It's also nature's medicine chest. Pharmacologists can't invent the compounds hidden in the roots there, and the bark, and the sappy leaves. There are researchers all around there scurrying through the undergrowth, climbing up the trees, asking the people that live there what it is they use for a lazy eye or a gimpy leg. Science going on all over the place.

"Though that's not why our father made the pilgrimage. There are certain projects which, while meritorious in the realm of pure science, may be unpalatable to society and the body politic. You can't refuse treatment to black men with syphilis to test your theories. You can't explode nuclear weapons and send clouds of fallout over downwind towns to examine radiation's effects. You can't give dying men placebos in a drug test for a fatal virus. Not in the Free World. Why, the public would be outraged.

"So you take your laboratory where the strictures against scientific inquiry are less inhibiting. At that time, in the forests of South America you were pretty much free as a bird in the pursuit of knowledge. This was before there was a coke factory and a druglord in every village. You could set up your own little empire. Also, some of the distinguished scientists and the financial benefactors our father worked with were a bit restricted in their choice of locale. They were careful not to peek their faces out from under the trees. They all had their pseudonyms: Mr. van Hoek, Mr. Pratt, the Blithes, the Crimples. They were all 'former colonels in the RAF,' or 'businessmen from Holland.'

"There were many experiments going on with an ample supply of subjects. There were the diamond mines, the plantations, all the roads being built, frontier towns full of unwanted children. Girls were easier to come by because the parents could at least conceive how boys might be useful to them one day. Our father's work used girls who had been raised to maturity and were ready for impregnation when he arrived. However, most of the subjects were little boys because several of the benefactors had certain personal predilections. Herr von Ruggen went through several boys a week. Afterwards, they were stored in the freezer and buried fortnightly in the forest. The jungle floor was forgiving of these excavations. It's all fertilizer to the trees, you know, Speck.

"Our father was trying to find the trigger that caused certain traits to be selected and others to be rejected in the formation of a fetus. Although his employers saw the control of this trigger as a means to purify the races, our father was mainly interested in the science. Unfortunately, he wasn't mapping DNA, as they do today; he was basically planting seeds and cross-pollinating smooth and wrinkly peas like old Mendel in his garden. Add sperm until conception was achieved, expose the fetus or the female carrier to some chemical or process, wait for the result, make observations, autopsy, then begin again with new parameters. Slow, tedious, and largely unrewarding work."

Chaz's feet withdrew from my view as he slid up to sit braced against the footboard. I began to shift my head to face him, then changed my mind and closed my eyes.

"So anyway, Muriel and I grew up there in the compound. We had a governess, Miss Black, and Frau von Ruggen kept her eye on us to see that we were not raised as savages without the civility of Aryan culture. She was lonely, I think. There were a few other wives from the Fatherland around, but many of the men had married natives. They would explain it to their fellow expatriates over cigars after dinner. Yes, she's a mongrel bitch, they would say, but every man needs a place to rest his pipe, ha, ha. Herr von Ruggen was usually in his lab with those little boys, conducting his experiments in sexual cognition. So the Frau took her little blond angels under her wing. We would sometimes stay at the von Ruggen house overnight, and I'm sure our father was relieved to have such a capable, well-mannered woman watching over the progress of our souls.

"My only memories of those years are of visiting the von Ruggen house. We would sit stiffly in the drawing room, and she would arrange Wagner on the turntable of her new Swiss-made stereo. She would synopsize the plot of each act, and then we would listen. Tea would be served with little jam cakes, strudels, and chocolate eclairs, and we would hide as many as we could in our pockets for later. One day I will take you to Bayreuth, she would say. We will stay at a fine hotel and have picnics and soak in all that rapturous music.

"We never got through the *Ring* cycle. My father had an argument with Herr von Ruggen, and the Bentley never arrived to take us to their house again. Then our father died, unexpectedly, in his sleep. People often died in their sleep in the enclave. And by a circuitous route, we were sent to live with his sister in the United States. And that was our childhood."

I felt the mattress shift as Chaz leaned forward. He kissed me lightly at the small of my back.

"My most vivid memory was one night we stayed at the von Ruggens'. We had finally finished *Siegfried*, and Frau von Ruggen led us upstairs and tucked us in. Later, when Muriel and I were certain that the von Ruggens had retired to their rooms for the night, we slipped down the stairs into the back hall and out the door. We walked the long, winding path through the garden, which led to Herr von Ruggen's private lab. Along the way, we ate our little cache of tarts and sticky, smeary eclairs, and when we got to the lab door, we found it locked. But the plank doors over the stairs leading down to the concrete cellar were not barred. We crept down quietly, holding hands against the dark, with only our great curiosity pushing us on.

"We found them there, in the light from the door thrown open above, the little boys in their pen. They were huddled naked in the corners of the cage, but they stood to look at us as we passed. Perhaps a hundred dark eyes under matted dark hair. We searched, but there was no way to open the pen. When Herr von Ruggen's pleasure required it, the boys were pulled up through a trap door in the floor of the lab above. We put our fingers through the chicken wire walls, and some boys came up to touch them. Muriel leaned her face in, and I copied her. The holes in the fencing were wide enough to accept our puckered mouths. And a few brave and hungry boys were able to lick the glaze of chocolate from our lips.

"And since then, Speck," Chaz said as he spread his body over mine to hug me, "we have dedicated our lives to helping others."

# Speck

# 76

I was sleeping on my back when they woke me. It was dark in the room and outside the window, but after Muriel peeled the covers from my shoulders, Chaz began to light candles and position them in saucers on the nightstands. Muriel moved to the stereo. "What do you think? Segovia?"

She slipped a silver disc into its drawer, and a guitar shimmered with a brooding, pensive etude.

"Just go back to sleep if you like, sugar," Muriel said. She left the room and returned with an armload of rolled towels. She shook one out and lifted me by the neck to spread it underneath my head and shoulders.

"Look," I snarled, "if you're not going to let me go home, at least let me get some sleep, all right?"

Both Chaz and Muriel were wearing white T-shirts and loose

white cotton drawers, and in the light of the candles they looked more celestial than ever, as if their clothes and faces and hair were emitting a golden effulgence into the room. But the story Chaz told me wouldn't leave my head, and I couldn't help picturing the Lambents as Third Reich youth from a Leni Riefenstahl film.

"Have you taken a look at yourself in the mirror lately?" Muriel whisked off the duvet and left me naked on the bed. She unfurled another towel and tucked it under my back while Chaz wandered into the bathroom and ran water in the sink. "No wonder your sister was shocked."

"My sister?" I sensed the truth but couldn't pull it towards me.

"After you left the dinner table, she said you had never looked so scruffy."

My sister and her husband. They were the guests at the party. I hadn't recognized Meg, and my behavior had been appalling. I heard myself shouting "ten-inch dick!" and winced. I hated the Lambents —at that moment—for their deception.

"How long has it been since you shaved?"

"What chance have I had?"

"Don't you worry about it, Peter. We'll get you ready in time."

"Ready for what?" I struggled from the last of my grogginess.

"Do you know the story of Hop-Frog, darling? It's Hans Christian Andersen or the Brothers Grimm or someone. It seems—"

"Not another story."

"Fine," she said peevishly. "You talk then. Tell us more about Brad. What was he like when you weren't jumping his bones?"

Chaz returned bearing a basin of steaming water, which he set on the bed at my side. "I don't want to talk about Brad," I said.

"You know, Speck," Chaz said as he dunked a washcloth into the basin, "sometimes you act like you're too good for this world. But if what you had going with this Brad was so fucking great, you must have done something pretty shitty to make him leave you. What was it?"

"Nothing. Leave me alone." I sounded defensive rather than angry. When Brad left me to move back to Portland with Alex, I had been dazed and uncomprehending. I had accused myself of a vague inadequacy—which was another means of blaming Brad for judging me too harshly. I didn't want to consider that I might have been more directly responsible.

"We ask only because we're interested in your past," Muriel said. At the end of the bed, she unrolled a towel bundle whose contents were concealed from my view by the piled bulk of the duvet and by the duvet's shadow in the mirror overhead. Chaz rubbed the wet cloth over my face, following the line of my jaw where a substantial growth of beard bristled.

"Okay," I said. "Brad left me because he decided he still loved his old boyfriend and didn't love me. At least not enough to matter. Not enough to take priority." My answer wasn't satisfying, and I couldn't bring much conviction to it.

"Do you think love is really like that, Peter?" Muriel asked. "Hierarchical?" She shook something in her fist. I looked down at her arm rapidly jerking a can of shaving cream.

"That's just what happened, is all."

"This interests me, though." Muriel pushed the button on the cannister and built a mound of blue gel in her palm. "I mean, do you think you love one of us more than the other? Do you think you have to choose?"

I didn't respond; I knew she was shrewd enough to recognize that I wouldn't discuss my love or lack of love for them.

She rubbed the gel over my face and neck until it made a rich foam.

Chaz ripped into a cellophane bag of disposable plastic razors. He selected one and dipped its head into the basin then shook it. "Hold still now." I acted as he instructed out of a deep fear of being cut. For his first stroke, he cleaned a path over my Adam's apple across my chin to my lower lip. In the mirror I saw my face and its soapy beard divided by the empty line.

Muriel continued with the wet washcloth, moving it under my spread arms and over my chest. She squeezed out another dollop of gel and rubbed it into my armpits and onto the slight patches of hair between and around my nipples.

"Don't do this," I said, realizing that they weren't listening. "You bastards."

"Oh, Peter," she said and looked along my stomach towards my groin. I followed her gaze in the mirror, although I didn't need to; I could feel my body stirring. "You love the attention."

While Chaz worked up to my ears and into the philtrum beneath my nose, she finished coating my chest, leaving my nipples free. She tweaked them with her filmed fingers. "They're so small and hard. Like berries in the snow. Ever thought of getting them pierced?" I must have flinched, because Chaz put his cast-encased arm against my shoulder to steady me, and Muriel lowered her voice to soothe me. "Don't worry, sugar. I don't have a proper needle."

Muriel took another razor from the package and began to cut through the hair under my arm. When Chaz finished my face, he wiped it off with the wet cloth, dried it with the loose ends of the towel beneath me, and carried the cloudy blue metal basin into the bathroom. He returned with clear water.

"Why are you doing this?"

"When we get all this off you," Muriel said, "you'll see what a beautiful body you have."

I watched them shave me in the heavy, dark glass above. With the Lambents hunkered over me I felt claustrophobic. But by observing my reflected self, I found the procedure became more distant and detached. Chaz moved down to the bottom of the bed to begin work on my shins. To reach the backs of my calves, he bent my knees slightly. I watched the razors scrape over me, sometimes tugging at a knot of hair when an edge grew dull. I separated the discomfort I registered in my skin from the movement of the blades I followed overhead. The blades skated like tracks in ice along my inner thighs and hissed smoothly over my stomach. Eventually, they discarded each stubbornly dull razor and removed a new one from the bag. In the glass, I studied them both kneeling near my waist as they worked towards my crotch: Muriel clearing the thick line snaking below my navel, Chaz holding my balls up to denude my perineum. In the flickering light, with my arms and legs outstretched in a martyr's pose, we were a classic tableau, although I couldn't say if I was being prepared for the crucifixion or anointed for the tomb.

I grew fully hard as they moved my penis from one location to another while uncovering my crotch. The escutcheon of hair I had been anxious to achieve as a young teen disappeared under the gel and the ministrations of the razors. I ceased considering what was happening to my real body and kept my eyes entirely on the mirror. Muriel spread the skin of my scrotum, and Chaz carefully cleared it of its fuzzy covering. The chill tingle I had felt over the rest of my body was magnified tenfold on the naked sack of my balls.

They removed the chains binding my wrists, and Chaz held my arms out before me while Muriel clamped on a pair of steel hand-cuffs. Then they turned me over to complete my buttocks, the crack between them, the tops of my forearms. I closed my eyes in the crush of the pillow. When they flipped me onto my back again, I relaxed, believing that the shaving was over.

They grabbed me by the slick hollows under my arms and slid me up until I was seated with my legs folded before me. Chaz spread a towel across my lap. "Just let your head fall forward, Speck," he said and guided me with his fingers twisted in my hair. I looked sideways at Muriel. She held a compact cordless clipper.

"Don't," I whispered futilely.

Beginning at the nape of my neck, she guided the clippers around the contours of my head until I was shorn. Then Chaz used the shav-ing gel and the razor to polish my scalp. As the disc of études faded in the stereo, he washed my head with water from the basin, and Muriel rubbed it with a towel. Then she stepped away from the bed to stare at me. They both did. "Behold the New Prometheus," she proclaimed without exposing any insincerity.

"Listen to me, Speck," Chaz said earnestly. "If the world weren't fucked and it was still possible to believe in anything, people would fall at your feet in worship just because of how you look." He walked to the nightstand under the Tiffany lamp and lifted a tube of lubricant from the drawer. He threw off his T-shirt and kicked off his pants. "I want to know you this way, Speck. I want to feel your body now. I want to give myself to it." Muriel had stretched her hand under her shirt with her eyes shifting from me to Chaz and back. He wet his fingers from the tube and reached his hand behind him. He cov-ered his mouth as if to stifle an excited cry, then climbed onto the bed and came to me.

We made love, the three of us, in a heavy, almost awed, hush. My skin felt shudderingly alive. Each hair that had been shorn was replaced by an active nerve. My journey behind the covered eyes of the mask had increased my sensitivity to the tactile world, and the shaving had left me with a bare canvas ready to be brushed with new sensation. As our bodies interpenetrated, I reached, as never before, into the Lambents' reservoir of grace. I felt the charge of their bodies ripple over me and wrap me like a cloak. I wanted to take them and them to take me, infinitely, as some erotic Ourobouros. I couldn't hate them; I couldn't feel anything but desire.

I was inside Chaz. He squatted across my hips while Muriel knelt astride my chest, facing me. Her spine nestled against Chaz; her crotch brushed my chin, grazed my lips. Whenever she rose up and leaned into Chaz, his dick nudged between her legs. She reached back and pulled it up towards her then pushed its slick head down against my stomach. She pressed her body into me and left wet trails across my cheeks. I looked down my nose to spy his hand as it emerged between her thighs to grope upward into her kinked thatch of hair.

She hummed and reached above and beyond me to her dressing gown, which hung from the edge of the headboard. She dragged the robe onto the pillow near my head and pulled the belt from its loops with a silky whisper. She rocked her pelvis against the fingers sinking into her and wrapped the length of fabric around my neck. "Why do this?" I asked quietly. She tied a small, quick knot. "Wait," I said heavily. But she didn't and cinched the belt against my throat. She rocked against his hand, and he began to ride me more rapidly.

She cinched the belt again, and I couldn't breathe. My face burned. My heart flailed in the vise of her knees. I fished my mouth desperately open and closed. Nothing left or entered my throat. I sensed a cloud of thick black ink approaching at the corners of my vision. "Why do it?" she panted. "Why . . . because you love us, sugar. And you would let us take you if we wanted. Take you out." Her tone was pure melodrama, but her fingers whitening with strain against the belt were real. She reined back tighter and stroked her breast's aureole with a single finger. "Go, sugar," she whispered. "Go." Her body shuddered above me. I realized I was broncobucking underneath them both. My muscles strained and flipped like wet eels within the casing of my skin. I came, driving upwards into Chaz. Exploding. Exploding with the dark sea in my head.

Muriel dropped the end of the belt and pulled at the knot twisted under my chin. I gasped air into my lungs in loud, painful bursts and felt Chaz's semen patter wetly between Muriel's legs and onto my stomach. He pulled off of me and placed wet palms on the bones of my hips. "It's a good thing you came when you did. You didn't have much time left." His voice was hoarse. "But I guess none of us does."

# 77

After they left me, I collapsed into a dense, unshifting sleep. When I woke, a faint dawn light crept through the interstices of the blinds. I had turned on my side with my hands settled next to me on the pillow. Something solid and heavy rested on the backs of my thighs, and I lifted my head to see Cissy's thick yellow body slumped against me. Her closed eyes were smushed into the puddle of her thick, wrinkly cheeks and jowls. When I shifted my legs, she muttered somnolently and pushed her spine against me again. Chaz and Muriel had been careful to keep the dog from the bedroom while I was held there, but when they left me that night, they had forgotten to latch the door. It remained open a dog's width, and I could see a thin rectangle of the hall's plain white wall. I also heard the sound of softly thudding music from somewhere in the house.

I reached up to scratch above my ear and was surprised, first, to find both hands pulling in one direction due to the handcuffs and, second, to touch the almost slick expanse of skin over my skull. I was reborn into an awareness of my hairless state and recognized the patches of slight irritation around my body as razor burn. I lowered my hands to feel my bare legs and groin and received a third surprise: the Lambents had forgotten to chain my arms to the rings again. I had previously considered my routes to freedom in all their permutations, and I was aware that if my arms were somehow freed I should be able to climb off the bed.

I rolled forward at my hip to escape Cissy. She growled without moving and flopped nearly onto her back with her legs poking out stiffly like an upended beetle. I sat up and stretched down to grab the chain at my ankle. To muffle the noise, I played it out carefully over the edge of the bed as I lowered my foot to the floor. I slid my other leg across the bed, but there was not enough slack in the chain for it to follow my first leg onto the ground. Holding the footboard, I stood tentatively on one leg with my other foot braced on the mattress. I ventured out into the room as far as I could until I was hanging from the chain at my ankle. But I could not reach the bureau to search for the keys to the padlocks. I hopped towards the door to the room. To near it, I needed to pull my furthest leg over the top of the footboard and allow the chain to slide along the top. Even with the protection of the silken sheath, the links would abrade the carved rim, and I paused to worry about damaging such a beautiful work. Then I thought, fuck that. If they were going to play with chains on an art treasure, any damage was the Lambents' responsibility. I tugged the chain over quickly but quietly and strained for the door.

My fingertips touched the edge about two feet above the bolt of the doorknob. I hesitated, listening, before guiding the door open further. I could see the empty upstairs hall with its unadorned white walls, the closed hall door to the bathroom, the closed door of a closet, and the half-opened door to the second bedroom. Light and sound were seeping faintly around the open margins of that final door.

I had seen inside the second bedroom only once, when Muriel slipped in to find me a book on Le Corbusier. The three inner walls were lined floor to ceiling with overflowing bookshelves. In the center of the room there was a tall black metal frame with a series of pulleys and cables, which I had assumed to be exercise equipment—Nautilus or that system advertised endlessly on cable television. Although I had given it little attention afterwards, I noted that Muriel was careful to shut the door behind her while she hunted for the book.

As I hobbled on one foot to find the best angle to look, I focused on the song arising from yet another stereo. Since the beginning of the evening, they had switched musical gears from Spanish guitar to some dark, trancelike electronic beat. Leaning far forward with my other foot stretching the chain almost straight out behind me, I found the best stance to catch a glimpse into the second bedroom.

Muriel hung upside down, her bare back to the door, with her legs spread and feet bolted into some kind of padded clamps at the top of the black frame. Her head dangled several feet off the ground and was bent weirdly out of my view until Chaz appeared beneath her. His hand was wrapped in her hair, which wound round and round his forearm like a tentacle. He squatted on his haunches under her, looking up; he snarled and his teeth were coated with crimson. He yanked her head from side to side by the hair. As her torso torqued, a long shadow whipped down from between her legs as if she had a tail.

I couldn't look any longer. I closed my eyes and paused there, my left leg hanging in midair. I rubbed unthinkingly at the abrasions on my throat. Distorted female voices slipped in a whisper over the music's drone: "And my love blooms death inside you. And my love blooms. And my love blooms death inside you. And my love blooms." Then the doorbell rang.

While Cissy scrambled to her feet on the mattress and barked malevolently, I pushed at the bedroom door with my fingertips to close it and stumbled to return to the bed. The chain caught on the edge of the footboard, and I bent awkwardly to free it. When I looked up, Cissy's claws dug at the edge of the mattress. She snarled and bared her spittle-flecked teeth near my face. I tried to slip around her, but she scuttled sideways and crouched on her haunches. She would not allow me onto the bed. Afraid that she might launch herself at me, I moved away until the top of the footboard stood between us and waited for her to grow bored and relax.

"Peter, what are you doing? You could break your leg if you're not careful." Muriel pushed and tugged me forcefully back onto the bed and sat straddling my chest. She looped one of the bed chains around the central chain of the handcuffs and locked it off with a padlock. She grabbed a thick fold of skin at Cissy's neck and pulled her off the bed. "We don't have time for these shenanigans," she said, a little breathlessly. "Irena twisted her ankle. She crawled all the way here from the carport. She's sitting on the cement outside the patio in pain, poor darling. And we need to take her to the emergency room. So you're just going to have to relax."

Muriel walked to the window while combing her hair back and gathering it at her neck. She wore her dressing gown, silk and swimming in green paisleys, with the belt returned to its place and cinched tightly at her waist. She reached behind the blinds and slid the glass open along its track. "Chaz," she called down. "I need you up here a moment."

She crossed the room into the bathroom and flipped on the lights. After she emerged with a glass of water and something cupped in her fist, she stared at me, her breath close and coarse, then turned to the door of the bedroom. Chaz appeared there wearing a tank top and cutoff shorts. "Hold him," she said flatly.

"Look, don't—" I began as Chaz crossed the room to me, but my throat clenched and stopped my voice. A phantom cord tightened. Chaz pressed my shoulders firmly against the bed.

"You need to relax, sugar," Muriel said. "It's not safe for you to be so agitated. Here's something to soothe you." She touched a pill to my mouth, but I held my lips tightly. She pinched my nose and waited patiently until I was forced to open my mouth to breathe. Then she dropped the pill onto my tongue and followed it with a large splash of water. She pushed at my jaw to close it and squeezed my nose again.

I held out for as long as I could. I tried to hide the lozenge beneath my tongue, but too much water swam in my mouth and I had to swallow. I imagined the pill making its slow course along my horizontal esophagus, then depositing itself softly in my stomach.

Chaz and Muriel walked together to the door, then looked back at me. "Night, Speck," Chaz said. I heard them moving through the house, making noises in the second bedroom, then more noises downstairs in the kitchen. I might have shouted, but I had no will. The hidden door onto the patio closed downstairs and footsteps clattered on the sidewalk moving towards the carports. Irena's wavering voice broke the dawn's silence. "Are you sure you can carry me, Chaz, with your cast and all?" Her voice receded. "Bless you, both of you, bless you."

# 78

My thoughts rose and rose like bubbles of carbonation in a slow stream up the side of a glass—up through the dark broth of sleep until the realm of air and light was visible beyond the tension of the surface. But the filmy spheres of drowsiness would not break to release the trapped gas of my consciousness into the waking world. I bobbed under the meniscus between real life and dreams . . .

At some moment in daylight, I looked over at Chaz. He was suddenly in my view by the bureau although I had been unaware of opening my eyes. The window blinds were angled half open, and between the slats I could see leafy branches transformed into green clouds of light by the sun. He stood with his arms folded over his chest, his free arm supporting the cast. I couldn't read the expression on his face. His eyes were lowered to look at me; his mouth was set with glum, even mournful, determination. I watched him shift his weight from the bureau and stand upright. He moved towards me, jangling metallically with each step. A key ring dangled from one of his fingers—a circlet festooned with brass and silver keys. "It's fucked, Speck," he said. And I wanted to shout, but the trigger for my tongue was missing. He tossed the keys near my head where they made a solid clank and a dent in the pillow. I wanted to reach for them, but my body made no motion, and my eyelids dropped like heavy, wet drapes . . .

Manjula Gupta loomed in the doorway with a square brown box balanced between her palms. "Here it is," she said. I don't recall if I heard her first or saw her, but when I realized that my eyes were open, I focused on the room. Muriel rose from a corner where she had been polishing my chair with a blue rag. She lifted the box from Manjula's hands and rested it on the dresser. Cardboard scratches varnish, I thought, dredging up an admonishment from someone in the past, my father, my mother, Gino Ardt.

Manjula wore a purple velvet vest over tight jeans, and Muriel unhooked the irregular obsidian buttons from their holes until the vest fell open to reveal bare skin underneath. Muriel peeled back the sides of the vest from Manjula's breasts and stroked her fingers in long arcs along the yielding skin beneath. Her breasts were larger than I had imagined and of a lighter shade than her face and arms, except for the nipples which spread wide with the color and sheen of coffee beans. Her nipples tautened at Muriel's touch and seemed to pull up the cones of her breasts.

Manjula touched Muriel's lips with her fingertips, then trailed them along her throat and behind her neck. She pulled Muriel closer and stroked her side through the thin screen of her T-shirt. She tilted Muriel's head to kiss her. And as the planes of their faces shifted, Manjula's eyes met mine. She made no acknowledgment except to place her hands on Muriel's shoulders and urge her down onto the floor.

Soon they knelt so that only their heads were above the rim of the footboard. While they kissed, Muriel glanced at me quickly, then grinned, looking at Manjula, who pulled Muriel on top of her as she slid onto the floor. I could see them lying together in the mirror, a jumble of angles, on the carpeting at the periphery of view. But the image was darkened and crackling, and I could not keep awake. "Don't worry about Peter, Guppie," Muriel said between the wet sounds of kisses. "We have no secrets from him." She laughed, and I shut my eyes again.

# 79

My vision was sharp. The room was etched as if with a black, razor-thin outline around each plane and contour. But accompanying the clarity was a dull ache, as if my skull were bound in a coil of thick metal wire.

I was sprawled fully dressed on the duvet. I studied my clothes in the overhead mirror, in the light of the grape cluster lamp. It was an outfit Muriel must have selected: a white T-shirt, worn black jeans, and a pair of heavily scuffed black work boots. A black jacket was carefully laid out across the bed at my feet. The jeans were mine; the other clothes I didn't recognize.

There were no chains on the bed, no handcuffs, no bonds of any kind. I propped myself up on my elbows.

I heard a crowd of people in the rooms below: talking, clinking china and glassware, switching from song to song on the stereo. To get out of the house would require pushing through a throng of the Lambents' friends. I considered using hysterics but decided to try camouflage instead. I pulled on the jacket and opened the door to the bathroom.

I looked in the mirror over the sink and rediscovered I was bald. I touched my white scalp hesitantly and realized I wouldn't have to worry about my hair. I returned to the bedroom and scooped up my wallet, keys, and pocket address book, which were laid out on the dresser, then stepped out into the hall and down the stairs.

The front room seethed with party guests—none of whom I recognized. The two distinct groups I had observed at the earlier party were still discernible from their dress and habits, but the trendy and the classic mingled more complexly than I had imagined. It was possible to look across the room and find a young woman with black Spandex bike shorts, a black leather bustier, and a tribal arrow tattoo on her shoulderblade speaking animatedly with a silver-haired man in blue flannel banker's attire. I was no longer curious to meet them; the envy I had felt at the earlier party had been leached from me.

The winged chair commanded the center of the room. The Lambents had built or rented a dais with a black metal frame and a blue velvet platform and had erected it in the middle of the floor. Several couples and groups sat on the platform's edge, and the chair rose from behind their backs like a dry fountain. Apparently, the party was in its honor.

I left the stairwell and took a tentative step towards the front door. Over the head of a woman wearing some kind of brimless green velvet cap and choker of pearls, I saw the white shocks of Chaz's hair. He stood at the door holding a wooden tray stocked with drinks. I wasn't ready to confront him; I ambled away around the other side of my chair and lingered in a corner. I was free of their chains, but I was still stuck in their house; it was ridiculous.

"So we consulted with the landscapers and decided to switch over to native vegetation. Xeriscaping, they call it. Although I'm going to miss the azaleas along the upper terrace."

"And your lovely roses! They won't really tear out your flower beds?"

The first woman nodded regretfully and sipped at her cocktail. Her other hand was tucked into the pocket of her floor-length skirt, black with twined gold and silver vines and flowers, and as dense as a Persian rug. Her light gray hair had been teased out into a corona of curls, almost an Afro, around her narrow face and aquiline nose. "We're getting coastal sage. Creosote. Buckwheat. And these plants with these tiny orange flowers—I don't recall the name."

"A perfect home for the gnatcatcher, huh? Or did they all get fricasseed in the brushfires?" The second woman had the bronzed, crepey skin of an old-guard California society matron. Her black hair was pulled back severely, perhaps to accent the huge gold lion's-head necklace at her throat. Her dress was shimmering emerald green organza, and she leaned her bare shoulder against the end of the cosy corner.

"Don't even *joke* about that bird around Floyd. He's invested—somehow—in building the toll road. And after about the millionth environmental impact statement, he made it very clear he didn't want to talk about endangered species ever again."

"But he's still going to go ahead and tear out your garden?"

"We entertain a lot at home. And he thinks it would help to seem ecologically sensitive."

The woman in green quaffed the last of her champagne and began to glance around, either for a place to put the glass down or for another drink. "It's something we all have to think about these days," she said pensively. "Donald Bren spoke about it at a function recently. He's such a wonder, that man."

"He is. Those environmentalists don't know how lucky they are to have him at the helm of the Irvine Company." The Persian-skirted woman touched the other's forearm above her bulky gold bracelet. "And speaking of the crème de la crème, I've heard the Aldencotts are going to endow a fine arts museum at the university. I'm sure Muriel will be tapped for the furniture collection when the time comes."

"I'm sure," the other said. "Have you looked at the new piece? What did you think?"

"It's so vulgar. Very Disneyland. Very Geppetto's Workshop. Still, he seems to have something. I could see getting something done for the guest house. For the grandkids when they come to visit. The artist is a friend of Muriel's?"

"He's here somewhere apparently. Her *petit ami*."

The two women laughed, and I decided that the conversation had grown entirely too personal to eavesdrop on further. I moved towards the sliding door behind the buffet table.

I spotted Zorna in an imposing gold lamé gown with a standing fan collar, moving down the food line, her long-nailed fingers clutching the rim of a beautiful bone white plate. She chatted with two dark-haired, olive-complected men. They were, I believed, the two men I had encountered making out in the men's room at the cabaret, and I didn't feel prepared to be introduced to them. I slipped away to the far end of the buffet.

A man dropped a plate of brightly colored marinated vegetables, and as he bent over to scoop them from the carpet, Manjula loomed above him in a saffron sari and offered a damp napkin. She stared at me and curled her lips slightly into a wry smile. "The man of the hour," she said. "I commend you on your beautiful chair."

"Thank you," I responded while considering a path around her that would take me out the patio door. I was both flattered by her comment and irritated at my positive response.

"You are the anomaly, Peter. A novice at the party and the guest of honor on the same night."

I stared down at the greasy spot the spilled vegetables had left on the carpet.

"Mrs. Rabindagore insisted on making dosas for you. She is quite taken with 'the young friend of Chaz'—as she styles you." She must have noticed my gaze darting furtively over her shoulder to the door. "I wouldn't leave before the presentation, Peter," she said, and although her inflection didn't change, something in the music of her voice made her words into a threat.

She turned away, and I crept quietly through the kitchen behind Mrs. Rabindagore and her daughter Jamma busily at work at the stove, and popped out the opposite door into the hall. For relief, I climbed the stairs and headed for the bedroom.

This is sick, I thought. Sick. I can't believe I'm going back upstairs.

If I had hoped to retreat, the bedroom wasn't safe ground. There were people there. Five or six in dark colors, all seated on or around the bed talking with each other. There were not enough people in the room and not enough intensity in the conversation for my appearance and immediate exit to pass without notice.

"Hi." A woman in a multicolored Peruvian vest, a fedora, and black jeans waved me in. "A friend of Chaz? Or a friend of Muriel?" she asked.

"Both," I said. "Sort of."

"The best kind," she said. "I'm Kavanaugh."

"Hello," I said dully. She continued to study me, and I realized that she expected me to identify myself. "Peter."

"Peter the Chairmaker?" Another pretty young woman with corkscrews of red hair and a man's green plaid sportscoat swiveled to look over the footboard of the bed at me.

"Yeah. I guess that's me."

"I love it! We were just talking about your chair. It's so fairytale!"

"*This* from a girl who read her first fairytale *after* reading Bruno Bettelheim." The man who spoke had at least four earrings, two piercings in his nose, a goatee, and a faded Voluptuous Horror of Karen Black tour T-shirt.

"I can't help that! We lived in Senegal. And my parents didn't want me poisoned with Western Culture."

"Poisoned. That's an interesting choice of words. We should bring that up next week in Derrida's class." The goateed man extended his hand, and I shook it. "Nice chair, man."

"Thanks."

A second man patted a space next to the headboard. "Come sit. Place of honor at the head of the bed." His brown hair was cut at one length and hung in long strings over his pale, beautiful face. "My name's Jim."

I skirted the group reluctantly and sat down where I was commanded.

"Fuck Jacques Derrida anyway!" Kavanaugh, the fedora woman, retorted.

"I'd love to," the redhead countered. "There's a woman who drives here from Arkansas every year for his seminar, and I think she hopes he'll give her a baby."

"A bouncing baby theorist," said a short-haired blond man in thick black-rimmed glasses who sat crosslegged on the floor.

"Personally, I would've wanted Foucault to fist me," stringy-haired Jim said. He sat with his thigh pressed against mine on the bed and his hand settled somewhere behind my back. "I would've pursued any limit experience with him. I'm serious."

"We know you are, Jim." Kavanaugh idly flipped one of the rings mounted on the footboard. "Jim," she clarified for my benefit, "has never had a sexual experience to our knowledge."

"One can imagine what our hosts get up to with those," the blond said.

"Shit." Kavanaugh studied the ring in her hand. "There's four of them and everything."

"S&M," the redhead said.

"B&D," the goatee man corrected her.

The blond man leaned forward with sudden enthusiasm. "I went to this seminar once at a leather bar. This huge guy had his slave boy crouched on the table in front of him, and he was showing the technique for all these knots. It was incredibly unerotic. Like watching Julia Child do a cooking demo."

"Hey, I get off on Julia Child," Kavanaugh said. "What about you, Peter? Have you ever done any bondage or anything?" She jerked the ring suggestively.

I felt as if my history were carved on my shaved head. I wanted to get up and run as far away from the bed as possible. But I didn't move. "Oh, I've done a little of everything."

"I know! Let's have Peter take our survey," the redhead shouted.

"Okay, it's professional wrestling," Jim said and slapped his hand to my thigh. "Who do you pick? Marcia Cross versus Sherilynn Fenn?"

"What?" I asked. I wasn't sure what response was expected of me.

"Okay, that was a tough one. How about the tag team of Luce Irigary and Hélène Cixous versus François Lyotard. Who will win?"

"That's so sexist," Kavanaugh scowled.

"No, Lyotard can take care of himself," the blond said.

"I'd have to go with the women," I said.

"All right," the goatee man said, "Elizabeth Clare Prophet or Marianne Williamson?"

"Don't know. But Zu-krall could whip them both," I said and pictured the Green One using its hammerlock. "You guys are grad students, right?"

They laughed in unison.

"Critical Theory," Jim said.

"Comparative Literature."

"Comp Lit."

"Film Studies."

"Comp Lit."

"How could you tell?" Kavanaugh asked, and they all laughed again.

# 80

When the students were ready to rejoin the party, I went with them, hoping they would act as a buffer on my way to the door. But at the foot of the stairs I ran into Muriel.

She was radiant in red, in a gown with a full skirt bordered by a frieze of black roses. She took me in her arms and turned me around in a circle. "Are you having fun? Do you like your party?"

I stared straight ahead. It didn't seem appropriate to protest my captivity in front of these people; I was forever a victim of etiquette.

"We have another surprise for you. Let me just say good-bye to Zorna and Polly, and then we'll get started."

The two ladies emerged from the large closet under the stairs, sweeping into their wraps: a lamé cloak fringed in black plumes for Zorna, a nubby peach cloth coat for Polly Morpheus. Polly's bouffant was actually smaller in diameter than that of the gray-haired woman I had spied on earlier. While Zorna was speaking with Muriel, Polly smiled at me pleasantly, although it was clear that she didn't recognize me from my brief intrusion into her dressing room.

Muriel said, "I'm sorry you have to leave so soon."

"I need to get home while my gardenia's still fresh." Zorna held up the corsage at her wrist.

"Thank you for coming." They air-kissed each other's cheeks.

When Muriel swerved to speak with Polly, Zorna stepped around her and loomed over me. "Isn't it past your bedtime, child?"

"What do you mean?" I felt expectant, but also slightly uneasy.

"Remember what I told you about making an early exit? You always want to leave the throng wanting more. Come walk out with us."

"Sure. That would be great," I said.

Muriel stepped beside me and locked her fingers tightly around my wrist. "But you can't take Peter away yet. We have plans for him."

I looked into Zorna's eyes, and she shook her head but said, "Suit yourself." She adjusted the faux-marabou collar against the golden fan at the neck of the dress. "I *do* like your chair. You've got a gift." She touched my chin with her nail then twirled around and out after Polly with a vexation of feathers and glint.

I looked away from the door and noticed the sounds of the party and the music again. A snippet of Madonna repeated over and over: "Stop, Bitch—Stop, Bitch—Stop, Bitch—Stop, Bitch." The two dark-haired men from the cabaret men's room and the man who had decapitated flowers on the stage were huddled like the Three Fates around the stereo system, toying with the CD player.

"Ready?" Muriel asked and hugged me to her.

"For what? You can't keep me here."

She offered me a smile of amused patience but didn't answer. "Excuse me," she said and walked to the stereo. From across the room, I watched her squeeze each of the men on the shoulder. They moved away without protest, and Muriel squelched the sputtering Madonna. She left the music off and turned to face the party. "Everyone! May I have your attention? We would like to start the evening's ceremonies. Our entertainment for you, and then the final course. We need you, please, to clear the floor."

Manjula swept around the corner from the kitchen. She orbited the chair's dais, speaking softly into adjacent ears, and parted the crowd with billows of deep yellow-orange chiffon. Murmuring, the guests found places against the wall or seated on the historic furniture. A few, including the woman in green organza and her husband, slipped discreetly to the front door and departed, as a solid block of party guests formed between me and the exit. Muriel had moved into the dining area to close the blinds across the sliding glass door.

Kavanaugh and a few other students jockeyed for places at my side. Jim draped his arm around my shoulder. "So is it time? What's this like anyway?" He batted hair from his eyes and hooked it behind his ears. "I can't believe they actually do it."

I didn't answer. My apprehension had toughened into a hard knot in my throat.

Chaz emerged from the kitchen holding Manjula's cardboard box. He was followed out by Jamma and Mrs. Rabindagore, who pulled scarves over their heads and rapidly, silently, left the house. Chaz rested the box on a corner of the dais, and the breathing cycle of all the partygoers grew noticeably unified and intent.

Chaz pulled up the folded flaps of the box and peered inside. Muriel had slipped through the kitchen to emerge from the hall door behind the circle of people. I twisted my head to watch her go to the stairs, and she found my face in the crowd and raised her eyebrows at me before dashing up.

The guests held a collective breath as Chaz reached both hands into the box. I sickened; a column of bile threatened to overflow my mouth. It was not immediately clear to me what he lifted out from inside the cardboard. It was small and black within his palms. He turned it so that it was draped across one hand, and he stroked it with the other. So that everyone in the room could see, he spun slowly on his heels. It was a furry black kitten, marked with a triangle of white on its chin and a diamond on its chest. "That's a good boy, Speck," Chaz said as he scratched between the kitten's eyes. "Don't be scared."

He rested the kitten gently on the white berber carpet under the dais and reached into his pocket. The kitten stood paralyzed with uncertainty for a moment, then began to pad gingerly across the floor. Chaz took out a pocket knife and unfolded the central blade.

Oh, my God, I thought, Oh, God. My body tensed; the tendons stiffened in my neck.

Manjula separated herself from the crowd and walked towards me. With her hands working at our shoulders, she parted the crowd between Jim and me until a channel opened from the center of the room to the bottom of the stairs. She adjusted a light switch on the wall.

The track lights, which normally provided soft pink-white illumination for the Hall of Chairs, rotated in their settings to converge on the dais. They produced a baleful blue pulsing light—a slow weird strobe.

Chaz moved through this flicker with his knife. Towards the kitten, which had curled up against the side of the dais with it legs tucked into its black fur. Chaz stroked the kitten delicately, then took its head firmly in his hand. He stretched the flap of its ear and slashed it with the knife. The kitten howled horribly. A line of purple wet dribbled down its face. Chaz touched the split ear with a finger, then released the kitten, which ran from him to wander randomly across the carpet. Chaz stood and strode in my direction through the blue strobe. The guests sighed.

I muttered, "Oh, fuck," and the woman next to me, with the Persian skirt and the gray corona, leaned close to whisper in my ear. "Don't worry," she murmured. "This is the worst bit. She has strong jaws. She usually breaks its neck with one bite. And the rest of it is very tolerable."

Muriel led Cissy on her leash along the corridor from the stairs. She must have been locked in the second bedroom. In the intermittent blue pulsing, I saw that the fur around her mouth was tufted with dry saliva. Her behavior was more frantic than I had ever seen it, and I wondered if they had been starving her of food and water since I last saw her.

Chaz knelt before the dog and patted her head. He held out his wet index finger—purple in the light. "There you are," he said. Cissy's tongue lashed out and licked the blood from his hand. "Little Speck is waiting for you."

Muriel detached the leash and looped a finger through Cissy's collar. The dog made a low, desperate sound. "Go, sugar. Go," Muriel whispered. She loosed her finger.

Cissy ambled forward into the pulsing blue room, her head slung low. I searched the room for the kitten, which had crept towards a corner. Someone kicked it out onto the carpet with the toe of his dress shoe. I sensed the strength of the crowd's shared impulse to observe, to watch the small, pathetic spectacle with the eyes of aesthetes. An inconsequential tragedy behind police tape. Irena Delgado squirming in a coffeehouse. A freak in a jar. I had always believed this detachment was an attitude I cultivated.

Cissy spotted the kitten and hunkered down on her haunches, snarling.

"Fuck this!" I shouted. "Fuck this!" I pushed between Kavanaugh and the Persian-skirted woman, who had edged in front of me for a better view. Soon, I was in the free space where blue light vibrated in my eyes. I ran around the dais on the side opposite Cissy's probable trajectory and scooped the kitten into my arms.

Cissy charged.

Then she stopped a few feet from me and crouched again. The audience grew restive for action. They whooped. But Cissy knew me. We weren't friends, but she knew me. She wouldn't advance further. She allowed me to back off across the room towards the door. I glanced behind me to see Manjula, her searing eyes, her hands holding a slender filleting knife and a white china serving platter arranged with wedges of lemon and pink rosettes of pickled ginger.

As small as it was, the kitten was frantic, and clawed and flipped in my hands. I glanced down to adjust my grip, and when I looked up, Muriel stood across the gap in the circle of guests. "You don't like the surprise? Don't sweat it, Peter. It's just a party game. Now give me that. Otherwise, there will be nothing for dessert."

She reached out when I stepped close enough, but I dodged her grasping hands.

She smiled. "Are you really this sentimental, sugar? To make a scene about a kitten?"

I punched her in the face and pushed through the crowd out of the house.

# 81

After I raced from the Lambents' with the kitten curled to my chest, I burst into my place, chained the door, and dived into the inner sanctum of the dressing room upstairs. I couldn't say what I expected to happen—whether I feared that the crowd would chase me down, whether I waited for Molotov cocktails to crash through glass downstairs. But my panic was real, however ill-defined its source.

I cowered behind the folding door panels across the entrance of the walk-in closet and stroked the kitten. His fur was gummed with drying blood, and his ear splayed open at the tip of the gash. His eyes had been sealed tight but now opened wide and flashed with fear. As he twisted in my hands, I wondered how I could make him understand that he had less to fear from me than from his previous guardians. I knew that I had somehow sealed his fate to mine and I could never give him up.

I listened for any stirring outside the house, but the night was quiet until the stereo resurged from the party across the walk. The volume must have been quite loud to penetrate my closed windows and the intervening wall of the closet. Ella Fitzgerald and Louis Armstrong sang a scolding, buoyant "A Fine Romance"—a message from Muriel, I assumed.

I lingered in the closet as my fear toughened into anger.

Anger first at myself: I had come too close to surrendering to the Lambents' petty cruelties.

Anger at the other party guests: I guessed at why they had come and why they stayed. Jim, the student of critical theory, wanted to creep out on the cliff of social behavior to watch someone else jump over the edge. The woman in the Persian skirt attended the party because it was expedient, either personally or politically, and remained to watch the spectacle because she knew that what did not impinge on her lifestyle did not require consideration. When the time for carving came, she would slip the smallest sliver of cat flesh between her lips and rub the fat from her fingers onto a linen napkin, sublimating her distaste. The other guests all had their excuses, their justifications, their secret desires and deficits of empathy.

But I reserved most of my anger for the Lambents: they acted as they did because they believed—correctly—that they could proceed without objection. They were *Übermenschen*, the consorts of angels, with the inhuman confidence accorded such creatures. And while they had both wept before me, their tears, like Christ's in Gethsemane, served to emphasize the uneasy accommodation of the Supernatural to a vessel of flesh. They floated so far above moral restraints that they might clamp Cissy's jaws upon *my* throat and serve my heart, red succulent muscle, without any greater protest from their audience. They chose to sacrifice a kitten, not because it was beyond their moral code to select something larger, but because a helpless, disposable being suited their purposes more aptly. It was their party ritual, apparently, to fling this scrap of life at Death's grinning face and demonstrate their lack of fear, their impermeable aura. As a jape, Chaz had named the kitten Speck, my pet name, to remind me of their powers.

Muriel called me sentimental; the Lambents would claim incomprehension at my actions. They would say their crimes were just the wickedness of children—spirited, endearing, almost wholesome—while my response was outsized and punitive. But I didn't care about their excuses. I swelled with disgust for them and stripped off my fear.

I stood and carried the kitten to the counter of the vanity. With a washcloth, I cleared the sticky blood from his face. With a cotton ball, I carefully swabbed his wounded ear. It would need a veterinarian, but for the time being, I looked in the medicine cabinet for salve. I noticed my toothpaste: squished in the middle instead of rolled from the bottom. Behind it lay a foreign blue toothbrush. They had let my sister into the apartment. It was just my sister, it was only toothpaste, but my fear returned.

I applied Neosporin to the kitten's sliced ear, then lifted him and held him close. He struggled for freedom, so I set him down.

I wondered if I had been the only person to defy the Lambents. If others had protested, what had become of them? The kitten crossed the room to the alcove with the tub and toilet, and his paws brushed over the amorphous stain in the rug—the legacy of an earlier tenant, very much like the red continental blotch Muriel had soaked up after the first party, but larger. I looked down at the stain and shuddered. Chaz and Muriel had no limits. I remembered the belt around my throat; I remembered Muriel's finger slipping casually from Cissy's collar. Go, sugar, she had whispered.

I stuffed clothes into my traveling bag, grabbed my briefcase, and slung the straps of both over my shoulder. I scooped up the kitten from underneath my desk. Before I left the bedroom, I called the police.

# 82

When the police arrived at my apartment, I had some difficulty convincing them that I was serious; imminent danger to a kitten is seldom a concern of law enforcement. One officer stood under the light at my kitchen sink examining the kitten's ear while the other crossed the walk to ask the Lambents to turn down their blaring stereo. When she returned, there was a silence followed by the sound of rapidly departing party guests. The officers wanted to impound the kitten, overnight at least, for examination. But I convinced them that the animal had suffered enough. They put in a call to a veterinarian and drove me to his office in yet another Irvine shopping center. They took photographs, and the vet sewed a few stitches into Speck's ear. I bought a short-term supply of food and a litter box. Upon returning to the Villas del Sol, I asked the officers to drop me off next to my car in the carport; I had brought my bags with me and had no intention of returning to my place. They asked me if I had any reason to believe I might be endangered, but I didn't want to tell them my story. I explained that I was just nervous. I gave them my mother's number, then checked under my car, in the hatchback, and in the shadows under the seats. I drove onto the freeway with the kitten napping on the floor of the passenger side.

When I arrived in Brentwood before sunrise, my mother was less shocked and confused than I had expected. She accepted the prospect of my extended visit cheerfully. She was initially dubious about extending her hospitality to Speck, but she was soon settled into the breakfast nook with the kitten curled on her lap. I told her a reasonably truthful version of the events that had brought me to her door —omitting the precise nature of my involvement with the Lambents. Although she wondered where I had been for the last month ("You never return my calls"), she nodded calmly throughout my story, as if my misadventures were more or less what she had anticipated when she sent her son out into the cruel landscape of adulthood.

I woke late in the morning. As I leaned against the kitchen counter with a glass of orange juice and studied the front page of the newspaper, I was somehow less shocked by the date—it had been three weeks since I last looked at the paper—than I was by the day. It was Wednesday. A work day. I immediately called in to my department.

The secretary responded with a derisive snort when she recognized my voice. "I'm sorry, Peter. You're up Shit Creek without a paddle. They fired you last week."

"But I wasn't . . . I . . ." I stumbled into silence, unprepared to explain myself.

"Don't you listen to your phone messages? Don't you read your mail?"

"I didn't . . ."

"Good luck elsewhere, kid," she said and disconnected the line.

I called in to check for messages on my answering machine, but there was nothing.

The police called me at my mother's that afternoon. They had checked their files and uncovered some curious reports. Alice Maynes, an old woman I had often noticed lurking around the Villas del Sol garbage dumpsters perpetually dressed in a crocheted brown stocking cap and a green cable-knit sweater, had driven to the police station in her rusted Chevy Impala at least twice after scavenging the complex for recyclables. Each time, she had torn into a cardboard box to find the mauled remains of a small animal: in one case, a puppy, with its flesh partially rent from its bones; in the other, skeletal remnants of a full-grown cat. No one had paid much attention to Alice beyond filing a perfunctory report, but with my story as corroboration, the officers were prepared to investigate.

The news upset me, and I lay all day in the spare bed in my mother's sewing room enclosed in the headphones of my personal stereo. I was bothered—I realized—because I still loved the Lambents. I was not proud of my devotion, but I could not contain it. I floated in despair until I noticed the white tape marking Speck beneath his ear's frayed edge. Then I found my anger again.

I gave my Irvine landlord a month's notice as required, then waited until the last weekend to drive down and collect my belongings. My mother did not understand why I had put the task off for so long, but the reasons were clear to me. I never wanted to see the Lambents again; I also didn't want to move away.

I rented a space in a storage yard and a small U-Haul truck to transport the larger furniture. After some justifiable grousing that I called only because I needed their muscles, Judy and Clara came with me for the heavy lifting, and although nothing was packed and we had to beg boxes from the supermarket down the street, we worked quickly and efficiently.

While Clara was busy wrapping newspaper around glassware in the kitchen, Judy cornered me in the bedroom. She closed the flaps of the box I was preparing to stuff a sweater into, and pushed her nose into my face. "What's up?"

"What do you mean?" I sputtered disingenuously.

"Bolt from the blue, we get this call from Peter Keith. Long time, no hear. And he says, 'I need you to help me move out.' 'Where you going?' we ask. 'To my mother's,' he says. Now I ask you, does anyone pack up in a rush to go live with his mother? Something's gone unsaid here. Granted, this place of yours is really . . ." Judy grabbed the thick wedge of bright red hair angling from the nape of her neck and looked around the room. ". . . really beige. But is that enough to send you flying out of the whole county? For that matter, if you're unhappy here, why have you stayed this long anyway? 'Cultural Wasteland' wouldn't be putting it too harshly."

Judy had covered so much ground that I had the option to respond to a less uncomfortable topic—although she clearly did expect me to answer because she kept her eyes on mine.

"It was tedious living here sometimes. That's true," I began. "But despite that, I always felt that there was something here. Under the surface maybe. But powerful." It was easy to speak this way: indirectly, ambiguously. "You know the Harmonic Convergence? It all had something to do with ley lines, points on the globe where power collects. And that's how Orange County felt to me. I mean, why are the ultraconservative Republicans into astrology and channeling? It's almost like they don't have any choice. There's a magnetism here that people need to explain to themselves. And this power attracts certain phenomenal . . . beings; it draws them down towards it. Towards here. It's only tedious on the surface." Judy scrunched her brows and tightened her mouth. "I'm not making sense, am I?" I pleaded. In fact, I didn't understand a morsel of what I was saying. I babbled like Irena.

"What the fuck, Peter! I'm sorry I asked." Judy shook her head and lifted her hand from the box.

"I can't tell you exactly what happened. Yet. But it was weird." I smushed the sweater around the edges of the black boots Muriel had dressed me in for the party. I had kicked them off in disgust that night, but now I had decided to keep them.

"Well, shit, yes, it does sound weird. Not your kind of thing at all." She grabbed the handle of the tape dispenser and squeaked out a long brown strip over the box top to seal it, then slung the box against her hip. "But don't you ever—ever again!—make fun of me for getting my tarot read twice a year." She pointed her finger at me, then slipped around the corner of the bed and gave me a kiss on the cheek. "And what's with the hairdo, baldy?"

# 83

We were loaded and ready to travel by early evening. During the whole excursion, I spoke with no one in the complex. Blinds and curtains were drawn across all the windows of the Lambents' house, and I made a concerted effort to contain my curiosity. My only contact was with the woman who lived at the opposite end of the Lambents' building. She stood in her upstairs window with her hair dripping from the shower and her hands on the hips of her polka-dot bathrobe, and scowled. I scowled back and carried my television out to Clara's VW van.

I went back the next day to wash down the counters and steam-clean the carpets in the hopes of receiving my full deposit from the landlord. I worked futilely at the stain in the bathroom rug; then I Windexed the mirrors and carried the cleaning equipment downstairs. I called Lonna at Beautiful Homes, who stopped by to accept my house key and place it in a Realtor lockbox on the front doorknob. Before I loaded the lingering odds and ends into my car, I propped the door open and walked out to the mailboxes to check on the mail I had neglected.

My box was crammed to capacity, and I pulled handfuls out and dumped them in a paper sack. I bent down to retrieve an electric bill that had missed the opening, and glancing along the cement, I discovered a pair of feet in simple black pumps and tan nylons.

Irena stood at the end of the row of boxes, dressed more stylishly than I had ever seen her in a maroon shirtwaist dress, with her black hair in a short, soft wedge cut close to her neck. I felt as if, in returning to Irvine, I had plunged instead into a parallel universe where the sky was clearer and bluer than when I left, the sun brighter, and Irena Delgado more tasteful and attractive. I looked up from the raw crystal pendant settled against the brown skin below her throat and met her eyes. "Oh," she said with unconcealed distaste. "You."

"Hello," I said. "How are you? I was sorry to hear about your ankle." I dropped the bill into the sack and rose to my feet.

"It's better," she responded. "No thanks to you." She opened her own box, lifted out her mail, and slammed the small metal door.

"Excuse me?"

"The Lambents were such a godsend to take me to the hospital. But you. Zu-krall told me about you. At the new seminar, he singled me out. But I didn't listen properly with my soul ears. He said a young male acquaintance was going to come back from a journey but still be in a different place. Now what might that mean, I thought. He said there would be trouble. I thought the young man must be Chaz, but you were the one who was gone. I should have warned the Lambents. The circle is only as round as it is." She finished by glaring at me accusingly.

"You know, Irena, I think you're full of shit." Given my speech to Judy, I couldn't stand on firm ground to criticize Irena for not making sense, but I had lost my patience. "I don't know what you're talking about. But you won't have to see me again. I'm moving."

"Well," she said. She turned and walked a few paces from the mailboxes, then spun around. "No. I won't walk quietly away from this. Do you know what you did to those poor people, Chaz and Muriel? The police came and picked through all their things. How degrading. How insulting! And did they find anything? Of course not! But they took their poor beautiful puppy away and destroyed him! Gave them a citation for disturbing the peace. And to add insult to injury, there was a brutal article in the *Register*. I hope you're satisfied! You and your grubby meddling in decent people's lives."

I silently folded over the top of my sack.

"They've moved now. They've gone. You've chased them away. Hounded them out of their home. Does that make you feel smug, Mr. Smartypants? I loved those kids like they were my own. And they were the lifeblood of the association. Roy and I had talked about doing something official." Irena glanced almost involuntarily towards the block of condos overlooking the guest parking lot. "Adoption or something. Did you know that they were orphans? Both of them."

"What you don't know about the Lambents could fill an encyclopedia," I said flatly.

"I don't want to hear any more of your bad-mouthing, young man!"

"You don't want to hear it because you're an idiot. Open your eyes! They're bad people! It's that simple." Yelling at her, I felt a great rush of release, joy.

"You know," she sputtered, "you know, when Zu-krall comes to change the past, I bet you'll be one of the bad people he erases from time. You'll never have existed. That's what I think." She twisted on her black heels and strode away.

I returned to the apartment and gathered the remaining sacks and boxes. When I reached the front door, Irena was lurking on my mat with a stamped envelope in her hand. "Oh, Peter," she said. I noticed thick tears in the corners of her eyes. "If you see them, if you hear from them, would you tell them to call me? Roy—Roy Garamilla, behind us—" She pointed vaguely. "—and I are getting married soon. I mean, it's only a matter of time because Roy has finally filed for divorce and our love's not a secret anymore. And I *do* want Chaz and Muriel to be there. Would you, if you find out, send me their address or phone number? Anything you hear?" She handed me the self-addressed envelope. Her rage at me had vanished; she wanted something from me, and anger didn't suit her purpose. "Oh, Peter. I feel broken. I feel lost."

She lingered on the porch with her eyes cast down to the adjacent flowerbeds as if she expected me to comfort her. I crossed my arms. Eventually, she glanced a last time in my direction and sulked along the sidewalk around the building. I pushed her envelope into my last bag of trash and tied the top.

Irena had cursed me with erasure—not such a bad fate, I thought—but I was more interested in what she had inadvertently revealed. Evidently, Roy Garamilla was the man Muriel had taken me to the coffeehouse to see. Muriel's story about Irena's husband was probably a total fabrication. She had not lied to me to decorate an essentially boring reality—Irena's covert liaison with our married neighbor was as surprising in its fashion as Muriel's fiction. She lied because she could. Because the act of lying was, by itself, what interested Muriel. I realized that every aspect of my relations with the Lambents had been forgeable and suspect. I could not even assume that my own emotions were anything but mirror tricks and the random flash of glitter.

# Tear Drops

# 84

Very little needs to be told about this period of my life. Like everyone else, I experienced the time as one day following another. Breakfast, lunch, and dinner. Shower, work, exercise, entertainment, and bed. Routine can mask the sting of many days, and I became adept at fostering a comfortable monotony.

I lived with my mother until I found a job. She was a satisfactory roommate; she did more than her share of the cooking, and we made a successful team for shouting answers at the television during *Jeopardy*, although she was rather more intrusive in the matters of my household cleanliness and grooming habits than I might have wished. I chose to think of our living arrangement in a somewhat impersonal manner because it made the actuality of moving into my parents' house more endurable. The fiction of my roommate status was undermined chiefly by the fact that I was unemployed and paid no rent. My mother and I were both living in limbo—I was looking for a job and a new life to begin, and she was waiting for my father to return or not return definitively—but our lives were advancing despite ourselves.

My mother and I traveled to Florida together to visit my sister for Christmas. I apologized privately to Meg and her husband for my behavior at the dinner party; the medication had made me delirious, I explained. Meg was forgiving, and, kindest of all, she had never discussed the details of that evening with our mother. She felt bad that her surprise had upset me.

Deborah doted on her grandson, Tyco, as if her years of objection and avoidance had been wiped from her mind. She had reconceived her family, and when she finally received a phone call from my father, she was prepared to set the divorce proceedings in motion. She negotiated a generous alimony settlement and occupancy of the house in Brentwood. My father was living with Miss Kensey on a Greek isle I had never heard of. He had bought Helen a potter's wheel, and he was making rope sandals and selling them to tourists for pocket money. He continued to send postcards.

After months of halfhearted searching, I was offered a position. Gino Ardt, my old professor, had taken over the curatorship of the privately funded Preston & Bracken Museum in Santa Monica. He called my parents' number looking for me, and I answered the phone. He needed a good draft artist and creative artisan to work with him and his chief designer on various shifting exhibitions and traveling shows at the museum. He said that he had always thought highly of me, and he wanted to know if I was available and interested.

I took the job at once and liked the work. I assisted on major decisions about wall placement and arrangement in the galleries, and I was awarded more autonomy in the design of fixtures, stands, and informative plaques. I recognized that few visitors would ever consider the secondary aesthetic experience that our work supplied—the art underlying the presentation of Art—but I was pleased by the anonymity. Our art was also ephemeral, changing every few months, and its disposability was a further comfort. I didn't feel like being bold in those days. I didn't want attention drawn to my handiwork.

As soon as my bank account could tolerate it, I found an apartment for myself in West Los Angeles. My mother understood my need to live on my own, and she was, I suspect, relieved to see an end to my habit of scattering clothes and open magazines around her home. Her one request upon my departure was that I leave Speck the Cat in her care. But I couldn't lose him. He was the reward for one action I could look back on with no regrets. Speck had grown into a sleek black being—part predatory projectile, part comfy companion—with only the slight forking of skin at the tuft of his ear attesting to the ribbon's width of fate between the triumph of his cathood and its snuffing. As a compromise, my mother bought me a tan plastic cat carrier and extracted an agreement that I would bring Speck whenever I visited.

I promised (and kept my word) and moved to my apartment with my cat. I hung my Kandinsky poster and another for Almodovar's *Matador*. I made myself at home—an accomplishment of attitude that I had never achieved at the Villas del Sol—and drifted into the binary code of days of gainful employment and nights of domesticity.

I spent a month compulsively scratching while my body hair grew in, but for a while, I kept shaving my head. I had never before received so many appreciative glances, and while I didn't particularly wish to pursue these smiles or cruising glares, it was a balm to my confidence. My mother said she had seen a fashion spread about it.

# 85

I saw Chaz twice during those days.

The first time I was still living with my mother. It was two or three o'clock in the morning, and she knocked gently on the door of the sewing room, then opened it with a slight squeak and creak. Because the narrow bed in the room was backache-inducing, I was sleeping on the floor. My futon took up most of the space in the tiny room, and as soon as my mother stepped in, the hem of her robe brushed the pillow near my ear. "Peter," she said. "Wake up."

"Huh?" I responded with the same incoherent irritation I remem-

bered from school mornings years before. I slowly opened my eyes
to the dark.

"I heard a car door."

"What? It's probably just those guys across the way getting home
late."

"No, it scared me," she said. "It felt like something swooped
across my grave." She crouched by the edge of the mattress. "Would
you take a look out front?"

"Okay. Just give me a minute." I didn't want my mother to see
me naked so I waited until she shifted out of the room, brushing the
walls with her hands. I felt around the floor for my briefs and pulled
them on.

As I stepped cautiously towards the front room, I sensed my
mother vaguely, standing at the other end of the hall in front of her
bedroom door. Her attitude made me more apprehensive than any
real sense of danger would.

Faint light spilled over the white puffy couches from a slight part
in the curtains, and I maneuvered gingerly around the furniture to
clamp one hand on a fold of the thick material. Sliding the curtain
sideways, I saw the snake neck of the streetlamp stretching from its
pole across the street and the black leaves of the intervening trees.
Monochrome hulks of cars lined the curb. And on the nearer sidewalk, almost obscured by a complicated fall of shadows, Chaz stood
staring at me.

His hands were tucked in the pockets of his bomber jacket; his
feet were firmly planted in his scuffed workboots. His stance gave
no indication of when he had arrived or if he ever intended to leave.

The Lambents must have copied out all the addresses from my
daybook, I realized. As I searched further along the street for Muriel,
I understood that she had not accompanied him. He was alone. And
although I couldn't actually see his eyes in the blank shadow smeared
across his upper face, I felt his beckoning. He wasn't threatening me;
he was offering proof of his isolation and abandonment.

I watched him until I recognized that he could see me much more
clearly in the light from the streetlamp than I could see him. I let the
curtain fall. I did not go out.

I walked down the hall to my mother's door and found her seated
on the end of her bed. I noticed her black satin nightgown through

the sheer, voluminous fabric of her robe, but I didn't want to consider her penchant for lingerie. "It's nothing," I said. "Just the college guys across the street, I think."

"All right," she said weakly, doubtfully. "Thank you."

"Sure," I said. I left her and collapsed on the futon.

I couldn't find my way into sleep again. I kept thinking about him. I got up after fifteen or twenty minutes and returned to the front window for a careful peek, but he was gone.

The next time I saw him was several months later. I was living in my own apartment, budgeting my paycheck carefully to last the month, and designing vitrines for an exhibition of art deco jewelry. Dale Briars, who worked in the publicity department at the museum, invited me to spend a Saturday with him in Laguna Beach. I was reluctant to accept his offer because I had been carefully avoiding Orange County, but Dale insisted: he'd love my company on the trip. I was flattered he asked.

We drove down and spent the day on the malted-milk sand. We ate sushi for dinner and went to a coffeehouse to hang out. I had wondered all day whether the excursion that Dale and I had undertaken could be considered a date, but when we moved on to the Boom Boom Room on the ocean side of the Coast Highway, the nature of our relationship became clear. We had a beer, then walked together onto the cramped dance floor. Before one song had segued into the next, Dale drifted off towards a blond man in a string tank top whose piledriver arms seemed appliquéd to his body.

I wandered away from the dancers and pushed through the throng of men to the bar. I drank a second beer and stared up at the low, dingy ceiling. When the press of bodies and attitude became too intolerable, I pushed my way outside to get some air. At the end of the street a flight of concrete stairs dropped to the beach. Halfway down, a few men leaned against the railing of a landing in the stance of nonchalance mixed with battle readiness that is the acme of cruising. I kept my eye contact to a minimum and eased down to the sand.

The beach was filled with men: couples holding hands or sitting on the lifeguard platform, small groups standing along the skirt of the surf, and other groups pressed into alcoves in the rocks. I decided to walk northwest on the hard-packed wet sand near the water. The ocean was a black sink that surged and sucked under the moonless sky, and I felt truly lost and aimless at its edge.

I moved further inland to avoid a large rock that was being dashed by the waves. A huddle of men filled a recess in the cliff face. Two of them looked out towards the water, acting as sentries. The light filtering down from the houses on the ridge above was dim, but I saw that two other men behind the sentries were fucking. The standing man was fully dressed in a white T-shirt and a vest with his jeans pushed down to his knees. The other man was naked and was bent over to grip a boulder with both hands. While the man in the vest was thrusting between the other's legs, more men jerked off onto the crouched man's back. The man rolled his neck, and the white waves of his hair caught the light. His locks were longer, but it was Chaz. His face clenched; his eyes squeezed shut. I stood frozen with loose sand slipping over my shoes, then recoiled with the same shock I had experienced when Muriel had sat on her Hepplewhite chair in her running clothes. In each case, I felt that something wholly exceptional was being mistreated as if it were meant for everyday use. In each case, however, I recognized that I had no authority to speak.

I stumbled over my footprints in reverse, and when I passed a curve in the rocks, I broke into a run. I doubted that Chaz had seen me, but I couldn't be certain.

I jogged along the Coast Highway to the well-lit fast food restaurant across the street from Dale's car and waited until he appeared on the sidewalk searching for me. I made him drive me home. The next morning I made an appointment for a full complement of blood tests—I knew I should have done it sooner. The results were all negative, but I remained vulnerable to any strain of the Lambents that might have taken root inside me.

# 86

I don't know what motive led me to the library—boredom, determination, a pigeonlike instinct to search out the same old coop. I browsed through the furniture and design section, but these books had lost their savor. Procrastinating, I tracked down the Orange County phone number for Timothy Crane, the hypothetical man from the ad agency whom Muriel had foretold. But I could hardly call him and say that a woman had tied me up and predicted we would have a bad relationship so we should get together and talk about it. Instead, I returned to my original plan and looked for Brad in the Portland phonebook. This was better than calling Information; I wouldn't need to say his name aloud.

I didn't find him, but I found his boyfriend's name, and after drinking a few Pacificos, I dialed the number.

Brad answered, and I was suddenly paralyzed with the seizure of a wounded heart—as if he had left yesterday, not years before.

Brad was surprised to hear from me, but he didn't seem angry that I had tracked him down or that I had waited so long. I listened to myself apologizing for unspecified wrongs. "Are you okay?" he asked. "You sound shaky, Peter."

"I'm good," I said. I had planned to tell him the truth of what had happened to me, but I couldn't find a way to begin. Instead, I sketched in the mundane details of my life and told him how much I had missed him. Somehow, on the fumes of hope and longing, I invited myself up to Portland for a visit.

Brad was silent, and I was prepared to withdraw my request, excuse my impulsiveness, smooth it over. Instead, Brad cleared his throat and spoke brightly. "Of course. Come on up."

I called the airlines, and we made plans. I clung to his words "come on up" as if they held the key to every future possibility. I had failed with Brad before, but I had changed. I was ready to put my new understanding of the world to the test.

# 87

The house Brad and his lover Alex rented had a manicured, miniature backyard. Through the casement window beside their kitchen table, the small square of grass looked like a blotch of vibrant algae, dense and dangerously green. Compared to the parched, precarious foliage on my street at home, their yard was threateningly lush, a hyper production of the earth's too-verdant glands. I sipped at the mug of spearmint tea I had been given and wondered what had made me want to come. Whatever mysterious fluid of expectation had swept me up and deposited me here in their kitchen, it had evaporated and left me in dry confusion.

Brad sat across the table from me with one leg raised on the seat of his chair. His knee was bent up, his elbow rested on his knee, and his hand cradled his head. He looked at me from a half-cocked angle, and the attitude imprinted on his face was either curiosity or lust— or perhaps I could no longer interpret his expressions. We had walked the city all day, and Alex had gone upstairs to take a nap before dinner; I sensed that it was a conscientious effort on his part to give Brad and me time alone.

But we hadn't spent our allotted hour very productively. Talking felt awkward—we had been close once, but I now sat in the chair of the lover who had come both before and after me. Our former intimacy seemed dubious and transparent. We talked haltingly about Judy and Clara, about gay politics, about my lack of hair. I hadn't managed to say anything about the Lambents. I studied his now longer, darker hair, which was tied back behind his head. The tilt of his face in the light from the window accented the lines that had deepened on his cheeks, around his eyes. I became aware that our time would run out before we made any statements that couldn't be uttered with Alex in the room, and I was resigning myself to think back on this trip from the vantage of work the next week as a long weekend where nothing happened, when Brad lifted his head from his hand and muted his voice. "I suppose we could all of us try it."

"Try it?" I asked, vaguely panicked.

"You know, go upstairs." He made an effort at a cosmopolitan smile, as if this were a regular proposition for him—and I wondered briefly if it was.

"You mean, the three of us?" I was unsettled, although I couldn't claim the experience would be entirely new to me.

"I talked it over with Alex, and he said it was cool with him. As long as it turned out he liked you. And after lunch, he said it was okay."

"I'm not sure it's okay with me."

"I understand," he said and looked down at the checkered tablecloth.

My head reeled from the thought that Brad had anticipated this proposal and gotten approval before he had even seen me again.

"It's just that Alex and me, we've discussed it before, as something to try. And I thought it would be okay with you. Because you know me, and it would be safe—loving even." He pushed away from the table and stood to clear our cups and the box of cookies which had sat unopened between us. "I thought maybe you'd changed. That you'd be willing to do something someone else wanted. To try something that didn't come out of your own head."

"I have changed." I followed him to the sink and watched him fish the teabags from our mugs and squeeze them with his thumb and finger, sending thin streams of greenish liquid into the drain.

"I guess I was wrong."

"Brad," I began. I touched his arm with the side of my hand— less a stroke than a light tap. "Okay, let's see," I finished, although I had no idea what I meant.

"Really?" He turned to me hopefully. He took my hand and led me up the steep stairs. I was thinking how different we were from the men we had been at the Consulate, how irrevocably changed. I had been manipulative then, when I thought I was blindly surrendering to him. Now I acceded to his plan but previewed the scene ahead with icy control. Brad turned to kiss me tentatively, softly, under the rosette window at the turn in the stairwell while I felt for his nipple beneath the pale yellow cotton of his T-shirt and twisted it sharply between my fingers.

# 88

Alex napped above the bedcovers on the left half of the bed, a four-poster in white pine that rose snugly between the sloping eaves of the room. He was curled fetally on his side in a pair of green gym shorts; his hands were clasped together before him, and his wide feet were crossed as neatly and symmetrically as Christ's on a crucifix. His chest was furry and so was his belly, but beneath the light brown hair, solid, tight, trained flesh was visible. He was very attractive, and I couldn't see why Brad would crave more than this—why he would crave me in particular. Yet as I disparaged myself, I didn't actually feel my own inadequacy—just reenacted my memory of it, nostalgically.

I stood next to a bureau topped with a row of vintage mallard decoys watching Brad peel his shirt from his lightly sunburned chest and kneel to encircle Alex's shoulders with his arms. He murmured into Alex's ear, and Alex rolled onto his back and stretched with the exaggerated prolongation of waking from deep sleep—although I didn't doubt that he had lain hyperconscious, straining to hear conversation from down the stairs and into the kitchen. Brad climbed onto the bed and knelt over him, one knee between Alex's thighs, the other foot poised near his hip like a runner's at the starting line. Alex reached up to stroke Brad's chest, his sunburn, tenderly with his fingertips.

I still couldn't hear what Brad was saying to him, but in response Alex slipped off the bed and helped Brad fold the patchwork quilt—a double ring, a wedding pattern—into a square bundle. Brad brushed by me to place the quilt on the seat of a Shaker-style chair. "Preserving the heirlooms," he explained.

When I looked back across the room, Alex had dragged the blankets to the floor, baring an expanse of white bedsheet. He had also stripped off his shorts and stood unselfconsciously naked at the edge of the mattress. Brad took my hand and led me over. While he squeezed my fingers in his fist, he gripped Alex's neck and kissed him deeply. He spun and kissed me too, working his warm tongue in between my teeth, until we had merged in a triumvirate of spittle in Brad's mouth. Then he moved slightly aside to allow Alex room to stroke my chest and shoulders. I marveled at how seamless and easy our introduction was; their experience with the protocol was obvious. Alex helped Brad and me take off our clothes, then we weaved into a knot on the bed.

As we weighed and tested each other's bodies, a rule of silence descended on the afternoon. Without talk, each man could be unknown, merely the flesh of desire and not the baroque convergence of lover, ex-lover, and ex-lover's lover. From their ease in action, I understood that this was normal behavior—not for everyone maybe, but normal for them. Nothing felt normal to me any longer. The room was so quiet beyond our breath that I could hear the rain start out in the yard and on the window ledge.

Within the push and tug of our three active forces, Brad and Alex managed to be tender with each other—a slow tracking of palm along spine, the lingering pull of lip on earlobe. They embraced each other above, beneath, and around me. I was a magnet clustering the shavings of their passion for each other. Although not reduced entirely to a breathing, sentient sexual appliance, I was kept outside a steady, translucent scrim that separated their coupling from its entanglement with me and sanctified it as unique. As we delved further into sex, the division made me edgy.

After Alex had finished, Brad knelt at the head of the bed. Alex lay with his head cradled on Brad's thigh, a slick curl marking his hairy stomach. I straddled Alex's chest and looked Brad in the face while I jerked off. Alex held Brad's dick in his fist and sometimes pulled it to his mouth. More rarely, he lifted his head to flick his tongue at my balls. I sunk two fingers into Brad's mouth then slid their wet tips down his neck and over the terrain of his chest. He closed his eyes and tilted his head. With my left hand, I squeezed myself harder. Brad looked down at Alex and smiled. Alex smiled back. A slow, enveloping, exclusive smile.

I slugged Alex across the cheek, then gripped Brad's shoulder fiercely as I came. "Fuck!" Alex shouted and struggled to move away underneath me.

Brad didn't flinch, but his face contorted into the mixture of disgust, fear, and awe with which I imagined Irena's cohorts first greeted their alien master. I hopped from the bed, scooped my clothes off the floor, and left the room.

I paused on the landing to pull up my jeans, then ran down and out onto the deck at the back of the house. I folded my arms against the rain, but it streaked across my head and onto my shoulders. The viral grass lapped it up hungrily.

Brad bounded down the stairs to the door. He had taken the time to dress in sweatpants and a cream fisherman's sweater. I expected him to rush out and pin me by the shoulders and shake me. But he slumped against the door frame and looked down at the wet line of the deck beyond the sheltering overhang of the rain gutter.

"Not what you expected?" I asked. I pulled my hands through my wet, close-cropped hair. "Not what I expected either."

I couldn't say anything else to him. I pushed past him to the spare room at the bottom of the stairs, changed my clothes and tied my shoes, then carried my bag to the front door. Brad silently drank another mug of tea while I stood in the kitchen to call for a cab. "It's not that big a deal," I said. "I don't understand why you're so shocked." I was being honest, but it was also clear to me that, once, I would have understood.

Alex never came downstairs while I was in the house.

At the airport, I stretched out on a blue upholstered bench and waited for 5:45 A.M. and the next flight I could get to Los Angeles.

# 89

After months of stillness, Muriel Lambent resurfaced in my life.

I had spent my third evening that week in West Hollywood skulking up and down the particular stretch of Santa Monica Boulevard where fit and beautiful men developed their muscles, pierced their nipples, imbibed espresso and beer, and danced and partied eternally. I had loitered in a trendy club beneath a neon sculpture drinking an overpriced draft and listening to a remix of the song I had once danced to on my bed. "Ri-ee-i-ee-i-ee-i-ee-i-ee-ide!" sang the woman in the machine, but now her endless wail was broken into bits by the motor of the song.

I remembered the Lambents watching me, unseen in the dark, and I looked down at my body, self-conscious again in a room full of strangers. I was wearing a slight variation on the basic outfit that Muriel had recommended to me. After returning from Portland, I had let my hair grow into brown spikes, but it was still much shorter than it had been before the Lambents exposed my bare scalp in their bedroom. I wasn't myself; I was a construction of those guardian angels.

And when someone attractive moved into view and I thought idly of going home with him, I saw Alex's face, red from my fist, as if some astral force had brushed by with its acid wing. My body had acted without my mind's direction, and I was afraid of this presence rising inside me. I knew its source; the Lambents had forced the lid of my soul and entered that private chamber against my will, rearranging the floorplan, introducing strange furnishings. I worried what I might say or do to any person I met—what I might allow them to do to me. I scarfed my beer and left the club.

All I had achieved by that Friday morning was a compounded hangover from three nights of beer and a sore throat from hours of passive smoking. My defenses were at their lowest.

A manila envelope arrived in my mail at the museum. It may have been its provocative thickness, or the absence of a return address, or the lack of a postmark across the stamps that led me to open it first. Inside, tucked between sheets of cardboard, was a square of familiar, spongy handmade paper. Centered on one side was a block of neat, somehow sinister calligraphy:

> *O Rose, thou art sick.*
> *The invisible worm*
> *That flies in the night*
> *In the howling storm*
>
> *Has found out thy bed*
> *Of crimson joy,*
> *And his dark secret love*
> *Does thy life destroy.*
>
> *—William Blake*

With a pair of scissors, I very deliberately sliced the sheet into threads.

A half hour later as I drowsed at the light table, the phone rang on my desk. My eyes were sewing shut with threads of sleep, and I was reluctant to resurface. I watched my hands float dark against the rising light, fingers spread and still amidst a flotsam of pens, paper scraps, and X-Acto knives. I counted the rings until the call was about to switch into the voice-mail system, then reached out to grab the receiver. "Peter Keith," I muttered.

"It wasn't too morbid, was it?" she said.

"Who's calling please?" I asked with the polite detachment of my work voice.

"Things aren't that dire, really. It just seemed fitting." The voice paused. "Peter, it's Muriel."

I didn't respond; I felt my headache building, gray and high, like a thunderhead.

"Am I to take it from your silence that you are taken aback?"

"It's been a while." I switched off the light in the table but continued to stare at the unilluminated surface. "What can I do for you?"

"Are you in work mode or something, Peter? You're so formal."

"I *am* at work, Muriel." I began to wonder how long our sniping could continue.

"Yes, I know you are," she responded more mutedly. "I'm really sorry, but I needed to reach you and this was the number Chaz had. It's about your chair. The back was damaged when it was moved. I hoped you might take a look at it. I wouldn't like to trash it."

I pictured the chair with its spreading fantail snapped and drooping towards the floor; I had always suspected that the base of the back was the structural weak point. It hurt to imagine the damaged chair-bird perched atop the garbage in a dumpster. But I resisted the impulse to volunteer my services. I never wanted to set foot inside the Lambent household again.

"So do you think you could check it out for me?"

"I don't want to see you again. I don't want to hear from you."

"I understand that, Peter. Saturday afternoon maybe?"

"You're not listening to me—"

"I cherish your chair. I think it's the best thing I have right now."

"Muriel! I can't forget it all this easily."

"You've heard that Chaz and I are no longer together? Another two hearts broken on the rack of love." She laughed briefly and joylessly. "And so she is thrown upon the mercy of the world without even her dog for company."

"It's too bad about Cissy. It wasn't *her* fault."

I meant my words to be caustic, but Muriel ignored them. "I

couldn't have kept Cissy where I'm living now anyway. But do please come down. Can I expect you Saturday?"

"I don't trust you," I stated baldly. I stood and paced the meager floor of my office.

"You have nothing to fear from me, Peter. We won't even be alone together. I'm staying with my mother."

"Your mother?" The existence of parents for Muriel shocked me more than any other possible revelation.

"We all have mothers, sugar. It's just that some of us would rather we didn't. Shall we say four o'clock? We're at 2021 Alta Rosa Drive in Laguna. Can you find it?"

"No."

"Then I'll meet you in the bank parking lot on Broadway just up from the main beach. See you." She hung up, and although it was too late, I held the phone to my ear for a few moments attempting to formulate a more definite refusal. I swept the scraps of paper and acetate from the unlit table and dumped them into the wastebasket by the door.

# 90

Muriel's tresses had darkened from honey cream to taupe. The tint of her braid closely matched the fading paint of Lady Lazarus, her decrepit El Camino. She may have colored her hair, but the deepening tone seemed a natural process like oxidation or erosion. As I watched her lean against the front end of her car in khaki safari shorts and a peach tank top, I saw that she was still beautiful. She had not aged. Her body remained fit and slender. But her aspect had changed. What had once seemed sculptural about her beauty was now architectural. Her curves had firmed into angles. Her plasticity had grown rigid. There was more to observe about her—she seemed no more fallible or human—but I had lost interest in objectifying. Although my curiosity had goaded me to come, the sight of her was too real and painful.

I parked in the space beside hers in the parking lot and killed my engine. My hand was shaking as I released the key. The Lambents' talent had always been to lure me into situations where I didn't wish to be, and now I was held captive by my inability to bear the thought of my chair being lost.

Before I could reach for the door handle, Muriel leaned her elbows into the window like a carhop. "Hi, Peter," she said. "Don't get out. We'll go up. Keep close behind me."

She smiled and trailed her hand through the air in a wave as she walked to her car and climbed in. She started from her slot and bolted for the exit around the row of cars before I had turned over my ignition.

I adopted a mode of aggressive concentration to force my Honda to keep pace with her as she slung her car up the steep, twisting roads into the hills overlooking Laguna Beach. At the highest crest, the road leveled off and reduced its curves to a modest squiggling. The houses lining either side of the pavement seemed unusually modest and unexceptional—unadorned one-story structures partially hidden behind an unbroken screen of privet hedges, brick walls, and wrought iron gates—until I realized that the buildings I saw were, in most cases, merely the garages for giant houses that dropped in terraced flights down the hillside below the level of the road. I was able to glimpse a few houses that seemed to levitate with one end braced against the hillside and one end poised on tall concrete stilts. Those on one side of the crest would be afforded magnificent views of the ocean while those on the other would stare off into the canyons beyond. Muriel spun around the cul-de-sac at the end of the street and parked the El Camino on the seaward side in front of a red brick wall mounted with three weathered copper lanterns.

I made the loop and pulled up into the long space between the end of her car and the start of the macadam drive up to the house. As I stepped out, Muriel moved in front of my car and beckoned me with her fingers. I walked towards her. She shook her head. "Sorry. Not you. Your car."

"What?" I peered down at the hood, baffled.

"Here, give me your keys." She held out her hand. I looked into her eyes then dropped the key ring from my palm into hers. "I just want to make sure it can't be seen around the wall." She climbed into the driver's seat and started the car. "Mother doesn't like to see automobiles out the window. Just go on in. Take a look around the yard. I'll be there." Very slowly, she began to shift my car a few inches forward along the curb.

I turned away, marveling at Muriel, a woman who had never been cowed by anything in my presence, not even—I imagined—by the blow I had delivered to her cheek (a blow that, so far, we had both avoided mentioning), but also a woman who worried that her mother might react to a glimpse of reflected sun in my car's taillights at the end of the drive.

I waited for her in the small, enclosed front court. The landscaping was Southern Californian—a few severely trimmed ficus trees, some spiky clumps of bird-of-paradise, impatiens, a bed of ferns. I glimpsed a small Zen garden bordered with a low hedge. Black boulders bulged from a field of white, but the sand had not been raked into integral order. There were no repeated furrows in its surface, only gentle dunes. Set down at either end of the oval bed of sand like the foci of an ellipse were redwood tubs of begonias. The effect was not soothing.

Muriel slipped past me to hold open the heavy wooden front door. As my eyes adjusted to the dim illumination inside, I noticed the stuccoed walls and the red tile floor in the front hall and the brighter room beyond. The lighting fixtures were black wrought iron chandeliers with frosted bulbs tapered to resemble candle flames. Muriel ushered me into the large back room, and I examined the Spanish modern furniture: bulky wooden tables and metal chair frames slung with straps of dark leather. The room reminded me of the cantina of a 1960s Mexican restaurant, although the cheesy effect was disrupted by the floor-to-ceiling glass overlooking the city of Laguna and the endless sun-limned blue water beyond. Nothing stirred in the room except for the ticking of an antique clock on a baroque mantel shelf and a soft directionless thudding.

"So how have you been, Peter?" Muriel asked. She led me to a broad staircase that curved down into the next level of the house.

"I'm okay," I responded without thinking. Then I realized that I had been too distracted by the act of observing and had forgotten where I was and why. I paused at the top of the stairs. "Oh, I need my toolbox."

"You can get it later. I'd like you to see the problem first." She continued onto steps of rough stone with a plush crimson carpet runner bleeding down the center.

I followed her. At one landing I looked through the portal of a formal sitting room worked up into a Louis Quinze froth of endless filigree, gilded cherubs, and delicate sofas on a thick rose carpet. We did not pause there but continued down another flight while I decided that the house's decorator was someone with contradictory whims and, unfortunately, ample funds to pursue them. But perhaps the money (or the desire) had run out some time ago; the appointments seemed well preserved but dated.

As we approached the lower landing, the thudding in the air became more insistent—a repeated bass beat with some sort of electronic snare snaking over the top. The rhythm was Latin and familiar, although I wasn't sure if it was samba or bossa nova. "Oh fuck, they're dancing," Muriel said in a low voice. She took my hand and pulled me down to her level so that I could see.

The curtains were drawn across the windows, but in the dim light I saw that the room was fitted with a parquet dance floor. An elaborate lighting system—including a mirrored ball—hung suspended from the ceiling. Across the room, a black box with various glowing numbers and blinking lights appeared to be the source of the beat. I noticed speakers mounted in the corners of the room, and also, pressed incongruously against one of the walls and in heavy shadow, four of Muriel's chairs: the Eames lounge chair, the crouching-woman chair, the De Stijl-era chair—and my own winged chair. At that distance, I couldn't see what the damage was; I took this as a hopeful sign.

My survey of the room was cursory because my gaze returned invariably to the two women dancing in the center of the floor. The diminutive white-haired one wore a navy dress with a white-and-blue nautical print scarf at her throat. The other woman wore black stirrup pants beneath an oversized white peasant blouse with the sleeves pushed up above her elbows. Her hair was legal-pad yellow and swept up into a startled pouf like the crown feathers of a cockatiel. She looked very much like the doyenne of Muriel's flock of intelligent bird-women.

The two dancers' bodies pressed close and rocked at the hips. It took me a moment to realize that, despite her stature, the tiny figure in blue was leading. She barked orders in a low, gravelly tone, "One—two—cha-cha-cha! One—two—cha-cha-cha! Now, back—two—three-four." The elder woman lifted her arm straight into the air so that the other could spin under it.

"Gumma!" Muriel called out and stepped onto the parquet. "Gumma, I've brought a guest to look at the chair."

The women stopped in midturn and twisted their heads to stare at us.

"Can he dance? 'Cause if a man can't dance, I ain't got no use for him," the old woman rasped, then offered us an open mouthed smile. "You can laugh. That was a joke."

Muriel snagged my sleeve and pulled me along behind her to the center of the dance floor. "Mom, Gumma, this is Peter. Peter, this is Martha, my grandmother, and my mother, Miriam."

The women accepted the introduction with a complete lack of interest. "Mary," her mother said, wiping her forehead with a handkerchief, "have you vacuumed the pink sitting room yet? Because if you haven't, remember to empty the ashtrays."

"The Pink Parlor is done, Mom. And I did the Father Serra Memorial Hall and the Fontainebleau Tribute Room as well."

"Don't be sarcastic, Mary," her mother scolded. "It lacks style."

"The girl has a point there, Miriam," the older woman said with her hands folded decorously at the belted waist of her dress. "I still can't believe I gave up my nice things to come live with you in a place got up like a Tijuana cathouse."

"Don't you start with me, Mother." Miriam touched the base of her blond eminence.

"You've got no taste for anything—except for money. You just can't wait to get your hands on my portfolio." Muriel's grandmother spoke with a vindictiveness that was chillingly calm. She shifted her feet in her homely black dancing shoes.

"Oh, Mother, I couldn't care less what you do with your money. You never were a real mother to me. I had to make my own way in this world."

"Gumma," Muriel said very loudly to break the bonds of the conversation, "is it all right if I switch on the light so Peter can take a look at the chair?"

"He's the repairman?" Her grandmother peered at me dubiously.

"He made the chair with the fan back, Gumma."

"You're a chairmaker?" She stared at me harder. "When we had the house in Pasadena, I had this gorgeous William Morris rocker. Oh, and a flawless mahogany secrétaire with zebrawood veneer in the front panels. As a student of furniture, you must understand the pricelessness of that. Do you know Regency, sir?"

"No, not much," I said. I did, but I had no desire to discuss design with Muriel's grandmother.

"I used to have such nice things," she responded, with a wistful sigh, a trace of malice.

"She's going to go off about that goddamn imported ceiling again," Miriam growled. "Come with me. We'll turn on the lights."

Muriel and I followed her mother to the wall where the chairs were displayed. She twisted the knob of a dimmer and tungsten houselights glowed from the ceiling. Next to the switch was a framed photograph of the Reagans in formal wear above a signed White House Christmas card. "I suppose I can continue to support Mary on the upkeep of her chairs. She puts such stake in them." Miriam spoke directly to me as if Muriel were an autistic child or otherwise absent from the scene. "I don't mind paying for something worthwhile. But I can't see shelling out good money for rent each and every month when there's plenty of room for her here. She spent too much too foolishly when she was on her own."

"Here, Peter," Muriel said, ignoring her mother. She pointed to the rear side of the winged chair. On the reverse of the spreading back, three parallel gouges stretched diagonally almost from top to bottom. They looked like the slashing of a marauding bear—or a calculating handrake.

"I was worried," Muriel offered in explanation.

"You need to fill in the scratches. Maybe some kind of wood glue would do it. Sand it. Stain. Resurface. If you do it right, you won't notice it." I was angry; I guessed that she had damaged the chair intentionally. Then, with apprehension, I wondered what Muriel actually had in mind for me.

"How much do you charge?" Miriam asked.

"I don't charge. I don't even have the supplies to—" I began.

Muriel interrupted me. "You need a shop, right? My friend has a workbench in the back of her antique store. We can take it there."

"I don't really do repairs. Why don't you just get your friend to—"

"You don't do repairs?" Miriam adjusted the cuffs of her blouse. "Why are you here then?"

"Don't say no, Peter," Muriel said. She pulled a pack of cigarettes from her shorts. She took one and handed the pack to her mother. Her grandmother shuffled across the dance floor to cadge one as well. When the pack came to me, I declined and returned it to Muriel. She passed around her lighter, a plain gold cylinder the size of a lipstick, and the others stoked up. For a moment the three women stood in a ring, puffing and trailing smoke like censers.

"God, that's just what I needed," her grandmother Martha said, slowly exhaling a huge pungent cloud.

"Come on, Peter," Muriel snapped. She dropped her cigarette to the parquet and crushed it with the flat of her loafer. "Let's go."

"Mary!" Her mother shouted with outrage, but Muriel hoisted the chair to her hip and marched across the floor without glancing back.

"You little hellion. You'll burn your mother's parquet," Martha warned, unable to conceal her spiteful pleasure at the thought.

I looked at the women, at their creased faces and hostile eyes; then I followed Muriel up and out.

She reached through the open window of Lady Lazarus and retrieved a blanket and a bungee cord. She spread the blanket in the bed and laid the chair gently on its back. As I watched her loop the cord deftly around the chair and hook it to the sides of the bed, I tried to imagine the vast coercive power of a woman who could get Muriel Lambent to vacuum for her.

# 91

We drove south through Laguna Beach on side streets, then onto the Coast Highway to the Aliso Beach Pier. "Muriel," I protested, "where's this shop we're supposed to be going to?"

"Were you always this impatient?" she said as she jumped out of

the car. "Seems like you used to spend hours in bed just contemplating the ceiling."

"That's easy to do if you're chained up."

"You really think that's why you did it, sugar?" She turned to
slink towards the sidewalk.

I sat in the cab of Lady Lazarus until I decided my feeble effort
at protest was going to go unheeded. With resignation but also a stab
of curiosity, I followed Muriel down the long walkway and out onto
a vaguely hexagonal loop of concrete alighted on thin posts over
the blue-green surf. The pier was white and delicate with an open
center like the frame of an enormous magnifying glass. I fantasized
fitting a lens across the opening so that the ocean beneath it would
boil.

The water lapped gently against the pillars, and the translucent
fishing lines of Vietnamese families glinted intermittently like loose
strands of spiderweb on either side of Muriel as she leaned against
the outer railing. The view slanted between the open sea at one end
and the beach at the base of the pier at the other. Over and over, I
asked myself why I had allowed Muriel to bring me here.

We stared at the water. Then back at the beach. Along the mild
curve of the sand, a hardy few had spread out their towels in the
hazy sun. Around the next curve of the coast was the gay beach
where Dale Briars had taken me. We stood and stared until it seemed
that Muriel had mislaid whatever purpose she had in bringing me
here. She lit a cigarette but failed to smoke it.

I decided to fill the gap in our conversation. "So how are you
doing anyway?" I asked.

Without looking at me, she responded wearily, "Oh my God, Peter." Her tone encompassed eons of tragedy: from Alberich's theft of
the Rheingold to Götterdämmerung. After another minute, she
flicked her half-incinerated cigarette from the railing where it had
languished. The butt pinwheeled as it fell, then plopped into the
ocean. "You probably think me incapable of sentiment."

She fell silent again as if she expected me to respond.

"I really don't know what you are capable of, Mary." I tested the
name her mother called her, but if Muriel had been stripped of a
layer of artifice, she did not acknowledge the absence.

"I'm full of feelings. I'm limp with feelings. I'm sodden." She pulled the doughnut of pink cloth from the end of her braid, sunk her fingers into the weave and freed her hair. She shook it out then scooped it against her palm again and resecured it in a looser fall. "I'm just not facile." She gripped the railing with both hands and rocked back on her heels. "Now Chaz . . . Chaz is facile. This is the beach where he picks them up. The men he wants to charm.

"You're lucky, Peter, that he treated you with some respect for your mind. The men he picks up here, after sex he takes them out to dinner, then for Irish coffees on the piazza of the Hotel Laguna or to the chic gay café for mochas. What this means to him is Romance. He cossets them. He dotes on them. And he hopes, I suppose, that they will respond in kind. He doesn't do this for love—not for love at all. He just wants to be nice to them. Nice. But to me it's capitulation, settling for less. Niceness is a failure of will." She choked on *niceness* as if the word were a gobbet of blood-clotted phlegm. Then she switched around to lean with her elbows on the railing and her lower back braced against the bar.

Her image of Chaz and his romances did not correspond to my vision of him on the beach, but I didn't speak. My throat throbbed with the aftereffects of three nights of clubbing, and I dug out a cough drop from my pocket. I untwisted its wrapper and tugged the lozenge from the sticky paper with my teeth.

"Chaz was never as . . . strenuous as I was. I don't know how else to put it. He wanted to come apologize to you. As if you would have respected that." She shook her head in disbelief while I sucked to dissolve the menthol onto my tongue. "When the police came, he practically volunteered Cissy into their custody. I think he wanted to concede the point to you. He would have gotten quite sentimental— if you'd stayed. His nihilism is just the slick, sour coating of his sugar-candy core. I think even if he killed someone, it would be a sticky, sentimental act."

"So you hate him now?" Inside my pocket, I crumpled the wrapper into a ball.

"Oh, no, Peter. I love him. More than ever. I'm just not sloppy."

"No. You're tough."

"When you evaluate a design—something practical, a car or whatever—you need to stress-test it up until failure. I'm sure you know this, sugar. When you're building new muscle, you exercise with weights until your strength gives out. You must make small painful tears in the tissue; this is necessary for growth. Otherwise, you don't advance. Otherwise, you don't know where you are." She looked down at her scuffed leather loafers. "I guess we found out, Chaz and I. We broke down. But we need to get back in the saddle. Even our failure was more interesting than the rest of this. We need to get to the bottom of it."

"The bottom of what?"

I asked, but she didn't answer. The image in my head was a mixing of reactive chemicals, a flash of light, a sonic boom, and smoke.

"We're reuniting," she said firmly.

"Where is Chaz now?"

She didn't answer this question either. She crossed her arms and rubbed her shoulders along the straps of her tank top. A stiff breeze had begun to blow off the ocean. "It's cold," she said. "Let's get some coffee." As she kicked away from the railing, she added casually, "I had the child."

"The child?" I floundered for the conversational rung that I had missed.

"Cid. C-I-D," she explained. "Named after Cissy. But changed because you have to give a kid some breaks in life. A cute baby." She strode rapidly towards the car.

As I chased after her, I had time to wonder whether Chaz was its father, whether it was mine, or whether the child was even real.

# 92

While we sat at sunset on the sheltered patio of the same beautiful, expensive, pretentious coffeehouse where Dale Briars had taken me on our "date," I forgot the reason Muriel had lured me to Laguna: my chair in the back of Lady Lazarus parked up the street. She had captured my attention.

"Chaz didn't want me to have it. He said he'd like our generation to be the last spasm of humanity to befoul the planet. But I was interested. I wanted to know what it felt like to have my uterus expanding, the fetus flipping around inside me, my breasts full of milk." She sipped at the froth in her cup. "Manjula was against me too. She demanded I come to her house for a D&C. But I wasn't about to let them decide what I should do with my body."

Just inside the open door from our table, a three-member steel drum band was playing a possibly ironic medley of Disney's "Under the Sea" seguing into "The Banana Boat Song." Across the table Muriel spoke in a loud, blunt voice to override the music. She kept her palms parenthesized around the wide bowl of her latte.

"I think the party for you was a last-ditch effort. I thought if we had our friends around us, the old rituals, we could make peace over my choice and everything would be like it was. Needless to say, it didn't work. We packed up the house together and drove off separately. He took the furniture, the bed, the mirror, and all. I took the chairs, and the few things that were Gumma's."

She related these events very dryly, as though they had transpired in the distant past and were now no more than fine print in the ledger of history. I was nonplussed that my capture and my actions at the party seemed to have played so small a part in the fracturing of Chaz and Muriel. I had been wrenched from the track of my life, but they had suffered only a failed diversion. Unless she was lying. I turned from her to watch pedestrians shifting from art gallery to art gallery along the street. Of course she was lying.

"I went to the desert to have it. It was really no big deal. An essentially anticlimactic experience. There was a hotel there, a small lesbian resort with misting machines in the garden to make it bearable to be outdoors. They gave me a job with a room and food, so I did maid service and light groundskeeping until I went into labor. I took a few weeks off to be with the kid, then got back to my usual rounds. It might have worked out, but my mother found out where I was. They let it slip about the kid at the front desk, and she kept leaving messages. I didn't respond. So finally Lori, the office manager, told me that she didn't care if I didn't talk to my mother, if I wanted my mom to fuck off, or whatever. But I had to get her to stop calling and hectoring everyone in the office.

"I told Lori I would take care of it. And I knew I would have to get out of there before they fired me or my mother descended. I'd already been lifting spending money from the rooms I cleaned, and I decided to pocket a stash of twenties some woman had hidden inside a Lucinda Williams cassette case in her backpack. I loaded my stuff in the Lady, and put the kid in the carseat, and took off. I didn't much care where to." She took a larger swallow of her latte, which had ceased steaming some time before. Where the lipstick had smeared off onto the cup, her lips showed flat pink through the glossy coral shade. I looked in the door at the band members, who were struggling into a spotty cover of "I'll Tumble 4 Ya."

"I was driving back towards the coast, and I stopped for gas near that place with the dinosaurs. Cabazon. Cid was crying, really bugging me. But I thought maybe I was just cranky from hunger and food would do the trick, so I took the kid in the car seat into the café. No one jumped out from behind the register to seat me. They never do in places like that. So I took it upon myself to find a menu and a booth. I put Cid's seat down on the bench and went to the restroom.

"When I got back, Cid was screaming. And I guess it was bothering the other customers. It sure was bothering me. Someone finally paid attention. The man behind the order window asked, 'Are you the mother?'

"I looked at the man, this fat man in his grease-spattered T-shirt and white cook's hat, and I asked myself the same question: Am I the Mother? The Mother. I'd never thought about it before. That sounds ridiculous, but it's true. I answered the man, no.

"And then to prove it to him, I just walked out of the café, got in the Lady, and drove. I drove all the way to Laguna without stopping." She slapped the sides of her cup rapidly with her fingers. "Back to Mom. A typical tale. But it's not like my mother has asked any questions. She believes she understands everything completely. She's put me on a tighter allowance; I don't get my own money anymore. She's got it all under control."

I winced at her story, although I doubted her words. The image of Muriel as a working mother with diapers to change and day care to schedule was as phantasmic as the tale of the Blond Woman she had told while I was captive. I felt ill thinking of her with a child to raise; I suspected her motives for motherhood were unwholesome, monstrous. "What about the baby?"

"Oh, I'm sure Cid's in a good home by now," she said flatly, without any active interest.

Wherever the truth lay, I felt my disgust surface. "So what do you actually want from me? Clearly, it wasn't to fix the chair."

"Are my motives so mysterious?" she asked, and I accepted the blitheness in her tone until I looked up into the fixed points of her eyes.

# 93

We drove back into the hills after nightfall—somewhere not so far to the southeast of the house where Martha and Miriam danced the bossa nova—and Muriel parked along the curb under a heavy screen of red-flowered hibiscus bushes knitted tight with vines of morning glory. The streetlamp smothered in this riot of vegetation produced a fractured green aura. She killed the engine and sat immobile for a moment. "Well," she said. Light and leaf-shadow spattered unequal stains of indigo on her face.

"This is the shop?" I asked although I knew it couldn't be.

"This is where Chaz lives," she said. "I'll go get him."

I had been pulled too easily back into the gravity of the Lambents' world, and I felt something wrench as if the sealed vessel inside me had cracked and split in the quake of reentry. "Forget it, Muriel."

She climbed out of the car. "I'll leave the key in so you can listen to the stereo." She crept along the street to the first break in the dense hedge.

"No, wait!" I called, but she had disappeared around the corner.

I sat fuming and thought of leaving. But I didn't. I turned the key in the ignition and fiddled with the station tuner. No signal rose far enough out of the static soup to be identified, but a tape lolled like a tongue from the cassette deck. I pushed it into the stereo, and dark synthesized drumming slammed out of the speakers. Old, solo Deborah Harry. Music for Muriel's soul. I turned down the volume and stared ahead at the blank street.

I couldn't divert myself with my usual time-eating activity of making an aesthetic assessment of my surroundings; it was too dark to discern more than the murkiest outline of the buildings on the street. I closed my eyes. Without stimulus, I was forced to swim in the claustrophobic pool of my thoughts, and it sickened me. I saw an infant screaming in an abandoned restaurant, its eyelids ridged with dried rime, its mouth a violet flap. Wet drops pattered on my face, and I opened my eyes and bolted forward in the seat.

Automatic sprinklers jetted through the hedge into the cab. I rolled up the window and watched the water slick the glass. Instinctively I twisted around on the seat and looked behind me into the open bed of the El Camino to check for danger to my chair. It was safely out of range. Beyond it, the oily black hulk of metal I had noticed from my first trip in Lady Lazarus still crouched in a corner. I looked down to inspect a box closer to the cab and saw a familiar face.

It was black, glistening, simian. I had seen it before in dreams when I looked in the mirror. The Beast Beholds Himself.

The face slumped on a pile of black fur, swollen hands and feet crammed beneath it. A gorilla suit. A costume I had worn in a dream, or not in a dream, on the checkerboard stage of the Ground Zero cabaret. I knew the face was empty, but drops from the sprinklers strayed now and then onto the surface, shifting and matting the hair. The nostrils seemed to flare, the lips to shiver. This was how the Lambents' god had come for me: as a dead wet face beckoning from the back of a car. I stared at it, hoping to catch its whisper, to find out what it intended for me to do.

My door opened with a brutal metallic click, and Muriel slipped cold fingers under the ribbed collar of my T-shirt. "Come inside, Peter." Her voice was as harsh as the doorlatch.

"I don't think so."

"I'm not asking. I can't do this without you." She pulled at my shirt.

"Leave me out of this."

"I told you my story. The Blond Woman needs her sultan."

"And look what happened to him!" I worked at her fingers to free my collar.

She pulled away suddenly and rubbed her fingers, wounded, with her other hand. "I thought you would do anything for us."

"Once, maybe," I said. I turned my head to stare at dark houses down the street; I couldn't look at her. "Not now."

I heard Muriel dig into her purse. Something cold nudged at my throat. I jerked my head to face a massive hunk of dark metal. A handgun—ugly, industrial, machine lathed and fitted with cross-hatched plastic on the grip. She prodded me. "Get out," she said.

I stared at her. "No."

She spoke more slowly. "We need to get back on course. But Chaz won't see it my way unless you come convince him."

I twitched. I hoped I shivered at the sight of the gun and not from the thought that Chaz might want to see me. I couldn't allow myself to care about them. And it was not because I was afraid of what they might do to me. I was afraid of how I might react. I remembered my fist slashing across Brad's lover's smile. I closed my eyes.

She brushed metal against skin along my cheek. She stroked the gun down my chest and pushed the barrel under the waist of my pants. "You know I could."

"We both know it." I wouldn't look at her because I knew my denial would frustrate her. If I didn't look, she was invisible. I felt her breath grate at my ear in incredulous rasps.

"Fuck you then." She pulled back and pressed the flat mouth of the barrel against my temple. A finger poking at my fishbowl, trying to lure me up to the glass. When I failed to flinch, she dropped the gun onto my lap. "You take it." I felt its dull weight against my thigh as I listened to Muriel stride away.

I shifted in the seat and allowed the gun to slip untouched to the floor, hoping the safety was on. As the gun settled between my canvas sneakers, I wondered why she carried it, what she expected to happen. I wondered if she thought she could anticipate my response: she might expect me to take the gun and go to them; she might believe I wouldn't dare.

I stumbled out of the car into the road. Away from the stereo, I heard shouting through the hedge. Nothing particularly loud, nothing that would alarm the neighbors. A staccato drumming of angry voices.

I couldn't leave the gun. I didn't want to touch it again, but I also didn't want to feel responsible for whatever the Lambents might do with it. I reached down through the open door and felt in the darkness until I found it.

I slunk towards the gap in the bushes, my fist tightly clenched around the barrel, not the handle, of the gun. I smelled something, ferocious and fleeting, but it could have been the bile rising from my stomach. I studied the bottom of the driveway, new cement, chalky in the moonlight. My steps hugged the corner, and a saucer of hibiscus flower brushed my face, its sticky stamen crawling along my cheek. I batted it off and saw Muriel, for an instant, fractured into a grid by the small square windowpanes—

—The wall beyond her was yellow and bright—To her right, the edge of the cosy corner cut the light in a dark vertical—Blood flowed in a thin, precise curlicue from a cut on her forehead—In a black frame above her shoulder, a sketch hung—a tortured torso—maybe Egon Schiele—She pulled something—a piece of jagged, broken crockery—from her mouth, couched in more, frothy blood—She wiped her lips and smiled—

—Then I lurched away. I didn't want to see Chaz. I didn't want to observe them. From the speaker in the car door Deborah Harry was singing, in strange, affectless, doo-wop harmony, "Tear drops, tear drops." The Lambents were not fooling. Or if they were fooling, it didn't matter. Like the fight in the parking garage where their lies had ended with Chaz's broken arm, their games always carried a tincture of the real in their rules of play. And I felt it—more clearly than I had ever felt the truth of any event that had not yet happened. Muriel had suggested my part for the evening, the face in the bed of the car had whispered it, but I didn't want to play the sultan or the beast. I knew how this night would end.

# 94

I suppose if the Lambents were angels, it was only proper that some seer would be on hand to warn, to forecast, to prophesy. But I had no one to tell. I wouldn't call the police or Muriel's mother. And I wouldn't care any longer. I walked away, steadily, down the street, down the hill.

A vast rosy Cadillac made a sudden stop with its tires riding over the sidewalk, and I edged out into the center of the road to avoid it. I averted my eyes from the figure emerging from the driver's side of the car. "Peter!" the woman said. I glanced up at a facet of crystal glinting with reflected streetlight.

Although I stared directly at the woman in her toast-colored tracksuit, it took time for me to identify Irena Delgado—perhaps because it was too horrible to believe she was here. Her crystal pendant vied for space around her neck with a pair of compact field glasses as she adjusted a wrap or heavy scarf patterned like a Navajo blanket more tightly over her shoulders. Her face looked different, harder, in the frame of her hair, and I assumed it was an effect of the weak light until I noticed that Irena had plucked her eyebrows and penciled them further up her forehead in sharp arched lines. "I didn't expect to find *you* here," she huffed, although she seemed neither upset nor unduly surprised to see me.

"Neither did I," I said.

"Still, I suppose you put two and two together like I did." Irena slammed her car door and took a few steps towards me.

I remembered the gun in my hand and concealed my fist against the small of my back. "What do you mean?"

"Zu-krall. His Descension. He must be manifesting tonight," she explained patiently. "I always told you the Lambents were special. And when I got that message from Chaz, well, it was the first ray of light for me since the wedding was postponed." She edged closer. "You see, Roy—well, Peggy, Roy's wife, went through a real cancer scare. So it hasn't been a good time for him to make his break. I was let down of course, but now I see it was all for a purpose. Roy is a doubter, and I need to be free of doubt if I want to help Chaz and Muriel out."

"Help them out?" I gulped air; I heard an uncomfortable echo of Muriel's appeal to me.

"Didn't you hear it from Chaz?" she asked, then pressed a finger to her lips. "All right, he didn't actually come right out with it in his message. But it's clear as day they are conduits for the Circle and they've invited me—us, I suppose—to go greet Zu-krall when he comes down."

"You misunderstood. You can't go." I reached under my shirt and pushed the gun into the waist of my pants. I had already seen what was about to happen—with such clarity that I could not let Irena go. I raised my arms to hold her back. "Let's get in the car. Give me a ride down the hill."

"Peter, if you so much as touch me, I will rouse the neighborhood. Are you on drugs? When you lost your hair, I thought it might be chemotherapy. But maybe . . ." Her words drifted off ominously. She backed away from me then turned and hurried up the street towards the house.

"Irena!" I called, but it was no use. She wouldn't stop. I squeezed my face in my hands. Sighing, I took off after her.

By the time I turned the corner, Muriel was already loading Irena into Lady Lazarus. She had one hand cupped beneath the older woman's elbow and pressed Irena's neck down with the other. "Watch your head now."

I looked towards the driver's side to find Chaz standing with crossed arms staring at me. His hair fell white almost to his shoulders in the moonlight. "Go home, Speck," he said. He spoke in a low voice, which wouldn't have been audible if the car stereo were still playing or the breeze had switched course, and I wasn't sure if I was meant to hear it.

Muriel lifted a folded square of paper towel and held it to her forehead. She looked across the roof of the El Camino to Chaz, then followed the angle of his gaze to me. "Where did you run off to, sugar? It seems we have another guest, but there's room for you too. Or you could ride in the back."

"We're not going with you." I moved forward until I could discern the puckered wound on Muriel's temple.

"Who's 'we'?" she asked and looked to Chaz as if he might have the answer.

"Irena and me. You're going to leave us here."

"That's naïve, Speck," Chaz said and reached down to lift a crumpled sack from the ground. As he tossed it into the bed, I heard chains shifting within the brown paper. "Would you like to stay with Keith, Irena?"

Irena's voice emerged muffled from her seat in the center of the cab. "He's being absolutely deranged. What is wrong with that man?" She kept her eyes locked forward and did not shift to look at me.

"I can't leave her with you," I insisted.

"Then you'd better come along and chaperone," Muriel said.

Chaz added, "Don't you think it's wonderful that this green being would come down from space to help us out with all our problems?" His voice trembled with respect and awe, for Irena's sake, but his smile—meant for me—was derisive and broad enough to interpret in the dim street. He twisted to climb behind the wheel and slam the door.

"Let her go." I reached back for the gun. I fumbled for the handle and aimed the barrel at Muriel.

She tilted slightly to speak into the cab. "Peter is quite insistent that you get out and join him."

"The nerve!" Irena shouted and rolled her shoulders. She continued to snub me with the back of her black wedge of hair.

"I'm afraid I can't convince her. But tell me, who put your balls in a vise and turned the screw, sugar?" As Muriel spoke, I noticed how thick and fumbling her voice was, as if her tongue had swollen to fill her mouth. "You know, you always were dismissive of our beliefs. The little pacts we make, the stories we tell, the talismans we keep to get through the day. What were we—just beautiful things to you? Your own interactive exhibit? You were never interested in our spiritual side, like Irena is. She's ready to let us bring heaven down for her. And what did you ever aspire to but a tender kiss before bedtime? We just fought over you, Chaz and me. You see, Chaz had already invited Irena because he thought you wouldn't come. I think he hoped you wouldn't. I defended you, but now I see he was right. You were just a waste of my time."

"You bitch!" My grip trembled around the handle.

"Oh, tough talk. Is this your proletarian moment, sugar?"

I aimed the gun to fire to the left of Muriel over the roof of the car; I wanted it to be a warning shot, but if the bullet went awry, I didn't care. If I had paused to think, insanity would have struck: I was shooting a gun for the first time in my life to rescue a woman I despised from a fate I felt churning in my stomach but couldn't imagine in my mind.

The gun fit comfortably in my grip, but the trigger was stiff, and I probed with my other fingers for the safety and flipped it. The trigger moved, but the chamber clicked with air. Nothing. I tried it several times. Nothing.

Muriel hadn't flinched. "Be seeing you." She laughed and slipped into the cab.

Chaz spun a U-turn around me to point Lady Lazarus down the hill. I turned the gun over and peered down to find that the bullet clip was missing. Chaz killed the engine and leaned out his open window. "That's not going to do it for us, Speck. We're in for something grander and more pathetic." He reached out for my arm and pulled me close. He kissed my cheek. "And she didn't mean to be nasty. Today's just been a disappointment. You have to wonder why she was surprised."

"Stop," I said—half a whisper.

But Chaz put a hand on Irena's shoulder—she avoided looking at me—then he released the brake. They began to roll downhill.

"Stop." Half a shout. I waved the gun then hurled it futilely after them. It disappeared with a clang beside my chair in the bed of the car.

I heard Irena's voice receding down the quiet street. Her head was already just a shadow in the cab. "What did he have, a gun? Would he really have hurt us?"

"His kind," Muriel responded as her voice slipped out of range, "they only hurt themselves."

I watched them go, then shut my eyes. When I opened them again I was more keenly aware of the moon's silver light bathing the world of objects, animating the surfaces of a dead and silent street.

# Tyger, Tyger

# 95

I walked a stretch of Laguna Beach along the Pacific Coast Highway, whose straights and slow curves mirrored the undulations of the coastline. I had come down to the ocean because I couldn't find a road to follow through the hills. When I reached the main beach, I was tired, and I wandered more slowly away from the water into the grid of the central village. I tried to remember street names, the names of galleries, familiar vistas of landscaping or commercial development—anything that would help me find my way back to my car.

I shifted from one dark street to the next, gradually climbing again. I looked for signs of Alta Rosa Drive, but I wasn't concentrating. I drowned in a new emotion. It was a feeling I had fully imagined, craved, anticipated since the night of their party. It was hatred. I hated the Lambents with a force black, toxic, and pervasive. I wanted to flush my pipes with venom. I wanted to vomit them out of me in chunks of burning creosote. I flung myself up steep sidewalks, exhausted but almost running, striving to break into a sweat of angry drops.

But what rose in tandem with the hatred inside me, pulling up from my gut, was love. Love tasting both sour and ripened to rotting, but love nonetheless. Thwarted and baseless, love ached in my stomach and crept to my eyes and wormed through the knots of my nerves.

My hatred made it possible to condemn the Lambents to their fate. Hate spread its viral tendrils to strangle any lingering sympathy I held for Irena. But love worked at me also—not with the wish to save them, but with the counterurge to assist them to a conclusion. That urge seemed the truer response, the deeper homage of devotion to them.

By the time I found a street sign for Alta Rosa, I was out of breath, and my mind no longer raged. I was too conflicted to know what to feel, and my heart just wheezed like a cold engine, barely able to coax out enough power to keep my body in motion. I trudged slowly from one widely spaced streetlamp to the next up the squiggling road to the cul-de-sac.

# 96

I saw my car sitting almost alone on the well-swept street; it glimmered with indefinable color in a light that dripped like weak tea from the lanterns on the wall beside it. My lungs heaved with relief at the sight of its condensed utilitarian shape, the familiar configuration of furnishings inside, the miniature Mackintosh ladderback chair and the museum parking permit dangling from a chain around the rearview. It looked like safety, a friend who had patiently waited.

As I fished for my keys, I looked up into the bowl of the cul-de-sac at the only other car in view, a huge tanker, perhaps a Mercury station wagon. My fingers tumbled the forty or fifty cents in the bottom of my pocket. I squeezed the balled-up cough drop wrapper in my other pocket and stood still waiting for my mind to catch up to the realization that already seeped into my body: Muriel had not given my keys back when she moved the car. I thought this coolly and recognized that she had done this purposely. She hadn't taken the chance that I might slip away before she was finished with me.

I stood there looking at my car as if it were a Chinese puzzle box, a sealed vessel that I might penetrate if I were clever enough. I could imagine finessing the door lock but not starting the car. I scowled at the tiny chair through the windshield and listened to the murmur of a breeze in the heights of the eucalyptus trees.

Then, listening closely, I realized the murmur wasn't breeze but voices, low but animated voices carrying through Muriel's family's garden on the other side of the wall. I walked to the entrance to the macadam drive but paused at the wall's corner outside the spill of light from the house.

"I couldn't believe the expense," a voice was saying. "Might as well have been plastic surgery."

"Well, honey, just so you know, you can get it done cheaper in Corona del Mar. So many salons there, they got to be competitive."

I looked around the edge, risking exposing my face to the light. Zorna stood at the edge of the Zen sandscape with her large hand around Muriel's mother's wrist. She carefully guided the woman's fingers into the beam of a garden spotlight as if she were handling something stunning from Fabergé.

"I wouldn't mind the price so much if it wasn't one of those Oriental girls," Miriam explained in the drilling nasals of a despotic socialite. She was dressed in a silky peignoir that shivered around her body as she stretched her arm into the light. "None of them can speak English, so you have to sit there in dreadful silence while they file away. Still, she did a nice job, I think."

"Lovely," Zorna said. She dropped Miriam's hand and rose to her full height, made more imposing by the tower of long, ribbon-bound dreadlocks on her head. She wore a dark-colored mini-dress in some velvety fabric that absorbed the light.

As I listened to their discourse on manicures, something in my head began to pulse. The irrelevance of their words to this night and this moment twisted with irritation inside me, and I began to feel a hard pressure building. It wasn't love or hatred. Its strongest, salient quality was determination. I wanted to be done with them: with the Lambents, their relatives, their friends, groupies, and confidantes. I wanted to get my car keys, go home, and forget.

I stepped out of the shadow and walked across the uneven paving.

Zorna saw me first and pointed in my direction. "Speak of the devil, and his hooves shall cleave the darkness. Honey, we was just talking about you." When I approached, she snagged my wrist and pulled me close to her. "Actually, Miriam was showing off her new nail wrap." Zorna spoke in her usual drawl of ironic sincerity, but her eyes fixed on mine with the fierce desperation of a hostage in a forced confession video. She batted her two-inch mascaraed lashes cryptologically. "But before that you was all we had on our mind."

"Are my car keys here?" I doubted Muriel had left them in the house, but I glared at Miriam anyway. I didn't care what they had been saying about me; I wasn't concerned how these two divergent worlds of Muriel's had come together. "Do you have any idea where she's gone with them?"

Zorna's hand continued to cling in an insistent vise around my wrist. "S'funny. Cause we want to know almost the same thing, honey. Where *is* that woman?"

Miriam peered skeptically in the direction of my hands. "I can't see how it would take this long to repair a chair. Are you sure you're qualified?"

"I just want my keys."

Miriam rose up on the balls of her feet and looked past my shoulder as if she had noticed for the first time that her daughter wasn't with me. "Where *is* Mary?" The spotlight coursed through her cockatiel hair, and it swelled like a tethered yellow cloud.

"I don't know." I bit harshly at my words.

"That seems rather irresponsible. I hope she hasn't paid you yet." Miriam swished away in her silk gown and stared expectantly down the macadam towards the street. "Mary, where are you? I always told you to work with licensed contractors."

With a clenched rage, I watched her search the yard. She was as monstrously single-minded as Irena.

Zorna must have detected the stiffening in my stance. She loosed her fingers from my wrist and replaced them with a hand on my back. "I'm sure she's just around the corner," she called to Miriam. Her hand guided me firmly away from the Zen garden. "Mr. Peter and I will go out and take a look-see."

"She shouldn't be difficult to find. You must have just left her somewhere." Miriam looked down to recinch the belt of her peignoir, and Zorna and I moved past her towards the end of the drive. "Not that it's any concern of mine. As I was telling Zelda a moment ago, she's a grown woman. She doesn't have a curfew—within reason."

"All right then, dear," Zorna said, "we'll just let you get back to that tome you was analyzing. Bye now!" Turning, she gave Miriam a sort of homecoming-queen wrist-pivoting wave.

"You tell her I'm locking up. She knows where the spare key is." Miriam padded away from us in her Isotoner slippers and sealed herself in behind the heavy front door.

We emerged into the brown lanternlight of the street. "Your wheels or mine, child?"

"I'm not going anywhere. She took my keys."

"My chariot then. Chariot of the Gods!" Zorna strode forward, and I followed her to the station wagon parked in the cul-de-sac. I waited while Zorna searched in a spaghetti strap purse and pulled out a key attached to a long, tangled pendant of feathers and shells. She pushed it into the driver's side lock, hesitated, shifted her weight in consideration from foot to foot in her crushingly high heels, then reached up to her brow with both hands.

What happened next startled me so that I held my breath. Zorna guided her fingers under her hairline and lifted the dreadlocks from her head. She set the wig carefully on the roof where it seemed to crouch like an angry dog in a collar of velvet ribbon. I stared at the mound of hair with repulsed fascination. I had known she was wearing a wig, of course, but it lay in shadow as unnatural as a severed limb. As I looked away at the hair, Zorna rushed forward to pin me against the side of the hood. "Now tell me what the fuck is going on."

Her voice didn't shift genders; Zorna's tone had always been more theatrical than feminine. It didn't drop an octave or lose its shape. But the notes once struck with felt mallets were now rung with steel.

She leaned against me with her hands pressed to the hood behind my back. The hairs on her close-cropped head glistened in the light from the distant streetlamp like a mesh of silver wires. "You going to answer me?"

"I don't know what's going on." I pushed at Zorna's chest to break free, and her breasts compressed with disconcerting realism under my palms. "I want my car keys," I added, somehow defensively. I continued to shove until she sprang back. I moved a few paces from the car.

"You'd better know," Zorna said and crossed her bare arms. "You'd better. Because some weird shit is going down, and I don't understand it." She leaned against the wagon's chrome trim and crossed long legs in front of her.

I cleared my throat. "Why are you here anyway?"

"Why am *I* here? Who's asking the questions, honey? Why am *I* here!" She roared and pushed off the car towards me. "I was doing my gig in L.A., right? I take my bows, my curtain calls, then I go to the phone outside my dressing room and call my machine. There's a message from Chaz." Zorna shifted into a pretty good imitation of Chaz at his most sardonic. " 'Well, well, little Zorna,' he says, 'things are looking up. Or down. Or whichever way damnation goes these days. If you were home, I could've told you about it.' Click. Buzz. End of message." Zorna ran a hand along the back of her neck and looked down past me along the street. "Now do you know how many times Chaz has called me up on the telephone? None. Never. Zero. Zip. Uh-uh. This was *un*-usual. I called Paul—Polly Morpheus—at once. He also got a recorded monologue from Chaz. Same message. Some student Paul talked to at the cabaret did too. Seems Chaz has been reaching out and touching everyone he can think of."

The news stabbed me; he had called Irena, and Zorna, and Polly, and perhaps every performance artist, drag specialist, socialite, and grad student in Orange County—and not me. I couldn't decide whether to be hurt or relieved.

"You know that feeling you get when something's so very very *not* okay it won't wait till the morning to get itself taken care of? I was *out* that stage door. Didn't even grab a wrap. So I get about halfway down the four-oh-five, Lakewood maybe, Bellflower, and I think, shit, girl, you don't know where the bastard lives. He didn't send out one of those change of address cards like you're supposed to. You just can't find that man 'less he wants you to.

"But Muriel, I knew a thing or two about *her*. It's hard to believe she ain't behind this drama somehow, so I scoot my ass up this hill and meet Lady Chatelaine, who's got her finger holding her exact spot in *Plein Air Woman: The Life of Joan Irvine Smith*. And what a fine finger it is. Nail wrap and all. She says she don't know where her daughter is, but I lure her out to the light to have a look at those cuticles so I can maybe squeeze an answer out of her. Then look what the cat drags in. Yourself." Zorna reared up to her full height and glared down at me. "So, Peter-boy, you gonna set my mind at ease, or what?"

# 97

In the station wagon on the way down the hill, I told Zorna the story of Muriel's call and its aftermath. I told her as few of the details as I could and still make sense. Editing the evening to its essentials wasn't easy because I didn't understand what was happening myself; I didn't know what to hide or what to reveal. I told Zorna that Muriel had invited me down. I told her that we had talked, although I was vague about the subject of our conversation. I told her that we had stopped to visit Chaz and that the Lambents had taken my old neighbor away with them. I had a dark, nasty feeling about it, I explained. I tried to stop them; I gave it my best effort. But now I just wanted my car keys so I could go home.

Zorna was dissatisfied, I could tell. She made little doubtful noises as I spoke, but she didn't question or contradict me. Perhaps she thought she had already pushed me too far. Or maybe she was saving her spleen to grill me later. In either case, I was reprieved from discussing the true extent of my involvement with the Lambents. I struck a reportorial tone that involved neither love nor hate for them, and I pretended to be satisfied with the result.

As I finished speaking, we arrived not at the police station, not at the locksmith's, but at Zorna's apartment in North Laguna, where she had taken me so she could change out of her stage clothes. We climbed a creaking staircase that led up from an alley to a studio above a garage. Zorna unlocked the door, then turned to look into my eyes. "You're saying Chaz lives in my town? What does he do? He don't go out. Least nowhere I go, and I've *done* Laguna from Cafe Zinc to Wahoo's Fish Taco. I've never seen him." She plunged into the dark apartment and flipped on a lamp.

The room was a mess. Clothing covered the matted gold shag carpet in an alluvial fan of fashion while the open cupboards in the kitchenette seemed to have disgorged their contents in a single torrent into the sink. "Don't look like the maid's been in."

She took my hand and guided me carefully around a tottering pile of *Interview* magazines and playscripts to a beaten green corduroy loveseat in the center of the sitting area. "Wait here. I'll change. Something less fetching, more—what's the word?—apposite." She disappeared behind a paper screen which half-concealed the bright floral sheets of a mattress on the floor.

I looked down at a framed picture on the coffee table: a postcard of four First Ladies in front of the Richard Nixon Library in Yorba Linda, each in some kind of shiny skirt-suit. Pat, Betty, Nancy, and Barbara. BEST WISHES, POLLY was looped in silver ink in one corner. On the wall before me was a poster of Billie Holiday in a recording studio looking old and frail and gripping a glass as if it held the Water of Life.

"So what do you think?" Her voice sounded faint and hollow as if she spoke from some further recess—the bathroom perhaps.

"What do I think about what?" I wasn't sure I had heard everything she said, so I stepped gingerly around some mysterious piles on the floor and approached the edge of the screen. Along one side of the bed was a long, shallow closet with two half-retracted folding doors. Inside were a series of gowns suspended in carefully wrapped plastic shrouds. On the shelf above the clothes rod, turbans and picture hats alternated with elaborately coiffed wigs. The closet was so tightly organized compared to the front room that it seemed two different people lived in Zorna's apartment. I supposed they did.

"Have you gone stupid or something, honey? Knock-knock. Anybody home behind those shiny little eyes?"

Zorna stood before me wrapped at the waist in a red towel—flesh silky, chest sleek and muscular—with a collection of lingerie and rubbery apparatus strewn below on the floor. Looking at Zorna bare-chested but in full makeup, I realized I had been avoiding the aes-thetics of drag. I didn't want to find myself diverted by any more false finishes or misleading veneers. But my resistance to the styli-zation of Zorna had obscured another sensation: attraction. It was no longer possible for me to dismiss him as a kind of artificial woman, as less than fully human.

I remembered the first time we met in the dressing room of the cabaret. My interest had flickered but soon buried itself in the Lam-bents. Yet now, desire flooded me from the same hard place where my thoughts of the Lambents dwelled. Beyond my uneasy confusion about the crossroads of Zorna's body, Zorna's costume, and the un-known personality that might lurk behind Zorna's performance, I wanted to put my hands on her—*his*—flat stomach. I wanted my mouth spread against his bristling scalp. Some control valve had bro-ken in me, an inner seal shattered, and the intensity frightened me. I didn't want to feel it—not on this night; the timing was unbearable. "Sorry. I didn't hear you right," I said.

"What . . . I . . . said . . . was," he drawled, "what do you think —about the Blond Ones?"

"I told you I'm not going to do anything. I want my car keys."

"Yeah, I think you mentioned your keys about, oh, sixty-nine mil-lion times." His eyes bore down on me. They were hot, intense and shining, like black coals ready to fall against a grate and break to show their fire.

I looked away.

"Stop skulking there and go sit down," he concluded and dis-appeared behind the screen again.

I paced down the path behind the couch and looked across the room at Billie Holiday. Her eyes searched the air—not into the cam-era lens but down and out-of-focus, as if she wondered how she had ended up at the studio and what the fuck she was supposed to do now. "Well, Billie," I said quietly. "I just don't know."

# 98

I sat on the couch while Zorna finished his transformation. I listened to him curse his inadequately appointed vanity table—"Where's the acetone, bitch?"—"Noxema? Noxema, you got?" Then he climbed into the shower. I spent the time trying not to think. The more inevitable it became that I would need to see the Lambents again, the less willing I was to consider it.

Finally Zorna emerged in black jeans and a T-shirt silkscreened with The Human Torch and his word balloon mantra: "FLAME ON!" He dropped down beside me on the couch, which creaked, displeased. "We got to think this out. You said the neighbor lady wanted to go see some green guy?"

"Zu-krall."

"Zu-krall, right. So where's he hang?"

"He's from space. He walks into people's bodies. He could be anywhere."

"Come on. Why you being such a shit?"

"Why do you care so much? So they've gone off looking for UFOs. So what."

"You know."

I did know. I knew what was going to happen; it had fallen like a blow as they drove away. Zorna must have felt it too. But I refused to care.

"You think this neighbor lady's worth less than a cat?"

I didn't look at him but felt his weight shift closer to me on the cushion.

"See, I heard what you did at their party after I left. And I must admit I admire your sense of style. I been called fierce before, but I'm not brave that way. You more than made your point when you took that kitty. You reached them. I don't know if anybody's done that before."

I pulled a pillow into my lap, crocheted with an approximation of a Fifth Dimension album cover.

His body vibrated against the couch with barely suppressed anger. "So you wanna just sit here? And when whatever happens happens, you gonna be comfortable with that decision?"

"If you think there's a problem, let's call the police."

"Sure." He stretched over to a table beside the couch and picked up a pink plastic princess phone, which he set on the pillow in my lap. "Here. You tell them what happened. You say, Officer, these three folks went off sightseeing for space people. And, no, her momma's not going to file a missing person's anytime soon, but I've got a real bad feeling. What do you think the cops'll do?"

"They took my keys. And my chair." I set the phone carefully on the coffee table.

"Okay, so make that your motivation then: you need your keys." With a puff of disgust, Zorna stood and moved through the apartment somewhere behind me.

I stared at the phone until his feet stepped into view in a pair of leather sandals. He crouched down and grabbed my shoulders. "Why're you here?" He shook me. "I mean it. Why did you come with me if you didn't care? We need to figure out where to look."

"She had a gun. She threatened me. Then I had it. And I would have shot them, if there were any bullets." I realized I was barely coherent, but the love-and-hate sensation choked me. I couldn't stop it.

"A gun? Look, I don't know you, Peter. But it don't take no expert to say you've been acting weird all night."

Zorna looked carefully into my eyes. I wondered why he was stroking my forearms until I realized he was trying to calm me down. I was shaking. "Okay," I said quietly.

"Okay?" he repeated, puzzled. He stood again. "Okay, let's rewind for a remix. So, Peter, where do you think they've gone?"

"Palm Springs." As I said the name, I had no doubts. All of Muriel's stories ended in the desert; there was no reason for this one to be any different.

"Palm Springs?"

"We should start in Cabazon. It's on the way." I thought of the baby, the café, the place where the thread of Muriel's maternal journey had snapped. The pressure to be finished with the Lambents resurged. I felt the need to act. I wanted to find my car keys. I wanted to take Zorna's head in my hands. I wanted to take my chair back and focus all my effort on repairing it. I wanted to squeeze something so tightly in my fists that my flesh and bone would fray to the wrists like the ends of a rope. Every impulse gathered into one inchoate throb.

He peered at me a moment longer, as if deciding whether to trust my odd certainty, then he touched his hand to my hair before moving towards the door. "All right. We'll get a map on the way. Let's go."

# 99

With one hand on the steering wheel, Zorna reached down for the purse that sat between us, rummaged inside it for a while, and emerged with a cassette. He held it up for me. "Here. Music." I took the tape and lifted it to the light of headlights behind us. The clear plastic casing was smudged with fingerprints of mascara and blush. M People. I felt for the slot of the tape deck and pushed in the cassette. The electrobeat of the intro to "One Night in Heaven" began —somewhere between a drum, a bell, and a wood block.

We were on the 91 freeway, nearing the interchange with the 15. Our route was PCH to the 73 to the 55 to the 91 to the 15 to the 10 and then, perhaps, the 111. Because distances are reckoned in Southern California not by counties or cities or streets but by freeways, I felt we had made some progress towards our destination—even if I didn't know exactly what the destination was.

We hadn't talked much—I didn't want to make my distress any more obvious to Zorna than it was—but the music shaping the silence beyond the steady knocking of the station wagon's engine seemed to energize Zorna. "You ever had your one night in heaven, Peter?"

"What do you mean?"

Zorna swiveled his head to give me what might have been a smoldering look if I could have seen it in the dark of the car. "You know what I mean. With them. With the Blond Ones."

M People had moved on to another song.

"I don't want to talk about it."

"All right. Just asking." I watched him looking straight ahead, bopping his head to the music. After a time I saw his lips move in profile, perfectly synching Heather Small's voice from the stereo. He flipped on his signal and shifted lanes to make the change from the 15 to the 10. "First time I almost had my heaven night was with Denny Newhouse. I was how old? Don't know. My daddy was still alive. High school in Anaheim. Couldn't drive. Musta been fifteen. It all happened cause I had to get outta gym. 'Stead of basketball— which they wanted me to play since I was, you know, tall and black—I was student aide to a coach who was also a math teacher. I got myself the job of tutoring Denny. He was on the wrestling team and failing pre-algebra, second time as a junior.

"So he was this dumb-fuck jock. But I *knew* he was queer—cause I know these things. And I wan-ted him. Oh, girl. He was all golden-colored under his little tunic, same color as the little dudes on the trophies. He had tawny hair, sorta wavy. Baby freckles on his cheekbones. And sprinkled here and there over his body were these cutest pale, pale hairs. You're not gonna ask me what class wrestler he was, are you? Fuck, you won't ask me anything, just gonna sit there inside your brain and ignore me.

"Featherweight? Flyweight? I don't know. I just know I wanted to pick him up and hug him till he squealed. Though I imagined him small but dense like a neutron star, and his muscles all squeaky and hard like rubber balls.

"We sat in Coach's office doing story problems. Denny in Coach's chair with his hand on this jockstrap Coach kept around to show freshmen at gym orientation. I thought that was a sign for something. So Denny tells me to come over to his house that night. His folks out of town, and he has something to ask me. I go, uh, okay. But I'm shooting sparks out my ass, know what I mean?

"I go, take the bus, and he meets me at the door in a button-down pink Polo shirt—this is the best part of Anaheim, here. He's got The

Cure on his stereo, and he gets me a beer. Löwenbräu. Dad beer. I'm all, sure is a nice place; shit, man, you got cable in your room? And my little heart is *buzzing*, thinking I'm gonna get at least a kiss outta this.

"We sit on the floor, talk and shit, and his stereo shuffles to Siouxsie and the Banshees. He looks down at the sculpture-shag carpet, and I see he's got these wiry eyebrows same tawny color as his hair. You're gay, right? he says. I make this little sound like a 'lectric can opener then say, uh-huh. I guess nobody in high school had a doubt about me.

"Denny Newhouse don't look at me, but his head makes these little nods like I gave the right answer, and also like he got a motor revving. And you're friends with Ted Gerome, right? he asks.

"And I shoulda known what was coming. But I wanted a kiss so much I didn't get it yet. Ted Gerome and I are touring elementary schools in *Huckleberry Finn* for Drama Club. Guess who I play? And me and Mr. Total Drama Fag Gerome spend lots of time sitting on a two-piece foldable raft.

"So is he gay too? Denny asks. And I finally get it. I feel all punched and airless. Denny Newhouse wants Ted Gerome's body bad—he tells me all this later—and I'm the good black fairy that's gonna make it happen for the boys. But it's not s'posed to go like that. Blond Denny drooling for pale little heart-faced Ted. S'posed to be opposites that attract, right? Ebony and ivory side by side on my pya-no.

"I sit there and hear The Dreams of Denny Newhouse starring Ted Gerome in Technicolor, and my soul just dies. Turns out I'm too gay for this boy. Too fem, too black. He don't exactly call me nigger, but he makes it clear we dark-skinned gentlemen don't even show on the radar. I see the future then. I don't fool myself this is the last time this is gonna happen.

"I take Denny to the *Huckleberry* cast party so he and Ted can end the night with their tongues down each other's throats. And I hate myself. I'd thought the world—if I could get a driver's license and a car—would be so cool and queer. Gothic drag. Nights prowling from one hot club to the next. Life as an endless dance mix. But it was shit. With no Denny Newhouse to take me away from all that, I got stuck in Orange County. A community college drama major. Poor Jeremy was in it deep for years till he met the Lambents." He was silent while the tape flipped over in the stereo. "That's my name, by the way. Jeremy. Case you was wondering."

# 100

I hadn't been wondering about his name or anything else he said. I listened to Zorna/Jeremy, but while I was glad to hear his voice—to fill the dead hours of the trip if for no other reason—I wasn't able to transform his strings of words into meaningful thoughts in my head. Maybe I didn't want to. Maybe I didn't want to hear the story of another lonely soul full of vague longings who was transformed by the ministrations of the Lambents.

"Nineteen years old, I'm just a boy with spandex shorts and attitude trying to flee the surfer skinheads on my roller skates," Jeremy continued as we sped out into the blank black desert. "My father was dying of cancer from the chemical shit he worked with at the plastics factory. My mother went back to teaching second grade to pay bills. No money for me to go away to school. But I couldn't stand it at home. I moved down to a winter rental on the Balboa Peninsula with three other student boys. There was Paul—you know, Polly Morpheus—and Carl, who was too queer, and Clint who was just sooo confused. We was all confused. I was in the drama program. S'posed to have color-blind casting, but I still couldn't get a decent part.

"Afternoons, I'd go to the Lady Cow, that coffeehouse, and sip on some iced tea and think about the department or Denny Newhouse or some depressing shit. And one day I notice across the room this blond woman giving me attitude. When I say blond, I mean ice queen. Whiter-than-Marilyn hair and all bound up her black leather skirt. She's casting eyes my way like I don't belong in her view. And my head's twirling, going, where's this racist bitch get off looking at me?

"Sometimes I lack what you'd call restraint. I sauntered up to her, and I was gonna dis her down, take her head right off. But I get there and she smiles up and says, 'I bet you look sensational in heels.'

"Well, shit. What can you say after that? So I just sit right down next to her, and she tells me about the outfit she's got all picked out for me. Pretty soon we're in the Lady Lazarus cruising down the Coast Highway to Laguna. She's seen this gown in a thrift store. These silver sandals with stiletto heels. I'm supposed to study for a biology midterm. Instead, I'm riding the fucking Whirl-*wind*. I'm stripped to my Hanes in the men's dressing room pulling on this green chiffon frock, and I think, what kinda woman would've worn this thing? Cause it fit me fabulous. Like it was made for me, you know? In three hours, the Divine Zorna was born.

"I'd never done drag before, never *thought* about it. All right, so maybe I thought about it. But it was my first time in chiffon. And it wasn't like the Blond Ones *made* me do it. They made me *want* to do it.

"They took me to the cabaret. Her and Chaz, the Blond Stranger. He was bored—you could tell—but he didn't say nothing. Just sat there with his arms crossed while some guy got pierced in the tits and covered with candlewax. But her, the Princess was swimming in her own pool. She said how I was a natural for the stage and that was where she wanted me to be. I wasn't in no costume—yet. I wasn't up there on stage—yet. But I was bound for lip-synch glory. No choice in the matter.

"Next weekend I went to their place with my Donna Summers, my Dianas and Dionnes, and my Gloria Gaynors, my palms all sweating over the sides of the jewel boxes. Chaz takes one look at my selections and says, 'I really don't care, you understand, but this won't cut it.' He goes to a shelf and picks out a stack of fifties jazz and pop. Chris Connor, he gives me. June Christy. Anita O'Day. 'Here's what you need,' he says. 'Women so cold and white they make your teeth ache.' I resist—no thank you, nothing but soul food for me—but he was dead-on right, *naturally*."

Jeremy stopped talking while he changed lanes and glided past the shimmering silver length of a semi propane tank.

Naturally, I thought, Chaz's musical instincts were right; naturally Muriel's choice of gowns was fabulous. The Lambents were masters of presentation and surface, with a refined sense of proportion and drama. They understood instinctively how to bring unifying structure to every aspect of their lives—even their desperation and despair. One of them had called me; the other had called everyone but me. Their actions were complementary, like echoing reflections in elegant mirrors. Although their approaches differed, their intentions seemed identical. I was certain they treated me as they did out of the strength of their feelings for me—whatever those feelings were. Muriel wanted me to share in their fate; Chaz apparently wished to exclude me from it. But beneath their divergence lay the mechanisms of an inescapable symmetry.

It sickened me to recognize the extent to which our current identities—mine and Jeremy's—were dependent on the Lambents' designs. His music and my chair. His gowns and my haircut. And if the Lambent-constructed world had broken down beneath its polished surface, as Muriel indicated, what did that mean to us? We might not have a choice but to continue the functions they had assigned to us. I burned with rage—rage forged of disgust at my obedience, and of desire to act. I wanted to be rid of them. At the same time, the size of my anger made me afraid to go on.

I looked around the headrest to the rear window where Orange County vanished more completely with each bend in the road and wished I could convince myself to urge Jeremy to turn back.

"The Blond Ones were twin stars," Jeremy continued, "and I was a satellite. For a time, a short time, I thought they was all I ever wanted. Fuck Denny Newhouse. Fuck racist Anaheim. Fuck the Drama Club. I had a gig. I was heading for the big time. I was Miss Zorna!

"So I was a happy boy. But even so I remembered my grandmother's saying. She wasn't the type of ole granny full of folk wisdom; she was up to date. She'd sit there with her feet up after work watching *In Search of . . .* or reading the *Weekly World News,* something about the yeti or ETs at Chappaquiddick. When I was still living at home, I'd tell her about some shit happened to me at school, and she'd look over the top of the paper. 'If you're dealin' with devils,' she'd say, 'you got to hold your nose so you don't smell the sulfur.'

"I don't know what she meant by that exactly. But I took it that sometimes if you need to play along with a game to get where you need to go, you may not like it, but you got to ignore who you're playing with.

"The old woman was full of useless advice, but this one little bit came back to me cause it didn't take me long to catch a whiff of that particular perfume on the Blond Ones. They had an underside. I didn't know what, but creatures of sun like they are, they cast mighty long shadows. Cold and clammy shade they can throw on you, full of slime and toadstools. I took care to stay out in the light, pretend there wasn't no dark.

"I was at one of their parties. My first one. I wore something real showstopping. It was always Miss Zorna, not Jeremy, went to these big affairs. I'm having a fine time. I *work* that room. Until it's time for Cissy. Time for some fun, somebody says. I ask this old woman in Chanel with braids wrapped on her head like earmuffs, what's next? She leans into me, confidential, and says, the Blood Sport. Lady's oh-so-droll. Very Roman, she says; I suppose they had something of the sort in Africa, too.

"Africa? Africa, honey? Charming lady. Knows just what to say to make me feel comfortable. I'd be ready to push her face in the punch bowl. But Zorna has all the social graces in the family, so she just keeps smiling through until Chaz brings in a puppy. A puppy and a pocket knife. Then Zorna makes her exit. Quickly. I never stayed for that. But I always came back, holding my nose. Even when I didn't need them, when Miss Zorna could stand on her own spike heels. I love the monsters."

"I don't," I spat out quickly. "I hate them."

"That I don't believe. Why else you driving three hours in the middle of the night if you don't care about them?"

I fidgeted in my seat. "I'm not doing it for them."

"You want to rescue the neighbor lady? Or you still worried about your car keys?"

"I want to get it over with. I want to be finished with them!"

I spoke more loudly and harshly than I had intended, and Jeremy's head swerved from watching the road to examining me in my side of the car. "You know, I like you, Peter. Have done since I first met you. I saw you with Muriel and thought, whoa, how's that gonna work? He's too nice for the Blond Ones. Won't know how to take care of himself. I liked that about you. You made a good impression on Miss Zorna. When I heard about you and the kitty, it made me think, he's tougher than I thought. And I liked you more." He reached out to touch my shoulder. I wanted him to touch me; I tried not to flinch. "But tonight, I don't know. You're not telling me the whole story. I get the feeling you know the Lambents a whole lot better than I do. But okay, I respect that. You don't know me. No one says you have to tell me shit. How-*ever*—" His hand pulled away from me. "—don't you think I got a right to know what you think we're gonna find when we get wherever it is we're trying to get to?"

I strove to speak quietly but carefully. "I don't know what will happen. Honestly. All I know is I have to get there." I slid my hand across the seat between us, past the purse, until the side of my palm grazed his leg. "I'm glad for your help." It was good to touch him, although it was difficult to keep the feeling separate from the other emotions surging in me.

I watched Jeremy reach down to poke very tentatively at the back of my hand with a fingertip. When I looked up, I saw the road sign. "Cabazon! We need to get off."

He jerked the station wagon into the right lane, and we coasted down the exit ramp. We turned onto a dark frontage road and drove until we reached a small cluster of buildings. "Muriel mentioned this place this afternoon. We should ask if they've been here. Just in case. Maybe get a map." Jeremy slowed on the blacktop. "You try the gas station. I'll check out the restaurant." Before he could park the car and tell me what he thought of my plan, I was already opening my door.

# 101

The manager of the café stood behind the back counter topping off pots of mustard with a spoon from a huge plastic jar. I had read somewhere that topping off condiments was now illegal, so it wasn't surprising she was doing it in the middle of the night. The waitress at the door had nervously deflected my question and pointed to the woman at the back. She wore the same peach dress with white piping as the waitress but lacked the stiff triangular cap across her hump of auburn hair. She acknowledged me with the briefest glance without raising her head from her task. "Kitchen's closed."

"Oh. I thought you were open all night." The sign on the roof said 24 HR EATS.

"We're open. We break the kitchen down for cleaning two to four. You can get coffee. Coffee and Danish. Whatever's in the case." She shrugged her shoulder towards a glass and stainless steel box suspended above the coffee pots behind her: banana cream pie, Jell-O with whipped cream, a plate of coffee cake shriveled and dry as a desiccated fetus.

"Actually I was supposed to meet some friends here, but I'm a little late. Maybe you could tell me if they were here. A man and a woman? Both blond. Very striking looking. And an older woman with dark hair and a kind of Navajo blanket wrap?"

"When?"

"Maybe two, three hours ago?"

"Not my shift." She scraped a knife along the top of the mustard pot to even out the contents, then screwed on the lid.

"Oh. Guess I'll just get a map of Palm Springs then. Do you have one?"

She started digging into the larger jar with her spoon again. "Rack by the register."

I lingered in the aisle. I had another question, which was the reason I had sent Jeremy to the gas station next door. I didn't want to reveal Muriel's story to anyone until I knew how to respond to it myself. The possibility of fatherhood made me uneasy—even speculatively, even in fantasy. I looked around at the formica-topped table booths with their plump vinyl cushions in optimistically mellow seventies shades of Harvest Gold and Avocado, and I felt the stab of family life—vacations, Sunday outings, nights when Mom was too tired to cook. I thought of Muriel in sensible flats, a diaper bag slung diagonally in a maternal bandolier across her shoulders, the handles of a molded plastic infant carrier in her grip. She was forced to live out a domestic scene rather than observe it, as she had with Irena, from the cool, cruel vantage of the sidelines. For a moment, the image was more vividly real to me than the vision of Irena and the Lambents on the move in the night. I felt responsible, but I didn't know where my responsibilities lay.

"There's something else," I said and stepped closer to the counter between two mushroom-capped stools. "I was curious . . ." My question was so odd I had to gather my courage to ask it. "Did anyone leave a baby here recently? I mean, just leave a baby in a baby seat and walk out and never come back?"

The woman looked up at me for the first time. I couldn't avoid staring at the pattern of red veins spidering in S-curves across the whites of her eyes. I had the distinct impression that her eyes had been trained to function only under fluorescent lights, that we had entered the unassailable territory of the night. "What kind of question is that?" she snapped.

"I just wondered. I'd heard something." I stumbled trying to think of a quick and reasonable explanation of my interest.

"What kind of question is that? Does this look like that kind of place? Where something like that could happen?" She pointed at me with her mustard spoon.

It looked exactly like that kind of place. Empty. Isolated in a pass between northern hills and mountains to the south. Buzzing beneath a thin, almost metallic Muzak, with the electric pulse of cash registers, light bulbs, the hotplates under coffeepots, the swoosh of water hosing down thick rubber mats in the parking lot outside. I could see Muriel looking down at her child, its eyes screwed up and rheumy with tears, a comma of saliva on its chin, toothless gums stretching across the gap of a scream. I could see her turn on her heels, gliding across the linoleum, her hand resting an instant on the metal doorframe, not looking back.

"Fine," I said. "It's not that big a deal." I backed away from the counter.

"Bastard. Asshole." The woman barked, and her eyes darted towards the front. "Did Tracy send you back? Tracy! This man wants to buy a map!" She shooed me with the spoon. "Go on. Get out of here. Rack by the register."

Tracy, the waitress I first spoke to, met me at the front desk and looked uncertainly from me to the manager and back. I lifted a map from an assemblage of postcards and giftbooks and handed it to her. She flipped it around in her hands, scanning its surface carefully for the price.

"It's on the front," I said. In large white numbers in a large white circle.

"Oh." She rang up my sale and took my money. My change poured from the side of the register, down a slide, and into a built-in cup. "Don't worry about her," Tracy said and bit the cuticle of her thumb. "She's the biggest bitch ever."

I smiled. I was about to ask about Muriel and the baby again when she leaned across the counter with her eyes twisted sideways to watch out for the manager. "They were here," she said. "Earlier. A pretty woman and her husband. And a sweet-looking lady with black bangs."

"Did you talk to them?"

She shook her head. "It's not my table. They're friends of yours?"

"But did you maybe hear them say where they were going?"

"No. But I remember the woman asked for a pen 'cause she took it with her, and Maeve—she had their table—had to borrow one of mine." She reached under the counter and pulled out a package of napkins. "Then after they left, I was on break. Outside with a cigarette. And the woman was in the phone booth looking in the book."

"Did you see what she was looking for? Or did she make a call or . . . ?"

The waitress didn't answer. The manager was bustling towards us, so Tracy squeezed the package of napkins in both hands and scurried at high speed across the room.

I left the café and crossed to the open space beyond it, where the massive dinosaurs rose up to meet the stars. There were no spotlights on, and they seemed more cloudy black masses than creatures. There was a gift shop in the body of the Brontosaurus—Closed. I had no idea what lurked inside the Tyrannosaurus Rex. I walked around them, between them, but they didn't come to life for me. They were just concrete.

I reached the lighted phone booth and slid past the folding door that was stuck half-opened. I pulled up the Yellow Pages on its chain. I knew where to look first: under H. Hotels.

But there was no Seraglio anywhere in the Coachella Valley. I had followed them this far to reach a dead end in a phone booth. I leaned heavily against the glass wall, with no will to move, and the phone book began to slip from my hands. A few pages flipped back.

In the lower left corner, on an eighth of a page, I saw a minaret. I spread the book open in both hands and stared at the ad. The Ali Baba Motor Court. Just off the Pines to Palms Highway, Route 74 in Palm Desert. There was a motto calligraphed in neat ballpoint on either side of the minaret's crowning spire: *Born in silks, the princess now lives in penury* . . .

I ripped the page out, squeezed through the broken door, and streaked for the car.

# 102

Jeremy was waiting in the station wagon when I arrived. He seemed to be asleep. He had cocked his seat back, and his head nestled against the headrest, his face half-turned to me in the dark, his eyes closed. I opened the door and climbed in, but he didn't stir.

I was about to wake him and tell him what I'd discovered and that we had to hurry. But for an instant, instead of panic—even though it seemed clear from the scrap of yellow paper in my fist that Muriel had anticipated me—I felt a quiet elation. My desire to find them and finish things was too intense for Muriel's manipulations to dissuade me. My blood rushed. I didn't understand what I was doing, but I stretched across the pull-down armrest separating Jeremy's seat from mine and fit my mouth over his. I used my lips to open his slack mouth and brushed the tip of my tongue across the slick plates of his teeth. I slid my hand between his neck and the upholstery to adjust the angle of his head, trying to unlock the chamber of his mouth with my tongue. As he woke up or roused himself, his jaw shifted beneath mine, half responding, half reluctant. I was too close to see if he had opened his eyes. "Found them," I breathed, then closed contact again over his mouth.

His hand rose to push at my chest, not hard enough to break away, but steadily. The pressure of the Lambents entered me again. Desire, disgust, and something I couldn't name, which burned very much like violence.

He pushed me off firmly. "Whoa, Peter." He wiped wet from the corner of his mouth. "Let's not forget what we're doing out here."

"I'm not," I said. But I did want to forget. My elation had faded. I didn't try to kiss him again. I slumped back hard in my seat and looked down at my map, at the map Jeremy must have found, and at the crumpled fragment of phone book, half in and half out of my lap.

"I fell asleep," Jeremy said as he started the engine. "The dude at the gas station saw them. Blond lady asked which exit to take to go up the mountains, then tipped him ten dollars." He backed the car out of the space and headed for the freeway entrance. "So I got directions on a map and looked for you in the café, but you weren't there. Then I got *tired*."

I wanted to forget. I wanted to pretend we hadn't found them; an hour before it had seemed unlikely that we would. But they could not be avoided. I wanted to cry out, although I wasn't close to crying. I wanted to call up Anthony, to jerk off and not think. I wanted to fuck Jeremy senseless. I wanted to ride his cock until I bled and red heat clenched my stomach and vertigo rocked my head. Anything to delay, to forget.

But instead, I would need to act. I couldn't avoid it. As we entered the empty freeway, all I could see was Muriel on her earlier trip as she turned the key in Lady Lazarus and drove away. "Bye, baby. Bye, sugar," she said and tossed the diaper bag out the window, where it bounced along the shoulder into the median. The El Camino drove on without touching ground, and the white windmills in the hills around Palm Springs sliced the air with celestial applause, the sounds of cupids clapping wings.

# 103

Palm Springs and its sister cities curved lushly along the base of suddenly rising mountains like a hallucinated Orange County coastline planted in baking desert sand. Their appeal to Muriel was obvious: the valley shimmered as impossibly as a magical Arabian mirage—if Scheherazade had seen fit to conjure endless golf courses and tennis clubs. There was something to appeal to Chaz as well: an undercurrent of sun-blasted impermanence, as if space travelers had colonized too close to a supernova sun and now awaited their millenial doom.

As we cut through the dark, along the broad, vacant streets of Palm Desert, my eyes were drawn to the entrances of one country club after another where lighted gatehouses were the chief signs of life. We had continued on the 10 and gotten off at Date Palm Drive because I thought we had gone too far. We turned left on Dinah Shore Drive, then made a premature right on Bob Hope and another left on Frank Sinatra. I had revealed our destination to Jeremy, but I was no longer sure I wanted to find it. I was tempted to lead us on a blind quest down Gerald Ford, Fred Waring, and Country Club Drive as well. But eventually we reached Monterey, which became the 74, and there were no diversions left to make.

At a turnout at the bottom of a steep hill, a simple painted sign cut in the shape of a minaret topped a cairn of rocks. Jeremy slowed the car and turned to me expectantly. I nodded. We started our ascent.

The road was paved but crumbling and rose sharply in a scar sliced across the face of the hill. Gravity pressed me back into my seat as the car made an extreme upward-tilting turn. Then another rising straightaway. And another banking switchback.

After a final precipitous climb, I saw the Ali Baba. It was nothing like the Vegas-Arabian fantasy Muriel had described. It was not the Seraglio. I was almost certain I had never been there. Across a weedy gravel parking lot, the buildings stood low and brown like barracks. A short drive led off the road to a similar but smaller brown structure with white letters painted on its doorsill: OFFICE. No lights welcomed us there, and there were no lights over the parking lot, only a dim streetlamp across the road in front and one lit window at the far end. As our headlights swept over the rectangle of gravel, I spotted a single car in the lot: Lady Lazarus—without my chair in her bed.

Jeremy pulled up to the office and shut off the engine. We paused in the sudden stillness.

"So what now?"

"Why ask me?" I said. "You talked me into this."

He snorted doubtfully and looked into his purse.

I got out of the car silently and walked down the drive and across the road to the opposite shoulder where the hill sheered away sharply into sand and scrub. I followed the road down with my eyes as it switched back and forth like a snake, then joined up with the highway below. Under clear starlight in one direction, I sensed the invisible surrounding hills open up to a spray of lights lining the streets of Palm Desert. The view was blank dark in the other direction, but I knew from the map that Route 74 climbed into the mountains up to the Idyllwild Ski Area. I wanted to flee into those mountains, into the cool, vast sky. I never wanted to turn around and face what lurked at my back.

Jeremy had crept up behind me, and when he touched my arm, I flinched forward. A few pebbles scudded audibly down the hill beneath my feet. I jerked around, and he put his fingers to my lips. "We should go take a look."

I followed him up the drive and past the station wagon in front of the dark office. We kept close to the side of the building under the overhanging eaves. As we neared the lighted window directly in front of Lady Lazarus, I stopped walking and shut my eyes. I didn't want to open them, but Jeremy pushed his palm between my shoulder blades. We crouched then and pushed our way through the tall weeds that spread before the concrete foundation of the building.

The curtains were a cheap, loose weave, like burlap, and the light hemorrhaged through them over our heads. Jeremy had brought us this far, but he lost his confidence. He squatted with his back against the wall, breathing hard, and motioned me to rise. "You first," he said.

I tilted forward to balance against the wall with my fingertips and rose up until my eyes were just above the sill. I winced at the window as if it were an open wound. Through the weave, I saw a cone of light around a squat lamp, on a nightstand, with a shade too small for its base. The geometrics of the room beyond this central glow grew less and less distinct. There was a bed on either side of the light. One was tucked neatly into a bedspread of garish diagonal rainbow stripes. The other had been stripped of its cover, and blankets, sheets, pillows, and bolsters were heaped together in a white pile on the bottom sheet. There might have been a passage or another door at the back of the room. From my vantage through the gauze of the curtain, the deep shadows there seemed tinted. Like the gloom of a dense forest, deep but green.

There was no movement in the room, no sign of habitation—no clothes, no purses, luggage, cigarettes, or plastic wrap from sanitized cups. I didn't see my chair. "No one's in there," I whispered to Jeremy.

He stood up slowly. "Seems like nobody's in the whole place."

I straightened up until I could balance without touching the wall. Further up, the two halves of the curtains closed unevenly, leaving a narrow oval porthole between them. I pressed my cheek to the glass and peered in with one eye. I saw the nightstand, the untouched nearer bed, the green gloom at the rear in an alcove leading to a closed door. Then as my gaze shifted, color in the jumble of whites on the far bed flashed like a bird darting dark across a bright horizon.

I had thought the pile was a fortress of pillows and bedcovers. But it was more than that. In the center of the heap, a flower of blood bloomed through a sheet, thick as a fist.

"Oh, fuck." I dropped to my knees and pulled Jeremy down. But not before he glanced into the gleaming pupil of the curtains. "What?" he said, then, "Oh."

I couldn't speak or breathe, just stared at the ground until he put his arm around me. I didn't relax into his embrace. My muscles tightened. My jaw clenched. I pried a harsh whisper out of my throat. "You need to get the police."

"Right. Let's go." He rose to a crouch and reached out to grab my hand.

"*You* go. There was a phone at the gas station down the hill. The last intersection."

"You gonna *stay* here?"

"What if they leave? Or what if they come back from . . . wherever . . . and take the . . . Irena. One of us has to."

He gave me one of his penetrating stares. "You brave or stupid, honey? I can't tell." But he didn't reject my plan as I hoped he might.

"Stay out of the way. I'll come get you. By the bushes, by the office." Then, bent over, he ran back along the building and across the pavement.

I waited as he turned over the engine, and turned the car around, and gunned it down the hill, loudly enough for anyone nearby to hear it. As I waited, hard pressure built in me until I didn't care how long it took Jeremy to find a phone. I preferred to have him out of the way. I had been able to save Speck; I couldn't save Irena. However, I wasn't too late to act.

I scrambled along the wall of the building, dodging weeds, and climbed onto the small wooden stoop in front of the door. My fingers closed around the knob. I assumed the door would be unlocked. It was.

# 104

"Boo."

Chaz said the word, but his voice, from inside the black rubber mask, was so wet and blubbery, so sonically compromised, that it sounded more as if he were spitting out a pit.

He crouched in the grommet-eyed mask and his briefs (maybe even the ones I swooned to my face in his bedroom) on the wood-grain plastic bureau that stood against the wall out of view from the window. He lurked like a part of Fuselli's nightmare: the little bug-eye who crushes the chest and steals the breath. He, or the mask at least, was staring directly at the door—at me—when I opened it.

His body was very still, his chest convincingly sculptural, although there were scratches all over his shoulders. His taut skin had the matte sheen of dried sweat, and one of his thumbs, which bracketed his knee, was blue under the nail, as if he had dropped a weight on it. Beneath and beyond him, a sickly green light leaked out from under the bathroom door.

I allowed myself to make these observations and distancing, painterly allusions because I needed the time to decide how to act.

There were options. The room was not as pristinely ordered as it had seemed from the window. If I was searching for something to grab, there was a length of rusty pipe with one end tightly wrapped in a clingy produce sack at the foot of the closest bed. On the near end of the bureau was a hunting knife; a column of viscous blood hung between the tip of the blade and the surface of the bureau like a thread of come between dick and belly.

Most tempting was the gun. My chair stood under a coatrack next to the door. I examined it, relieved to see it was unharmed, and found the gun sitting in its lap. This time a bullet clip protruded a few inches from the handle like a sample of fruit sliced to reveal its black flesh and ordered row of golden seeds.

I avoided looking at the bed across the room, where an almost indetectable curlicue of black hair emerged from the top of the twisted but utterly motionless sheet. I breathed through my mouth to avoid the room's sickly perfume of copper and meat.

"I hate you," I said.

Chaz scuttled a few inches, crablike, along the bureau top, then dropped to the floor. He strode towards me with his dick half full in the pouch of his briefs. He raised his arm to push me out the door, and as his fingers dug into my clavicle, I wrapped mine around the doorjamb.

"Get out," he said, pressing his head to the crook of my neck. "You're not invited." He pushed his hissing, slurping, dark, wet farts of sound into my ear. My body was canted back over the stoop, the muscles stretching and screaming in my gripping arm, when green light exploded in a corona around the bald pate of the mask.

"That Peter, sweetie?" Muriel asked from the back of the room.

Chaz stopped pushing. He twisted away and leaped onto the unrumpled rainbow bedspread. Facing into the room, he looped the waist of his briefs under his balls and started pulling at his dick.

"I forgot to give your keys back," she said. "Sorry, sugar."

Green light poured from the bathroom behind her. Wet tendrils of hair dripped over her forehead as she felt around the waist of her dressing gown.

I stepped deeper into the room and shut the door behind me.

"Complacencies of the peignoir," she said. "I wear this every day and still can't find the pockets. Ah, here." She pulled my keys from a slit at her hip and came towards me. When she held them out to me, I flinched. She shrugged. "Whatever." She set them next to the knife on the bureau and walked away.

I watched Muriel's back. I watched Chaz jerking his dick at Muriel's back. I looked at the gun.

Muriel entered the bathroom, entered the insectile light. There was a swishing, scraping sound; then the light went out. She returned holding a green lightbulb by the glass end with a washcloth. She looked at the rosette spreading steadily across the bed sheet. She spoke to it. "May I present Zu-krall, dear." She tugged the sheet until I saw that the curlicue of hair was not Irena's but the gorilla's. The simian mask was inhabited now by glassy eyes. A silk-wrapped chain collared its throat. Muriel dropped the bulb at the foot of the bed. "You might have waited till you actually saw the fucker before you took your clothes off, silly woman."

With both hands, Muriel scraped her wet hair back into a cap on her skull. Turning, she scrunched her face in irritation at Chaz's erection, at his mask, then smiled at me. The cut on her forehead also smiled. "We got bored waiting for you to get here. We tried to carve OH ECSTASY on Irena's thigh with an X-Acto knife. It's harder to do than it sounds. We didn't finish. It says O HEC. Guess we should have picked something simpler."

Chaz came in short, ropy driblets. They landed on the bedspread and maintained their querulous shapes on the slick, probably Scotch-guarded surface. I saw there was no bottom to the Lambents. Their souls stretched down and down into an unquenchable well. In answer, pressure boiled up from the depths of me. I reached for the knife.

I picked up my keys instead. I put them in my pocket and looked back at Muriel.

"Peter! You asshole!" she screeched. "Aren't you ever going to *do* anything?"

My understanding came as quickly and definitively as a bullet clip snapping into place. The pressure inside me. My determination. It was *their* feeling. *They* had put it in me. *They* had cultivated it. *They* wanted it to blossom. All these weapons, all in easy reach.

They were begging for it, and the only way I could imagine to save myself was not to give them satisfaction. If I had learned how to lead my life from the Lambents, I had also learned not to pretend that my choices weren't my own. I no longer wished to be the mannequin my father posed and studied at the trade show. I was not under glass; I was a real boy now. And if I raged among all their chains and masks, I would become just another angry puppet in their cabaret.

Muriel rushed towards me, her hands in claws, her face in an openmouthed grimace.

I grabbed for the knife instinctively, but Chaz pounced on her before she reached me. They fell to the ground at my feet and scuffled. Chaz pinned Muriel's arms with his knees and sat on her. He lifted the pipe off the floor, and I thought he would stave her head in. Instead he laid the bar across her throat and scooted up her body to press it down with his knees. From that position he could reach out towards a pile of clothes and pillows near the other bed. He seemed to have difficulty locating the pile through the mask.

While he searched, Muriel's arms and legs kicked and flailed through the air like a bug's with a severed head.

Chaz found a set of manacles and flopped back onto Muriel's stomach. He began to work her hands into the rings. The cross-hatched plastic of the knife grip started to hurt the web of flesh at the base of my thumb.

Muriel jerked her head up, and the pipe fell from her throat and thudded on the carpet. She kicked me in the shin with her bare foot. Not very hard. "Do it, Peter! Do it!" Her voice was hoarse, strangulated. "This isn't baroque enough for you?" She dropped her head heavily onto the rug. She sighed. "I have such bad taste in men."

"I'm taking my chair," I said. I dropped the knife and touched the chair's fan of wooden feathers; this was what I wanted.

Chaz dragged Muriel until she was sitting upright with her back against the bed.

I ran my fingers along the ridged top of one of the chair's wings. Then I grasped the back and tilted the chair forward. The gun slipped from the cushion. It didn't fire when it hit the carpet; it made a disappointingly hollow thunk, like a toy.

I reached behind me to open the door. They didn't notice. While Chaz stepped away to pull on his khaki shorts, Muriel somehow managed to pick up the fallen knife. When he returned, she poked him in the side, in the ribs. A small but steady stream of blood coursed along the ridged path of his serratus muscle. He smacked her across the face. He let her keep the knife.

Chaz ripped the sheets and pillows from the heap on the bed. I looked for an instant below the gorilla mask at tanned leathery skin, yellow-sheathed bonds wrapped around and around, and blood. Chaz began to pull at the chains.

I carried my chair outside and shut the door.


# 105


It was quiet in the parking lot of the Ali Baba Motor Court. Every window remained dark but the one behind me. Unless they were deaf or distressingly uncurious, there could not be any other guests to hear the noise from Room 108. Maybe Muriel had rented the entire motel for the night. Or bought it. It didn't matter.

It was so quiet that I heard the knocking of Jeremy's engine from a distance and lugged the chair over to the edge of the road to look down. There were headlights pulling up the road near the minaret sign. I decided to meet the station wagon partway. I didn't want to wait.

I stumbled down the steep road with the chair held out in front of me; it was heavier than I remembered. I started in the gravel of the narrow shoulder, but the ground dropped away too uncertainly at my feet. It was easier to walk and balance the seat rail against my hip on the pavement.

When I was out of sight of the Ali Baba, I heard the engine of Lady Lazarus awake with a cough, reluctant to come to life. Below me, Jeremy's station wagon had made the lower switchback and was now climbing steadily.

Tires squealed; a motor roared. I looked back up the hill. It was hard to see past the blazing lamps in the front grille, but there must have been some light filtering from the streetlamp above. Chaz was visible driving the El Camino, still in the rubber mask. Muriel writhed at his side, trying to gain control of the steering wheel, possibly the gas pedal. But she could only flail ineffectually within the confines of the manacles. I couldn't tell if she still held the knife. To complete their theatre of the absurd, they had taken time out to lash Irena's naked, masked body across the hood like a hunting trophy.

Lady Lazarus wasn't moving very quickly towards me, but fast enough.

I glanced down. Jeremy was just entering the last upward curve; he couldn't yet see me or the car on the road above.

I wondered where to jump out of the way. The El Camino was weaving across both lanes. I thought if I stayed in the middle of the road until the last moment . . . I don't know what I thought.

Muriel started clawing at the rubber expanse of Chaz's head, and I realized that I could see them as well as I did because they had flipped on the overhead light. Their cab was lit up behind the windshield like a little stage. Punch and Judy.

Tufts of fur on the gorilla head whipped horribly in the air speeding over the hood. Zu-krall in flight.

Muriel stopped abusing Chaz and looked down the road at me. "Go! Go! Go!" I heard her shout at Chaz over the engine. "For you, Peter! For you!" The station wagon pulled out of the turn, and Jeremy must have seen me because I heard the sharp whine of his brakes.

I had been clutching the chair to my chest, but I dropped it with its feet to the ground and ran. I scrambled to find a foothold over the sheer side of the shoulder, then looked back at the chair standing in the dark, its tail and wings rising from the pavement.

Chaz slowed the car and turned his head in my direction. His expression couldn't tell me anything. It was just a pattern of silver beads on black. He punched the accelerator, and Lady Lazarus barreled down the road. I worried for Jeremy. I thought I should shut my eyes for the collision. But I didn't. With an idiot impulse, I rushed out to save my chair.

"Yes! Go!" I heard Muriel again, closer now. Chaz's mask watched me as I was bathed in the headlights. He touched his fingers to the inside of the windshield, then he jerked the wheel. The Lady made some horrible, grinding protest as she shot to my left and vanished over the side of the road.

I ran to the shoulder.

The horizontal of the road below was not enough to stop them. Or the one below that. They had momentum. At each cutback, I heard a crunching boom and saw a flash of spreading fire in the engine block. These intermittent portents allowed me to track their descent as they plunged with cervine swiftness into the darkness.

Jeremy parked the station wagon across the road and ran to stand beside me in time for the final thud and flame.

"Couldn't get the police," he panted. "Phone was out of order."

"Well," I said, "it's over." They had come to earth a few hundred yards from the intersection and the minaret sign; we wouldn't have to pass the wreck on our way back to Palm Desert. I didn't want to see it; I didn't want to stay. But we couldn't bear to leave.

I shifted several wig heads and a box of feathers and put the chair in the back of the station wagon; then we stood and watched. If we had left we wouldn't have seen her. A streetlight shone on the highway near the crash, and Muriel dragged herself towards it. Her robe had spread open as she crawled across the pavement, and although the pole was some distance away, the cloth dully reflected the light.

Jeremy spun around to jog for the car. "We gotta help her." I threw my arms around him, but he didn't stop.

I had to pull him to the ground.

"No, we don't," I said. I still loved her enough not to ruin her story. When I saw that Jeremy was going to stay put, I stood and walked to the edge again.

This last look haunts me: she was alive as a delivery truck approached. I watched it grind towards her. I waited with her. Chaz was gone, and we waited for the truck. As we waited, I guessed at what I meant to them. They cared for me. In their own ways both of them had shown it to me, offering life or death, offering something that mattered. If it wasn't love, it was distilled from whatever syrup drains through the hearts of angels. But the knowledge gave me no comfort.

I imagined Muriel looked up through the smoke and darkness to find the truck descending upon her, the beams of its headlights smeared into crosses by tears and the snakes of hair in her eyes. The beams came flying towards her, paired creatures of light, their arms outstretched to bear her up and unite her with a brilliant, immaculate canopy of stars.

# Trespassing Angels

# 106

After a death, it is easiest to function on the firm ground of ritual. The recovery of bodies. The ceremonies of burial. The dispersal of property. The appointment of guardians. It was no different with the Lambents.

My last look at them was in a morgue in Santa Ana.

Jeremy drove me home that morning to Los Angeles. I told him everything about the Lambents and me. I described what they had done to me, how I had responded. I tried to explain what they had meant to me, although I didn't have the words. Jeremy said almost nothing. He was more subdued than I had ever seen him—as if Zorna had also gone off the side of the road and he wasn't sure how to continue without her.

We parted without saying good-bye or making any plans to speak in the future. I went inside and fell asleep in my clothes. When I woke, it was late morning, but the sky showing through the slats of the blinds above my bed shone a hazy silver blue as if, above the screen of clouds, the sun had not yet decided to rise.

I took a shower. As I wiped steam from the mirror with the end of my towel, I noticed the wall of the bathroom behind me, a hint of red shiny shower curtain at the periphery, and I did not know where I was. I cartwheeled in space, my face caught in the glass like a cosmic ray—etched as a fleeting footprint on a photographic plate—before I sped off through the planet as if the earth were vapor, as if the earth were nothing. Until I finished shaving in a trance and fussed with my hair, I didn't realize that this weightlessness was the beginning of grief and loss.

Speck scraped his whiskers proprietarily against the doorjamb, then rubbed the length of his body beseechingly against my leg. I lifted him to my chest and held him tight, fur against flesh.

I called Amtrak and took a train to Irvine and a taxi to Laguna to retrieve my car. I gave the name "Alta Rosa Drive" and allowed the driver to search her maps and find the street for me. When I spotted my Honda parked at the curb, I paid the cab driver and sprinted across the road, gripping the keys in my pocket as if they might otherwise dematerialize. I jumped in, prepared to speed onto the freeway and leave Orange County behind.

If I hadn't rolled down my window to clear the mist from the glass, I would have missed Miriam's shouts.

"Mister! Mister, excuse me, are you certified to work on Mercedes?" Muriel's mother strode up to stand stiffly outside my window, holding tight to the shoulder strap of her purse. "It won't start. I think it's the wet air."

"I don't know anything about cars," I said and reached out to twist the key in the ignition. I looked in the rearview at Muriel's grandmother standing at the end of the drive in a belted raincoat, her hair encased in a clear plastic hat.

"You're a handyman, aren't you?"

I peered up at her, puzzled that she hadn't thought to ask me what had happened after Jeremy and I left her. But to Miriam, I was just a man who fixed things. "I only do furniture," I said.

She fumed. "Look, mister, my daughter is dead. The police called, and I need to go to the county morgue for the body. And you're telling me that you can't fiddle with the alternator or the gearbox or whatever it takes to get me there? Is this some union thing? Because I'll pay through the nose if I have to. Just get it going." Her blond crown frizzed in the wet air.

"I'll drive you." I was more shocked than she was at what I offered, but my reason was simple. I wanted to see them if I could.

After pausing, no doubt to mull over the social consequences of accepting my proposal, she said, "All right." I unlocked the passenger door, and she stepped around and yanked it open. "Are you coming, Mother?"

The older woman responded with a moan, "I hate hospitals."

"A morgue is not a hospital. You're probably afraid they'll put you in a drawer if you stop moving."

"I'm going in." Muriel's grandmother slunk away around the wall, shaking her plastic-wrapped head wearily.

"Suit yourself." Miriam settled in, not deigning to buckle her seatbelt.

She guided me into Santa Ana to the lot where the police had instructed her to park. She stepped carefully out into the misty air. I opened my door. "It won't be necessary for you to accompany me," she said, but I ignored her and followed her across the blacktop to the entrance.

We were shown to a gray-tiled room, and after fifteen minutes in which Miriam made a concerted effort to ignore me, two orderlies wheeled Muriel in on a stainless steel cart. A blue sheet was folded decorously across her clavicle. Her eyes were sealed shut and her mouth closed, but her jaw hung slack within the flesh of her cheeks. There was the night's first cut, gaping but bloodless, on her forehead. Her hair had been pushed back roughly behind her ears, and some trauma hid beneath her blood-darkened tresses. She was not sleeping; she was definitely, utterly still; but it was possible for me to look at her and believe she was not dead.

"What happened to my baby girl?" Miriam asked herself, but her voice did not waver and, in fact, seemed to shimmer with righteous glee.

She gripped the edge of the sheet and yanked it from Muriel's body with a flourish. I glimpsed her naked torso—her crushed and mangled flesh, the crude seams of the autopsy—then I turned away.

Miriam must have noticed I was staring at a blank wall. "Do I shock you?" she asked. "Well, it shouldn't surprise you. I'm her mother. I deserve to know everything." She stared down clinically at her daughter's corpse.

Orderlies pushed another cart into the space along the wall next to Muriel's. "Here's the John Doe," one of them said as they left. Miriam didn't even glance up; perhaps she thought they had brought him in for me.

Chaz was covered with an identical sheet. His face, framed in matted blond locks, was less battered and more serene than Muriel's. But it was equally vacant; he still seemed to wear a mask.

"Oh, enough of this," Miriam said. She craned her head into the hall. "What do I need to sign to get out of here?"

She exited the room, leaving Muriel naked, Chaz ignored. I immediately followed her down the corridor to the front office. I did not want to stay with them alone. The Lambents had left their bodies, left the room, but I couldn't shake the feeling that they might soon return.

# 107

Their story was violent, lurid, and baroque enough to merit media attention. Although I didn't have a television, I found I couldn't avoid the articles in the newspaper.

In the press, Muriel was identified "by relatives" as Mary Louise Ludlow. Her survivors were her mother, Miriam Kent Ludlow, and her grandmother Martha Carlyle Kent. Her grandfather was the late Oliver Kent, a noted plastics industrialist. Her father was the late actor Myron Ludlow, who under the stage name Brent Harker starred in two popular television series of the late sixties, *Dark Horse: Pop. 63* and *Concealed Weapon*. Ms. Ludlow was also involved in the arts as the owner of a nightclub/performance space in Santa Ana. According to the article, Mary had been a doctoral candidate in comparative cultures, awaiting the completion of her dissertation.

The male occupant of the car was initially tagged as a "John Doe." At the request of unspecified authorities, his status was later changed to "name withheld." The man had apparently been relocated to California as part of a witness protection program, and he could not be identified until it was certain the revelation would not compromise the safety of officers and agents currently involved in long-term investigations. The deceased was the chief suspect in the double homicide-suicide; although his head had been entrapped in some kind of head restraint, both women were bound and thus appeared to be his victims. His body was being turned over to unnamed relatives for burial out of state.

In Irena Delgado's obituary it was requested that, in lieu of flowers, donations be made to the Interplanetary Research Fund of Costa Mesa, California.

Jeremy and I were never mentioned. No one suggested that there were other participants in the event or other interpretations of its meaning. I wasn't part of the story.

# 108

Muriel's burial service was well attended—partly as a result of my efforts. Miriam's number was listed in the phone book, and I called her the day after our trip to the morgue to find out about the funeral.

She was reluctant to provide me with the details. It was to be a very intimate graveside memorial, she explained, for the family.

I told Miriam that I desperately wanted to attend. I explained that I was not just a handyman, that Muriel and I had dated. I implied strongly that we were lovers. And this statement, in its fashion, was undeniably true.

Miriam laughed, a quiet mirthless chuckle, and said briskly, "You may have *thought* she was your girlfriend, but I happen to know that

Mary was a lesbian. She's been that way since college. You must have been fooling yourself."

Yes, I thought. I kept my silence for a moment before responding in a quiet voice, "I hope you'll consider letting me come."

"Well, I don't really see what harm it could do," she said regally and gave me the time and the address of the cemetery.

I was struck with an inspiration as I sat distracted in my office at work shifting miniature vitrines around a model museum. I found the number of the Ground Zero Cabaret and informed the woman who answered the phone of the details of the funeral. I urged her to spread the word to Chaz and Muriel's friends; I hoped Jeremy would hear through this connection because I couldn't find his number. It was only fitting that the audience who cheered Cissy's frenzy should witness Muriel's interment. It would be my tribute.

On the day of the burial, the freeway traffic was denser and slower than I had anticipated, and I arrived late at the cemetery in the hills above Newport Beach. At the chapel, a woman in mauve silk informed me that the mourners had already progressed to the gravesite. I followed the curving drive through the acacia and jacaranda trees and rows of low-set headstones to the mausoleum vaults. I studied the brass lettering above each stuccoed portal arch and located Seraph Court. I passed by the Alcove of the Lily into an open-air courtyard and found the funeral party gathered beside one of the towering tan marble walls. The faces pressed close around the casket were largely familiar. Either because I now knew them better or because of the solemn occasion, the Lambents' acquaintances seemed less motley, less distinctly subdivided, than they had at the Villas del Sol. Their homogeneity was aided sartorially by the fact that they were all dressed in black—one of the rare occasions when the color was appropriate for everyone. I wondered if they were all Muriel's friends alone, or if they sensed, as I did, that the memorial was for Chaz as well.

Muriel's mother and grandmother were seated opposite me, and Miriam glared intermittently over the glazed shell of the casket at the assembled audience as if she were appalled at the riffraff Muriel had attracted to her funeral.

Over Miriam's left shoulder, Jim the Graduate Student pushed strings of hair from his eyes, spotted me, and waved sheepishly. I stared at him impassively (I hoped), then shifted my gaze.

The minister began his sermon. He offered the simplest appeals to dust and ash, and I knew that Muriel's elements would not be found in compost, so my thoughts fled his words. I looked up to see Jeremy, tall and suave in a black camel-hair jacket and gray silk tie. He stood behind Miriam, behind Jim, much taller than anyone.

Soon the sermon was over, and attendants in plain suits lifted the casket in order to push it into a slot opened in the wall. I wandered through the slowly dispersing crowd, looking for Jeremy. A few people I didn't recognize gave me piercing looks; perhaps they remembered me from the night of the party.

Vases of fresh blooms were arrayed along the wall on either side of the vault. I decided to take some to give to Jeremy—to thank him for his help that night or for some other motive I didn't choose to consider too deeply. I was willing to operate on impulse. Muriel wouldn't begrudge me the flowers, I thought. Then I decided that she probably would. But I didn't care. I lifted a generous spray from one arrangement and carried it away casually, hanging it down at my side.

The woman from the party with the corona of gray hair stopped me abruptly before the bronze plaque memorializing *Those at Rest at Sea*. "You were the artist, weren't you?" she asked, pointing at my heart. "You made that remarkable chair."

I nodded vaguely and looked through an arch at the distant silver strip of ocean.

"I wonder if you do bedroom sets. We're refinishing a guest house and want something unique. Would you be interested?"

"I'm not sure," I said doubtfully.

"Perhaps now is not the time. Do you have a card?"

I made a ritualistic pat of my empty inner jacket pocket. "Sorry."

"Well, here's mine," she said and extracted a pale yellow business card from her purse: BETTY SARACEN, Realtor. "Do call." She zipped her purse. "It's such a shame. A loss for all of us." She smiled at me wanly, then turned and headed for the drive.

I pocketed her card and prepared to leave myself. Scanning the sheltered walkway for Jeremy, I found the triangular grouping of

Manjula, Jamma, and Mrs. Rabindagore blocking my path. I hadn't seen them at the service, but they may have been hidden in the crowd. I stepped back into the courtyard. But Manjula had already noticed me and detached herself from the others to flow towards me in a wash of gray and airy black.

"Peter," she said, smiling coolly, "I'm impressed. I would never have thought you capable." A fold of black cloth covered her hair and shaded her eyes; she turned it back so that the afternoon sun bathed her face.

"I don't know what you're talking about." I squeezed the stalks of the flowers.

"They could not have accomplished it without you, you know."

"Just what is it you think I did?"

"Not much, I would wager. No more than was expected. All they needed was a catalyst."

"I think you're full of shit, Manjula." I brandished the flowers as if I might strike her, but I refused to be riled. "They should've chained *you* to the fucking hood."

"Oh, you break my heart, Peter," she laughed and whisked away to offer her arm to Mrs. Rabindagore.

At the gravesite, the last mourners had departed, Miriam and Martha among them, but Jamma, looking ashen in her gray sari, had slipped away from her mother and sister-in-law to stand before the blank marble panel that had been fitted over Muriel's vault. Her fists were balled tightly at her waist. "Bitch," she said quietly, cursing Muriel for some unknown but likely just reason. She spit, and her saliva stuck then spread down the polished face of the wall. She spun around and chased after her relatives, glaring at me darkly as she passed.

I trailed Jamma at a distance down the sloping roadway, sensing but not studying the green hills and graves spreading out on either side of me. As I opened the dented blue door of my car, Jeremy swooped down towards me, his black jacket flapping open at each step. "Don't you even think of sneaking away without talking to me."

"I was looking for you," I said. "Here." I handed him the bouquet.

He peered at it suspiciously, then scooped it into his arms. "These for Muriel?"

"*From* Muriel, you could say. I thought you might like them."

"Stolen flowers from the Ice Princess? You devil." His smile was the dam stretched before a deluge; it stirred the first frond of happiness I had felt in days.

"I just ran into Manjula."

"My sympathies," Jeremy said.

"She made it sound like it was my fault."

"So what? You gonna believe *her*? Woman has no credibility."

"Yeah, but."

"Yeah, but you got the idea they needed you to be there, right? Maybe so." He shifted the flowers from the crook of his arm and pointed with the blooms up the hill to Muriel's vault. "I don't know about her. Don't know if she's even capable. But he musta loved you."

"Come on."

"No *doubt*. Why else would he take a dive in the car 'stead of hitting you?"

"That's love?"

"For the Blond Stranger, it is."

"I'm sorry. It doesn't matter. That's not enough."

"It's gotta be enough if it's all you're gonna get. They're dead and gone, Peter. You can't ring them up and ask them."

"I mean it's not enough to make me forgive him. I think I understand—sort of—why they did it and how they felt about me. But that doesn't make it okay."

"Well," he said. "No one's saying you gotta *forgive* them." He turned his back to me and stared at gravestones sunk in the grass. "I want to ask you something. When you kissed me there, in the car, what did that mean, exactly?"

"I don't know what anything means exactly."

"Just tell me you didn't do a Denny Newhouse on me. Making use of me so you could get at the Blond Ones."

I moved over to join him at the edge of the lawn. "It was real. I meant it."

"Good," he said. "Good." His eyes bore into mine. He raised the flowers and nodded towards them. Then he walked away to his station wagon further down the road.

# 109

I gave the chair to my mother.

I got out my toolbox and found a screwdriver. The plaque came off the seat rail fairly easily, and while two pinholes and a vague rectangular outline marred the varnish, you wouldn't notice them if you didn't know where to look. I filled in the scratches on the back, restained, and refinished. I put the chair in my hatchback and drove it over to my mother. I didn't want it squatting in the corner of my room any longer. I was glad I had saved it, but every time I looked at it, I thought of the Lambents.

My mother was thrilled when she saw it. She circled the chair with the broadest smile she had ever managed lighting her face. She patted the chair's back, then patted mine. Although I wasn't sure what it meant that my mother expressed more enthusiasm for my chair than for anything else I had ever done, I was pleased. She called my sister and praised me while I sat drinking coffee in the breakfast nook. She invited me over to dinner to celebrate. "You can come and bring your boyfriend, or significant other, or love buddy, or whatever-you-call-it. You can meet Victor." It was the first time she had mentioned him—Victor Muñoz, the man she was seeing. She had been considering opening a floral design studio and had met a handsome wholesaler at the flower market downtown. Her life was moving on, and I was happy for her.

I wished that I could enjoy the moment more, that I might find complete satisfaction in it, that I could cocoon with my mother and our respective boyfriends in front of the home entertainment center. But I didn't, and I couldn't. Not yet.

# 110

Something lurked unfinished in me, like a broken melody or an unrealized blueprint. Maybe it's something I'm still waiting to complete. The frustration in traveling the one-way street of love is that you can never return along the same route to the place where you started out with a full tank and fresh anticipation. You can't escape recalling the places you have been or resist imagining those you might have reached had you continued on the same road.

I had reason to hope that I had found a new route to travel: my mother, shaken loose from her past by my father's absence, had become more considerate than she had ever been, and my friendship with Jeremy had arrived in my life unbidden like a sign of grace. I knew these discoveries could serve as posts to which I could anchor the unspooling future's glossy, frail, but tangible lines. They would provide the comforts and disappointments of the real world.

Yet I still waited expectantly near the old path I had followed with the Lambents. Muriel's story of her child held me in place. Whether the child was mine or Chaz's or neither of ours, I judged myself its protector now. If it was difficult to believe in the baby entirely, it remained the last landmark connecting me to them.

One Monday when the museum was closed, I drove out to Cabazon and visited the sheriff's office to search through the missing-children files. The deputy at the front desk was a young woman with creamy brown skin and a short, well-managed Afro. While I made my request to search the files for any abandoned child who might have turned up in the area in the last year or so, her eyes darted curiously over my face. I intuited that the sudden interest in the fate of a discarded baby by a male stranger was the sort of behavior to raise immediate suspicions in her mind. I doubted, however, that a straightforward explanation of my visit would bring me any further into her confidence.

Instead, I told her I was a freelancer researching an article on lost children and that a young woman at a homeless shelter had told me a story I wanted to corroborate.

Deputy LaPlante leaned her chair back against the side of a tall filing cabinet. "You can't just walk in off the street and look at our records, you know. Just because you say you *may* be writing a story which *might* be published in some L.A. paper I've never heard of, doesn't mean I have to give you names and addresses."

"Just tell me what you can," I said mildly.

She studied me again before pushing away from the cabinet. "I think I know where there might be something like what you're talking about."

What she found was not conclusive. There had been a child brought into the station about three months earlier. It had been found by the highway with scratches on its body and twenty dollars in the pocket of its overalls. The child had been placed in the care of foster parents in Riverside until, about six weeks later, a couple from out of state appeared, claiming to be the child's grandparents. Either for jurisdictional reasons or due to some undisclosed but convincing evidence, the child had been remanded to the custody of the couple.

Deputy LaPlante was not forthcoming with any other details; she would not provide me with names or addresses. "Doesn't fit the story you heard, huh?" she asked smugly.

"Not exactly."

"Maybe that informant of yours was a liar. Can't always trust them."

I knew that to be true. Muriel had actually told me very little about this child; she had told me exactly enough to envelop me in mystery.

∞

After the sheriff's, I drove out past Palm Springs to the date farm in Indio where Brad and I had once waited patiently for the educational slide show. The food counter was closing, but I persuaded the elderly woman behind the register—although she had already re-moved her regulation hairnet—to blend me the last date shake of the day. I sat on the hood of my car to suck at the drink in the declining light, pausing occasionally to remove an obstructing chunk of date from my straw. I watched traffic zoom by on the roadway, out, fur-ther into the desert.

The Lambents had driven me this far into new terrain. Other peo-ple would not have traveled the same distance. They would have marked their boundaries—the perimeter of the possible—much closer to home. In the Lambents' company, I had acted in ways I had never imagined, created what I had only dared to dream, and left the protective jar of my self-consciousness behind. I had uncovered places inside myself that I would confidently visit again, lifted fears from my life that might have bound me forever. I had accompanied the Lambents willingly out to a point where I could venture no further.

I hoped that my final defiance meant that I was different, in es-sence, from them. I clung to the distinction between us: the road they followed disappeared into a refinement of darkness, a desert of pu-rity, that I could not—I chose not—to enter.

Yet there at the edge of the highway under the darkening mask of the sky, I continued to wonder what messages remained capable of recrossing the wastes that cordoned the heavens from the living world, the predators from prey—what stories, what tokens, what ghosts.

I thought how I might someday see a car flash by, driven by someone who resembled Muriel—Muriel and Chaz perhaps, or Mu-riel and me. The driver would be a rock star. She would be a Member of Congress. He would be a painter whose pigments were milk, and rust, and blood. She would write psalms in ballpoint on the palms of her hands. Behind the glare on the driver's window, I would glimpse the face of a baker. A nanny. A serial murderer with a com-plex and fascinating modus operandi. A beautiful idiot. A merciless genius. A trespassing angel. And I would understand. I would learn what kind of life might persist after a heart's illicit union with the celestial.

· A NOTE ON THE TYPE ·

The typeface used in this book is a version of Palatino, originally designed in 1950 by Hermann Zapf (b. 1918), one of the most prolific contemporary type designers, who has also created Melior and Optima. Palatino was first used to set the introduction of a book of Zapf's hand lettering, in an edition of eighty copies on Japan paper handbound by his wife, Gudrun von Hesse—also a type designer of note; the book sold out quickly and Zapf's name was made. (Remarkably, the lettering had actually been done when the self-taught calligrapher was only twenty-one.) Intended mainly for "display" (title pages, headings), Palatino owes its appearance both to calligraphy and the requirements of the cheap German paper at the time—perhaps why it is also one of the best-looking fonts on low-end computer printers. It was soon used to set text, however, causing Zapf to redraw its more elaborate letters.